GARTH MARENGHI'S
This Bursted Earth

About the Author

Garth Marenghi was born in the past, graduated from his local comprehensive (now bulldozed) with some O levels in subjects. He taught for nine years at his local library reading group before becoming a full-time horror writer. He has published numerous novels of terror (too numerous to list, nay count), over five hundred short stories, and has edited thirty anthologies of his own work, which have all received the Grand Master of Darkdom Award. He wrote, directed and starred in *Garth Marenghi's Darkplace* for the Peruvian market, which subsequently aired on Channel 4 and has not been repeated due to its radical and polemic content. He commenced work on *TerrorTome* during the late 1980s, continued on it alone and unaided by editors throughout the 1990s, and on into the early 2000s, then the mid-2000s. He continued that vision with *Incarcerat*. He continues that vision, again, with *This Bursted Earth*. He is an honorary fellow.

Also by Garth Marenghi:

Garth Marenghi's TerrorTome
Garth Marenghi's Incarcerat

GARTH MARENGHI'S
This Bursted Earth

CORONET

First published in Great Britain in 2025 by Coronet
An imprint of Hodder & Stoughton Limited
An Hachette UK company

The authorised representative in the EEA is Hachette Ireland, 8 Castlecourt Centre, Dublin 15, D15 XTP3, Ireland (email: info@hbgi.ie)

1

Copyright © Matthew Holness 2025
Map copyright © Alisdair Wood 2025

The right of Matthew Holness to be identified as the Author of the Work has been asserted by him in accordance with the Copyright, Designs and Patents Act 1988.

All rights reserved. No part of this publication may be reproduced, stored in a retrieval system, or transmitted, in any form or by any means without the prior written permission of the publisher, nor be otherwise circulated in any form of binding or cover other than that in which it is published and without a similar condition being imposed on the subsequent purchaser.

All characters in this publication are fictitious and any resemblance to real persons, living or dead, is purely coincidental.

A CIP catalogue record for this title is available from the British Library

Hardback ISBN 9781399721936
ebook ISBN 9781399721950

Typeset in Bembo by Hewer Text UK Ltd, Edinburgh
Printed and bound in Great Britain by Clays Ltd, Elcograf S.p.A.

Hodder & Stoughton policy is to use papers that are natural, renewable and recyclable products and made from wood grown in sustainable forests. The logging and manufacturing processes are expected to conform to the environmental regulations of the country of origin.

Hodder & Stoughton Limited
Carmelite House
50 Victoria Embankment
London EC4Y 0DZ

www.hodder.co.uk

CONTENTS

Introduction
ix

Bonelord
1

The Black Steeple
137

SpeciMen
289

For my Dad

For my Dad.

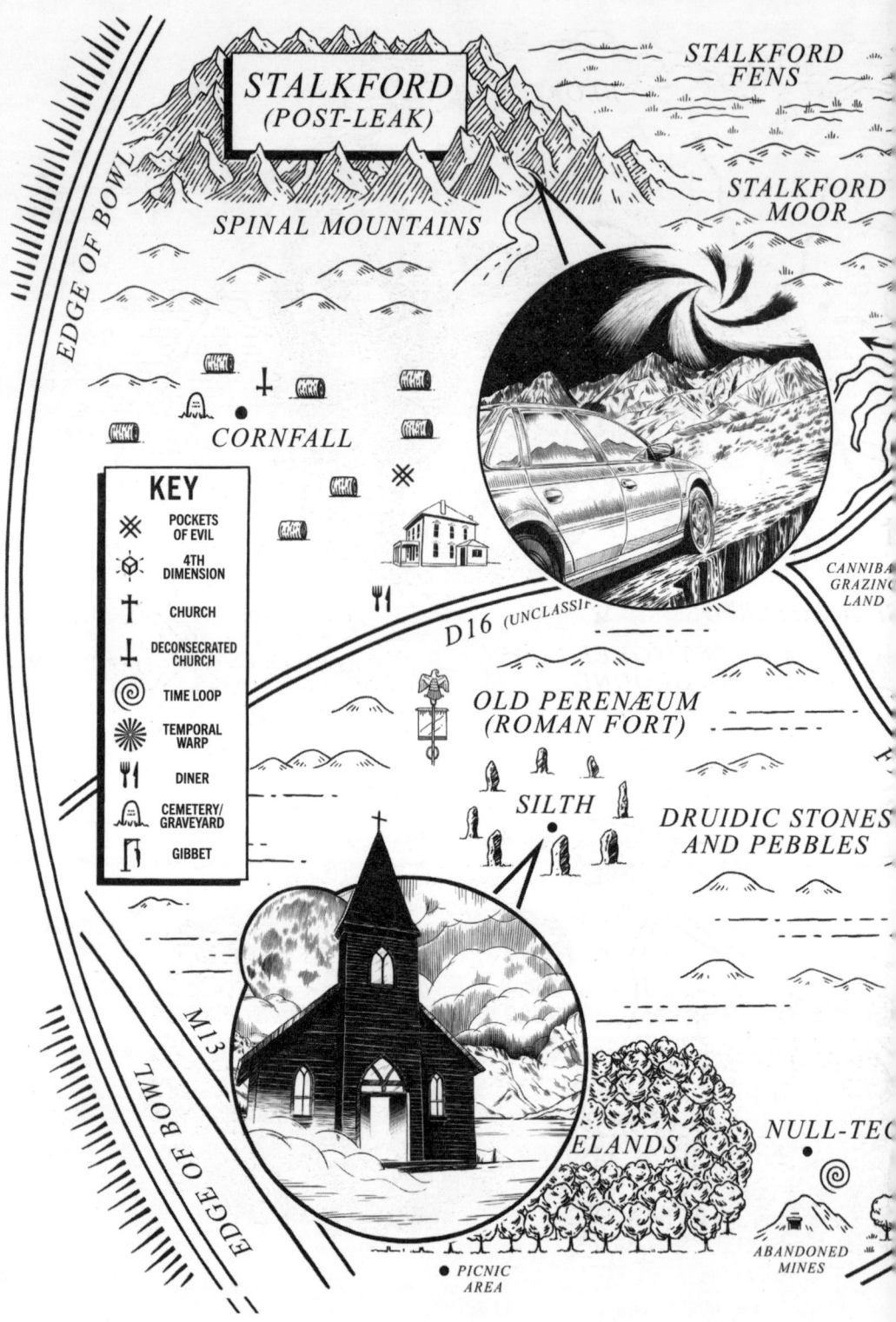

INTRODUCTION

I WARNED YOU.

Didn't I warn you? Yes, I warned you, alright. Oh, how I warned you. There's warning and there's warning and, believe me, I *warned*. I warned *you*. That's right, friend. *You*.

Yes, *you* were warned. Yes, you *were*. How dare you imply that you weren't warned when I know full well that you were, very specifically, warned.

You were warned, friend, about what would *happen*. Ah, I see you're starting to remember, now. That's right, pilgrim. I warned you about what would happen to this *Earth*.

That's right, *This* Earth. Not *that* Earth, or another Earth somewhere way over there that no-one's even seen or heard about. No, I warned you about *this* Earth. This Earth that's been *bursted*. That's right, pilgrim.

THIS BURSTED EARTH.

Look around you, friend. Are you seriously trying to tell me that this Earth *hasn't* been bursted? That it's somehow in 'fine fettle' or apparent 'good shape'? Seriously? *Seriously?*

GARTH MARENGHI

Seriously???

You are serious, aren't you? You're seriously trying to tell me that this Earth, *This Bursted Earth*, has not remotely been bursted.

You Fool. You poor, poor fool.
But I am not a fool.
I, pilgrim, am The Warner.

The Warner O' Mankind.

And I, The Warner, warn you now, as I warned you then, that this Earth hath been bursted.

For this be a Bursted Earth. An Earth so bursted that it shalt forever be known, heretoforth, as *This Bursted Earth*.

Look around you again, pilgrim. Only this time *really* look around you. Here swells Misrulerage. Unfair-ity. Despotatos. And loft, 'pon yonder horizon, doth ride the five Horsemen of Armageddolypse.

What's that, you say, friend? How might you be saved?

Heh heh heh.

Too late for that, pilgrim. Too *damned* late. As I say, I did warn you multiple times.

All I can advise ye now is to follow me, friend. Follow me in my Dance of Doom. For I 'twilt now dance the Dance of Doom across *This Bursted Earth* for all Eternitum i.e. the foreseeable.

INTRODUCTION

I doth warned ye, pilgrim.

Yet heed me did ye nay.

Disapprovingly,

Garth Marenghi,
Bewarner of Mankind
(Or Ladykind
If that be thy poison)
C/O Flat 9B,
New Spa Heights,
Drummond Mansion Developments,
Staines.

BONELORD

CHAPTER ONE

Nick Steen woke with a scream and immediately checked his balls. No longer on a snooker table being potted by Steve Davis, Ray Reardon and Dennis Taylor in hooded robes, thank God.

Another nightmare, then. Like the one he'd had last month about being incarcerated in some secret government medical research facility run by the sinister Dr Barbara Nullman.* A place that existed *for real* now, Nick recalled with horror, thanks to his imagination continually leaking out into reality from that portal to another dimension situated somewhere in the middle of his own head.

And in the same way that Nulltec was now part of Stalkford's

---

* See *Garth Marenghi's Incarcerat*, the events of which should now be discarded as merely the figments of a protracted dream or nightmare, Nick being a passive figure throughout and Roz Bloom herself being chief protagonist in one of the tales – which, as I warned Ken Hodder on numerous occasions, WOULD NOT SELL. GM

everyday world, situated just south of the town centre on the borders of Chokewood Forest, waiting to entrap Nick for real someday, soon a satanic Steve Davis, rabid Ray Reardon and demonic Dennis Taylor would be joining it. More hellish figments of Nick's escaping imagination somehow made manifest.

For that's how things were now, Nick reflected bitterly. Exhausted as he was from continually battling the demonic monsters of his own paperback novels, which were escaping at all hours through a huge portal in the centre of his brain, the grim fact remained that his *un*published works were also starting to manifest themselves. Now every single nightmare Nick suffered had the potential to come to terrifying life as well, alongside the already-rampaging demons from the pages of his existing books.

Which meant the task of destroying all these escaping figments of his imagination was getting harder. And that wasn't the worst of it – because now there were *additional* horrors coming to life. Horrors Nick could neither recall writing *nor* dreaming up. Monsters buried so far down in the murky depths of his id that even Nick's subconscious mind was unaware of their existence. But they were coming to life, that much was certain. Even if he didn't know what, or where, or why, or wherefore they were.

Like the creature he was currently hunting. A terrifying unknown entity that seemed to strike out of nowhere, attacking entire gatherings of people at once with no hint of warning. Physically deboning all and sundry in a bloody whirlwind of giddying, exploding gore.

First had come the massacre at Stalkford's public swimming pool. The victims were so thoroughly mangled that all the police were able to retrieve from what used to be water were a pathetic collection of shredded Speedos.

Then came the mass evisceration of Stalkford County Council's Board of Members at their annual budget review, resulting in an unprecedented seventy-five per cent increase in spending owing to the clean-up bill alone.

BONELORD

This was followed by the garden centre deboning, initially presumed by investigators to have been caused by an altercation over the exorbitant asking price for a 2006 *Michael Flatley Live DVD*,* but which had eventually been traced to their organic food kiosk – at which point both the police, and Nick himself, had lost interest.

Then there was the ill-fated booze cruise, the decks of which were still being sluiced. And that was followed almost immediately by what newspapers had dubbed the 'Meat Raffle Massacre', a crime proving almost impossible to investigate as much of the physical evidence had been consumed inadvertently during the killings themselves.

Finally, there were those mass slayings at the Raunch Pot, Stalkford's notorious, run-down, cinematic sleaze-pit. Police Commissioner Bob Kettlestrom hadn't considered this worth spending his already-overstretched manpower on, though a large stash of X-rated films were immediately seized and distributed among members of the initial investigating squad.

Six massacres. Six multiple-crime scenes. No witnesses. And not a single one of the victims remotely identifiable. Just pile after pile of the mortally deboned. It was proving to be Nick's toughest and messiest challenge yet, and so far he didn't possess a single clue as to what was going on, or what particular monster was deboning Stalkford's unsuspecting soon-to-be-deboned.

Nick needed help from somewhere, yet he knew deep down that help was no longer forthcoming. For all those who'd assisted

---

* Sadly, since writing this, Covid has wrought near-total devastation on the UK garden centre-based DVD entertainment industry. Where once you could find out-of-print classics like 2008's 30th Anniversary Tour DVD of Jeff Wayne's *War of the Worlds* (featuring Justin Hayward and the virtual reanimated corpse of Richard Burton), as well as the in-many-ways-superior 2012 *New Generation* version featuring Marti Pellow and the voice of Gary Barlow, these days it's just jigsaws of World War Two bombing runs and colouring books for adults. Go figure. GM

Nick in the past were either dead, like Bruford* and Capello,† or now sworn enemies, believing they somehow deserved equal praise for helping destroy wave after wave of Stalkford's hellish supernatural assailants. Sure, they might have picked up a shotgun here or there and helped Nick blaze away at assorted marauding hellspawn, but did those hangers-on share any of Nick's private pain? His sporadic moments of self-reflective anguish and occasional inner torments? Of course they didn't. Hence Nick steadfastly refusing to grant any of them credit where credit was apparently due. But though Nick's pride might be intact, there was no denying that the task of battling numerous demons single-handedly was getting tougher by the day.

And given that Commissioner Bob Kettlestrom held Nick personally responsible for this latest slew of appalling crimes, claiming they could only have originated, like all these other monsters of late, from the author's escaping subconscious, Nick couldn't even call upon the local police force for aid.

And despite Nick's having convinced Roz Bloom, his erstwhile female editor, to give up her career in publishing and join the cops in an attempt to plead his cause and help get Kettlestrom off his back, she'd proved as useless as ever, Nick reflected, rolling himself off the bed to check once more that his balls really weren't still being potted.

For it had been Roz who'd informed him that Bob Kettlestrom was now after Nick's blood. And it was only a matter of time, she'd warned Nick, before Kettlestrom's public lobbying for a return of the death sentence would finally reach sympathetic ears in the Senate,

---

* A psychic dugong bodily exploded in *The Dark Fractions*. See *Garth Marenghi's TerrorTome*.
† A live-wire Italian talk-show therapist turned crazed vigilante, killed fighting an army of Boners alongside his shredded brother Dwayne in *Bride of Bone*. See *Garth Marenghi's TerrorTome*.

now that Stalkford City Council's replacement board had been sworn in and were already hellbent on preventing a second massacre from occurring during their inaugural meeting.

'First item on the agenda?' Roz had warned. 'Restoration of the death sentence.'

'Whatever,' Nick had replied.

'And the second?'

'Hit me.'

'The immediate arrest and execution of Nick Steen as suspected chief orchestrator of the current supernatural crisis.'

'Forgive me while I yawn, Roz.'

And Nick *had* yawned. But it had been a fake yawn. A yawn born of mere bravado. Because Nick wasn't naive enough to presume he'd get a fair trial if the authorities decided to slap him in chains. Hell, he wouldn't even get an *unfair* trial. Because what Police Commissioner Kettlestrom was proposing, Nick had learned from Roz, was the power to execute, or 'whack', a suspect without due process. To whack them at will, and without warning. In other words, the authority to conduct summary whackings without fear of repercussion.

And unless Nick could somehow solve this particular series of murders single-handedly, thereby showing Kettlestrom that victory over the powers of supernatural evil was possible via Nick's leadership alone, then it was merely a matter of time before the authorities came looking for him. And though a simple stop-and-whack might well destroy Nick's supernatural mind-portal once and for all (Roz told him they were also considering pile-driving his head into the ground), Nick couldn't bear the thought of a world continuing without his fiction, incarnate or not.

Nick Steen wasn't prepared to die yet, damn it. He still had so much to offer. More books, for a start. And then the sequels. Then *more* books. Followed by *even more* books. Damn it, Nick Steen *had* to survive.

GARTH MARENGHI

He crossed the room and pulled back the curtain, staring out over row upon row of moonlit rooftops. It was the dead of night, and in the far distance Nick could hear the distinctive wail of racing police sirens. The old saying Nick had just invented was still true: Stalkford never slept. And neither did he anymore. As Nick glanced upwards, towards the glaring white disc of a full moon overhead, he thought he sensed something strange about its surface. Something that unnerved him, though for the moment Nick couldn't tell what precisely that was.

Maybe the moon demons from his novel *The Moon Demons* had finally set their eyes – and bared arse cheeks – upon the shores and oceans of distant Earth. Or perhaps the vast cosmic eye from his novel *The Crust from Nowhere* was about to blink down at him from some distant moon crater, dislodge a vast ball of 'sleep' from its giant tear duct, then send it, and a subsequent shower of deadly eye discharge, spiralling towards Earth on an unstoppable path of destruction.

But before Nick could decide exactly what the problem with the moon was, the phone in his bedroom rang.

Nick yanked the receiver from its cradle on the bedside table and spoke.

'Nick Steen, demon-slayer?'

'Nick? It's Roz.'

His former editor's voice sounded unusually fragile, as if she'd recently suffered a shock of some kind. Presumably Kettlestrom had informed her that make-up and slingbacks weren't standard-issue uniform.

He was wrong.

'There's been another deboning.'

'*Another* one? Whereabouts?'

'That's what's so awful, Nick. It happened right here, at this very police station. Every single prisoner in our cells is now a splotch of eviscerated meat, as well as most of our police officers. Including the head of Stalkford's FBI Office.'

'So why aren't *you* dead?'

'I was working late at the morgue, Nick. Attempting to identify the remains of all these previous debonings. Now, thanks to this fresh massacre, my workload's increased exponentially.'

'Tough titty, Roz. You took on the job.'

'I know, Nick. I really should stop complaining. And I guess there's a good chance of promotion now, at any rate. Who knows, if I play my cards right, maybe I can become the new head of Stalkford's FBI Office? And on another plus side, I guess I already possess some initial clue to the identities of these particular victims, given that a huge number of them are my former work colleagues.'

'Please tell me Kettlestrom's dead.'

'I'm afraid not, Nick. He was out with a surveillance team, arranging a secret wiretap on your house.'

Nick sighed, angrily. Of all the cops to escape a mass deboning at the police station, why did it have to be Kettlestrom?

'What do you want *me* to do about all this?' he asked.

'Well, obviously, we're seriously undermanned now, Nick. There are hardly enough officers left to mop up the remains, let alone conduct any sort of investigation into the massacre. We need your help.'

'Uh-uh. This is Kettlestrom's problem, Roz. Not mine.'

'It *is* your problem, Nick. Because unless Kettlestrom's wiretapping plans have been temporarily curtailed . . .'

'Which they haven't,' said a gruff voice, interrupting Roz from somewhere else along the line.

'You see, Nick? They're already listening in on you as we speak. And given that you and the police aren't getting on too well at present, they may just regard you as chief suspect in this latest deboning.'

'Me?'

'The monsters are oozing from your head, after all, Nick. So if I were you, I'd come down to the station right now and start doing your level best to solve this case.'

No way, thought Nick. *No way am I being dictated to.*

'You just said, Roz, that most of your fellow police officers have been deboned, including the head of Stalkford's FBI Office. So maybe they don't quite have enough constables left to arrest me on some trumped-up charge, either. Even if they want to.'

'Yes, we do,' said that same distant, disembodied voice.

'Fine. I'll be over in ten minutes,' said Nick, slamming down the receiver hard so that whoever was wiretapping him would know he was annoyed.

Nick sighed, tugging on a clean black shirt and freshly-weathered leather blouson. It looked like he had little choice but to investigate this latest deboning, after all. At least it might provide some temporary respite from his recent run-ins with the police. And maybe he'd finally get a chance to unmask the killer's true identity, be that some form of crazed psychotic, or a dimension-hopping hell-demon.

One thing was certain, at least. If the killer, whatever it was or consisted of, had now gone and attacked the police themselves, then it was clearly frightened of their investigation and, presumably, of its true identity being discovered. Which meant Nick would need to take extra care when conducting his own enquiries. Because if the thing was capable of deboning the entire contents of a working police station, it would have no trouble eviscerating him as well. No matter how virile and action-packed he might be.

Nick grabbed his .44 Police Detective Special from under his pillow, followed by a phial of holy water from beneath his bed. He had no idea yet whether his assailant was human or not, so he had to prepare for any eventuality. For good measure, Nick opened his bedside drawer and yanked out his harpoon, just in case the killer was a sentient flying shark, then made his way to the door of his apartment. He glanced once more through the curtain to stare boldly up at the moon, daring whatever horror might be hiding on its surface to reveal itself.

But there was nothing there. Just a collection of far-off crevices and craters which looked, now that Nick's nocturnal fears of the unknown had abated and the task at hand was upon him, no more tangible or solid than a shadow.

A shadow, Nick suddenly perceived, tearing his eyes immediately from the glass pane, of a vast and terrifying *skull*.

Swiftly, he followed the sound of the sirens.

(Which were on their way to the police station.)

((Where the recent deboning had occurred . . .))

CHAPTER TWO

Nick stepped into the basement holding cells in police-issue waders. Except that now there weren't any cells. For the fragmented remains of the metallic cage walls that had once kept Stalkford's worst offenders at bay currently lay submerged beneath the shallow pool of human viscera through which Nick now sloshed.

Roz followed him down the steps, angling a large pumping mechanism in her hand towards the crimson liquid. Nick realised the device must be connected via hosepipe to a portable container unit they'd passed in the corridor above.

'Shouldn't you be dusting for prints first?' said Nick.

'The killer doesn't leave any,' Roz said. 'We used these suction pumps on the swimming pool case,' she added, depressing a button on one side of the machine. 'We had to hire sixteen of them.'

Nick winced as the liquified remains currently lapping at his ankles started to bubble and eddy around him. Then a loud sucking noise gurgled from the pump as the brimming pool of human remains began shooting up its spout. Within seconds, the thing had jammed.

'Hold on,' said Roz, switching off the machine before fishing about in the nozzle with her gloved hand. She yanked out a kidney stone. 'That's the only solid we're likely to find,' she said, popping it into her breast pocket.

Nick gazed down once more at the surrounding human soup. 'What the hell do you expect me to detect in here, Roz?' he said, moodily. 'This is a total waste of my time. If there aren't any clues left to find, and you won't let *me* use the sucker pump, then I'm tempted to go back to bed.'

'Like I told you before, Nick,' said Roz, switching on the pump again, 'we hardly have any officers left to investigate this latest deboning.'

'Speak up, will you, Roz?' shouted Nick. 'I can't hear you over the gurgling.'

'I said, all the cops upstairs have been eviscerated!' Roz shouted back. 'But that itself gives us a clue. You see, whoever the killer was must have gained access via the main door upstairs, massacred the officers first, then headed down here immediately afterwards.'

'You mean *whatever* the killer was,' said Nick, correcting her and dismissing her attempt at identifying a supposed 'clue'. 'This is hardly the work of a human fiend, Roz. I should know. I regularly battle the supernatural denizens of my own brain, remember? And with regard to your alleged '"clue"': how do you know the beast that did this didn't massacre these prisoners *first*, then go upstairs to attack the police afterwards? You're making assumptions, Roz. Frankly, that's not the sort of behaviour befitting a member of The Royal Majesty's police force.'

'But there's no door to the outside down here, Nick. They would *have* to have come down from above.'

'Bullshit,' snapped Nick. 'The killer could have been a gas. Or an alternately materialising-slash-dematerialising demonic spirit. Wake up, Roz.'

'I'm sorry, Nick,' Roz said, her chastised voice growing quieter and less self-assured than before. 'I didn't consider those options. I guess I'm starting to apply scientific principles to a range of phenomena that defy rational logic, despite having joined the police force specifically so that I could advise the authorities on the ways in which supernatural assailants might challenge, if not outright oppose, the typical explanatory parameters of routine police investigations.'

'Then shape up, Roz. Because we're facing something *untoward* here. A force of *un*-nature that can potentially materialise in an enclosed space and systematically eviscerate an entire building of people without leaving the merest trace of its identity in its wake. If we attempt to defeat this threat with mere truncheons and whistles, we'll end up as extra condiments in the next bowl of human soup. The fate of our entire civilisation, specifically Stalkford, rests upon our ability to embrace the irrational as *bona-fide* reality. Now, if you won't let me use the pump so I can suck up what's left of these chumps, I'm definitely going back to bed.'

'You're going *nowhere*, Nick Steen,' said a voice from the doorway. Nick turned to see a short, rotund figure in thigh-length waders splosh down awkwardly into the flooded cell space. The man wore a C&A suit, its bulky jacket not quite concealing the presence of a .38 Special nestled inside a leather shoulder strap.

'I'm Police Commissioner Bob Kettlestrom, former head of Stalkford's FBI Office,' he said, stepping into the light. Kettlestrom's hair was neatly parted like an early school photo, and his thriple chins wobbled with each swish of his small legs. Yet appearances could be deceptive, thought Nick. For the cold, icy tone of Kettlestrom's voice told Nick he meant business.

'Officer Roz didn't bring you here because we needed *your* help. She brought you here so I could get a good look at you.'

Kettlestrom sloshed past Roz, moving closer to Nick. He had some trouble doing it, Nick noted; the tops of the lawman's waders were evidently chafing against the apex of his inner thighs.

'I'd trim those down a bit if I were you,' said Nick. 'Maybe an entire foot or two.'

BONELORD

'But you're *not* me,' retorted Kettlestrom, coldly. 'And I wear chafing waders on purpose, because it keeps me on edge, Mister Steen. *Literally* on edge. This way, I don't miss a beat. Besides, I don't like comfort. This world has little comfort in it. My job is to make sure those who *do* have comfort don't have that comfort taken away from them by those who crave their own comfort by sowing *dis*comfort. Understand what I'm saying?'

'Sure. You don't get comfort from people taking personal comfort from stealing other people's comfort?'

'That's right. Makes me very *un*comfortable.'

'Likewise.'

'It's not likewise at all. This whole mess is of *your* making. I've seen the books you write. Hell, I impounded stacks of them when they were being swapped round high schools. I know the kind of sick filth you've been pushing on society all these years.'

'It's not sick filth. It's largely horror, with occasional sections of potent horrotica. I agree that the latter probably shouldn't have been swapped between pubescents.'

'I don't care about your books anymore. I care about the *contents* of your books. Specifically, the contents of your books that are now coming to life. Because of your sick mind, mister. What kind of pervert sleeps with a goddamned typewriter?'

'It was a *cursed* typewriter,'* Nick countered. 'Big difference.'

'And what is that difference?'

'Well, for one thing, a ghost inside the typewriter spoke to me.'

'What did it say?'

'I'd rather not say.'

'Say it.'

'No.'

---

* See and then ensure that you read (and/or hear via critically acclaimed audiobook) 'Type-Face, Lord of the Prolix' in *Garth Marenghi's TerrorTome* (also critically-acclaimed).

'Say it, or I'll arrest you.'
'Do it, bitch.'
'Okay, you asked for it.'
'No, that's what the *typewriter* said.'
'It said, "Do it, bitch"?'
'That's right. "Do it, bitch."'
'Do what?'
'Do what it wanted.'
'And what did it want?'
'Me to do it.'
'To do what?'
'To do things to it.'
'What things?'
'Naughty things.'
'Dirty things?'
'I guess you'd call them dirty.'
'Well, were they dirty things or not dirty things?'
'They were dirty things.'
'Disgusting things?'
'Depends what you mean by disgusting.'
'What do *you* mean by disgusting?'
'Well . . .'
'Well what?'
'Well, you know, doing dirty, disgusting things . . .'
'To what?'
'To a typewriter.'
'Doing dirty, disgusting things to a typewriter. Am I right?'
'Right you are.'
'Thank you, Mister Steen, that's all I needed to hear. Sign this.'
The police commissioner held out a small notepad and pen.
'What is it?' said Nick, taking them from Kettlestrom's hand.
'A confession.'

'But I haven't confessed anything.'

'You just confessed to doing dirty, disgusting things to a cursed typewriter. Officer Roz here witnessed that confession. Am I correct, Officer Roz?'

Kettlestrom wasn't looking at Roz, Nick noted, but she somehow still seemed to be feeling the full force of his gaze.

'Correct, sir. I witnessed Mister Steen admitting to doing dirty, disgusting things to a cursed typewriter. Plus, I was there at the time, so can vouch for the alleged offence in a court of law.'

'So sign it,' said Kettlestrom, still staring at Nick.

What the Hell is Roz playing at? thought Nick. *The damned traitor* . . .

'I said sign it, Mister Steen.'

Scarcely able to believe what he was doing, Nick sensed himself being forced into submission. Maybe it was the memory of that evil, dominating presence that had brought so much calamity to Nick's world . . . the demonic spirit that had single-handedly bursted his own Earth. Yes, it had to be. It had to be that dark memory Nick could never shake. The memory of those things that Type-Face, Lord of the Prolix, had made him do, back when Nick was thirsting for dark knowledge to fuel his own horror writing. Things that had subsequently brought terror and ruin to Stalkford, burrowing a hole through Nick's brain in order to fill reality with the powerfully destructive figments of his own imagination . . .

Whatever it was that was now sapping Nick's inner strength, whether it was indeed the spirit of Type-Face, or simply the relentless pressure of what had once been the finest interrogative mind in Stalkford's FBI Office, Nick found his strength of will waning, wilting like a sprayed garden weed, in a way that it had never done before.

Surrendering, he signed the confession.

'That'll be all, Mister Steen,' said Kettlestrom, snatching the sheet of paper from Nick's hand. 'For now, this'll count as evidence once we recruit enough new officers to arrest you. We'll be in touch. And remember,' he added, pointing the pen directly at Nick, 'we're watching you.'

With that, Kettlestrom sloshed back through the human soup and, with some difficulty, lifted his waders up each step before disappearing into the upper levels of the station.

'Thanks a bunch, Roz,' snapped Nick, once the police commissioner had finally departed. 'You landed me in it good and proper.'

'I can't help that, Nick. I'm a police officer now. I must tell the truth or I might be severely reprimanded. And you *did* confess, after all.'

'He coerced me into that confession, Roz! The guy's a damned pit bull.'

'Well, whatever he is, Nick, unless you can solve this case soon, he's going to have you arrested and whacked without trial. It's only because most of our officers have been murdered that they aren't out whacking you right now.'

At the thought of that, Nick decided it was time to leave. He wasn't going to be able do anything to solve this case by working with the police. Or Roz, for that matter, who seemed to have turned into some sort of right-wing fascist overnight. No doubt she already had her eyes set on that vacant position as head of Stalkford's FBI Office ... And as far as the authorities were concerned, Nick, by unwittingly unleashing whatever supernatural being this particular perpetrator was into the heart of Stalkford, had technically made himself an accessory in a conspiracy to debone. For that reason alone, he had to get as far away from the police station as possible.

BONELORD

'See you whenever, Roz. Thanks for nothing.'

But Roz failed to hear him. For at that very moment, a large sucking sound could be heard once more inside the sucker pump's nozzle. Another blockage.

'Another kidney stone, I think,' said Roz, fishing around inside the mechanism. But what she pulled out from the pumping machine was something else entirely. As she rubbed it briefly against her uniform and held it up towards the overhead lights, the object in her hand began to shine and sparkle.

It was a golden locket.

'Let me see that,' said Nick, snatching it from Roz's hand. He flipped open the smooth oval case to reveal a miniature black-and-white portrait of a noble-looking elderly woman clothed in an archaic Renaissance-style gown with her grey hair tied up in an elaborate period beehive.

'*Countess Signora Margarita Mantovani*,' said Nick, reading aloud a row of tiny, ornate lettering carved into the metal beneath the woman's portrait.

'Somebody's girlfriend?' asked Roz, moving closer to examine the picture.

'Hardly,' Nick replied. 'This withered old crone can only be someone's grandmother. Tell me, was there a prisoner here with the surname Mantovani?'

'Not that I can recall,' said Roz. 'Prisoners generally have working-class surnames, Nick. Like Stubbs or Greaves.'

'There's a Mantovani somewhere in town, if I remember rightly,' muttered Nick, his contemplative gaze drifting idly over the pool of mangled remains slopping around his feet. Suddenly, his stomach rumbled involuntarily at the sight of what resembled a floating meatball tangled up in strands of delicious spaghetti. 'That's it!' he said, turning his attention back to Roz. 'Giuseppe Mantovani. He owns an Italian restaurant slap-bang in the middle of the Italian district –

and, if I remember correctly, he is also the head of a notorious mafia crime syndicate. Are you sure there was no prisoner here named Mantovani?'

'I'm certain of it, Nick. Let's see. There was a Gavin Tucker, a Lenny Bends. Even a Strangler Bates. But no Mantovani.'

'Then this locket must have belonged to the killer instead,' said Nick. 'Dropped accidentally, no doubt, while he or it committed this mass deboning. I suspect Giuseppe Mantovani knows a thing or two about this massacre.'

'But Nick,' said Roz as he sloshed past her towards the steps. 'There's a chance this locket could have been *stolen* by the killer. Did you ever stop to think about that? Maybe the Mantovanis had absolutely nothing whatsoever to do with this particular deboning? Maybe this locket was merely a piece of lost evidence from some previous case, uprooted from some forgotten drawer by all these slopping innards?'

'Careful, Roz,' warned Nick. 'You're beginning to sound like a bad apple. In case you didn't know, the Mantovanis are one of the oldest and most infamous crime families in the history of Stalkford's murky underworld. It won't hurt to ask them a few questions about these shocking debonings – by which I mean, interrogate them harshly under threat of imminent violence.'

And, thought Nick to himself, even if the Mantovanis had nothing to do with these killings, grilling them would at least convince Roz that Nick was doing something constructive to apprehend the killer. Right now, he needed time to think, and to do that he had to ensure Roz kept Bob Kettlestrom off his back. Currently, the only way to do *that* was to convince her that Nick's own life was worth saving.

'I'll inform Commissioner Kettlestrom,' Roz said as Nick waded past her. 'Perhaps if you come up with a lead or two, it'll keep him off your back for now.'

BONELORD

'I hope so,' said Nick. 'For *your* sake, Roz. Because if I can't solve the mystery of this phantom deboner soon – I'm not calling it that, by the way, it's not *The Two Ronnies* – you and Kettlestrom may not have time to whack me, even if you wish to. Because by that stage, we might *all* be stone dead.'

'Stone dead?' repeated Roz, fearfully.

'By which I mean, *deboned*.'

He left that thought to linger, then made his way outside.

★

Nick yanked open the door of his Honda Civic and slumped himself inside. It was still dark, and most of Stalkford's restaurants would currently be closed. But if Nick knew anything at all about Stalkford's mafia, it was that they'd most likely be operating an illegal late-night lock-in, allowing customers to purchase soft lagers and bottles of cheap Chianti after hours.

No wonder the world was in such a mess.

As Nick keyed the ignition and drove out into the neon-lit streets of Stalkford town centre, he thought once more about Kettlestrom's relentless interrogation technique, and how he'd cruelly coerced Nick into signing his apparent 'confession'. No one had put Nick under that kind of pressure before (with the exception of Type-Face, Lord of the Prolix himself, who at one point had turned Nick's body into a liquid). It was only because Roz believed so fervently in the rule of law that he hadn't slammed her superior officer into the wall and kicked his squat, belligerent arse out into the street. Hell, there were currently no cops around to intervene, after all. But that wouldn't solve the matter of these debonings. No, the only way to solve this case was to uncover the identity of whatever it was that was committing these crimes, and then flame-throw it.

GARTH MARENGHI

Nick looked up into the night sky. The moon above was still full, appearing, disappearing, then reappearing between passing banks of cloud.

He could see the face in its surface more clearly now: that giant skull that somehow seemed to be forming from the shadowy contours of those distant craters.

A skull, Nick was increasingly convinced, that grinned.

Grinned at *him*.

I.e. Nick.

CHAPTER THREE

Nick's Honda Civic braked hard against the kerb, propelling a wave of rainwater from an overflowing gutter towards the front door of Mantovani & Sons Restaurant. The sign in the window said 'Closed', but Nick spied a faint glow of light emerging from a small gap in the drawn, smoke-stained curtains.

He exited his vehicle, hunching his shoulders against the heavy rain, and hurried across the pavement. As he arrived at the door, he drew out his revolver.

'Nick Steen, demon-slayer! Come out with your claws up!' he yelled, bracing himself against the edge of the doorframe. There was no response from inside, but Nick could now hear the faint sound of distant opera singing from within, and the clatter of stabbing cutlery.

His suspicions confirmed, Nick took a step back, then propelled himself forward, kicking the door inward. When it failed to break open, he shot off its lock and kicked again. This time it finally opened, but a freshly aching toe had put Nick in a bad mood.

'Freeze, Giuseppe,' he snapped, levelling his gun at a man in his mid-thirties who was holding out a plate of steaming spaghetti. The restaurant behind him was jammed with patrons, most of them chic young hipsters in ironic Lycra, all too busy stuffing their faces on disposable incomes to have noticed Nick's entrance.

'I'm Luigi,' said the man, evidently a mere waiter. Then he pointed his plate of spaghetti at an older male manning the restaurant's glowing bar. 'Pop's over there. Hey, Giuseppe!'

'Whatta the 'ell is a-happenin' here?' puffed Giuseppe, moving out from behind the bar and heading over in Nick's direction. The man was overweight and largely bald, save for several strands of dyed, coal-black hair stuck fast to his perspiring forehead.

He looks annoyed, thought Nick. *Best show my balls.*

The last thing you did with the Stalkford mafia was refuse to show them your balls. Because when they finally got hold of those balls, they invariably lopped said balls off. But if you showed the mafia your balls outright, practically waving both balls in their faces, then they showed those balls some respect.

Not that Nick was going to show Giuseppe his *actual* balls. Nick was still a writer at heart, and was merely thinking metaphorically.

But he was absolutely going to show Giuseppe his metaphorical balls. He was going to wave them at him *right now*.

'I'll tell you what's happening here, Giuseppe. You and your sons are operating a late-night lock-in, and allowing these unsuspecting patrons to consume assorted pasta shapes doused in tinned tomato pulp and basil *illegally*. Not to mention selling wicker carafes of boxed wine and tepid bottles of lightly bubbled lager after hours. Now we've got you.'

'You need-a da warrant, *asshole*,' barked Giuseppe. 'You can't-a come in here a-waving your balls in my face.'

'I'll damn well wave my balls if I want to,' said Nick, maintaining his tough and resilient composure. That was crucial if any strategic ball-waving was to continue.

'You need-a to show me a *warrant*, not your balls!' Giuseppe snapped back at him. Suddenly, the restaurant owner's hand shot outward, slapping the barrel of Nick's gun aside. 'And putta that thing away!'

Nick considered shooting him dead on the spot. For he himself had now been openly disrespected, Giuseppe having slapped away what might well be construed as Nick's metaphorical member, alongside both his figurative balls. But if Nick did that, he might risk losing track of the one clue he currently possessed on his one-man mission to uncover the identity of the mystery deboner.

'Let's all calm down, Giuseppe. I don't need a warrant, because I'm not a police officer.'

The Italian's face turned an even deeper shade of red. 'Not a police officer?' he cried out, incensed. 'Hey, Marco!' he yelled behind him, at another one of the waiters. 'Cutta this guy's balls off and put 'em in a sauce.'

'I wouldn't do that if I were you,' said Nick, icily, aiming his revolver directly at the approaching Marco. 'Because if anyone's balls are going into a sauce, it'll be yours.'

Marco, evidently another of Giuseppe's sons, stopped mid-stride and gulped.

Nick quickly pointed the revolver back at Giuseppe. 'Then yours, too, Giuseppe,' he said, before pointing the gun at Luigi as well. 'Followed by your *one* ball.'

Luigi looked mortified. For Nick knew Luigi had lost one of his in a previous bar fight with the Corbuccini mob, and now only had a single ball left to swing at potential enemies. One foot wrong and he'd be completely ball-free.

Giuseppe took a step forward, looking like he'd be happy to sacrifice both of his own balls in an attempt to rip off Nick's personal pair – but then his expression eased, and the redness of his cheeks dulled to a light pink.

'Hey, lessa all-a calm down. He ain't the law, so no need for anyone to lose any balls.'

'I'm a private investigator,' said Nick. 'I also slay demons and monsters of the mind. I'm currently tracing the last known movements of a professional deboner.'

'What is this ... *dee-bonair*?' said Giuseppe.

'Don't play dumb, Giuseppe. You know full well what a deboner is. A person, or *thing*, that's been deboning people all over the city.'

'Ahh, yes, atta the swimming pool ...' muttered Giuseppe, nodding his head while evidently recalling the recent news bulletins.

'Exactly,' said Nick. 'Followed by that mass deboning at the local council meeting ...'

'*Mamma mia*, of course ... the local council meeting deboning,' whispered Giuseppe to himself, making the sign of the cross over his chest.

'Then the garden centre slaying, followed by the booze cruise and meat market massacres. Plus the cinema ripping ...'

'A terrible business,' sighed Giuseppe, clicking his fingers at yet another waiter serving on the far side of the restaurant. 'But all of this has nothing to do with me.'

'Doesn't it, Giuseppe?' snarled Nick tersely, stepping forward suddenly to grab the restaurateur by the scruff of his neck. 'Sounds a bit like a mafia hit to me. A scrub-out. Using what might just be, but probably isn't, a traditional mafia method of murder – the ritual deboning. *Il ritual del disossamento*, Giuseppe. That's right, you heard me. *Quelli che devono essere disossati*. "They who must be deboned."'

'Bulla-shit!'

'Is that what this is about, Giuseppe? Was there some rival don in that morning swim session, perhaps? Or maybe your mole on the town council refused a bribe to alter this restaurant's health and hygiene rating? Maybe those garden centre killings had something to do with their popular organic food kiosk driving up the cost of your own imported veg? Then there's the booze cruise. Were you managing the career of their resident lounge singer, Giuseppe? Was Bing "Perry" Bennett no longer giving up his percentage? Was he being wined and dined by some rival manager from the Corbuccini mob when you finally decided to off him? What exactly do you serve in those meatballs, Giuseppe? Is it horse? Did someone at the meat raffle do some digging and pluck out a hoof or two? Was that why you topped them all, Giuseppe? Was it? And then, when the heat was finally on, did you and the Mantovani boys try and off the entire police department in one fell swoop in an effort to get them off your back?'

'The police-a department?' cried Giuseppe suddenly, his eyes starting to well up.

'That's right, Giuseppe. The deboner's struck again, and offed an entire squad.'

'Hey, you,' said a voice behind Nick. 'Droppa the gun.'

He heard the distinct click of a weapon being cocked, and realised he should have kept one eye on the waiter to whom Giuseppe had just signalled.

Releasing Giuseppe's collar, Nick lowered his weapon as two more waiters from the far side of the restaurant closed in, surrounding him.

Marco reached over and yanked the revolver from Nick's hand, before smoothing Giuseppe's collar back into place. Luigi handed the restaurant owner a tissue.

'What is all-a this-a you say-a about-a the police department?' croaked Giuseppe. 'You mean-a the police-a station, right?'

Jeez, thought Nick.

The guy looked like he was about to *weep*. Not the reaction he'd expected from a mafia don learning about the mass wipeout of an entire police force.

'Like I said, Giuseppe. Both the police and all prisoners at the Stalkford precinct have been wiped out.'

'No!' yelled Giuseppe, bursting into tears. 'Not the prisoners, too! It cannot be!'

'Whatta you a-wanna us to do with this asshole, Pop?' asked Marco, holding the gun agitatedly against Nick's head. 'Shall I start-a a-wasting his balls?'

Roughly, Giuseppe wiped away his tears and glared sternly at Nick. 'I tell you what I'm-a gonna do, mister. I'm-a gonna personally shoot-a both your balls and stuffa 'em inside a big meatball sauce, and make-a you eat-a them one after the other.'

The five gathered waiters cheered loudly, four of them each grabbing one of Nick's limbs while the fifth headed straight for his testes.

'Get your stinking paws off my marbles!' Nick bellowed. But no sooner had Nick sensed a strange hand clenching at his globes than he felt it drop away again in favour of the golden locket situated an inch or so to the left of his scrotum.

'Hey, whatta the hell is this?' cried Marco, withdrawing the glittering item of jewellery and holding it up to the light. "I know this locket!"

Nick sensed a swelling of fresh sibling aggression as Marco flipped it open, exposing the black-and-white photograph of the countess within.

'It's a picture of Nonna!' yelled Marco. 'Hey, Pop!' he cried, addressing Giuseppe. 'I think it's *his*!'

'*His*?' replied Giuseppe. 'What the hell is *his* locket a' doing here?'

His? thought Nick. *Who the hell are they talking about?*

But before Nick could figure out an answer, there was a sudden roar of anger, and he felt himself being dragged across to a waste bin beside the main bar. Were they gonna do it right here, he wondered? In front of all the restaurant customers? Customers who'd largely finished their mains and would soon be demanding desserts? Were they actually about to yank off Nick's balls in public and start mixing up a fresh sauce when it was almost time to roll out the cake trolley?

Giuseppe leaned towards Nick's head, thrusting the locket in front of his face.

'Where-a the hella you getta this from?'

Nick winced as a hand once again grabbed at his *cajones*. 'In the jail cells,' he gasped.

Immediately, Giuseppe let out a howl, joined immediately by similar howls from his surrounding sons. Then, all at once, Nick felt the collective grasp upon his body loosen, as the men burst into mutual tears and commenced hugging each other.

'*Mamma mia!*' wailed Giuseppe. 'They come-a for him too, now!'

'What the hell do you mean?' asked Nick. 'Who's been a-coming for who?'

But instead of answering Nick, the assembled captors turned as one to face him, their tear-streaked faces morphing into ugly expressions of primal fury. Then all of the Mantovani boys, except Marco who was already holding Nick's gun, reached beneath their individual serving towels and drew out personal Berettas.

'Go blast-a his balls!' ordered Giuseppe. 'Then bring-a them to me on a plate!'

As Giuseppe's boys took aim at Nick's nether regions, the author cried out in vain. 'You're making a mistake!' he yelled, realising it was already too late to stop the inevitable. He braced himself for the imminent double-crack of exploding gunfire and decimating testicle.

But the noise that followed was something else entirely.

'Hey! Whatta the hell you think you're doing, Giuseppe?'

Nick turned his head to the left. This new yet strangely familiar-sounding voice emanated, he sensed, from the restaurant itself. One of the customers was now rushing towards them between the tables, a tomato-spattered napkin still tucked inside the neck of his shirt.

Nick could hardly believe his eyes. For the man's face, along with its thick, brown moustache, were instantly familiar.

Hell, they'd even been buddies, once. Because this guy with the overgrown painter's brush was none other than Stalkford's burned-out 'talk' therapist turned violent street maverick, Cliff 'Livewire' Capello.

But that couldn't be ... *could it?* After all, as far as Nick could recall, Capello was *dead* ...

'This here is Nick Steen, goddammit!' yelled Capello, reaching the group of waiters and immediately batting away their gun arms from the vicinity of Nick's balls. 'Put those guns away, you *assholes*! This guy saved my life!'

This wasn't exactly true. Technically, Nick hadn't really saved Capello's life at all. In fact, he'd more or less left him to die during their joint battle to defeat the sinister machinations of Dr Nelson Strain and his army of Boners.* But right now, Nick had to admit, Capello was in the process of saving *his*.

'Come along with me, Nick,' said Capello, ushering the waiters away before yanking Nick's gun back from Marco's hand. 'You were gonna blow the man's balls off with his *own* gun? Where is the goddamned respect these days? This man saved my life, God dammit!'

Embarrassed, Giuseppe shoved his sons aside, grabbing the accumulated tips from their respective shirt pockets before stuffing them deep inside Capello's jacket.

'I'm-a so sorry, Cliff,' said Giuseppe. 'We are just-a so upset.'

'Sure, okay, okay,' said Capello, smoothing things over with the restaurant owner. Both men kissed each other on the cheek, then Capello kissed the respective cheeks of Giuseppe's sons before waving them off towards the kitchen area.

'I'm-a gonna cook up some special meatballs, just for you, Capello,' said Giuseppe. 'And for my beloved *fratello*.'

Fratello? As in brother?

The mention of the word (either '*fratello*' or 'brother') caught Nick's attention. Was this brother the guy Giuseppe and his sons had

---

* See *Bride of Bone* in *Garth Marenghi's TerrorTome*. GM

been crying over? If so, then presumably the locket he'd found in the prison cell had belonged to Giuseppe's sibling? Gradually, things were starting to make the slightest bit of sense. Giuseppe had sobbed because he believed his own brother had been torn to pieces in that doomed jail cell.

Meaning the Mantovanis hadn't committed the police station slaying, after all. Rather, they'd been *victims* of it! Evidently the locket's owner, one of Giuseppe's many brothers, had perished in the massacre.

But Roz had *insisted* there had been no one called Mantovani imprisoned in the cells, hadn't she? Unless the Mantovani in question, of course, had given the authorities a *false* name... This was the mafia, after all, Nick reflected grimly. For them, no crime was too base.

While Nick pondered all the above, Capello nodded sombrely at the retreating restaurant staff, then turned to face Nick, handing him back the golden locket he'd surreptitiously lifted from Giuseppe's pocket mid-hug.

'Thanks. But please don't kiss me, Capello.'

'And you don't be an asshole, Nick Steen,' Capello replied, grabbing Nick's cheeks in his hands and planting two big wet ones either side of the demon-slayer's face. 'You're my *brother*, dammit.'

Capello's *brother*. *Fratello*. That hit Nick like a big sock filled with snooker balls. To be called Capello's brother was the ultimate compliment from a man who'd given his own life to die alongside his *genuine* sibling.

It was, indeed, the highest mark of respect Capello could show Nick, short of asking him to sign one of his novels.

And maybe, just maybe, this much-revered loyalty between siblings also explained why Giuseppe had been so torn up about his *own* brother's demise – whoever the hell Giuseppe's brother was. But, given the man was now a thoroughly deboned ex-felon, Nick ultimately had no real interest in finding out.

'Come on, Nick, let's break-a some balls. *Meat*balls, I mean.' Capello laughed raucously.

Nick laughed too, although he knew, deep down, that if he could break genuine human balls with anyone else in the entire world, it would be this man alone.

He just had to find out one thing.

Why Cliff Capello was no longer dead.

CHAPTER FOUR

'So, how come you're alive?' asked Nick, plunging his cracked bread stick into a plateful of steaming meatball spaghetti.

Capello, shreds of flat-leaf parsley peppering both cheeks, held up one finger, his lips still in the process of sucking up multiple strands of sauced pasta. As the spaghetti disappeared at speed below Capello's moustache with a satisfying *schmack*, Nick ducked to avoid another arc of spraying tomato.

They'd only been chomping for two minutes, but Capello's napkin already resembled a piece of misplaced homicide evidence. Nick watched as his former buddy wolfed down another mouthful of ball, poured a second full glass of corked Chianti from their mock-wicker carafe, then double-chomped both breadstick ends together, creating a cloud of crumbs that stuck to Capello's moustache like falling snowflakes. The Italian angled the wine bottle towards Nick.

'Not for me, I'm slaying,' said Nick. 'I have to stay in control.'

Capello grinned widely, exposing a mouthful of mashed meatball. 'That's what I like about you, Nick. Always slaying the demons.'

'I remember you did, too – *once*,' said Nick. 'And you haven't answered my question.'

Capello looked momentarily confused. 'What question was that, Nick?' said the Italian, immediately forking up another mound of spaghetti.

Capello knew damn well what question Nick had asked. Could this famously unpredictable Italian hothead really be so preoccupied with Giuseppe's meatballs that he hadn't heard? Nick knew it was possible, of course, himself having once ignored his own internal voice while allowing an entire flotilla of Her Majesty's navy to be wiped out by the telson* of a giant tiger prawn as Nick's conscious brain paused to savour the flesh of a titanic red Carabineros† he'd been battling all morning after his giant prawn warfare novel *The Big Prawn-Off* had come to terrifying life last June. And though Nick had insisted on at least a mouthful or two mid-battle, plus a dash of lemon to enhance flavour, in order to restore his body's stamina for the main event (the titular prawn-off), the internal voice of his own subconscious had never let Nick off the proverbial fishing hook.

But Capello was hardly in need of extra stamina, by the look of things. No, for some reason Nick sensed Capello was bluffing.

'I asked you why you're not dead?'

'Wrong, Nick,' said Capello, grinning up at him again, mouth once more half-full of spaghetti. His napkin looked even worse. 'You asked me why I'm *alive*.'

Then Capello *had* heard him.

'The last time I saw you, Capello, you were hurling yourself into the fray with an army of Nelson Strain's Skeletorian Guard in an attempt to rescue the headless form of your deceased skeletonised brother.'

'That's true, Nick. And it all worked out well.'

That's not how Nick remembered it.

'That's not how I remember it, Capello.'

'Well,' said Capello, pausing to burp semi-politely into his napkin, 'how do *you* remember it?'

Damn it, was Capello *stalling*?

---

* Look it up. GM
† Again, look it up. I'm not your science teacher. GM

BONELORD

'The way I remember it, Capello, is that as soon as Roz and I managed to escape from that place, we were immediately pursued across the outer swamp by an army of raging Boners. Those very same raging Boners whom we believed had just torn you and your skeletal-yet-still-sentient brother to pieces. But maybe that's not how it happened. Maybe you two ran away and left them to pursue us?'

'It may have looked like that, Nick. But I *promise* you, we did our best to stop those Boners from following you.'

Capello's smile had faded, and Nick thought he could see tears welling in the Italian's eyes. Maybe it was *guilt* that Capello was hiding from.

'The trouble is, *you* were the one they were after, Nick. Not us. They immediately abandoned our fight and focused on chasing you instead. Then, by the time I'd emerged from that secret army research base, you and Roz were long gone. I thought *you* were dead, goddammit ...' The Italian reached up suddenly with his napkin to wipe away tears.

It checked out, Nick guessed.

'Don't sweat it, Capello. How *is* brother Dwayne?'

'He *did* die, Nick,' whispered Capello, pausing mid-spaghetti-suck to wipe another tear from his eye and make the sign of the cross under his bespattered napkin.

'I'm sorry,' said Nick, even though in reality he was essentially indifferent. The guy had been a skeleton, after all.

Capello brushed away a second tear. 'I thank you, Nick, for letting us have that last moment together, brother to brother, fighting against an army of killer skeletons. Not many people can say they've done that, right?'

'I guess so. Except me, of course.'

'Of course,' agreed Capello, his expression serious. 'It meant the world to me, Nick. And Dwayne.'

'No sweat, buddy,' whispered Nick, gripping Capello's shoulder manfully and fixing him with an understanding stare. Capello smiled deeply, and reached forward to grip Nick's own shoulder manfully, fixing him with a similarly understanding stare, if one tinged with an additional aching melancholy.

'It's like old times, *paesano*,' said Capello, smiling wistfully. Then he snapped into his usual wide grin. 'You old pirate!'

Nick was a *paesano*, certainly, but not technically a pirate, and he suspected Capello was mixing him up with some previous buddy. And Capello still seemed distracted for some reason. Nick needed to know why.

'How are things otherwise?' he asked, twirling a forkful of spaghetti against his spoon.

Capello watched him do this for a moment, then vainly tried to copy him. 'I'm good, Nick, even if the knowledge that I've only ever been a figment of your imagination does cramp my style.'

'Wrong, Capello. *That's* what's cramping your style,' said Nick, pointing to the Italian's fork, which had failed to maintain its coiled spaghetti and had sent everything dropping down on to his plate again, the impact immediately daubing Capello's napkin with yet another spattering of tomato sauce.

'Thanks for saving my life, by the way,' said Nick, realising he'd forgotten to say anything at all about Capello halting his altercation with Giuseppe and his boys.

'Hey, you saved mine, Nick. That means we're quits.'

'*Quits?*' said Nick, suddenly troubled. When did former buddies ever speak of being 'quits'? 'You mean even, right?'

'Even! That's what I said, Nick.'

'No, Capello. You said "quits".'

'Quits? Even? What's the difference?'

Capello began to laugh. To Nick, it sounded like a *false* laugh.

'No difference,' said Nick, dropping the subject.

BONELORD

'So, what got them all riled up?' Capello asked, knocking back yet another full glass of piss-poor Chianti.

'This damned locket,' said Nick, sliding it over the table towards the Italian. Capello picked up the jewel, flipped open its case to expose the black-and-white photo of the old Italian countess, and winced.

'Something wrong?' asked Nick.

Capello said nothing for several moments, his eyes still fixed on the old woman's intimidating countenance.

He looks frightened, thought Nick.

'It's their mother, Nick. I mean, Giuseppe's mother. His sons' grandmother. A very vindictive lady. Rumour has it that she was some sort of witch. Luckily, she died last year. So you see, they are still very upset.'

'Well, they should man up a bit. Christ, she looks like she's about to croak in that photo.'

'You say you found this at the police station?' said Capello, examining the jewel more closely.

'That's right. Like I told you just now.* There have been multiple massacres taking place across the city.'

Capello looked up sharply. 'Massacres?'

'Specifically, debonings.'

'*Debonings?*'

'Like I've already told you, Capello.† Gatherings of people across the city are being eviscerated by a person, persons or demon unknown, and their bones scattered to the four winds. So violently, I might add, that only the tiniest flecks of bone marrow remain, largely stuck to distant fence panels and overhanging telegraph poles.'

---

* Between chapters three and four, to save on unnecessary expository repetition. Don't go looking for this conversation earlier, because it doesn't exist in the pages of this book. Just take it from me, it happened. GM

† See previous footnote. GM

'Heaven protect us . . .' whispered Capello, once again making the sign of the cross below his now largely orange-tinted napkin.

'The police station deboning was the latest. My hunch is that the killer, or killers, or walking monstrosity, or gas, attempted to destroy the investigating officers because someone there was getting too close to identifying its identity. Now the squad in question is severely depleted and the investigation back to square one. Still, on the plus side, it looks like they accidentally took out one of the Mantovani boys at the same time.'

'You're right, Nick. This locket belonged to Giuseppe's brother, *Roberto* Mantovani.'

'A mafia goon, Capello,' said Nick, rising suddenly from the table. 'He and Giuseppe had it coming. Here, you might as well hand this back to them.' He tossed the locket down on the table. It was useless to him now. Not remotely the vital clue he'd been hoping for.

'Wait, Nick,' said Capello, grabbing his arm suddenly. 'No matter what you might think of the Mantovanis, they didn't deserve this – for one of them to be completely deboned by some wandering monster in an enclosed cell.'

'That's a matter of opinion, Capello.'

'Maybe, but whatever that thing is, Nick – whoever it's killing – it needs to be stopped.'

'Can't argue with that,' Nick said – and then he was struck by a sudden thought. An appalling thought, admittedly, but one that possessed a crazy kind of insane logic. 'What if I asked Giuseppe and his boys to help me?' he said. 'With the police out of the running, it would mean a lot of extra muscle on our side.'

Especially, he thought, *if – no, in fact, when – Kettlestrom comes calling with his whack warrant.*

'I don't think they would agree to that, Nick. And even if they did, I might not be around the next time they make a grab for your balls.'

'Yeah, maybe,' admitted Nick, dismissing the notion.

BONELORD

'Unless ...'

Nick glanced back at Capello. 'Unless what?'

'Unless *I* help you, Nick. If there are no more cops around, this killer's going to be hell to catch. Let's team up, like old times. We don't need the Mantovanis *or* the police on our side. Just you and me, Nick. Gun to gun. Ball to ball. Pistol *paesanos.*'

'Thanks, Capello,' said Nick, patting the Italian on his shoulder. 'But I work better alone.'

Nick wasn't looking at him, but he could sense the hurt on Capello's face and did his best to ignore it. It wasn't that Nick was averse to teaming up *per se.* After all, he'd only just considered throwing in his lot with the Mantovanis themselves. But Capello was an old buddy of his, and right now Nick didn't know exactly what they were up against. No way could he risk Capello getting deboned until he had a clearer idea of who or what their adversary was.

'Don't be a fool, Nick!' Capello insisted. 'I *can* help you. I know I can.'

'Can you, Capello?' asked Nick, forcing himself to look his former buddy in the eye. After all, it was the honourable thing to do, given the circumstances. Then he transferred his gaze to the Italian's tomato-covered shirt front. And the swelling paunch below it. Damn it, Capello was no good to Nick, anyway. The Italian was enjoying the good life too much. Besides, with Capello's knowledge that he was merely a fictional character, brought to life by Nick's leaking imagination, his abilities might be badly affected at some crucial stage of proceedings. This terrible knowledge alone could put Capello off his aim at a key moment. Or force him to explode violently, precisely when Nick wanted to explode violently instead, and thus take all the glory that was rightfully Nick's.

But his initial concern for the Italian reigned paramount. Nick didn't want Capello dying unnecessarily on his watch. If this deboning entity ultimately came for Nick, then he or she or it would inevitably take out anyone in his vicinity as well. And Nick wasn't going to do that to any man he'd gripped shoulders with.

'Not this time, buddy. Enjoy your meatballs.'

As Nick headed out of the restaurant towards his waiting car, he realised there was another reason, too, why he hadn't wanted to team up with Capello. A reason he could hardly believe he was even contemplating. But the truth was that, for some reason, when Nick had looked Capello directly in the eye mere moments before, the Italian's orbs had immediately darted left to avoid his own. Meaning Nick Steen could no longer fully trust any of the things Cliff 'Livewire' Capello had just been telling him ...

★

'Identified anyone yet?' asked Nick, striding into the main operating theatre of Stalkford county morgue ten minutes later. Roz looked up briefly, then returned her gaze to the sieve in her hand.

'Nothing yet,' she said, observing the last dregs of human liquid drain through the wire mesh, leaving nothing whatsoever behind.

Nick's eyes took in a giant glass vat, filled with what looked very much to him like a tankful of the tomato sauce he'd just been consuming. He stifled a sudden feeling of nausea.

'I presume that's the deboned,' he said, tapping one finger against the glass while averting his eyes, noticing that the shelves usually storing row upon row of Stalkford's deceased had been dismantled in order to allow space for this giant contraption.

'And that's just the police station massacre. The previous debonings are housed in separate vats – and, in the case of the swimming pool slaughter, the pool itself.'

'They've got you working overtime, I see,' said Nick, trying to make light of things.

'I haven't slept for three days, Nick. It took hours to suck up all the physical evidence, then pump it into this giant vat. Now I'm trying to separate each individual blood cell in order to identify those multiple victims sloshing around inside, which is proving nigh-on impossible. At this point in time, I've only been able to isolate enough red cells to reconstruct someone's left knee.'

'Have you run that through the police knee database?'

'Of course I have, Nick. But it turns out to be someone who recently had a knee *replacement*. The knee donor himself died six months ago, so now I'm right back where I started.'

'Maybe a bigger sieve might help?'

'I doubt it, Nick. I'd need other police officers to hold the sides, and those are all currently deboned inside the very tank I need to sieve.' Roz sighed, exasperated. 'How did you get on?'

'Well, lucky for you, Roz. I found out the identity of *one* of your victims, at any rate.'

'Really?'

'Yes, using that locket we extracted.'

'Correction, Nick. The locket *I* extracted.'

'Jeez, Roz. You need some sleep. That locket belonged to Giuseppe Mantovani's brother, *Roberto* Mantovani.'

Roz shook her head firmly. 'Nonsense, Nick. I told you before that we didn't have any prisoner incarcerated here under the name of Roberto Mantovani.'

'And I'm telling you he was here somewhere, Roz. Giuseppe and his sons were weeping like little girls when they heard he'd been killed. That woman in the picture was Giuseppe's mother, the Countess Margarita Mantovani. Apparently she was a right old witch. *And* an old witch.'

'And *I'm* telling *you*, Nick Steen, that we definitely had no prisoner here under the name of Roberto Mantovani. We had a Gripper Stubbs, an Alfie "The Strangler" Bates, a Nobby the Chomper, but no Roberto Mantovani.'

'That's because he used a *false* name, Roz.'

'I don't think even the mafia would stoop so low as to use a false name, Nick,' said Roz, ascending a small ladder in order to scoop out another saucepan of liquid remains from the top of the giant vat. 'And besides, family pride would never allow that, surely?'

'No? Then tell me how the hell a locket containing a photo of the mother of Giuseppe and Roberto Mantovani ended up inside that police cell if Roberto Mantovani wasn't present in the cell in order to drop it?'

'Simple, Nick,' Roz replied. 'Because the locket in question was in fact stolen from Roberto Mantovani by one of these deceased prisoners, prior to them being arrested.'

'You and your "stolen locket" theory, Roz.' Nick sighed, shaking his head. 'You really need to put that one, and yourself, to bed.'

In fact, Nick was aware that Roz was probably right, but he wanted to keep her on her toes regardless. Because if he could force her to work even more overtime, she'd most likely get increasingly tired and leave all the decent clues for him to uncover.

'Well, I'm going to look into it at any rate,' Roz huffed.

'Thattagirl,' said Nick, winking at her. 'I'm off to get some shut-eye. Good luck with sifting through all that lot.'

'Wait, Nick,' said Roz, her expression suddenly darkening. 'I almost forgot to tell you.'

'Tell me what?' Nick replied, gruffly.

'That Police Commissioner Kettlestrom has obtained an arrest warrant.'

'An arrest warrant?'

'For you. In fact, it's not technically an arrest warrant. It's more of a whack warrant. A warrant to whack you, Nick. A warrant to whack you at will.'

'Yeah?' said Nick, scornfully. 'If he has any hope of catching me, he'll need to climb out of those waders first.' And with that, he turned to leave.

BONELORD

Until the phone on Roz's operating table rang.

'Officer Roz?' she announced poshly into the receiver, once she'd climbed back down from the vat.

Nick's former editor listened to the voice on the other end for a few moments, then slammed the phone down.

'That was Kettlestrom,' she said, her face a sickly shade of pale. 'I guess you won't be going to bed after all, Nick. There's been *another* deboning.'

'*Another* deboning?' Nick gasped.

'Another *mass* deboning. Everyone inside the restaurant was completely deboned.'

'*Restaurant?*' stammered Nick, an ominous feeling rising in his stomach – alongside a sudden upsurge of semi-digested spaghetti. For already, deep down, Nick knew exactly which restaurant it was.

'That's right, Nick,' said Roz, watching the expression of terrified disbelief spread across his face as she spoke. 'It was Mantovani and Sons ...'

CHAPTER FIVE

Capello's in there, thought Nick, trying not to panic as he slammed the car's brakes hard outside the Italian restaurant he'd only just departed. *Or somewhere in there*, he corrected himself, remembering that the chances of extracting Capello's remains from those of Giuseppe and all the other deboned victims, including hipsters, waiters and assorted mafia capos, plus forty to fifty semi-digested heavily tomato-based Italian meals, were practically negligible.

Having mentally prepared himself to wait twenty minutes or more for Roz to pull up in her police-issued panda car, he was surprised to find her already there.

'You can't drive anywhere near as fast as I can, Roz. What gives?'

'As a police lady, Nick, I do get certain privileges. One is to drive at illegal super-fast speeds completely legally in a souped-up vintage 1970 Austin 1300.'

Odd, thought Nick. He hadn't seen one of those cars operating since the late 1970s, having written about them in the earliest days of his writing career. Then, at one point in the late nineties, he'd insisted on updating his characters' vehicles in 'modernised' versions of his earlier works in an effort to reflect changing times, resulting in a massive drop in sales. Now here was Roz, beating all the odds by trouncing the performance of Nick's modern vehicle in a seemingly defunct auto-mechanical relic. It certainly had little to do with Roz's innate driving ability, which was well below the usual low standards of more conventional lady motorists.

BONELORD

'Don't let it get to your head, Roz,' Nick warned. 'I've a hunch you're about to be ordering a new giant vat.'

Nick wasn't wrong. As he and Roz stepped past the yellow police tape in fresh waders and entered the restaurant, both were shocked to discover that the deboned remains of the restaurant's clientele came up to their thighs.

'Damn it, my waders are almost entirely submerged, Nick,' said Roz, trying not to make any fast movements in case she accidentally created a mini tidal wave that might propel a mixture of Bolognese sauce and human offal into her boots.

'You're going to have your work cut out here, Roz,' said Nick, swishing the contents of the flooded restaurant through a police-issued fishing net. He lifted the rod and extracted several clumps of shredded Lycra from the net, then let the blood drain free through its gauze to reveal a semi-consumed serving of Mantovani meatball, Giuseppe's signature dish.

'It's not just a case of separating individual blood cells this time,' he continued. 'Now you have the remains of everyone's meals to contend with as well, most of which consist of tomato sauce, assorted pasta shapes and miniature chunks of unspecified meat. Including, if I'm not mistaken' – Nick slid a finger between the lasagne's layers of pasta and dabbed a trace of the mince over his tongue – 'horse.'

'This is *dreadful*, Nick,' sighed Roz. 'How am I even supposed to start looking for clues in all this gore? All our usual crime-scene investigators were wiped out entirely in that last deboning, and now all I have at my disposal are a group of fresh cadets, two traffic officers and a community police volunteer named Gabriel. Who is not the angel his name might appear to suggest.'

'How so?' said Nick, wondering if the officer was another fictional character come to life from his angels vs demons tetralogy *Armageddolypse*, in which escaping heavenly hosts and demonic hordes bring about the end of the Earth as we know it. Twice. At the same time.

'He's after that head of the Stalkford FBI job as well, Nick. Thinks he can do it better than me. Claims he works three times more efficiently.'

'I don't believe that for a second, Roz,' said Nick. '*Two* times more efficiently, maybe, but not three. He's just a community support officer.'

'Even so, Nick, I don't want him helping me out on this case. With our numbers down, I may well be in line for that promotion soon, but if Kettlestrom were to find out that Police Community Support Officer Gabriel is even two times more efficient than me ...'

'Maybe two and a half.'

'Whatever the final number, Nick, I don't want Kettlestrom handing Police Community Support Officer Gabriel my own personal patch to pound. And I certainly don't want to see him made head of Stalkford FBI's Office. That position is mine alone, I tell you. Mine.'

'Fair enough, Roz. Then it looks like it's just you and me,' said Nick, rallying his one troop. 'Correction: just you. I'm here to find what's left of Capello, then I have to go.'

'I understand, Nick,' said Roz, taking the fishing net from his hand to sift elsewhere through the ocean of blood with bits of hipster Lycra in it.

'I just can't believe I was in here talking to him only an hour ago,' said Nick, wading across to the small table at which he and Capello had sat chatting and scoffing.

He reached down into the lapping pool below to retrieve what looked like a sodden, orange rag. It wasn't Lycra, Nick realised. That colour would be too ironic, even for bloody hipsters. Then he saw what it was.

Capello's napkin.

All at once, he was fighting back tears.

'He saved my life, dammit. Only sixty or so minutes ago! Why did it have to happen, Roz. *Why?*'

'I hate to say it, Nick, but maybe whoever did this—'

'Or *whatever*,' Nick interrupted, turning his grief-stricken rage on her.

'Or *whatever* did this may have known that *you* were in here. Maybe they—'

'Or *it*.'

'Or *it* believed that you were inside the building when it attacked.'

'You mean the deboner was coming for *me* on this occasion?'

'It certainly seems a possibility, Nick. Perhaps, even though you haven't thrown up one single cogent clue concerning the attacker's identity as yet, it suspects you're on the right trail.'

Nick could see why the police had hired Roz, for her female tack was sharpening by the day. It was a good job she was no longer his editor, because at this rate of mental development, the chances were strong that Roz might start believing more fervently in her own editorial judgements, too, which meant she'd probably start insisting Nick stick to her proposed editorial changes despite his passionate and occasionally violent protests to the contrary. Thankfully, now that she'd joined the police force, he wouldn't have to sack her on the spot.

'Well, whatever it is that's been deboning all these people, Roz, the fact remains that they've angered me in a way they never anticipated I'd be angered. I couldn't give a flying one about minced hipsters – in fact, I welcome their demise – but by killing my soul buddy, Cliff "Livewire" Capello, the killer's practically *guaranteed* their own destruction. Because I will never rest, Roz, until whoever, or whatever—'

'Or whomsoever.'

'Forget "whomsoever", Roz. I'm not writing a solicitor's letter.'

'Sorry, Nick. Go on.'

'I will not rest until whoever or whatever, but not whomsoever, is dead. Killed by my own bare hands, if a shotgun or automatic machine gun aren't to hand.'

Barely had Nick uttered these words than the sound of an approaching police siren was heard outside.

'I thought you said there wasn't anyone else available to help with the investigation, Roz? Unless this is Police Community Support Officer Gabriel arriving, to improve your evidently already ailing efficiency rating?'

'No, Nick. It's far worse. Worse for *you*, I mean. For that particular police siren is the *louder* police siren. The one that gets put on the super squad car, as opposed to our more normal panda cars. That police siren belongs to the police commissioner himself!'

Kettlestrom. That's all Nick needed right now. Here he was, standing alone in a fetid pool of yet more recently deboned victims. How on earth would Kettlestrom not suspect that Nick himself was the one committing these mass debonings?

'You'd best explain that I'm standing here in the middle of the deceased for a reason, Roz. Because right now I have these victims' literal blood on my hands, and am liable to be locked up by Kettlestrom *tout suite*, which is French for "toot sweet".'

'And there's no escape,' said a familiar voice from the doorway.

Nick looked over at what seemed at first glance to be a small ball perched on the end of a pair of giant black marker pens. As his eyes adjusted to the glare of the neon street lights shining behind the bizarrely shaped silhouette, he realised the figure was Bob Kettlestrom himself, wearing a pair of slightly taller waders that now came up to his armpits.

'No way out at all, Mister Steen. As you can or cannot see, I have here in my hand a warrant to whack you at will. We have you surrounded. There are no exits in the main restaurant area, and Officer Roz is standing between yourself and the kitchen, so you can't flee that way, either.'

BONELORD

Nick assumed Kettlestrom wasn't lying about there being no exits other than the main door. Given that the restaurant's recently deceased proprietor, Giuseppe Mantovani, was one of Stalkford's most notorious mafia dons, the police must know this place back to front. Yet surely, as an aforesaid notorious mafia don, Giuseppe and his deboned sons would have constructed a secret getaway route in case of a sudden police raid like this? If only Nick could somehow find it, he *may* be able to escape ...

'We suspect there was an altercation between you and the Mantovanis shortly before they were deboned,' said Kettlestrom, striding forward into the room and sending a small tsunami of human soup rushing forward, seeping over the top of Nick's waders.

'But you have no witnesses,' countered Nick. 'Because I'm standing in them.'

'I can vouch for Mister Steen's innocence,' interrupted Roz, trying to ignore the sensation of deboned customers now slopping inside her own waders. 'He's only just arrived here, with me. Even if I was a bit faster than him.'

'Balls, Roz,' snapped Nick. 'Your car's been souped up.'

'Don't lie to me, mister,' said Kettlestrom. 'You didn't "just get here" at all. We've had this place wiretapped for a while, and we heard the whole thing. We know full well you were here a mere hour before these debonings took place.'

'If you had the place wiretapped,' said Nick, 'then you'll know that someone – or something – other than me deboned these people. Because I'd left before any of that happened.'

'We'll check the tapes later, of course,' said Kettlestrom. 'But right now you're our chief suspect, and we're taking you into custody so we can whack you at will back at the station. Officer Roz? Cuff him.'

Surely not, thought Nick. Surely Roz wouldn't do as her superior officer commanded and arrest her former author on some trumped-up charge, for a crime he definitely hadn't committed?

'I'm sorry, Nick,' she said, stepping towards him through the liquid gore. 'But I erroneously vouched for your innocence just now, and if I have any hope of protecting my integrity as a police officer and potentially becoming head of Stalkford's FBI Office in a matter of mere days, I must obey without question the command of my superior officer.'

'I'm warning you, Roz,' said Nick, getting panicky. 'If you arrest me now, there'll be no one left to investigate these debonings other than yourself and that increasingly efficient Police Community Support Officer Gabriel I keep hearing about, who's similarly hell-bent on becoming the new head of Stalkford's FBI Office.'

Jeez, even *that* couldn't persuade Roz.

'In any case,' Nick went on, 'I can guarantee Kettlestrom here isn't going to lift a finger to help you.'

'Is that so?' said Kettlestrom, wading forward. 'You think because I'm the police commissioner, I somehow don't like getting my feet dirty once in a while?'

'Dirty, maybe. Bloody, no.'

'Well, that's where you're wrong, Mister Steen. Because I was all set to arrest Giuseppe this week for his crimes against humanity. I knew he operated the late-night lock-in racket, and apparently had also been "accidentally" reducing the number of meatballs in his signature sauce from the advertised five to barely four.'

'Yeah, I noticed that, too,' said Nick, still feeling short-changed. 'And if I was you, I'd be running an additional DNA check on the balls in question.'

'Whatever Giuseppe puts in his balls doesn't interest me, Mister Steen.'

'Even if it's horse?'

'Who hasn't eaten horse at some point in their lives? I'm talking about a *deboning*, Mister Steen. And the bottom line is Giuseppe didn't deserve getting deboned, and neither did his sons. Hipsters? Who gives a shit? But as likely chief imaginer behind whatever this thing is, I'm holding *you* entirely responsible.'

With that, Kettlestrom whipped out his .38 revolver.

'Now hold on,' said Nick, realising his chances of locating an alternative exit somewhere towards the rear of the restaurant were long gone. 'I only came here to chase up a clue for Officer Roz, who found it at the police station slaying.'

'A clue?' snapped Kettlestrom. 'What clue?'

'A locket, sir,' said Roz, sheepishly.

'A locket? What's this about a locket?'

'It belonged to the Mantovanis, sir,' Roz explained, evidently starting to fear for her imminent promotion. 'I found it floating about in the police cells.'

'And you gave it to *him*?' said Kettlestrom, pointing his gun even more forcefully at Nick. 'That was vital police evidence.'

'Hardly,' said Nick. 'It was just a picture of their mother.'

'Whose mother?'

'*Their* mother.'

'The Mantovanis' mother?'

'Yes, the mother in the locket.'

'Are you lusting after their mother?'

'Why would I be lusting after their mother?'

'Maybe you're lusting after *my* mother?'

'Why would I be lusting after *your* mother?'

'Are you saying my mother's ugly?'

'I'm sure your mother's very attractive.'

'You *are* lusting after my mother.'

'Look, this is just an excuse to whack me right here, isn't it?'

'You saw him, Officer Roz,' snarled Kettlestrom, pulling back the trigger on his levelled .38. 'Mister Steen was resisting arrest and lusting after my mother.'

'Roz!' Nick pleaded, hoping she could help in some way. But his former editor was already removing a pair of handcuffs from her belt and angling them in the direction of Nick's arms.

'Don't bother with the cuffs, Officer Roz,' said Kettlestrom. 'This is an immediate whack job.'

And before Roz could object, the police commissioner opened fire.

But Nick was no longer in front of him. Sensing what was about to take place, Nick had braced himself for the inevitable, opted for the least appalling alternative option, and dived headfirst into the pool of deboned remains.

'Where is he?' cried Kettlestrom, squeezing off several rounds into the swamp of swirling, bubbling viscera.

Roz gasped, watching as jets of crimson liquid burst upwards with each impact, the entire pool below them now a seething, frothing mass of frenzied, frantic motion. Amid a rush of bubbles and floating breadsticks, Roz dimly sensed a swirl of fluid pass by her feet as a dark form slid through the murky liquid below her, then passed between Kettlestrom's parted waders.

Then a rush of liquid sounded as something large rose from the bloody pool, over by the restaurant's front door.

It was Nick, she saw, drenched from head to toe in what she hoped was predominantly ten tins' worth of chopped tomatoes.

Run, Nick! she thought, not daring to utter those words aloud.

And by the time Kettlestrom himself had realised what had just occurred in front of his very eyes and fired off his remaining rounds in the direction of the risen felon, Nick had done precisely that.

CHAPTER SIX

Nick raced past the door of Mantovani's towards his waiting Honda Civic, realising there was no way he could avoid staining its interior. He was covered from head to toe in deboned remains, after all, and no amount of industrial-strength car shampoo was going to shift human innards from the upholstery.

Luckily, someone washing a nearby vehicle was so startled by Nick's scarlet appearance that they lost control of their hosepipe and accidentally doused him with water, cleaning off his body entirely, so Nick was now completely clean as if he hadn't just swum through a load of blood at all.

Without pausing to thank the guy (he only had time to berate him), Nick yanked open the door of his car, jumped inside and keyed the ignition.

As Nick floored it past the restaurant, he caught sight of Roz emerging from the doorway, knowing Kettlestrom would be close behind her, give or take a few seconds owing to the size of those new waders of his. If Nick could somehow make it out of Stalkford's Little Italy, he might be able to lose the pursuing cops in Little Chinaland or Little Igloo, the town's rarely-visited Inuit district.

He looked into the rear-view mirror to check on Roz's progress – and was shocked to see someone sitting in the back of his car.

It was Capello.

'Hi, Nick.'

'*Capello!* I thought you were dead,' gasped Nick, swerving the car right into Little Igloo. He glanced at the rear-view mirror again. The moustachioed Italian was still wearing his spaghetti-stained napkin.

'I think I'm in shock, Nick.'

'What happened?'

'Seconds after you left, I went for a wee-wee in the alley outside – the toilets at Mantovani's restaurant are *obscene* – and when I came back in, everybody was in pieces, Nick. So I went out again and telephoned the police. When I saw your car draw up outside, I decided to climb in when you weren't looking – which I managed despite the door being locked, which always happens in your horror thrillers. Then I waited for you.'

'Thank God you survived,' said Nick.

'Tell me about it. I was terrified that whatever had deboned those people would come looking for me, too. But I knew that if I could just hold out long enough, my old buddy would be back here once again to save my life.'

'Don't get too misty-eyed, Capello. I have a suspicion that whoever or whatever, but not whomsoever—'

'What about whatsoever?' interrupted Capello.

'No. "Whatsoever" is an adverb used for emphasis, deployed most often after a negative phrase to add emphasis to a notion that's being expressed.'*

'Sorry, Nick. My English is no good – *whatsoever.*' Capello guffawed loudly at his own witticism, though Nick refused to join in, still annoyed by Capello's initial interruption.

'Whoever or whatever – but not whomsoever, and not remotely whatsoever – deboned those people in Mantovani's was after *me*, Capello.'

'*You*, Nick?'

'That's right. And if you'd been in there at the same time, you'd

---

* Look it up, like I did. GM

have been deboned too. And all because the deboner was trying to get to *me*. Hell, everyone's out to get me at the moment, Capello. Even the police, who think *I* must have done this with my leaking imagination. I've no memory of writing a book like this, but this evening the police commissioner himself was out wiretapping my house. So don't start feeling too grateful towards me, Capello, even if I did subsequently help you with some basic grammar issues.'

'It's not your fault, Nick. I know if you had a chance in hell of killing whoever, whatever, but not whomsoever—'

'And not remotely whatsoever,' added Nick, helping out yet again, as was his wont.

'Not remotely *whatsoever* this thing is, you'd have done it by now. That's why I insist on helping you with this case, Nick. You need a buddy by your side. You can't beat this thing on your own.'

'I know,' Nick whispered to himself, so quietly that Capello couldn't quite hear. He hated admitting any sign of weakness, especially in public, even if Capello *was* his buddy.

'Let me help you beat this thing, Nick,' said Capello, leaning forward in the chair to grasp Nick's shoulder manfully. 'I know I can beat your thing.'

'True, we've beaten each other's things before,' said Nick, slowly coming round to the idea.

'Then let me beat your thing now.'

'You *really* want to beat my thing?'

'Are you crazy? After all those times *you* beat *my* thing? Of course I wanna beat your thing.'

'Fine, so let's beat each other's things,' said Nick, breathing a deep sigh of relief. It felt good to have Capello on board again, he had to admit. For together, they always helped each other beat their respective things. 'You know, I thought I'd grasped your shoulder manfully for the last time, Capello,' Nick said, 'but even so, can you stop grasping mine now? You're greasing up the leather.'

'Sure thing, Nick. I'll grease leather with you another time.' And with that, Capello removed his hand from Nick's shoulder and eased back into his seat.

As Capello's frame moved away from the rear-view mirror, Nick felt a sharp stab of angst at the sudden appearance of blue flashing lights closing in at speed from behind.

'The fuzz,' spat Nick, slamming his foot down on the accelerator.

'Go easy, Nick!' cried Capello from the rear, but Nick knew there was no time for caution. He only hoped that most of the Inuit population of Little Igloo were either tucked up safely inside their frozen ice-houses at this time of night, or out fishing.

'Hold on to your hat, Capello,' said Nick, wrestling the vehicle into a nearby sidestreet, its fishtailing rear slamming several cardboard boxes of harpoons halfway across the road.

'I'm not wearing a hat, Nick!' yelled Capello. 'What the hell do I hold on to instead?'

'Hold on to anything, Capello.'

He couldn't quite reach Nick, so Capello opted instead for cupping his own balls, which somehow did the trick.

'Go for it, Nick!' the Italian yelled as Nick approached a rounded igloo at speed. With the sound of police sirens closing in behind, Nick braced himself, released his seat belt in case he needed to exit the car in a hurry (and because it made sense dramatically), then vaulted the Honda Civic skyward, over the igloo's roof. With a crashing thump, the car hit the ground at speed, several yards past the igloo. But Nick realised it was already too late.

For ahead of them, blocking the road, was Roz's souped-up Austin 1300 panda vehicle.

Nick slammed on the brakes, swerving the car sideways to avoid clipping Roz, who stood firm, waiting calmly by the side of her vehicle.

As Nick's Civic skidded to a final halt and the dust began to clear, Roz tapped firmly on the driver's-side window.

BONELORD

'Damn it, Nick, I think you were speeding,' said a worried Capello, from behind.

'Let me handle this, bud,' said Nick, winding the glass partition downward. He immediately let rip at Roz. 'You were speeding just as much as I was, Roz,' said Nick, electing to go on the offensive, like they do in chess. 'In fact you were speeding *more* than me, because you somehow overtook me while I was vaulting that igloo.'

'Relax, Nick. I'm not here to issue you with a speeding fine – although consider this an official caution. Keep your speed low and within legal limits at all times.'

'I will, Roz. I promise.'

'I do hope so, Nick. Because this is a residential area full of Inuit, huskies and wandering polar bears.'

'Yetis, too, if you remember, Roz,' said Nick. And Roz did remember, recalling that they'd both been in Little Igloo only last year, battling a giant yeti family from Nick's arctic thriller *Frozen Horror and the Handersons* – even though Roz had pointed out on several occasions that those yetis were, geographically speaking, native to the Himalayas and not Antarctica, as Nick stubbornly, and ultimately victoriously, maintained.

'Yetis migrated en masse during the first ice age, Roz, from the frozen plains of Antarctica to the even more frozen peaks of the Himalayas. I paid a researcher to come up with that, remember, so you're still wrong.'

'Regardless, Nick,' said Roz, evidently pressed for time, 'I came to inform you that I'll attempt to hold Kettlestrom off for as long as I can, but he's ordered everyone in the police force to whack you on sight. Including me.'

'You?'

'Of course, I won't do that just yet, Nick. Maybe tomorrow, or, if you're lucky, the following day. But you'd best speed up with solving this case, in case I'm forced to whack you when you least expect it.'

'Well, I have orders, too, Roz – from myself, no less – to whack *the police* on sight. So put that in Kettlestrom's pipe and smoke it.'

'I'd rather not, Nick. I'm having enough trouble with Police Community Support Officer Gabriel insisting on doing that at all hours of the day and night, as well as fetching his superior's slippers whenever Kettlestrom asks for them. Anyway, I came to tell you something else, too.'

'Shoot.'

A Beretta appeared beneath Nick's ear, aiming squarely at Roz.

'Not you, Capello,' said Nick.

'Sorry, Nick,' the Italian replied, lowering the gun again.

'Carry on, Roz. What else did you come to tell me?'

Roz slid her own half-drawn revolver back into its holster and continued. 'That there *was* a witness to the Mantovani deboning, after all.'

'A witness? How? And more importantly, who?'

'Someone who was in the restaurant toilet when it all happened, Nick. Unable to locate a bar of soap in either of the lavatories, they came through to the kitchen area and managed to glimpse whoever or whatever, but not whomsoever—'

'And definitely not whatsoever,' piped up Capello again, from behind.

'—the person, or *thing* was.'

'Where's the witness now, Roz?' asked Nick.

The amateur police lady winced visibly, as if afraid to give Nick the answer.

'Up at the state asylum ...'

*

The man was insane. Totally insane. And what he was describing was even more insane. But given he'd apparently been completely sane before he stepped inside Giuseppe's restaurant – or, at least, as completely sane as a hipster could claim to be, which was only partly sane – Nick had a duty to hear the guy out.

'Let me run over this again,' said Nick, eyes roaming once more over the hastily-scrawled notes he'd taken down while the patient before him ranted, raved and foamed continually at the mouth. 'You saw what you think was a *big skeleton* . . .'

'Yes!' the man raved.

'A big skeleton . . . in a *red cape*?'

'Yes! Yes! A big skeleton in a red cape!' the man ranted.

'A big skeleton in a red cape that slashed the occupants of the restaurant apart with its bare, fleshless hands?'

'Yes, damn it! That's exactly what I said!'

Nick nodded as the struggling hipster chained to the wall in a Lycra-themed straitjacket shook himself frenziedly in a futile attempt to escape his bonds.

'Please,' said Dr Tentacles, who'd allowed Nick access to the asylum and was observing his interrogation, 'there's no need to put my patient through further distress. He's had quite enough for one day. As have I. You have no idea how difficult it was sourcing close-fitting "mad-wear" for ironic purposes.'

'I just wanted to confirm he said it was a big skeleton in a red cape.'

'And you have your information now, Inspector. So please leave our asylum.'

Nick sighed, frustrated. Where was Capello when you needed him? For the moustachioed, napkin-necked Italian had left the asylum over an hour before, and was waiting outside in Nick's Civic, apparently still troubled by personal memories of the infamous 'Crazies' breakout, during which he'd personally witnessed the insidious and invidious escape of Dr Nelson Strain.*

---

* See *Bride of Bone* in *Garth Marenghi's TerrorTome*. I'm actually starting to get a bit cheesed off with having to remind you all to read my previous stories. Take the hint. GM

'Is there anything else he can give me?' said Nick, shoving the straitjacket abruptly with his hand in an attempt to jolt the patient out of his lunacy. 'Apart from an "ideal" TDK cassette that requires an understanding of multiple levels of ironic disassociation in order to ascertain that it is anything *but* the "ideal" TDK cassette?'

'We don't shove patients anymore,' said the doctor sternly, reaching out with one hand to smooth the tight folds of the patient's straitjacket back into alignment. 'This isn't the Dark Ages. If there's the slightest trace of damage to this restraining device, we'll be invoicing you personally.'

'You don't appear to understand, *Doc*, that Stalkford is under attack from supernatural entities. This big skeleton in a red cape might just be the most dangerous of them all.'

'Nonsense, Inspector,' the doctor replied, Nick having pretended to be a police detective in order to gain entrance. 'That whole affair was cleared up over two years ago following Dr Nelson Strain's escape from this very asylum. I can assure you that nothing like that will ever happen here again.'

'But it *is* happening again,' insisted Nick. 'Not here, maybe. But if what this patient is telling me is true, some form of skeletal warrior in a cape is deboning large social gatherings with impunity and without warning. It's my job, now that I've uncovered the who and the what, to find out the why. Plus the where – and, ideally, the when.'

'That's all the information you're getting from this particular patient, Inspector Steen. In my professional opinion, he went insane as a result of the poor sanitary conditions of Mantovani's toilet facilities. Not because of some supposed supernatural slaying.'

'You have to *listen* to me!' yelled Nick, as his arms were grabbed by a gathering of gruff, asylum orderlies.

'If you don't leave this asylum right now, Inspector Steen, I shall have no option but to regard that as an act of madness itself, and have *you* incarcerated here!'

BONELORD

No, thought Nick. *Not that. Anything but that.* The nightmare he'd experienced about his imprisonment at Nulltec had given him more than enough indication about what being deprived of his freedom meant regarding the ultimate fate of Man- and Ladykind.

'Fine,' Nick said. 'I'll go quietly.'

Suddenly, a huge scream erupted from the mouth of the bound patient. A scream, followed by what sounded almost like words. Garbled words that ran essentially as follows:

'*Its face! Its face!*'

'Whose face?' said Nick. 'The face of the big skeleton in the red cape?'

'*Yes! Yes!*' replied the patient, his eyes fixed on some far-off mental vista behind Nick's shoulder. '*Its face! The thing's face! Something else ... about the thing's face!*'

'A skull, right?' said Nick. 'That's typical for big skeletons in red capes.'

'*Bonelord!*' screamed the patient, staring out of his asylum cell window towards the full moon. '*Bonelord!*'

'Bonelord?' repeated Nick.

'*Bonelord!*' replied the patient, still staring wildly up at the moon.

Nick suddenly recalled that strange, leering skull he thought he'd glimpsed staring down at him from the face of the lunar globe earlier that night. Could it be that the giant skull had somehow been *real*, and not merely a figment of the author-come-demon-slayer's overtaxed imagination?

'What about this ... Bonelord?' Nick asked, relieved that the asylum's doctor was similarly transfixed by the unfolding events, leaving him a decent window of time in which to get some pertinent questioning in. 'Specifically,' Nick added, 'who *is* Bonelord, and what does Bonelord *want*?'

Nick had already asked himself these two questions, assuming initially that the emergence of any supernatural being must be related to some novel, horrific idea or fevered dream from his past. But he couldn't recall a single instance of having created a literary monster known as Bonelord.

'*Its face! Its face!*' cried the patient, again.

'Yes, you've already mentioned its face. What *about* its face?'

'*Its face! Bonelord's face! The face . . . of Bonelord!*'

The patient was juddering and shuddering violently in the silvery white glow of the falling moonbeams, barely held still by the orderlies who had now let go of Nick's body, and were instead reaching for the patient in an effort to stop him from toppling over.

'Bonelord's face . . . has . . . has . . .'

'Has what?' snapped Nick.

'*A moustache!*' cried the patient, gibbering incoherently, his mind and soul now fully broken.

'A moustache?' Nick repeated, his mounting suspicions growing darker by the second. 'What do you mean, a moustache? How can a big skeleton have a moustache?'

But it was no good. The patient was as good as useless now. Fit only for the asylum's incineration pipe. Nick left them then, stepping back into the vast asylum corridor beyond, which itself was lit only by the beams of silvery moonlight shining down through angled windows far above.

'Capello?' Nick called out, uncertainly.

But answer came there none. For the Italian, Nick would discover upon returning to his vehicle, had vanished without trace.

CHAPTER SEVEN

Back at the morgue an hour later, Nick was growing impatient.

'I'll be with you in just a moment, Mister Steen,' said Roz, staring down the eyepiece of a microscope while separating two minute areas of liquid on the specimen slate in front of her with what looked to Nick like a pair of metal chopsticks. 'There,' she said, dunking said chopsticks into a glass of sterile liquid before scraping each mini-pool on the specimen slate into separate bottles of blood. Taking off her radiation goggles, she finally looked up at Nick. 'Another batch of blood cells separated.'

'How many bodies have you identified so far?'

'None. Though I'm now able to separate individual corpuscles, at least, with these recently invented clever metal chopsticks. But as far as reconstructing the bodies themselves? No way.'

'I thought you said Lorenzo in pathology had some special glue designed specifically to adhere unknown sections of mortal remains?'*

'Blood cells take a little longer, Nick, as they're a bit more fiddly. But Lorenzo's getting there, by degrees. If you stop by his office on your way out, you'll see he's already managed half of an arm.'

Nick wasn't remotely planning to stop by Lorenzo's office to examine half of an arm. As soon as Nick could, he was going to leave the county morgue entirely. For although he'd been here before, this place gave him the creeps, alongside all those other police forensic

---

* She didn't. If you don't believe me, go back and check. GM

laboratories and pathology departments conveniently located in the same building.

'Are you seriously telling me, Roz,' said Nick, 'that until Lorenzo can rebuild the bodies of every single person deboned in these multiple killings, we'll be none the wiser regarding their individual identities? Including whoever it was at the police station slaying who "stole" Roberto Mantovani's locket? I told you that theory of yours was a dead end, Roz. With the emphasis very much on *dead*.'

'Hold your proverbial horses, Nick. Because I've since been exploring a completely different alley.'

Nick's stare tightened. 'What alley are you talking about, Roz?'

'I've been running various blood tests on those groups of cells I've managed to isolate and bottle up so far, and they've provided me with some rather interesting d*a*ta.'

Nick winced at Roz's pronunciation of the word. 'It's "data", Roz. Like "pot*a*ta".'

'I say "pot*a*to", Nick.'

Nick refused to indulge that shit any further. He already had enough on his plate with these multiple debonings and the terrifying prospect that the perpetrator in question was some form of living skeletal warrior called Bonelord. A living skeletal warrior that may or may not be connected to his missing former buddy, Cliff 'Livewire' Capello. All he elected to take from Roz's incorrect pronunciation of 'data' was that she was becoming increasingly up herself. Then again, Nick thought, she *had* been separating individual blood cells since two o'clock this morning, and it was three o'clock now. Nick decided to let her burgeoning arseholery ride.

Temporarily.

'So what information have you gleaned, Roz? And note that I didn't say "data" again, because I don't want you to keep saying "d*a*ta" back. I regard your particular pronunciation of that word as incorrect and, frankly, the behaviour of a burgeoning arsehole.'

'I'd be careful how you talk to me, Nick,' said Roz, her tone suddenly icy cold. 'I'm an officer of the law now, in case you'd forgotten. And though I let you off a traffic violation earlier with a mere caution, insulting a police officer is also an offence. One that's even worse than insane speeding, and one that I may yet decide to act upon. Don't forget, I have a licence here to whack you on sight.'

What the hell's gotten into Roz? Nick asked himself. A few days in uniform and she was fast turning into a fascist. No doubt the Kettlestrom effect was rubbing off on her, too. Either that or the lure of possible promotion meant she was working overtime to ward off the competing efforts of fellow Police Community Support Officer Gabriel. If he wasn't careful, she might well just whack him without warning, when he least expected it. Somehow, he had to get on her good side.

'Don't forget, Roz, that I operate *outside* the law,' said Nick. 'Meaning that if you need someone you can trust to lower Police Community Support Officer Gabriel's efficiency rating, I'd be more than happy to frag him in the back, no questions asked.'

Nick was privately ashamed of his blatant attempt to placate Roz. He loathed giving his former editor any hint of an idea above her station, but if he had any hope at all of tracking down this sinister entity known only as Bonelord, he had to know what information Roz had discovered from testing those separated blood cells. Even if that meant feeding her swelling, fascistic ego.

'I don't require any assistance from you, Nick, thanks very much. And speaking of operating outside the law, I have it on good authority from Dr Tentacles up at the asylum that you appeared on his doorstep last night pretending to be a detective inspector. Impersonating an officer of the law is yet *another* felony you've committed. I'm not sure how many more of these crimes and misdemeanours I can tolerate, Nick. Frankly, I'm tempted to whack you right here and now and have done with it.'

'But if you do that, Roz, you won't learn the vital *clue* I discovered up at the asylum.'

'Oh, really? And what clue is that?'

'Let's trade, Roz. You first. What d*a*ta have *you* found?' He pronounced it her way, i.e. the wrong way.

'Some very interesting d*a*ta, Nick. Come this way.'

Nick followed Roz over to her desk and sat down beside her as she pressed a button on her big police computer.

The screen lit up with various graphs outlining Roz's recent findings.

'I fed our most recent d*a*ta from the restaurant deboning into the police blood-cell identification d*a*tabase I mentioned last time you were here, Nick, and it came up with some rather interesting information. By some bizarre stroke of luck, I must have somehow bottled up Giuseppe Mantovani's blood cells first, because the d*a*ta I fed in came up with an instant match. See?'

Roz pointed to the screen, where it said 'MATCH' in big shiny letters. Nick nodded, though he wasn't quite sure what 'MATCH' indicated.

'A match with what?'

'I'm coming to that, Nick. After you left the station earlier to explore Mantovani's, I started to feed yet more d*a*ta into the police blood-cell identification d*a*tabase. This time from some of the *earlier* debonings. And, as luck would have it, I must have also bottled up *their* blood first, as well.'

'*Their* blood? Whose blood are you talking about, Roz?' asked Nick, anxiously.

Roz pressed another button on the big police computer, and the name 'MANTOVANI' lit up in large flashing letters.

'The Mantovani *family*, Nick. See where it says "Mantovani"?'

'Tell me what all this means, Roz.'

'By lucky chance, those very bottles of blood I'd managed to separate from all the assorted mass debonings contained blood cells from members of the *same* family. The same *crime* family, Nick. The Mantovanis.'

'I thought you said you hadn't identified any bodies yet, Roz?'

'Bodies, no. Blood cells, yes.'

'But what about the police station deboning?'

'That's what's so strange, Nick. There was no Mantovani blood *at all* at that particular deboning.'

'None at all? But what about the locket?'

'As I said before, Nick. It must have been stolen by one of the deceased prisoners. You see, my "stolen locket" theory still has legs.'

Nick had to face facts. It looked as if Roz might be right, after all.

'Now, back to our trade. How about *your* clue, Nick? What vital titbit of information have you found out?'

'Well, as you know, Roz,' Nick began, reluctantly, 'you told me there was a witness to the restaurant deboning imprisoned up at the asylum. So I went along to question them – and yes, mayhap I *did* gain entrance by pretending I was a police detective inspector, but that's because security, as you know, Roz, is tight up there ever since the Nelson Strain breakout. Anyway, I thought you'd just deputise me in the morning and we could clear up any loose ends that way.'

'Unfortunately, I'd need to run that past my superiors, Nick – if I had any intention of deputising you, which I don't.'

'Please yourself, Roz. Anyway, the witness told me, between sarcastic jibes and occasional jazz scatting, that everyone at Mantovani's was deboned by a big skeleton in a red cape.'

Roz nodded, jotting down the information. 'You know, ordinarily, Nick, I'd have dismissed such wild claims immediately out of hand, or at least subjected you to some sort of lie-detector test. But seeing as I myself have been abducted previously by a living skeleton – and,

indeed, formed a passionate romantic relationship with one to boot*
– I'm prepared to take those details on trust. Please go on.'

'That's about it, Roz. I can't for the life of me recall ever writing about a living skeleton, other than in those Nelson Strain novels which came to terrifying life two years ago. But I never named one Bonelord, or put it in a cape, so frankly I'm as stumped as that half of an arm in Lorenzo's laboratory.'

'And you have no further information other than that?'

Nick could see Roz was needling him. But there was no way he was going to tell her about the skeleton having a moustache. That was Nick's clue, damn it. He'd found it, and he was going to keep it to himself. Otherwise, Roz might steal said clue and solve the crime before him. And he wasn't going to tell her about Capello, either, whom Nick knew *also* had a moustache. A big painter's-brush moustache. And who now, since the clue's discovery, had mysteriously gone *missing* ...

'No further information whatsoever,' Nick said.

'So who was that man in the back of your car last night?' said Roz, sharply. 'The one who stuck a Beretta revolver in my face?'

Damn it, so she *had* caught sight of Capello, after all. Well, it was no use trying to stall Roz any further, if he had any hope at all of gleaning what clues she herself had uncovered. Not to mention staving off a summary whacking.

'Okay, Roz, I'll level with you. That man was Cliff "Livewire" Capello. If you remember, he and I rescued you two years ago from that army of Boners led by the sinister Dr Nelson Strain.† Well, it turns out he didn't die alongside his brother at the dramatic denouement of that strange and mysterious series of events, but in actual fact *survived*. I happened to bump into him at Mantovani's, and we caught

---

* See *Bride of Bone* in *Garth Marenghi's TerrorTome*. I mean it about not reminding you again. From now on, you're on your own. GM
† I said you're on your own. GM

up over some meatballs. When you later gave me the news about the mass deboning that had taken place there, I automatically assumed Capello had died for real this time. But it turns out he kicked Death's arse a *second* time, having nipped outside to relieve himself in a nearby alley.'

'Though technically illegal, that was a wise decision,' said Roz, recalling dim, terrifying memories of her own experiences of Giuseppe Mantovani's lavatory facilities. 'If a bit convenient, Nick. Don't you think?'

'I was coming to that, Roz,' said Nick, realising she was snapping at his wavelength again. 'See, when Capello and I reached the asylum, he immediately cried off, saying the place was evoking sad memories of his lost brother Dwayne. Killed, as you know, in that very battle with the Boners which he himself survived.'

There was no way Roz could forget Dwayne, Nick knew. After all, she'd slept with the guy and planned to get married and have his baby skeletons one day.

'I told Capello to wait outside for me, but by the time I came out half an hour later, he'd completely vanished.'

'Perhaps he went to relieve himself up another alley?'

'No, he did that just before we got there. A number two, I think.'

'Then maybe he simply walked home?'

'It's possible, Roz, but I think he might have *run* home instead.'

'What do you mean?' asked Roz, writing ever faster and more frantically in her notepad.

He wasn't sure why, but Nick elected to tell Roz about his extra clue, after all. Maybe he was taking pity on her and that horrendous workload of hers. Or perhaps he was banking some capital against any potential steps Kettlestrom might make towards whacking him without warning. Whatever it was, Nick went with it.

'Something the witness said in his description of the perpetrator chilled me to the bone, Roz,' said Nick, 'if you'll pardon the expression. Something that's led me to believe Capello *himself* might have something to do with these continual mass debonings.'

'Go on,' said Roz, flipping her notepad over to the next page. 'I'm listening.'

'The witness said this big skeleton in a red cape calling himself Bonelord also had ...'

'Yes, Nick?' Roz replied, anxiously awaiting the clue. 'Also had what?'

'A *moustache*.'

'But that's impossible, Nick. A moustache? On a *skeleton*?'

'Human hair has been known to continue growing from the bones of a corpse, Roz. Long after the rest of the body has rotted away. But you're missing the crucial point.'

'Which is?' Another flip of the notepad.

'That Cliff Capello *also* has a moustache. A big one.'

The notepad slipped from Roz's hands.

'Something I said, Roz?' said Nick, smiling grimly.

'Tell me, Nick. Have you noticed anything strange about the *moon* recently?'

An odd question, thought Nick. Although he had indeed noticed something strange about the moon recently.

'As a matter of fact, I have noticed something strange about the moon recently, Roz. I've been convinced I'm glimpsing the features of a skull somehow superimposed upon its lunar surface. A vast, grinning skull.'

'A grinning skull, Nick? Don't you think that's some sort of coincidence, given the apparent existence of a big skeleton in a red cape committing all these murders?'

'I hadn't thought of that, Roz,' said Nick, ashamed of himself. For that particular clue had been right in front of his nose all this time. Even more so when he was physically looking up at the moon itself.

'Tell me,' Roz continued, 'have you ever written any novels where a moon featured prominently?'

'You know I have, Roz. *The Hairy Moon* for a start, my ten-part werewolf series. Other titles include *Snarl of the Bitchwolf* and *Howl, Silvermane, Howl*.'

'What about that book I sold abroad for you, Nick? *A Hamburgian Verevulf in Stalkford*, I think it was called.'

'Yeah, I remember that one, Roz. The one where a Hamburgian prince has to kill eight members of the same aristocratic family who placed the curse of the verevulf upon him.'

'If I remember rightly, Nick, it also featured numerous mass gorings in various public places?'

A cold, uncanny feeling washed over Nick as memories came flooding back.

'That's the one, Roz. Turning all its victims into literal hamburgers. Did you ever sell that book in the end? Because if you did, Roz, and I didn't receive any hard cash from the transaction, that's a crime, too, and I'll be instructing Police Commissioner Kettlestrom to arrest *you*.'

'I *attempted* to sell it, Nick, but the Italian publisher I mailed it to turned out to be a money-laundering front for a local crime syndicate — and *they* stole the book instead.'

'What the hell?' roared Nick, reaching for his revolver. Then he slid it back into its holster, realising there was nothing around him he could shoot for not paying him his authorial dues. Other than Roz, of course, but that would only get him into further legal trouble with Kettlestrom.

'They hired some hack — some "Fernando Corbuccini" — to rework the entire plot, rename all your main characters and turn the titular *verevulf* into . . .'

'A skeleton?' said Nick, hardly believing he was saying those words. 'In a big red cape?'

'Precisely, Nick. What we are dealing with here, I think, is a *rewritten* Italian version of your unsold verevulf novel. The living incarnation of a book you wrote but no longer recognise, as it was changed via illegal Italian translation into some kind of supernatural gothic crime mystery. One in which the Mantovanis are essentially the aristocratic family from your original novel. It's they who've placed this dreaded supernatural curse upon some lowly peasant, turning him into a terrifying *vereskeleton*. A terrifying vereskeleton that is now thirsting for revenge. By killing each member of the Mantovani family who originally placed that very curse. By *deboning* them.'

Things were starting to make sense, Nick figured. Bonelord was deboning various members of Stalkford's Mantovani crime family, who'd evidently somehow become entwined with the incarnated version of the Italian bastardisation of Nick's original novel, and who had seemingly placed, some time in their past, a supernatural curse of eternal Bonelordery upon him (or it). And the worst of it all was that, somehow, Roz had come up with the solution to this case before Nick had been able to. Plus, she'd invented the phrase *vereskeleton*, which Nick would have happily used if he'd come up with it himself, but which he now resolutely refused to mention again in case it gave Roz delusions of grandeur.

'Why didn't you tell me all this before, Roz?' Nick snapped unnecessarily for good measure.

'I had my suspicions, Nick, but I was waiting for further evidence before reaching my conclusions. That's basic police method, I'm afraid. And there's still one aspect I can't quite explain.'

'Which is?'

'Why there was no Mantovani blood present at the police station slaying.' Roz withdrew the hand she'd been resting her chin on quizzically, and swapped it for her other hand. Then she gazed up at the ceiling again, still quizzically. 'Also, why on earth is Capello involved? So two things, actually.'

'The second one's easy enough to answer, Roz,' explained Nick. 'When I was writing *A Hamburgian Verevulf in Stalkford*, I couldn't be bothered to think up a new character, so I simply made Capello from my previous book the verevulf and told you to sell it to some foreigners who wouldn't notice.'

'Oh, yes,' said Roz, remembering. 'You said, "If I say it's an Italian-German verevulf, it's an Italian-German verevulf — and if you don't like it, woman, sell it some place where no one knows up from down."'

'Precisely. And for that reason, Capello's now a were-skeleton. With a moustache. And he doesn't even know why.'

'Bonelord,' added Roz.

'Bonelord ...' double-added Nick. 'Capello is ... Bonelord.'

'Where are you going, Nick?' asked Roz, as Nick strode manfully towards the door.

'To find him, Roz. This madness has to stop. I need to locate Capello before the next full moon. Before, once again, Cliff "Livewire" Capello turns into ...'

He stopped mid-stride, then turned round to face her.

'... *Bonelord.*'

CHAPTER EIGHT

Nick swore loudly and flung the almanac he'd just purchased into his bedside bin. Nothing but full moons all week. Meaning that if he couldn't locate Capello during the hours of daylight, he was looking at a nocturnal tête-à-tête with his former buddy – along with the ever-present threat of that becoming a sudden skull-a-tête.

Nick had looked everywhere he could think of during the day, wracking his brains to figure out where Capello might be hiding. But after twenty minutes or so, he'd become hungry, hit up a carvery and then gone back to bed for a bit, realising he'd need to be fully alert for whatever the night ahead might throw at him.

Now, he'd woken up before his alarm clock's third snooze cycle, and was lying in a pool of his own sweat – a result of the pork roast, he assumed, before realising his reeking perspiration was instead coming from an intangible sense of *fear*. A sense of fear, he now saw, caused by those rays of silvery light passing through his apartment window between the partly drawn curtains.

The beams... of a full moon.

Nick kicked back his bedcovers, pulled back the curtains fully and gazed up past the drifting clouds.

There it was again: that gleaming, grinning, death's head smile. A smile Nick now knew was the hallucinatory visage of the all-powerful, formerly fictional Bonelord. A demonic murdering skeleton Nick had originally conceived as a Hamburgian verevulf. Sure, Nick had penned any number of fictional skeletons over the years; had, in fact, created the very army of Boners that eventually came to terrifying life when the portal in his brain first opened, releasing his horrific fictional imaginings upon an unsuspecting humanity.

But Bonelord was different. Bonelord was some crazed and unholy crossbreed between Nick's Hamburgian verevulf and a gothic Italian crime mystery penned by some cheap, thieving literary hack. Nick would naturally be pursuing his own vendetta against this 'Fernando Corbuccini' as soon as the blood was dry on his current assignment, but he had to give the guy some credit, at least. The name 'Bonelord' had a certain ring to it, after all. In fact, Nick couldn't help but feel an icy chill freeze his spine as he gazed up into that cold and distant orb above, and whispered the name aloud . . .

'Bonelord . . . Bonelord . . . Lord of the Bone. No, that's not quite as good. Lord Over All Bone . . . Scratch that. *Bonelord* . . . Yep, fair enough. Bonelord it is.'

As Nick said 'Bonelord' once again for the hell of it, the telephone on his bedside table rang. He grabbed it and cradled the receiver against his shoulder.

'Yup?'

'Nick!' said a familiar voice.

'Capello!' Nick said back. 'Where the hell are you, bud?'

'Where you just said, Nick. In hell.'

'What, Hell itself?'

'In hell, Nick. I am in hell.'

'I know that, but do you mean literal Hell or figurative hell? If you're in literal Hell I can't do anything about it at the moment – not until I track down a late-night satanist. Which will be tough right now, as it's the witching hour.'

'I'm not in literal Hell, Nick. I'm in . . . the other hell.'

Capello's voice began to waver, and Nick could hear tears beginning to well in the Italian's eyes. 'But I may be in literal Hell soon enough . . .'

'So, just to clarify, you're talking about being in *figurative* hell?'

'I think so, Nick. To be honest, I don't know what "figurative" means.'

'Yes, you do, Capello. You said, "I'm in hell," by which, presumably, you meant you aren't in literal Hell, but instead a hell of your own making?'

'Yes, Nick.'

'Then that, Capello, is *figurative* hell. Hell that is not literal, but essentially still hell for you, because it constitutes some form of internal psychological hell.'

'Yes! Yes! That's exactly the kind of hell I'm talking about.'

'Great. We got there in the end.'

'Thanks, Nick.'

'Any time, Capello. I'm a writer at heart, so words are my business. Consider my help on this one an introductory gift.'

'Nick, I need to talk to you.'

'We're talking now.'

'Not on the phone. We need to talk . . . in person.'

Is that what this is, Capello? A chance to debone me, as well? The one person getting close to curtailing your continuous debonings? Am I to be your next debonee?

But however much Nick might be dreading an unwanted violent altercation with his old buddy, Capello was still that: Nick's buddy. And Nick would never, *ever*, abandon a buddy in need. After all, this might be Nick's only remaining chance to find some way of helping Capello. If he could find out what exactly made Bonelord tick – or, more specifically, click – he might thereby discover some way of lifting the dreaded curse.

'Where are you, Capello? I'll come straight over.'

'I'm in the Italian cemetery, Nick. The literal Italian cemetery. Not the figurative one.'

'I know it well, Capello.'

BONELORD

'Meet me at the Mantovani mausoleum.'

There was a click as the phone line went dead.

Great, thought Nick. *The Mantovani mausoleum.*

The one building in the entire cemetery that the moon *shone directly down upon* . . .

*

Nick pulled up outside the cemetery gates with his Honda Civic's headlamps extinguished. He wanted to be able to locate Capello unseen, not the other way round. But the unwieldy luminescence generated by the rays of the full moon above essentially rendered that plan useless, so he switched them on after all. Then instantly switched them off again, as it was time to kill the car's engine and step out of the vehicle.

Nick made his way slowly through crumbling rows of elaborately carved gravestones, pausing occasionally to examine names he could still recall from various local news bulletins. Those corpses of mafia families either electrocuted by the authorities, or machine-gunned to mince by distant relatives in the seemingly endless turf wars and blood feuds that had plagued Stalkford's underworld for decades. It took a while for Nick to realise he'd yet to pass a single stone tablet commemorating the memory of the Mantovani family – but then he also realised he'd yet to arrive at the mausoleum itself.

Spying a silvery sheen of reflected moonlight glowing brightly from the sloping marble roof of some distant structure, Nick continued onward, through the graves. As he drew closer to the building up ahead, he began to perceive around it a number of ornately sculpted plinths and columns, formerly resplendent examples of Roman-style architecture, now crumbling into ruin.

'*La Famiglia Mantovani* . . .' said Nick, reading from a weathered crest set below the triangular arch of the stone mausoleum, tinged by age and decay with an eerie, greenish hue. Within its dark interior, Nick knew, lay the rotting, web-strewn tombs and dusty crypts of Countess Margarita Mantovani and the long-deceased members of her infamous crime clan.

'That's them, Nick,' said a familiar voice, directly above him. 'The Mantovanis.'

Nick looked up to see a thin, wasted-looking, moustachioed figure crouched on the roof of the mausoleum. It was Capello. He was still wearing the same bespattered napkin he'd put on at Giuseppe's joint, though he looked physically emaciated now, as if the hot-headed Italian had eaten nothing else in days, even though in actual fact it was just the one day.

Nick ducked as Capello leaped suddenly from the roof of the mausoleum, over his head, to land a short distance behind him. Nick turned with him, realising his own body was now trapped between Capello and the mausoleum's yawning entrance.

'I'm guessing they've all been deboned by a sentient giant skeleton in a red cape,' said Nick, coming to the point immediately in order to prevent any tiresome small talk or unnecessary fencing. 'A sentient giant skeleton in a red cape, who goes by the name of *Bonelord* . . .'

'How do *you* know?' said Capello, eyes darting wildly left and right in a manner Nick assumed to be caused by either anxiety or terror, but which was actually due to a persistent floater Capello was attempting to periodically shift from his central vision.

'That hipster witness, Capello. Up at the asylum. The one you refused to meet because you knew all too well that he'd seen you, and you *alone*, deboning all and sundry inside Mantovani's restaurant.'

'Hey, that wasn't *me*, Nick.'

'Quit stalling, Capello. I know full well you're currently embodying the fictional-protagonist-slash-antagonist of my lost werewolf novel *A Hamburgian Verevulf in Stalkford* — a book chopped up and re-penned by some Italian chancer who turned my titular lycanthrope into a giant skeleton in a red cape called Bonelord.'

'So you *do* know …' said Capello, wearily.

'That you're the one behind all these mass debonings, Capello? Yeah, I know that. And I also know you're doing it to exact revenge on those members of the Mantovani family who placed this curse upon you. But why take the lives of innocent bystanders, simply to wreak your own bloody path of vengeance on the Mantovanis?'

'Believe me, Nick,' said Capello. 'I have no memory of what I'm doing when I do all this deboning …'

'The pools of blood are a good clue.'

'Yes, Nick, but I cannot *remember* my debonings. It is as if I am possessed by the skull of Bonelord himself, with no mind of my own.'

'No "it is as ifs" about it, Capello. You *are* possessed by the skull of Bonelord.'

Without warning, Capello took a sudden step forward. Instantly, Nick whipped out his .44 revolver and aimed it at the Italian's heart.

'Silver bullets, Capello,' said Nick. 'So no tricks.'

'Silver bullets cannot save you, Nick,' Capello replied, looking at Nick as if he was about to pounce at him. 'Silver bullets might have worked on a mere verevulf, but they are useless against the mighty mincing marrow of *Bonelord*.'

'Want to test that theory, Capello?' said Nick icily, refusing to lower his gun — even though he knew deep down that Capello was right. He'd need bullets filled with powdered osteoporosis to even think of tackling Bonelord.

'*Nothing* can destroy Bonelord, Nick. Bonelord is undefeatable. *Immortal*. The ultimate supernatural demon, cursed to wander this earth as a giant skeleton in a red cape.'

'With a moustache,' said Nick.

'You said it, Nick. A giant skeleton in a red cape with a moustache who does nothing but debone all the time.'

Suddenly, the expression on Capello's face began to soften, and Nick could see tears slowly welling in his buddy's eyes.

'Why me, Nick? Why am *I* Bonelord? I thought I was a character from one of your Nelson Strain novels come to life when that brain portal of yours opened up. But this week I'm no longer dead, and am suddenly a giant skeleton in a red cape with a moustache. What gives?'

'I can't answer that, Capello,' said Nick. Actually, he could – but Nick didn't want to risk Capello deboning him right here and now in some sudden rage about Nick having scraped the bottom of his creative barrel for a premade character that he'd then immediately hawked to some distant foreign market. 'But I'm here to help,' he added, placatingly.

'No one can help me, Nick. As far as I can tell, I have one choice only. One way alone to free myself from this curse. *You* know what that is.'

True, Nick did know what that was. And yet there was still something Nick didn't know. Something he intended to find out, if only to get one up on Roz back at the station. Something that would explain the distinct lack of Mantovani blood present at the police station slaying.

'You need to kill all eight Mantovanis,' replied Nick, stalling for time.

'Just like your book says, Nick. I must kill and debone those eight members of the Mantovani family who placed this curse upon me. Only then will the curse of Bonelord be lifted. And if I have to take out gatherings of innocent people along the way? Well, them's the breaks.'

'Except for one thing, Capello,' Nick countered. 'Eight members of the Mantovani family have *already* been deboned – and yet you're still Bonelord. Eight massacres, eight Mantovanis.'

'Wrong, Nick. I have killed only *seven* Mantovanis.'

At last, thought Nick, sensing an imminent revelation that might somehow explain the police station blood-related anomaly...

'Seven?' he said aloud. 'Count them, Capello. The swimming pool slaying, the city council AGM, that garden centre deboning, the ill-fated booze cruise, the unholy meat raffle chow-down, the Raunch Pot, the police station massacre and Mantovani's restaurant. That comes to eight. Eight massacres. Eight dead Mantovanis. With the exception of the restaurant slaying in which Giuseppe Mantovani's multiple sons also died, but I assume you're just focusing on the eight that cursed you specifically.'

'I made a mistake, Nick,' said Capello, gravely. 'At the police station deboning. I missed one of those eight Capello-cursing Mantovanis.'

At last, thought Nick again, welcoming Capello's imminent revelation that was no longer imminent.

'Nonsense, bud,' he bluffed, baiting Capello for further revelations. 'Roz found Roberto Mantovani's locket in the human swill. She's separating blood cells as we speak in the hope of identifying him formally.'

'But she will never find him, Nick. Because Roberto Mantovani was not in the building at the time.'

'Not in the building?' queried Nick, sensing he was getting close to a more important and potentially terrifying plot revelation.

'You told me yourself, Nick. The Mantovani in question was away from the station because he was out ... *wiretapping your apartment.*'

Nick gasped, incredulous, as said more important terrifying plot revelation kicked in.

'You mean ... *Bob Kettlestrom?*'

'Real name, Roberto Mantovani, Nick. Giuseppe Mantovani's brother.'

'But he's the police commissioner, Capello. How can a member of a leading mafia family be that – and also former head of Stalkford's FBI Office? Unless ...'

Suddenly everything made sense. For there were bad apples on the force, and then there was Bob Kettlestrom. No doubt it would be a cinch for Stalkford's mafia to run illegal late-night lock-ins if the head of the entire police force was a secret member of its very own mafia clan. And, unwittingly, Roz was now part of that endemic corruption plaguing Stalkford's constabulary. Or what was left of it.

Jeez, thought Nick. Hadn't most of Stalkford's officers just been wiped out by Bonelord? No doubt Kettlestrom had suspected he might soon be in Bonelord's firing line, given that the demon was actively hunting down each member of the Mantovani family who'd placed the curse, and had therefore taken to making himself scarce via regular covert operations. Evidently he'd thought nothing of risking the safety of those upstanding, incorruptible officers he'd left back at the station, because if they got accidentally deboned in his absence, he could simply start filling his rotten barrel with a malleable batch of freshly festering apples.

Law and order in Stalkford had been completely eradicated, Nick reflected grimly. Unless . . .

Unless Bonelord could get to Kettlestrom after all.

'Roberto Mantovani still lives, Nick,' said Capello. 'And until I can debone him, too, Bonelord also lives. To kill again.'

Capello had that manic gleam back in his eyes, Nick noticed. The Italian was looking wilder now, his moustache twitching with mounting excitement. Hell, he looked *dangerous*.

'Help me, Nick. Help me debone one last time. Help me commit one final deboning, and this curse will be lifted. I *promise*. You owe me that, Nick. As a buddy, and as the author of this entire terrible tale.'

'Careful, Capello.'

'I mean terrible as in "full of terror".'

'Carry on.'

'Help me *kill* Police Commissioner Bob Kettlestrom, also known as Roberto Mantovani, and you will hear from me no more.'

Naturally, the idea of offing Kettlestrom appealed to Nick, especially now he knew that the police commissioner was a secret member of Stalkford's mafia elite. Similarly, he could also justify the deaths of those innumerable bystanders who'd inevitably get minced in the process, given these would now consist largely of corrupt police officers. And, in truth, Nick cared nothing for Police Community Support Officer Gabriel, or those new police cadets Kettlestrom had just hired, who'd probably all be dead in a week, anyway. But if such a clutch of surrounding officers were to be deboned in the process of deboning Kettlestrom, there was nevertheless a strong likelihood that *Roz* would be standing in the police commissioner's immediate vicinity – and Nick didn't want his former editor's complete bodily evisceration on his conscience.

Whatever the cost to Capello, deboning Roz was absolutely not an option.

'I'm sorry, Capello,' said Nick, tersely. 'I can't allow that.'

'Okay, Nick,' said Capello, in a voice that suddenly wasn't quite his, dropping several pitches downwards before rising multiple pitches past his normal range. 'In that case, you must also ... *DIE!*'

CHAPTER NINE

As Capello lunged towards Nick, Nick reverse-lunged backward from Capello, meaning there was still exactly the same distance between them as there had been when Capello had first uttered the words, 'In that case, you must also . . . *DIE!*', even though no one had even started to lunge at that point. This gave Nick an advantage, but only a slight one. For he would need to reverse-lunge away from Capello each time Capello subsequently lunged forward at him in order to maintain the same distance, or else reverse-lunge himself backward from Capello *more* times than Capello was able to lunge forward at him in order to increase the distance of their comparative lunging in Nick's favour.

But Nick knew that behind him stood the mausoleum of the Mantovanis, so even if he could reverse-lunge backward a sufficient number of times to evade Capello's future lunging, he'd only be reverse-lunging backward into an enclosed space in which the ability to reverse-lunge *further* backwards beyond that point would soon be curtailed indefinitely, leaving Capello free to lunge forward at will several more times and thus ultimately closing the lunging margin in the Italian's favour.

Nick had to do something other than a further reverse-lunge – and fast.

But no sooner had this thought entered his mind than Capello lunged towards him again. Operating on instinct alone, Nick took a second reverse-lunge at *precisely* the same time as Capello's second

BONELORD

forward lunge, meaning they were still no closer to each other than before, and gaining Nick a few further precious seconds to contemplate the probability of a further reverse-lunge.

Which was ultimately an *im*possibility, he figured. For he could already feel the mausoleum step against his heel, and knew that his next reverse-lunge would effectively imprison him *within* the enclosed vault of the Mantovani family's dead.

As he sensed Capello gearing up for another forward lunge, Nick decided to appeal to his former buddy's better nature.

'Please, Capello, don't continually lunge at me. You know I'd help you if I could.'

'I know you would, Nick,' said Capello, eyes staring manically at Nick's own. 'But I can't help it, you see. Bonelord is ... *inside me.*'

As Capello uttered those words, Nick saw the Italian's body twitch violently as if suffering a sudden electric jolt, popping his shoulder joint abruptly out of place.

'Bonelord ... He – or it – is coming, Nick,' added Capello, twitching violently again.

Nick saw that Capello's shoulder joint had failed to return to its former position. In fact, the entire shape of the Italian's bodily frame was changing, Nick realised. He caught sight of something white protruding from Capello's former shoulder blade. As he watched, the stitching on Capello's jacket elbow tore open, exposing a bleached substance that appeared to be pulsing upwards from below.

Bone.

No sooner had Nick identified the texture of the bursting appendage than the jacket material on Capello's other shoulder pad also split asunder, forced apart by a second expanding shoulder bone. The Italian reached up and did his best to stuff one of the expanding shoulder joints back down, but as soon as he had forced it back into place, the bone immediately shot upwards again.

'Help, Nick ... I'm coming apart.'

At the literal seams, thought Nick, but there was no time to vocalise his quip, especially as Capello probably wouldn't get it anyway, given the Italian's poor grasp of basic English grammar.

The other joints on Capello's body were starting to twitch and thrash violently now, as if moving of their own accord underneath his fragile flesh.

'He – or it – is coming ...' cried Capello, his face a mask of terror now as his arms and legs suddenly tore open and lengthened, the skin and muscle falling away to reveal a swelling frame of still-lengthening yellow bone matter beneath. Then Capello's face itself began to expand, mutating horribly with the shifting motion of a strange mass coming to life below it. And as Capello's mouth assumed an unprompted rictus grin, the plate of the Italian's forehead began to expand at speed, before the skin housing his own skull cracked and flopped open, revealing a giant-sized replacement skull beneath it. As the remains of the Italian's visage fell in fleshy strips to the floor, Capello's discarded mouth cried out some final words.

'Run, Nick! Get the hell out of here!'

'But what about you, Capello?'

'CAPELLO IS NO MORE!' shrieked a different voice, one that sounded like the Devil himself yelling outward at humanity through his own voiding bowels. Then the giant skeleton that Nick knew only as Bonelord began to climb out of Capello's flesh-suit. A burst of flapping red material followed from the departing skin, whirling about the emerging were-skeleton as it finally shed all trace of what had formerly been Cliff Capello. Now, a demon in a crimson cape stood before Nick, its skull enshrouded by a dark, scarlet-coloured hood. As Nick watched, transfixed, the thing began to move the mandibles of both jaws, opening then slamming them down loudly, clacking the teeth together as it produced a terrifying shriek that seemed to rise from somewhere within the darkest depths of Nick's mind.

'CALL ME ... BONELORD!'

BONELORD

Without warning, the red-caped skeleton lunged at Nick. Bonelord's lunge was a larger lunge than Capello's lunge, easily out-lunging Nick's own instinctive counter-lunge. But Nick was ahead of the demon, having anticipated the unnatural increase in lunge-ivity and elected to substitute his anticipated reverse-lunge for a side-lunge instead, mindful that Bonelord intended to trap him inside the mausoleum of the Mantovanis immediately behind.

Nick opted for a left-lunge instead of a right-lunge, moving away from a pile of cat-dung his nose had suddenly detected, which would otherwise have turned aforesaid right-lunge into a *wrong*-lunge.

As Nick's body therefore lunged sideways towards a leaning gravestone, the corner of his eye caught a passing flash of scarlet red as Bonelord's forward lunge sent the caped demon flying into the dank darkness of the mausoleum interior.

'BALLS!' shrieked that same voice in Nick's head, as Bonelord realised his — or its — mistake. But Nick couldn't pause to savour victory. For in no time at all, he knew that Bonelord's forward lunge would come to a stop, and the demon would either reverse-lunge through the mausoleum doors, or instead whirl its caped body 180 degrees around inside and then repeat another forward lunge through the doors that way instead.

Nick took to his heels and ran.

As he dashed through the mass of slanting gravestones, he could already hear the tell-tale click-clack of snapping joints, along with the whip and swish of Bonelord's whirling cape, as the skeleton pursued him relentlessly through the surrounding tombs.

Bonelord was only a few feet behind him, Nick sensed — and, in a sudden panic, he realised he was now fleeing *away* from that side of the cemetery where he'd parked his car. Instead, he was sprinting towards the cemetery gate on the *opposite* side.

A gate which led, Nick realised, directly into the neighbouring grounds of Stalkford's vast *elephant graveyard*. Long considered a no-go area for human beings, Nick realised that if Bonelord deboned him there, no one would ever know, and Nick's own bones, scattered among the larger bones of giant trunks and Dumbo-style ears, might never be found.

Therefore, Nick elected to veer right instead, hoping he would emerge from the cemetery on the furthest edge of the elephant graveyard, where the mourning elephants themselves were granted official access to the area by a keeper not dissimilar in appearance to TV's Terry Nutkins. Nick hoped that perhaps he could lose himself between the giant stumpy legs of some approaching herd member, while using its higher-density deboning potential to distract the pursuing Bonelord.

Then Nick remembered the *other* graveyard. The graveyard immediately adjacent to the elephant graveyard, which local schoolchildren had constructed for any dead roadkill they were able to find, and which last month had been completely destroyed by tramping elephants en route to their own graveyard. It had then, as a result of Nick's escaping imagination, become haunted by the unearthed bones of the interred roadkill. There was no way Nick could risk dodging the combined dangers of thundering elephants, ghost stoats and phantom chickens, as well an avenging Bonelord.

And he could hear the skeletal demon closing in. He was trapped again, he realised. Doomed to endure a complete deboning in either one of two alternative bone-filled graveyards.

Unless . . .

Like his body, Nick's mind raced as he fought to recall some distant detail calling out from the back of his mind . . .

And then he felt a deep and distant rumbling under his feet. Of course! Stalkford's underground system ran *beneath* the very ground over which he was fleeing! And if Nick remembered rightly, the 'Elephant and Graveyard' tube station was located just outside the main cemetery gate.

BONELORD

Feeling adrenaline course through his body, Nick forced another spurt of energy outward and raced towards what looked like the cemetery gate up ahead. Bracing himself, he vaulted the metal fencing, having gained a solid foothold several inches above ground level and climbing slowly from there. No sooner was he over the fence than Nick heard Bonelord shriek at him from somewhere behind in his – or its – customary unearthly, demonic tone.

'COME BACK HERE RIGHT NOW, NICK STEEN!'

As Nick's feet hit the ground on the far side, he flung himself towards the station entrance immediately ahead.

Pausing briefly to purchase a ticket from the machine, Nick cursed himself for accidentally selecting a one-day travel card, which granted him full access to the entire underground network, even though he would most likely be making just the one trip. Yet there was no time to complain at the kiosk and insist they give him an immediate refund or else, before starting the entire process again. For Bonelord, Nick knew, was close behind him. So, as soon as the ticket was in his hand, Nick sprinted for the entrance barriers and slid his lithe, leather-clad frame straight through the 'heavy luggage' gate towards the nearby escalators.

The station was deserted at this time of night, but as Nick leaped on to the descending metal stairway, he risked a brief look behind him and glimpsed something tall in a bright red cape reach with its long, bony hand towards the *very* ticket kiosk Nick had just been using . . .

Nick felt his heart rate increasing all the while. At this rate, he might not be able to generate enough space between himself and Bonelord to allow him to leap on to a tube carriage and watch the doors slam shut against his approaching assailant just in the nick of time.

His instincts told him to start running down the escalator, but the rules against such activities were very clear, displayed prominently on signposts and billboards throughout the underground system, so there was no chance of Nick gaining any time advantage that way. He'd only be able to gain speed again once the escalator had reached the bottom.

And yet, Nick realised, Bonelord would not be hampered remotely by any rules and regulations set by TfS (Travel for Stalkford). After all, Bonelord, by his – or its – very nature, acted illegally as a rule, especially when deboning multitudes of innocent bystanders. As Nick finally reached the bottom of the escalator, he risked another glance back, and was deeply relieved to see Bonelord standing motionless on the rolling stairway. This was not out of any respect for underground rules, Nick saw, but because both of his – or its – bony hands were now forced to hold up the folds of the scarlet cape, keeping the crimson robe well clear of the escalator's edges, and the grinding internal mechanism beneath.

Hopefully this would buy Nick the time he needed. With renewed vigour, he raced off under the nearest archway and sprinted out on to the neighbouring platform. The concourse ahead of him was completely empty save for a single elderly gentleman with an umbrella sitting by himself on one of the platform benches.

There was no sign of any train.

Nick glanced up at the announcement board, which was itself completely blank. *Of course,* Nick realised grimly. At this late hour, the night staff would no doubt be reading magazines, gossiping among themselves and otherwise neglecting their essential duties, resulting in the inevitable abandonment of anything approaching a regular schedule. Which meant that Nick would now have to duck back through the archway in the hope of catching a train from the *opposite* platform.

But before he could reach the far side, Nick heard a familiar, spine-shattering shriek from the vicinity of the escalator. It echoed terrifyingly through the abandoned underground and stopped Nick in his tracks, catching him like the proverbial rabbit in the headlights just before it gets slam-dunked by a whooping motorist. Nick sensed the train in front approaching just beyond his field of vision. He could hear it slowing towards the platform, and considered whether it was worth him sprinting past the escalator in the hope of leaping aboard. But in the same moment he saw that Bonelord was now almost at floor level, and realised he'd never make it past the demon in time. He stepped back instinctively, hearing the distant train depart soon after as he backed away from the approaching Bonelord. Moments later, he was back on the same platform he'd just left, only with the caped demon now following him in from behind.

'YOU ARE POWERLESS TO RESIST THE MIGHT OF BONELORD,' said that strange voice as, once again, the were-skeleton's teeth began clacking up and down in its skull.

'We'll see,' said Nick, before turning and sprinting along the platform towards the gaping mouth of the distant underground tunnel. On the way, he passed the figure of the elderly gentleman, still snoozing gently in his seat, and realised he had effectively condemned the old man to death by re-entering the platform – unless Nick could somehow make it to the tunnel before Bonelord caught up with him. Maybe if Nick could make it past the old duffer, Bonelord wouldn't even notice the geriatric in his insatiable desire to debone Nick himself. He had to take that chance, he decided, and so he continued along the platform towards the dark, distant tunnel entrance.

But as Bonelord leaped through the archway and gave another soul-splitting shriek, the pensioner's eyes snapped open.

Before Nick could yell out a warning, the old croc had risen to his feet and was swiftly extending his umbrella in some lame attempt at a defensive stance.

'Don't open that up in here!' Nick yelled, helplessly. 'It's bad luck, and right now we need *good* luck!'

But it was too late. The dying codger began to twirl the extended canopy, no doubt hoping that the patterns of rotating multicoloured fabric created through the circular motion might somehow distract or entrance the advancing demon. But Bonelord was not to be so easily duped. And, as the giant were-skeleton whirled its cape and shrieked again, the almost-deceased must have sensed the sheer hopelessness of his predicament. For in that moment, he gave a wild battle cry and charged his assailant head-on, using the pointy end of the umbrella as a makeshift bayonet. But what use was a bayonet substitute made from cheap aluminium? What use at all, against the mighty marauding marrow of this towering, cape-clad bone-warrior?

As Nick watched in horror, the condemned pensioner appeared to vanish completely amid a sudden whirlwind of lightning-fast motion. Nick saw an exploding cloud of what looked to him like scarlet-coloured dust, and then, as aforesaid dust began to settle, he realised it wasn't dust at all, but instead the showering fragments of eviscerated human matter: flesh and bone ground to a fine powder, itself having been ground to a fine mist. The substance seemed to float, then descend, in soft, rolling clouds of scarlet dew. All that was left of the old man after that, Nick saw, was a mere splash of red across the grey, unwashed surface of the platform.

Suddenly, Nick heard the tell-tale clickage of bones on tiles, and realised that the triumphant Bonelord was even now advancing along the edge of the platform towards him. It was a matter of mere seconds, he realised, before the skeletal demon finally caught up with him.

Nick froze, terrified at the sight of the caped and hooded Bonelord advancing along the yellow edge of the neighbouring track. Then, as if someone had poured the contents of a bottle marked 'miracle juice' over his exhausted body, he heard the tell-tale sound of another approaching train.

BONELORD

Maybe, thought Nick, if he stepped closer to the edge of the track, he could somehow trick Bonelord into inadvertently stepping *over* the yellow line – a practice that the underground's rule expressly forbade. If Nick could time it right, the approaching train might possibly just snag the tasselled hem of Bonelord's scarlet cape in one of its doors and drag the wailing were-skeleton into the tunnel behind him.

But it was a useless suggestion, Nick realised, cursing himself inwardly. For the train would be *slowing* on its approach, not speeding up, and those doors on its carriages would have to pause and open before they even thought of closing again, accidentally trapping the edges of Bonelord's red cape between them.

No, Nick thought, despairingly. He hadn't thought things through well enough.

There was only one option left.

Nick saw the lights of the train carriage approaching from the far-off tunnel. He would have to somehow avoid the relentless advance of Bonelord until the train itself had ground to a halt on the platform, then dash on to one of the opened carriages in the full knowledge that he would have no time to shut the door in Bonelord's face and effect an escape that way.

Instead, Nick would have to face Bonelord *inside* the carriage. He just prayed there would be enough passengers on board to distract the caped skeleton while Nick scrambled past them towards the driver's cabin. Yes, hundreds would probably be deboned in the process, but Nick saw those eviscerated souls as a necessary sacrifice in his relentless battle against Bonelord – and, ultimately, they weren't his problem.

As the train rushed out of the far tunnel, Nick prepared himself to leap on board.

Then gasped, incredulous, as the train failed to slow.

He only had time to glimpse the words 'NOT IN SERVICE' before the train was past him again and ploughing into the tunnel behind, leaving Nick once more alone in the underground station with ... Bonelord.

'IT'S THE END OF THE LINE FOR YOU, NICK STEEN.'

'Not quite, Bonelord,' said Nick, leaping down from the platform edge on to the track itself, then sprinting down the tunnel after the departing train.

He heard Bonelord leap down after him, realising that this was where it would end. Alone, in an underground tunnel, deboned by a demonic skeletal lord, with no one ever quite knowing that Nick had put up the fight of his life, single-handed, to protect the innocent lives of Stalkford's yet-to-be-deboned.

As the sound of bony footsteps hitting electrified rails fizzed and crackled behind him, Nick prepared himself to leap on the rails himself. Better to be fried to a crisp by the train's electrical signal than be ground into liquid beef by a crazed and predominantly marrow-based warlord.

And then he saw lights ahead. Surely he wasn't catching up with the train in front? That would be impossible, even for a man as lithe and fit as Nick. But then he saw that those very lights were coming *towards* him.

What the . . .? thought Nick. Surely there was no way a train could be coming *downaways* on the very same track on which a recent train had been travelling *upaways*?

And then Nick realised, as those lights got closer, that they were *blue* in hue. And flashing.

A police car? thought Nick.

Surely not. Surely a squad car driven by a member of The Royal Majesty's police force wasn't somehow driving along the tunnel tracks towards him?

But it was. And as the car screeched and swerved, then skidded to a final halt, a youthful police officer with a neat parting leaped out of the driver's side and bellowed through a loudspeaker as he leaned over the squad car's door.

BONELORD

'This is Police Community Support Officer Gabriel! Throw down your weapon, Nick Steen, and surrender!'

Observing that Police Community Support Officer Gabriel was armed with a truncheon only, Nick ignored the warning, slid himself over the police car's bonnet like they do on TV shows, and landed on the far side, whereupon he immediately sprinted off again. He would have yelled, 'Run!' to Police Community Support Officer Gabriel as well, but recalled what Roz had said about the man's constant attempts to get himself promoted over her, and so left him to fend for himself.

'Freeze!' yelled the terrified Police Community Support Officer Gabriel as Bonelord approached the squad car at speed. 'Cast down your cape and stick your carpal bones up!'

As Nick heard the distinctive sound of Police Community Support Officer Gabriel being ground to powdered mince in the tunnel behind, he burst through into another station concourse and swung himself up on to its main platform. Then he raced up the exit escalator, ignoring all official signs not to run.

For this was a world turned upside down now, Nick figured. A world where bone alone ruled. A world where 'Do not run' meant: 'Actually, run like hell.'

Bursting through the exit barriers, Nick fled the station, hearing Bonelord closing in once more from behind. But he had gained precious time at last, thanks to Police Community Support Officer Gabriel's recent deboning, and as Nick boarded a passing bus, which pulled out from the kerb mere seconds before the sprinting scarlet-caped were-skeleton could leap aboard, he allowed himself, at long last, a second to breathe.

Then he flipped Bonelord the bird.

CHAPTER TEN

Three blocks further on, the bus drew to a sudden halt. Before Nick could understand what was happening, he caught sight of blue flashing lights blocking the road ahead. Moments later, a stocky figure in oversized waders struggled up into the vehicle.

'You're under arrest, Mister Steen,' said Kettlestrom, aiming his police-issued revolver at Nick's head as he shuffled awkwardly down the bus's aisle towards him.

Roz was just behind the police commissioner, Nick saw, also aiming a gun at his head.

'Thought you had us, didn't you?' said Kettlestrom, yanking a pair of cuffs from his belt and holding them out for Roz to take. 'We caught you on CCTV entering the subway at Elephant and Graveyard. We sent Police Community Support Officer Gabriel down in a squad car, but I guess you evaded him somehow. Still, we got you in the end.'

Roz stepped forward, snapping the cuffs around Nick's wrists. He looked up at her with barely concealed – in fact, not remotely concealed – contempt.

'*Et tu*, Roz?' Nick said, as his former editor withdrew the handcuff key from her pocket and, on Kettlestrom's order, threw it away.

'I'm sorry, Nick, but with all these mass eviscerations of late, there are hardly any police officers left, as you know – which means I'm currently getting very close to a promotion.'

Nick nodded, grimly. 'I'd say *very* close, now that Police Community Support Officer Gabriel's finally out of the running. I imagine you played a personal part in sending him down there without back-up?'

Roz smiled wryly to herself. 'Like you always said, Nick, you can't afford to let anything or *anyone* get in the way of personal ambition.'

'You've changed, Roz.'

'Just doing my job, Nick.'

'You're lucky we're not whacking you right here on this bus,' said Kettlestrom, signalling for Nick to get to his feet. 'But Officer Roz thought we should do things by the book and whack you properly back at the station. I guess it'll give me a chance to mess you up a bit in the holding cells first.'

'If you saw me on CCTV entering the underground station,' said Nick, as they shoved him into the street and manoeuvred him towards Roz's waiting panda car, 'then you'll also have seen that giant skeleton in a red cape running in after me.'

'I didn't see that at all,' said Kettlestrom nonchalantly, pressing down on Nick's head as he prepared to shove him into the vehicle. Nick pushed his head upwards at the same time, creating a temporary head-pressing vs hand-resisting stalemate.

'Supernatural manifestations frequently challenge the mechanical limitations of audio-visual technology,' said Nick, wondering how long Kettlestrom could keep up the pretence, 'but what's left of Police Community Support Officer Gabriel in the subway tunnel below – *if* there's anything left – might convince you that your mystery deboner has in fact struck again. *And is getting closer all the time,*' he added, pointedly.

'You're the one behind all this, Mister Steen,' said Kettlestrom. 'The sooner we whack you back at the station, the better for everyone.'

Nick suddenly felt a heavier force exerting pressure on his head, and saw that Roz, too, had now placed her own hand on top of

Kettlestrom's, doubling the strength of the downward force currently battling with the resisting pressure of Nick's ever-defiant neck muscles.

In response, Nick flexed his digastric, scalene, stylohyoid, omohyoid, thyrohyoid and sternohyoid muscles against the combined exertion of Roz and Kettlestrom's lumbrical, thenar, hypothenar and interossei muscles. The sinew-based stalemate was holding for now, but Nick sensed the police commissioner's patience was fast running out.

'Let's quit fencing, Kettlestrom. Or should I say ... *Roberto Mantovani?*'

'Okay, that's it,' Kettlestrom said, finally snapping. Removing his hand from Nick's head, the cop levelled his revolver and cocked the trigger. 'You leave me no choice.'

'Are you just going to stand there, Roz, and let this trumped-up Elmer Fudd whack me on a public thoroughfare?' asked Nick, staring accusingly at his former publisher. 'Or are you in on it, too?'

Roz glared back coldly, removed her own hand from the author's head and levelled her own weapon. 'I don't know what you're talking about, Nick.'

'Haven't you twigged that this guy's a bad apple? That he's a fully paid-up member of the Mantovani crime family, and therefore personally responsible for Bonelord's mindless, bloody rampage?'

'I'm sure you're mistaken, Nick,' replied Roz. 'What's more, the sooner we can eradicate the *ultimate* source of all this supernatural activity, the sooner we'll be able to clear up all the outstanding remnants of your escaping imagination, and bring peace and prosperity to the people of Stalkford.'

'You're now promoted to Detective Inspector, Officer Roz,' said Kettlestrom, handing her a badge from his pocket with his free hand. 'I mean, *Detective Inspector* Roz.'

BONELORD

'Why, thank you, sir,' Roz replied, beaming as she pinned the badge to her breast pocket.

'Right,' continued Kettlestrom, 'now let's whack this arsehole.'

As Roz cocked her gun and Kettlestrom cocked his a second time, Nick realised it was now or never.

'Wait!' he yelled. 'If you kill me, you'll be killing yourself, Kettlestrom. The mystery deboner will come for you personally, whatever happens to me. I'm the only one who can stop him.'

Kettlestrom wavered for a moment, his gun barrel lowering visibly by a couple of millimetres.

Roz also noticed the police commissioner's hesitancy. 'What do you mean, Nick?' she said, warily.

'Like we discussed previously, Roz, Bonelord is a supernatural were-skeleton from my novel *A Hamburgian Verevulf in Stalkford*, transformed via its mangled Italian translation into a chilling were-skeleton known as Bonelord, intent on wreaking bony vengeance on the eight members of the Mantovani family who placed a curse upon a poor lowly peasant called Cliff Capello, who'd fallen behind in his protection payments, turning him into the aforesaid Bonelord.'

'I know all that, Nick.'

'But what you don't know, Roz, is that Kettlestrom here is one of the eight Mantovani family members who placed that very curse. He's since made himself former head of Stalkford's FBI Office and police commissioner in an attempt to allow the Mantovani family to commit crimes with total impunity. But what the mafia can't control is Bonelord's relentless thirst for revenge.'

'You've got it all wrong, Mister Steen,' said Kettlestrom.

'Have I? You see, what the Mantovanis created was a supernatural being that would ultimately destroy *them*. Only they didn't realise that when they signed on the dotted line with Satan. You signed a *Faustian* pact, Kettlestrom. Meaning that by placing supernatural curses on others, the Mantovanis would ultimately be paying for it with their *own* lives. Now Bonelord wants revenge on you all. For only if Bonelord can destroy all eight members of the Mantovani family who placed the initial curse will he – or it – ever be freed from a state of permanent were-skeletonery.'

'Keep talking,' said Kettlestrom, icily.

'*Seven* of those eight family members are now dead, Kettlestrom. The eighth – that's you, Roberto Mantovani – was out wiretapping my apartment when Bonelord came thrashing. Wiping out, conveniently enough, what was left of Stalkford's upstanding, incorruptible police officers.'

'I don't know anything about that,' snapped Kettlestrom.

Nick knew he was lying, knew that somehow the police commissioner had sensed Bonelord's approach and deliberately condemned his incorruptible officers to their ritual deboning. But he could still use Kettlestrom's denials to his advantage.

'Either way, Kettlestrom, if you hadn't been out at the time, you'd have been caught up in that particular deboning, and would no doubt now be housed inside one of constable Roz's human soup vats. You might almost say that it was *me alone* who saved your life.'

'Is this true, sir?' said Roz, transferring her gun's aim towards her superior officer. 'Are you really a bad apple?'

'I tell you, he's got it wrong, dammit,' snapped Kettlestrom. 'Sure, I'm a member of the Mantovani family. But I turned my back on our criminal past after placing that damned curse and devoted myself to a life of fighting crime. I wanted to make amends to society for all the bad things the Mantovanis did over the centuries – especially that completely unnecessary supernatural curse we placed on poor old Cliff Capello.'

'My heart bleeds for you,' said Nick. 'But innocent or not, if you whack me now, Kettlestrom, nothing's going to prevent the

BONELORD

all-powerful Bonelord from completing his – or its – mission and deboning the last remaining undefended member of the Mantovani family, i.e. you.'

'It's true, sir,' said Roz, handing her superior officer a dog-eared Italian horror paperback. She'd had it flown in directly from a second-hand bookshop in Naples earlier that afternoon, and it had just this very second been handed to her by a passing police cadet. 'Look, it's all here, written down in the very book Nick has yet to be paid for.'

'So you're part of this, too?' said Kettlestrom coldly.

Roz's face's dropped, her cheeks flushed with embarrassment.

'Consider yourself demoted, *Officer* Roz,' snapped Kettlestrom, snatching back the Detective Inspector badge he'd just given her. 'For aiding and abetting a known felon.'

Roz gathered herself suddenly, standing straight with her head fully raised. 'Felon or not, sir, I really think you need to let Nick save your life a second time.'

'We'll see,' said Kettlestrom, placing his gun back in its holster, before flicking idly through the old Italian paperback. 'How does it end, then?' he asked Roz. 'Do I get deboned?'

Roz tried to smile encouragingly, then gave up. 'Only half of that is Nick's work, remember, sir,' she said. 'And as long as Nick stays alive, I'm sure he'll be able to think up some other conclusion to this particular story now playing out for real around us. One in which you ultimately *survive*. Right, Nick?'

'Maybe so,' replied Nick, cracking a smug smile at Kettlestrom's expense. 'The only question is, do I want to?'

*

'There's to be a police benefit ball,' said Kettlestrom, handing Styrofoam beakers of coffee to both Roz and Nick. They were seated in his main office, Nick's hands now free of their cuffs, Roz having at long last located the keys she'd previously thrown away.

Not that Nick and Kettlestrom had exchanged much in the way of words while Roz had been searching for said keys. Instead of pumping Nick for possible alternative endings to this ongoing real-life saga of Bonelord, the police commissioner had refused to listen to anything Nick had offered up, insisting he would sort out his own affairs, rather than enlist the aid of someone whom he regarded as a criminal mastermind.

He's scared I won't save him, thought Nick. *Scared I'm gonna let him die regardless. That's why he's not interested in any of my alternative endings. I guess I should never have hinted as much in that last sentence of the previous section.*

'It's all arranged for this evening,' continued Kettlestrom. 'I've hired out a mansion in the country that used to belong to Nigel Mantovani, former chief councillor of Stalkford City Council. Alas, now one of the deboned,' he added, with grim emphasis. 'Like Giuseppe, he, too, was my brother.'

They'd all been Kettlestrom's brothers, Nick knew. And without Kettlestrom allowing Nick the chance to create an alternative ending, the only way out of this mess was for that *eighth* brother to die – i.e. Roberto Mantovani, i.e. Kettlestrom. So what was the police commissioner planning to do about it?

'It'll be a recruitment drive for new officers. There'll be a big dinner and dancing, followed by a prize raffle.'

'Sounds like fun,' said Roz.

'Not for Cliff "Livewire" Capello, it won't be,' Kettlestrom said, ominously.

'Bonelord, you mean,' said Nick, sipping his coffee. Part of him was enjoying watching how the commissioner operated. For if Nick hadn't been a horror author, or full-time demon-slayer, he quite fancied the idea of a career in the police force. Especially now that summary whackings had been allowed.

'It'll be tough on Bonelord, too,' said Kettlestrom, indicating a large map hanging on the wall behind them. In the centre was a rectangular structure which Nick took to be the mansion itself. Surrounding that was what looked like a complex network of signals, traps and intruder alarms.

'The whole estate is rigged up to a computer system housed in the mansion itself. From inside this main hub, we'll be able to detect whatever enters the estate from all sides, then track its progress from one sensor to the next. If Bonelord attacks—'

'*When* Bonelord attacks,' Nick interrupted, before taking another sip of coffee.

'*When* Bonelord attacks, we'll be waiting for him. He'll fall right into our trap.'

'What trap?' said Nick, not bothering to point out anymore that Bonelord could also be an 'it', as it was too tiring for all concerned.

'Excuse me?' snapped Kettlestrom.

'I said, "What trap?" How the hell do you think you're going to be able to stop a supernatural mincing machine, Kettlestrom? The claws on the end of each phalange are razor sharp. They can slice a propelled bullet into small slivers before you've even clocked the cloud of ejected cordite.'

'You leave that side of things to me,' said Kettlestrom, cryptically. 'As far as you're concerned, Nick Steen, that's classified information.'

'Fair dinkum,' said Nick. 'But you haven't quite explained my part in all this. If you're not prepared to let me come up with an alternative ending, or let me in on whatever plan you've personally laid down for trapping and disarming the all-powerful Bonelord, I fail to see why you need me to tag along.'

'Because you're my bait, Mister Steen,' said Kettlestrom, with a cruel smile. 'I need you to lure Bonelord in.'

'No way,' said Nick, shaking his head emphatically and placing his Styrofoam beaker on the desk in anticipation of rising up and walking out. 'Capello's a buddy of mine. I appreciate the need to stop Bonelord in his tracks – and my sympathies, frankly, were somewhat eroded when he came after me personally last night – but I won't be party to the murder of a former buddy of mine who once saved my life. Get some other lackey to do your dirty work, Kettlestrom-slash-Mantovani.'

'You'll lure Capello in, or I'll have you whacked right now,' said Kettlestrom. 'Frankly, now that you've helped fill me in on Bonelord's MO, and shared your advice on a few technical and culinary matters, I have no real further need of you.'

'So let me go.'

'You think I'm gonna let you walk out of here so you can go and warn Capello off? What's to stop you and him getting rid of me and carrying on your little love affair with the curse lifted and me finally out of the way? I'm not as dumb as you are, Steen. You'll stay right here by that phone on my desk and wait for Capello to call. Then you'll tell him all about the police ball, and that I'll be hosting things *personally*. You'll make sure Cliff Capello, and Bonelord, walk right into my trap.'

'How's he gonna know to call me here? If Capello's going to get in touch with me to apologise for almost killing me last night, he'll call me on my home phone number. Not a police phone.'

'I could accompany Nick to his apartment, sir, and wait there with him for Capello to call?' offered Roz.

'No chance,' said Kettlestrom, reaching down to pull open the drawer of his desk. 'And also, no need.' He reached in with his hand and pulled out, to Nick and Roz's joint surprise, Nick's very own bedside phone.

'I had this tapped and rewired all the way from your bedroom to my personal police office here at the station. Even did the cabling myself. You see, Steen, there's nothing I don't think of. So now all we have to do is sit here and wait for that call.'

'And then?' asked Nick.

'Then *you* spring my trap,' Kettlestrom replied, pointing his finger at Nick for emphasis. 'You, Nick Steen, will bag me a Bonelord.'

CHAPTER ELEVEN

The call came through around lunchtime. As Kettlestrom hit the record button and Roz listened in on police-issued headphones, Nick began the conversation he'd been dreading.

'Nick Steen, demon-slayer?'

'Nick!'

'Good afternoon, Capello.'

'Wanna grab some lunch? Mantovani's is still soaked through, but Bagacelli's on Fifth and Thirty-Second is largely blood-free. What say we slam some more meatballs together?'

'I'm not hungry, Capello,' said Nick, coldly. 'And I'm not sure I want to meet you for lunch, or even coffee, frankly.'

Kettlestrom jabbed a finger at Nick's written brief, glaring at him. But Nick shook his head, sternly. He'd do this *his* way.

'To be honest, Capello, I'm not even sure we can be best buddies anymore.'

'No longer *best buddies*? This is about last night, right?'

'Maybe it is, maybe it isn't,' said Nick, playing hard to get.

'Hey, that's why I'm calling you about the meatballs, Nick. I want to apologise.'

'And I should think so, Capello.'

'Believe it or not, Nick, I didn't want to chase you through the subway in the form of a gigantic skeleton in a red cape.'

'And yet you did,' muttered Nick moodily.

'I know, but that's because I was *Bonelord*, Nick. I had no choice in the matter. When that all-powerful bony warlord feeling comes over me, I'm powerless to resist. Frankly, you're lucky to be alive.'

'No thanks to you. But aside from me, there's an umbrella-wielding war veteran dead, plus an eviscerated police community support officer of the law, although that one's technically Roz's fault.'

'He knew the risks when he took on the job,' interjected Roz, before Kettlestrom immediately shushed her.

'Who's that?' snapped Capello suddenly, his voice instantly growing suspicious.

'No one, Capello,' Nick replied, covering for Roz's unprofessional slip-up. 'Just some crackling on the wire.'

'Maybe the authorities are listening in on us, Nick,' said Capello. 'Maybe your line's been tapped.'

'Nonsense, Capello. And even if those authorities were listening in, I have *their* line tapped, so I'd be able to hear their tap via my tap.'

That wasn't true in the slightest, but Nick was having to improvise.

'You can hear their tap via your tap?'

'Sort of, Capello. I don't actually hear their tap via my tap, because my tap effectively scrambles their tap.'

'What if their tap scrambles your tap that scrambles the original tap?'

'You mean a second tap?'

'Yes, another tap tapping your tap of their tap.'

'I *also* have a second tap, Capello. A tap to tap their tap of my tap of the original tap.'

'Four taps?'

'Plus the scramblers.'

'Scramble*rs*, Nick? I thought it was just one scrambler.'

'They'd need to scramble my scramble, Capello. And if they did that, then I'd also need a scrambler to scramble that scramble of my original scramble.'

'Plus a descrambler, I presume.'

'Correct. To descramble all the scrambled scrambles.'

'My mind's scrambled too, Nick. Please explain.'

'I'd need a descrambler to descramble their previous descrambling of my original descramble of the various scramblings.'

'All that, *plus* the taps?'

'Correct. Look, I have it all covered, Capello, so stop worrying.'

'Okay, Nick. But you must understand, I'm under a lot of stress with this curse. I'm sorry I chased you into the subway, buddy, but I had no control over that. When Bonelord calls, Capello falls. That is why I have to destroy the Mantovanis if I'm to have any hope of returning to the Capello of old. If I can somehow kill Roberto Mantovani, the curse will be lifted.'

Nick could feel Kettlestrom bristling beside him, the commissioner's hand reaching instinctively for his gun. Nick grabbed the lawman's hand, shaking his head.

'Like I said last night, Nick,' Capello went on, 'I need your help.'

'That's what I've been wanting to talk to you about, Capello. I've also been thinking about our conversation in the cemetery last night. About your proposal.'

'About helping me kill Roberto Mantovani?'

'Correct. Despite the risk to the wider public, I've decided to help you out after all. We may barely be buddies anymore, but technically we're still buddies at some level.'

Capello breathed an audible sigh of relief on the other end of the phone. 'My God, Nick, that is fantastic news. I'm so happy, my moustache is twitching of its own accord.'

'Listen, Capello. We don't have much time. There's to be a police ball tonight.'

Nick looked over at Roz and Kettlestrom, feeling suddenly sick. The dreaded moment had come. He was now betraying the trust of Capello, a best buddy who'd routinely saved his life on numerous occasions. Nick had saved his life back, of course, multiple times, but it was a good arrangement. And Nick would have preferred to continue implementing it in his fight against supernatural evil, were it not for his imminent betrayal. But Nick's life was on the line. When it came down to it, it was him or Capello.

Kettlestrom signalled for Nick to keep going.

'A police ball, Nick?' repeated Capello through Nick's earpiece.

'At the big country mansion once owned by Nigel Mantovani, the Stalkford city councillor you minced to pieces last week.'

'Bonelord minced him to pieces, Nick. That wasn't me, remember?'

'Of course, Capello. Sorry. Well, like I say, there's a police ball happening there tonight. There'll be dancing, meatballs, plus a raffle.'

'Musical chairs?'

'I believe there'll also be musical chairs,' said Nick, looking helplessly across at Roz, who jotted down 'musical chairs' on her ball preparation itinerary.

'I *love* musical chairs, Nick.'

'You'll love this more, Capello. Bob Kettlestrom—'

'You mean Roberto Mantovani?'

'The same. He'll be hosting the evening as a way of recruiting some fresh cadets for his hugely depleted police force.'

'Then it won't matter if Bonelord debones them all, will it, Nick? As far as Bonelord is concerned, those working for the police commissioner himself are all viable targets. Hey, by the way, that's Bonelord speaking through me, Nick. I, of course, think that deboning everyone at the ball is an awful idea.'

'So do I, Capello, and never forget that,' snapped Nick. He couldn't help himself. For the truth was that Nick would also be there tonight. Roz, too. And if anything went wrong, and Kettlestrom-slash-Roberto-Mantovani couldn't manage to stop Capello-slash-Bonelord in his bony tracks, then he and Roz would be deboned as well.

'I won't forget, Nick. I promise,' said Capello. 'And thank you for helping me out with this. I vow to you, as Bonelord is my witness, one more mass deboning and then you'll never hear of this Bonelord again. That is, presuming Mantovani dies, of course. If he ducks out at the last minute like last time, then we'll have to arrange the entire thing again.'

'He won't duck out,' said Nick, glancing up meaningfully at Kettlestrom. 'I can categorically promise you Roberto Mantovani will be there.'

'Great, Nick. Now, how about those meatballs?'

'Not today, Capello,' said Nick grimly. 'I seem to have lost my appetite, somehow.'

'Next week then, Nick. When old Capello will be back, and Bonelord will be no more.'

'I'll drink to that, bud,' said Nick, placing his bedroom phone receiver back on the police station cradle. Even if, Nick reflected moodily, that was to be his final drink ...

'It's done,' said Nick, emptily.

'Good. Now that wasn't so hard, was it?' Kettlestrom-slash-Mantovani replied.

'You'd best have a damned good system in place for catching Bonelord,' warned Nick gruffly. 'Because if you haven't, Kettlestrom, we're *all* going to be deboned by the end of play today.'

'Relax,' said Kettlestrom, rising to his feet. 'Everything's in hand.'

And with that, the police commissioner left to start making preparations for the upcoming ball.

★

Later, Nick drained his glass of rum punch and watched as the young men and women in dinner dress scrambled wildly to seat themselves on the final remaining chair.

BONELORD

'It's sad, isn't it, Roz?' said Nick, addressing his former editor, who stood beside him in a silky velvet frock that had already turned several eyes at the ball. 'To think that all these young hopefuls might, in less than an hour or so, be completely deboned – and in front of each other.'

'Don't be so morbid, Nick,' said Roz. 'After all, Kettlestrom said he has everything in hand.'

'Then why is he still wearing those waders? If he's so confident of catching Bonelord in his so-called trap, why's he preparing for yet another bloodbath?'

'He's become quite attached to those waders, Nick,' said Roz, steering Nick away from the rum punch counter and towards the prize raffle stall. 'Quite literally attached. He's too short to prise them off with his own hands, and he can't find a way of removing them now that all the other officers are dead.'

'How about *you* helping him out, Roz?' asked Nick. 'You're still employed by the police department, after all. And it might even get you re-promoted.'

'I'm not sure I can cope with that level of responsibility again, Nick. Power corrupts, as they say, and I did almost whack you myself, remember?'

'I remember all too well, Roz.'

'Frankly, I'd prefer to let my hair down for a bit. Plus, I do miss my slingbacks.'

'Understood. Fancy a go on the lucky dip?'

'I already own a revolver, Nick. Unless you want to try nabbing a walkie-talkie instead?'

'It would only be a tapped one, Roz,' said Nick, walking away from the large bucket of sand. 'And I've had quite enough of being tapped for one day.'

'How about a dance then?' said Roz, taking Nick's hands in hers. 'You can sweep me off my feet, if you like.'

Roz was enjoying this far too much, Nick decided. She wasn't on the ball enough, if he excused the expression, which he did, given that at any second, the marauding figure of Bonelord would be interrupting proceedings in a potential whirlwind of violent death.

'Sorry, Roz. Perhaps another time.'

'Oh come on, Nick. You can watch me go all glittery under the chandelier.'

'Can it, Roz. That dress is far too becoming for a police officer. I think you're too swept up in the party atmosphere, to be frank. You're not on the ball, if you'll pardon the expression.'

'Nonsense, Nick. And I definitely *won't* pardon that expression. I'm simply enjoying a bit of free time, that's all. And why not, I ask you? I've been working hard all week separating blood cells, remember? Heck, I deserve a bit of downtime.'

'It could be the last downtime you ever have, Roz.'

'Not that again,' said Roz, moving away from the dance floor. 'I told you before, Nick. Police Commissioner Kettlestrom-slash-Mantovani has everything in hand. He assures me that both the bait, and the trap, have been set.'

'And has he told you what exactly that trap is, Roz?'

'No, Nick. He hasn't. But that's classified information, as you know.'

'But you're the only police officer he currently has left, Roz. If he hasn't told *you* anything about how precisely he's going to catch Bonelord in the act, how do we know whether that plan even exists, let alone works? I have a bad feeling about tonight.'

'The plan exists alright, Nick. One thing I *have* been party to is overall preparation of the alarm sensors. Come along with me and I'll show you.'

Nick followed Roz through the main ballroom, aware of yet more heads turning as they passed through the crowds of police wannabes in their early twenties.

'It's up here,' said Roz, ascending a large sweeping central staircase leading up to an upper balcony overlooking the main ballroom below.

As Nick followed her up, he heard several wolf-whistles from behind as the crowded dancers observed the couple ascending.

Most probably wolf-whistling Roz, Nick thought. *They'll need to curtail that kind of activity if they have any hope of sustaining a professional police career.*

Then he decided to turn round and tell them that.

'You'd best cut out that kind of behaviour if you have any hope of sustaining a professional police career!' he bellowed down at them. But instead of a chastised silence, Nick's ears were met only with a resounding chorus of increased wolf-whistling. So they'd been wolf-whistling *him*, not Roz. Nick knew he had a reputation, but believed that was as a result of his demon-slaying activities, not the shape of his butt, which he knew, Roz having told him on several occasions in the past, was perennially uptight.

'Forget them, Nick,' said Roz, taking his arm again and leading him further up the stairs. 'They're just having a good time.'

'For now,' said Nick, grimly, following Roz up on to the upper balcony. 'Maybe later, not so much.'

Reaching the top, Nick observed a corridor running off towards the rear of the house on the left-hand side.

'It's down there,' said Roz, heading towards it.

Nick followed her to the end of the corridor and waited as she opened a door leading into a dark inner stairwell. Then Roz hitched up her skirts and commenced climbing the spiral staircase, followed by Nick. At the top of this second stairwell was yet another door, and Nick waited again as Roz gave a professional knock.

'Police Officer Roz,' she announced.

'Enter,' said a voice from within. Roz pushed open the door and Nick followed her into a vast office, lined on all sides with banks of computer monitors and glowing television screens. On each screen, Nick saw grainy, green-tinted closed-circuit camera feeds displaying assorted areas of the mansion's vast outer grounds.

'This is my observation room,' said Kettlestrom-slash-Mantovani, whose voice had ushered them both in. 'From here, I'm able to detect anyone or anything that might come crashing through our sensors.'

The police commissioner indicated the desk in front of him, over which was arranged a further bank of monitors displaying various graphs and tables, replete with chirping electrical signals and an array of flashing, multi-coloured lights.

'A lot of these are just for show,' Kettlestrom said, pointing to an area of constantly flickering bulbs. 'That one's actually a copy of the *Simon*™ game glued into this main bank, in case I get bored with all this observing. But that won't happen tonight.'

'And what *is* happening tonight?' asked Nick. 'It's all very well tracking Bonelord. Observing him – or it – as he – or it – triggers all those electronic sensors in the mansion's grounds, but how are you going to *trap* him – or it? I realise I vowed to stop saying "or it" earlier on but needs must.'

'That's *my* business, Mister Steen,' said the police commissioner, attempting in vain to sit down in the main observation seat, hindered by those vast, oversized waders he couldn't take off.

'Do you want me to help you with those?' asked Nick, stepping towards the giant rubber boots.

'No thanks. They're fine as they are.'

'It'll only take a minute,' said Nick. He was sensing, as he'd suspected, that the police commissioner was stalling for some reason.

'I said they're *fine*, Mister Steen,' Kettlestrom replied. 'Leave my waders alone.'

Nick sensed an ominous feeling deep down in his gut. The lawman was doing everything in his power to keep those waders *on*. Which meant only one thing, Nick realised. Kettlestrom was expecting a bloodbath.

'I asked you what plans you had in place to catch the all-powerful Bonelord,' said Nick, tersely.

'And *I* told *you* that's classified information,' growled Kettlestrom. 'Now back off, mister.'

But Nick wasn't going to back off. Nick Steen was going to find out precisely what plan the police commissioner had in place, one way or another. Even if that meant forcing the issue, right here and right now.

Taking a deep breath, Nick braced himself to leap forward and prise free Kettlestrom's waders from the lawman's tiny legs.

But he never got there. For just before Nick could physically launch himself forwards, towards the rubber boots, an urgent bleeping noise sounded from a nearby monitor. Then, every single alarm in the room erupted as the various sensors placed around the mansion's grounds went suddenly wild.

'This is it,' said Kettlestrom, watching a trail of red light advancing at speed across a vast map of the estate. 'Bonelord has breached the perimeter.'

'Bonelord?' said Roz, nervously.

Nick turned to face her, a grim expression on his face. 'Bonelord,' he whispered, attempting to contain the palpable edge of rising terror in his voice. 'Here comes Bonelord . . .'

CHAPTER TWELVE

They traced the swift progression of illuminating LED lights as Bonelord made his – or its – virtual way across the map.

'Now what?' said Nick, turning to Kettlestrom. 'At this rate, he – or it – will be here in three minutes or less.'

'Relax,' said the police commissioner. 'Like I said before, it's all in hand.'

'Precisely what is "all in hand"?' Nick snapped, tired of the lawman's oblique turn of phrase. 'Some sort of advanced-tech super-smart skeleton trap you haven't told us about, I hope. One in which we can contain Bonelord indefinitely. Or maybe a tactical thermo-nuclear device concealed somewhere in the ballroom below us, because that's what it's going to take to stop Bonelord in his – or its – tracks, Kettlestrom.'

'Neither of those things,' said the police commissioner. 'Just watch.'

Kettlestrom reached up and yanked a cord hanging from the overhead rafters. Immediately, a section of the ceiling began to slide back, exposing a slim patch of moonlit sky. Nick felt a sudden waft of cold air and realised, in horror, that Kettlestrom was in fact opening up a gap in the ceiling itself.

'What the hell are you doing, Kettlestrom-slash-Mantovani?' barked Nick. 'It looks to me like you're opening up a gap in the ceiling itself, through which Bonelord can leap down and subsequently debone us.'

'Wrong,' said Kettlestrom. 'I'm opening up a gap in the ceiling for another purpose entirely. Bonelord won't have time to get anywhere near us, believe me. This room is my late brother's observatory, and that slowly widening gap in the ceiling is where he used to train his telescope.'

Nick shivered against the icy coldness now filling the room, an ominous feeling taking hold of his senses. Evidently Roz could feel the chill too, because at that precise moment Nick felt her grab his arm and hug his body close to hers for warmth. He quickly shrugged her aside, sensing he'd soon be needing his own body free for immediate physical action. What precisely that immediate physical action might be, however, Nick didn't yet know. But as the ceiling panel retracted past the halfway mark, admitting the sudden bright rays of a cold and icy light, he began to have a good idea.

'The moon,' he said, as the three watched the panel retract fully at last, exposing the cold, white orb far above.

'That's right,' said the police commissioner, grinning to himself. 'And a full one, too.'

Nick turned towards Kettlestrom, noting that the lawman's eyes looked wider somehow, the Earth's luminescent lunar satellite now reflected in both orbs.

'What's this all about, Kettlestrom?' said Nick.

'My real name, Mister Steen, is Roberto Mantovani,' said the lawman.

'What's this all about, Roberto Mantovani?'

'Survival,' said Mantovani, breathing in deeply, as if to suck up the gleaming rays of the moon overhead. 'For there's only one of us left now. One Mantovani in all of Stalkford. A once all-powerful crime family, soon to be no more.'

'But I thought you were the white sheep of the family, Mantovani,' said Nick ironically. 'The one who joined the police just so you could put your powerful family behind bars.'

'Didn't think I'd convinced you,' said Kettlestrom, still staring up at the moon. 'I became police commissioner so the Mantovanis would *never* be troubled by law and order again.'

'Like I said in the first place. A bad apple.'

'Top of the whole rotting tree. Only there's a problem. Like I said, there's just one of us left. My mother, Countess Margarita Mantovani, should never have made her boys place that curse on Cliff Capello for falling behind on his protection payments, but she did, and now that lowly peasant's poised to destroy us all.'

'As the all-powerful Bonelord.'

'You said it. All-powerful. That has a quite a ring to it, don't you think?'

Nick realised Kettlestrom was *still* staring up at the moon, his face now looking increasingly *crazed*.

'What do you mean, Mantovani?' said Nick, sensing they were nearing yet another terrifying revelation.

'Watch,' said Kettlestrom. Almost immediately, the lawman's upper torso shot towards the ceiling, stretching by a distance of around three feet. *Hell*, thought Nick. Kettlestrom was suddenly *tall*.

Then he noticed the lawman's arse bone. It had somehow burst through the seat of his trousers, along with both thigh bones, extending outward to increase his overall height by an *additional foot*.

Then the lawman's arm bones burst through his uniform, too, and Nick realised the expanding skeleton living inside Kettlestrom-slash-Mantovani was beginning to climb out.

'Bonelord!' croaked Nick. 'You're *another* Bonelord!'

'*THE ONE AND ONLY BONELORD!*' shrieked Kettlestrom, strips of his former face flesh starting to curl off and fall away from the giant skull swelling stiffly underneath. 'THE ALL-POWERFUL BONELORD!'

Two Bonelords! thought Nick.

How the hell could there be *two* Bonelords?

Unless the police commissioner had, out of sheer desperation, and having realised his own survival was ultimately doomed, decided to place the very same curse the Mantovanis had originally placed on Capello on *himself too.*

'Double Bonelords?' Roz piped up, beside him.

'Yes, double Bonelords, Roz. Bonelord-C, i.e. Capello's Bonelord, and Bonelord-K, i.e. Kettlestrom's Bonelord.'

'Shouldn't that be Bonelord-M, Nick? In other words, Mantovani's Bonelord?' asked Roz.

'Technically, yes, Roz, but if we're not careful, we'll both start referring to Bonelord-M as Boney M., which might in turn make us think of Rasputin – or Daddy Cool, for that matter.'

'How about Bonelord-KM? And Bonelord-CLC for Cliff "Livewire" Capello?'

'Fine, Roz. Whatever you want. Just be quiet, please. I'm figuring out all the implications internally at present, and your interruptions are extremely disruptive, especially as you've contributed sweet Fanny Adams to this entire observatory-based conversation thus far. Pipe down.'

'Of course, Nick,' said Roz, suitably chastised. 'I'm so sorry.'

Nick would accept Roz's apology later. Right now, he needed to get his thoughts together, before Kettlestrom deboned them both prematurely, prior to a further deboning by Capello's original Bonelord.

So, figuring there was only one Mantovani family member remaining, Kettlestrom had decided to fight fire with fire in order to survive. Or, more specifically, Bonelord with Bonelord. Meaning that what was about to occur was some sort of final reckoning between the two.

'Too bad Capello didn't debone you at the police station,' snapped Nick, backing away with Roz from the ever-expanding Kettlestrom. Nick realised the former lawman was now the correct bodily height for those waders he was still wearing – and things were only going to get worse.

'CAPELLO DIDN'T COMMIT THAT PARTICULAR DEBONING,' roared Kettlestrom, whose voice was starting to distort into the distinctive throaty rattle of a part-living skeleton. 'I DID IT MYSELF! JUST BEFORE I WIRETAPPED YOUR APARTMENT. THAT'S WHY I WASN'T PERSONALLY DEBONED. I DID IT TO KILL ALL THE POLICE OFFICERS UNDER MY JURISDICTION.'

Of course! thought Nick, reeling from yet another terrifying plot revelation. For hadn't Capello mentioned only yesterday that he possessed no memory of the debonings he'd committed? All along, the Italian had presumed he'd been the one who'd attacked the police station, when it had in fact been the corrupt police commissioner himself...

'But why?' said Nick. 'You were the bad apple *tree*. No one below you could possibly have been a threat.'

'WRONG. FOR NEW OFFICER ROZ BLOOM WAS CLOSING IN ON ME, MISTER STEEN. SHE'D BEGUN TO SUSPECT I WAS IN FACT OPERATING *OUTSIDE* THE LAW, AND NOT WITHIN IT.'

'That's true, actually,' said Roz. 'I definitely had my suspicions. Sorry I didn't pipe up about it previously.'

'I'm tempted to say pipe down, Roz,' said Nick, still backing away from the emerging Bonelord. 'But on this occasion, I want you to continue to pipe up. Please explain.'

'You see, Nick, when Kettlestrom first mooted the idea of whacking you on sight without any supporting evidence, I suspected something untoward might be going on.'

'I'll say.'

'Wrong, Nick. *I'll* say. This is my turn to talk.'

'Fine,' said Nick, backing down again with a huff. 'Just make it brief, because Kettlestrom-slash-Mantovani's emerging Bonelord has almost fully climbed out of his body, and Capello's advancing Bonelord is already halfway across the perimeter.'

'Very well, Nick. I began to suspect Kettlestrom had rumbled my own particular law-abiding game when I suggested whacking all the prisoners we had in the cells immediately in order to curry favour with him, which at that point included several members of the Mantovani crime family. He resolutely refused, and subsequently released those very Mantovanis later that evening, citing lack of evidence. Something wasn't adding up, I figured. Why would he whack you without warning, yet spare some of Stalkford's worst offenders from an even worser whacking?'

'A fine piece of deduction, Roz.'

'So, when Kettlestrom told me that he was leaving the police station temporarily in order to commence the wiretapping of your apartment, Nick, precisely when we already had our work cut out investigating the recent booze cruise deboning, I began to grow even more suspicious. Sensing Kettlestrom might be intending to whack me as well at any second, I requested an immediate transfer to the police morgue detail, precisely when I knew he wouldn't be at the station himself to contravene said request. It just so happens that that was the *very* same night the police station deboning occurred. A deboning that ultimately spared the previously incarcerated Mantovanis – and destroyed all of Stalkford's rival crime families and law-abiding officers in one fell swoop. A deboning that was also meant to have deboned *me*!'

'But why didn't you mention, Roz, that there'd *previously* been Mantovani prisoners incarcerated in the cells when I asked you whether there'd been any Mantovani prisoners incarcerated in the cells on the night in question?'

'The fact was that there *weren't* any Mantovani prisoners incarcerated in the cells on the night in question, Nick. They were all over at Giuseppe's restaurant, celebrating their recent release. And as a police officer, I have to deal in facts alone.'

Nick nodded, sagely. 'And as Capello retains little to no memory of whom or what he's deboned when he transforms back into himself the morning after an all-night mass deboning, he wrongly assumed in this case that he himself had committed the police station deboning, and somehow missed deboning the intended target of that particular deboning, i.e. Bob-Kettlestrom-slash-Roberto-Mantovani.'

'Precisely, Nick,' said Roz. 'Now I'll happily pipe down again.'

'Meaning now we have two Bonelords intent on deboning each other in order to save their respective lives and prevent themselves turning into Bonelord again.'

'WRONG!' shrieked Kettlestrom's Bonelord, who had now stepped out of Kettlestrom's body entirely. 'I PLACED A SLIGHTLY DIFFERENT CURSE ON MY OWN BODY, MEANING THAT IF I WIN THIS FORTHCOMING BATTLE WITH CAPELLO'S BONELORD, I WILL REMAIN AS BONELORD FOR *ALL TIME!*'

Roz screamed as the demonic bone-warrior rattled towards them at speed. Kettlestrom's Bonelord was strikingly similar to Capello's Bonelord, Nick observed – only this skeletal demon didn't have Capello's moustache, and instead of a red cape, wore huge rubber waders. But it still looked all-powerful.

'Run, Roz!' yelled Nick. 'Down those stairs we previously came up!'

As Roz darted across the observatory floor towards the door, Nick prepared himself for what was to come. He didn't think he'd have time to make it across the room himself, and knew he'd have to distract Kettlestrom's Bonelord somehow in order to give Roz extra time to escape. Maybe if he caused some sort of technical commotion, the ensuing confusion might distract the demon long enough for Roz, and Nick too, to effect an escape. Decision made, Nick hurled himself towards the banks of computers and ran his hands and splayed arms across the buttons.

Immediately, the various screens went haywire and alarms began sounding throughout the building as Bonelord-KM parted its mandibles and laughed. The voice, as before, seemed to resound from somewhere deep within Nick's head.

'THAT WON'T HELP YOU. BONELORD MAKES NO DISTINCTION BETWEEN DIFFERING TYPES OF MATTER. FLESH, BONE, PLASTIC AND/OR INTRICATE METAL CIRCUITRY, IT'S ALL THE SAME TO ME.'

'Except that you now only have two seconds to memorise and repeat that sequence of lights flashing on the *Simon*™ interface,' yelled Nick.

At once, a confused expression crossed Bonelord-KM's face, even though Nick couldn't see it, skulls being essentially motionless. The all-powerful bone-warrior was clearly struggling, through the sheer unexpected urgency of Nick's request, to distinguish between its immediate priorities. And as Bonelord-KM's hand reached out to observe and repeat the sequence on the *Simon*™ interface, Nick made a dash for the door.

'CURSE YOU, NICK STEEN!' roared Bonelord-KM, realising he – or it – had been temporarily duped.

Nick heard the rattling of bones behind him, along with the telltale squelch and squeak of rubber waders, and knew that Bonelord-KM was already giving chase. But he and Roz now had one small advantage. For no being on Earth – or Hell, for that matter – could rush down a spiral staircase in rubber waders at speed. This meant that he and Roz now had a sporting chance to flee downwards to the upper balcony area.

As they broke out on to the upper landing, Nick could see that the ball below them was in full swing. The crowds of hopped-up youths were playing yet another round of musical chairs – completely oblivious to the horror that awaited them, Nick realised. Especially as Capello *loved* musical chairs, and if Nick's former buddy retained any influence at all over the mind of the marauding Bonelord, he'd be making a beeline for the hall below.

'Run!' Nick yelled as he and Roz flew down the grand staircase into the ballroom below.

'Everyone run for your lives!' Roz shouted as loudly as she could – but her shout wasn't nearly as loud as Nick's own shout, meaning hers was far less effective. In fact, it was hardly beneficial at all. 'Bonelord is coming!'

'Correction,' cried Nick, charging across the floor of the main ballroom in an attempt to break up the still-partying throng. 'Bonelord-KM is coming! Soon to be joined by Bonelord-CLC!'

But no one was listening, Nick realised. They were all too busy having a good time, not caring the tiniest bit about the presence of two demonic, all-powerful skeletal warriors heading their way, soon to be dicing and slicing them all to liquified bits.

'It's useless, Roz!' yelled Nick, hardly able to make himself heard over the screams of mocking laughter coming from the overexuberant youths. Then he heard the distinctive sound of yet more wolf-whistling. 'They think this is all a big joke, Roz. They're even wolf-whistling again at what they perceive to be my tight arse.'

'It *is* particularly tight, Nick. Especially in those leather trousers of yours.'

'I hardly think laughing about my tight arse – which, by the way, Type-Face, Lord of the Prolix would have assured you is not tight at all, but actually kind of cute – is conducive to solving crimes of a horrific nature, Roz. Frankly, I'd hesitate to recommend any of these wannabe recruits as likely police officer material.'

'I guess you're right, Nick. Then what should we do?'

Nick didn't have time to answer, as a sudden demonic shriek, followed by multiple screams, roared out from the bottom of the grand staircase. All at once, Nick, Roz and all those beside them were showered with a vast spray of desiccated flesh and bone fragments, along with pints and pints of crimson, copper-scented blood.

'What'll we do now, Nick?' cried Roz, 'I imagine it'll be *us* being deboned next. In fact, I'm sure of it.'

'The rum punch table, Roz,' said Nick. 'We can hide under it together. Hopefully, Bonelord-KM won't think of looking for us there. And if he – or it – does, we can at least drink all the rum punch in one gulp, and hopefully at that point our subsequent deboning won't seem quite so bad.'

'Crikey, Nick, we're really stuck between a rock and a hard place, aren't we?'

'Not exactly, Roz,' said Nick, smoothing eviscerated matter from her eyes so she could see him properly. 'I'd say we're stuck between Bonelord and Bonelord.'

Roz nodded, trying her hardest to appear brave, even though Nick knew she was obviously quaking.

'We'll make it yet, Roz,' he said, giving her chin a soft, encouraging tweak with his manly knuckle. 'And if not, that's a damned fine dress you've worn for our final dance together, Roz.'

'Oh, Nick,' she said, swooning into his arms. And although, amid the heady mix of primal terror and spraying gore, Nick would have liked to have done it with his former editor right there and then, surrounded by panicked crowds of screaming debonees, he knew he had to prioritise the welfare of others. Plus any future working relations with Roz, for that matter. Any potential nookie opportunity would just have to wait.

Gathering Roz in his arms, Nick staggered across the blood-strewn ballroom, ducking in and out of groups of fleeing police hopefuls, until at long last he stood before the table of rum punch. Sliding Roz gently underneath it, he picked up the bowl of rum punch in his free hand and climbed under the table beside her, using the giant brimming cocktail receptacle to mask both their bodies from the chaotic, violent deboning taking place before them.

As the blood level on the ballroom floor began to rise, Nick realised they might soon drown. Thinking quickly, he reached up with one hand to the surface of the table above and grabbed a couple of plastic straws. Handing one to Roz, he shoved the other in his mouth and breathed through that as their heads became completely submerged.

Floating amid the bloody pool, Nick could just discern, through the distorted prism of the mixed cocktail bowl in front, a pair of rubber waders standing amid the brimming pool of human remains. He could see no more than that, and hoped this also meant neither he nor Roz could be seen by the owner of Bonelord-KM's waders.

'NICK STEEN! OFFICER ROZ!' shrieked the voice of Bonelord-KM, from somewhere deep inside Nick's head. Then he saw the distant waders begin to slosh and squelch about the bloody pool as Bonelord-KM began searching for his missing victims.

'Keep quiet, Roz,' mouthed Nick, immediately stopping himself from speaking as a tell-tale rush of bubbles shot to the surface.

But it was too late.

For Bonelord-KM had seen those bubbles, and now knew precisely where Nick and Roz lay hidden.

Nick watched, helpless, as the waders changed direction, making their way towards him . . .

CHAPTER THIRTEEN

But before the all-powerful Bonelord-KM's rubber waders could reach the vicinity of the rum punch table, Nick and Roz heard a second catastrophic shriek from the ballroom above, distorted as it was by the waves of blood lapping at their respective eardrums.

Nick watched Bonelord-KM's waders stop mid-stride, then turn forty-five degrees in the direction of the grand staircase. Realising they were momentarily safe, Nick grabbed Roz in his arms again and surfaced amid the tide of human remains. Carefully, without risking any sudden movements that might draw Bonelord-KM's attention, Nick and Roz peered round either side of the rum punch bowl.

The sight that greeted their eyes filled them with terror. For there, on the grand staircase leading down into the deboned remains of the minced-up party guests, stood Death triumphant.

A gigantic skeleton in a scarlet cape.

More specifically, *Bonelord-CLC* . . .

'Bonelord!' whispered Roz, awestruck. '*Another* Bonelord!'

'Bonelord-CLC, Roz,' Nick whispered back. 'Remember? Capello's own all-powerful Bonelord. See the moustache?'

Roz peered through the red mist at the two twirling clumps of brown over the skeletal warrior's upper jaw. 'Oh yes, Nick. I see it now. But if there are now two Bonelords here, what chance in hell do we have of escaping? No doubt we'll be deboned in front of each other by separate Bonelords!'

'I don't think so, Roz,' said Nick. 'Look.'

Roz followed the direction of Nick's pointing finger as Bonelord-CLC commenced his – or its – descent down the grand staircase.

But instead of marching gracefully yet eerily, as a scarlet-caped all-powerful skeletal demon might be expected to do before its final supernatural deboning, Bonelord-CLC instead began to falter at each step, as if some other force within his – or its* – skeletal frame were attempting to resist the intended movement.

'*Capello*,' said Nick. 'It must be Capello's influence. He's attempting to battle his own Bonelord from within.'

'But why, Nick?' asked Roz, incredulous. 'Surely if Capello has any hope of lifting the curse upon him, he must somehow defeat Kettlestrom's own rival Bonelord in combat? How can one Bonelord beat another Bonelord if the aforementioned Bonelord is effectively deboned from within by the spirit of its own Bonelord?'

'It's because Capello knows *we're* here, Roz. Or, more specifically, me. He's attempting to defeat his own Bonelord internally so that he doesn't immediately debone you and me in the forthcoming battle. I don't think he cares so much about you, Roz, to be perfectly honest, but he and I are former buddies and have a mutual life-saving agreement in place. Which might be the reason he's doing this.'

'But that can only end one way, Nick,' said Roz. 'By quietening the ferocity of his own Bonelord, Bonelord-CLC, he's simply leaving himself vulnerable to attack by Bonelord-KM.'

'I know that, Roz,' said Nick forlornly, watching helplessly as Bonelord-CLC began kicking out its skeletal legs dramatically with each downward step, as though performing a striptease at some sideshow burlesque. 'Look, Roz, Capello's even twirling that moustache

---

* I'm going to abandon this again, going forward. From now on Bonelord will be 'It'. GM

of his. He's trying to fight Bonelord-CLC with every psychic fibre of his immaterial body.'

Just then a round of applause came from the far end of the ballroom as a couple of inebriated youthful police-force wannabes, evidently mass-debonement survivors like Roz and himself, began belting out 'The Stripper' at the top of their voices, each vocal boom mirroring the beats of Capello's Bonelord-CLC's outward kicks.

'The fools,' whispered Nick. 'They have no idea what they're doing. Though they're putting Capello off his literal stride, they've inadvertently revealed their position to the prowling skeletal form of Bonelord-KM.'

As if sensing Nick's appraisal of the situation, Bonelord-KM turned and strode at speed towards the two drunken, carousing youths in its skeletal waders, which the extended leg bones now handled perfectly.

Before Nick could even think about how to warn the pair without giving away his own position, the two had vanished completely in one explosive spray of their own disintegrating selves as Bonelord-KM's skeletal claws and jaws went to work.

'That settles it,' said Nick, stepping out of his hiding place.

'Nick! What the hell are you doing?' Roz cried, as her former author sloshed forward into the middle of the bloody ballroom.

'It's our only chance, Roz. We have to give Bonelord-CLC full control of its internal marrow if it has any hope of destroying Bonelord-KM, and thereby lifting the curse of being Bonelord. We just have to hope and pray that that happens before Bonelord-CLC debones us as well. If Bonelord-CLC can debone Bonelord-KM in time, then Capello's curse will still be lifted, and you and I – and Capello, too – can go home, preferably via a Wimpy for a celebratory thrice quarter-pound chow-down.'

'No, Nick!' cried Roz. 'It's too dangerous!'

But Nick had already made his decision. Staring up at the grand staircase in the direction of Bonelord-CLC, Nick yelled out at the top of his voice, hoping that the spirit of Capello inside the strutting skeleton could somehow hear him.

'Give it up, Capello! You have to surrender to Bonelord's will. I know you're trying to save my life, bud, but you can't help me this way. Bonelord-KM will simply debone Bonelord-CLC – that's you – before deboning me as well, plus Roz. The only chance you have to save my life again is to let Bonelord-CLC have his – or its – wicked way.'

That's all the time Nick had, for already he could hear the sloshing waders of Bonelord-KM approaching fast behind. He reeled round to confront the oncoming form of Kettlestrom's Bonelord as it poised itself to leap towards him. Instinctively, Nick leaped sideways at the same time, precisely as he'd done with Capello's Bonelord the previous evening, in an effort to defer his imminent deboning.

But for once, Nick had calculated wrongly. For on that previous occasion, when Bonelord-CLC had assumed that he – or it – could trap Nick in the enclosed walls of the family mausoleum, this new Bonelord (Bonelord-KM) knew that Nick was already aware of the other danger immediately behind (Bonelord-CLC), as he had, after all, been addressing Capello within it for the last few seconds. This meant Bonelord-KM had pre-empted Nick's movement, and therefore leaped sideways *with* Nick's leaping self, as opposed to leaping towards him.

However, Bonelord-KM had *also* miscalculated, leaping sideways towards the *opposite* side, i.e. leaping left when Nick had leaped right. Meaning Nick was currently still safe, and Bonelord-KM was now facing an imminent skûll-a-skûll with the fast-approaching Bonelord-CLC.

'Hold on to your frilly dress, Roz,' said Nick, diving back under cover again behind the submerged bowl of rum punch. 'Here comes Skellageddon.'

BONELORD

And Skellageddon it was, as Bonelord-CLC and Bonelord-KM commenced their mutual debonings of each other's demonic marrow. Unearthly shrieks met with otherworldly howls as the two demons ripped and rent at each other's carcasses.

But instead of bursting waves of blood and mangled flesh, the air in the grand ballroom was now filled with exploding joint cartilage and cascading bone fragments. A murderous enfilade of propelled osseous matter whipped violently in every single direction, as though each Bonelord were feeding the other into an industrial tree-chipper.

'Keep your head down, Roz!' cried Nick, shoving their faces under the pool of human soup once more as a million razor-sharp bone fragments peppered the goo around them.

Beneath the ocean of blood, Nick kicked out desperately, hugging Roz close to his own body as deadly, lethal shards of killer bone shot into the plasma pool around them, like machine-gun bullets in that World War Two film. Each shard missed their bodies by mere millimetres as Nick plunged himself right, then left, then up, then down, diving then rising between swiftly ascending bubbles from each propelled bone fragment. He did his best to stay submerged for as long as possible, but knew he and Roz would have to come up for air soon.

And as the bone-peppering slowly began to abate, Nick took his chances and kicked upwards again, breaking through the surface of the human pool.

Amid a cacophony of demonic screaming, Nick ducked immediately as a fragment of Capello's red cape tore past his head, then re-ducked as a shred of rubber wader followed it, embedding both itself and the shred of cape in the back of the ballroom wall.

As Nick turned around, he ducked again as what was left of the overhead chandelier was struck by half a flying femur, collapsing into the bloody pool below it and sending a small tsunami of human remains washing across Nick's head.

All the while, that terrible sound of demonic double-shrieking continued to tear at Nick's eardrums, and he was about to dive further under the waves to rid himself of the killer din, when, all of a sudden, the sound suddenly ceased.

Thankfully, the strangeness of the sudden silence helped warn Nick that the recent tsunami he'd endured would inevitably carry with it an even more powerful aftershock. He braced himself, clutching tightly with both hands to a sodden rag that was all that remained of Capello's red cloak, then held on for dear life.

As the second wave of blood roared across Nick's body, plunging him even more deeply below the sea of human soup, he wondered if he'd be able to hold his breath long enough to rise upwards a second time.

For now, he'd been cast into the deep, and was so weak that he didn't think he'd have enough strength left to kick his way back to the surface.

This was it, then. Nick Steen was going to drown in human soup.

Then he saw something ... Something in the bloody water just ahead of him. A pale, floating ball of some kind, ascending slowly through the gore towards the distant surface.

A life-buoy, Nick realised. A float! A float that could pull him out of here! Realising he had little time left, he reached out with both arms and grabbed it.

Then immediately gasped in horror, breathing out his remaining precious air.

For the thing he'd grabbed was a *skull* ...

As Nick began to sink away, back down into the depths, he suddenly felt a sharp tug on the sleeve of his leather blouson. Then he felt himself rising once more, behind the ascending skull. As he finally broke through the surface, Nick realised his jacket had become snagged between the jaws of the floating skull.

Jaws, Nick realised, that had clamped down on his sleeve by themselves, saving his life.

Jaws, Nick now saw, that were partly covered by the drooping hair of a sodden moustache ...

'Capello,' Nick gasped in the peaceful calm of the silent ballroom, realising that the place was now entirely free of warring Bonelords.

For inexplicably, the seemingly impossible had happened. Both Bonelord-KM and Bonelord-CLC were no more.

Instead, in the middle of the ballroom where the pair of skeletal warriors had recently clashed in violent, bony fury, there floated two severed skulls. Two severed skulls that, as Nick watched, ceased to be skulls, slowly re-acquiring before his very eyes, layer by layer, the original flesh-strips of their human victims. In seconds, the departed bonces of Roberto Mantovani – aka Bob Kettlestrom – and the moustachioed head of Cliff 'Livewire' Capello bobbed like upturned barrels in the swishing plasma.

'They've cancelled each other out,' said a voice, behind him.

Nick turned to see Roz swimming towards him from the far side of the room.

'Each Bonelord beat the opposing Bonelord,' she said.

'Meaning both curses are now lifted, Roz,' added Nick, still in shock. 'Except that the men who endured them have both been beheaded.'

Nick swam over to the floating remains, reaching out tenderly to grasp Capello's bobbing head.

Which was still, somehow, *alive* ...

'I got him, Nick,' said Capello, turning in Nick's hand to face him, gasping for breath from lungs he hadn't yet realised he no longer sported. 'I killed Roberto Mantovani. The curse, at long last, is lifted ...'

'I know, Capello,' said Nick, lifting his buddy's head above the blood-line so he could stop taking in so much human soup, which was currently liable to choke Capello to death long before he passed naturally. There were still things Nick needed to say to his buddy of old.

'You saved my life, Capello. You took the hit so I could live.'

'Hell, you saved my life too, Nick,' coughed Capello, 'even though that life won't last too long, given I've been almost completely deboned.'

'You look good from where I'm treading blood, bud,' said Nick reassuringly, not telling him that he'd already taken a good glimpse of the total nothingness extending downward from Capello's mangled neck stump.

'I guess we never got to grab those meatballs, huh, Nick?' croaked Capello. 'And all I really wanted to do was grab some meatballs with you. Now you'll have to grab those meatballs on your own.'

'I'll grab them, Capello,' promised Nick, choking back tears. 'I'll grab those meatballs, don't you worry about that, bud.'

'For me, too, Nick. Grab some meatballs for me, too . . .'

'I'll grab your meatballs too, Capello.'

'That's the old Nick Steen talking,' said Capello, staring up at what remained of the blood-spattered chandelier (essentially just the light-fitting) as a smile broke out across his decapitated features. The last smile, Nick knew, Capello would ever give.

'And that's the old Capello talking, too,' said Nick, placing a tender Italian kiss on Capello's forehead.

'I see him, Nick,' muttered Capello, his voice becoming weaker and quieter as each second ticked by. 'I see my brother Dwayne, waiting for me. Calling me, Nick, from beyond the veil . . .'

'That's great, Capello,' croaked Nick, unable now to stop the flow of tears. 'That's really great. You say hi to Dwayne from me, okay? You just goddamn do that.'

But Capello was already dead.

Nick howled. Then howled again. Then continued to howl until he couldn't howl anymore.

BONELORD

Finally, after a failed attempt at yet another large howl, he stood up, Capello's head still in his hands, and stepped over to Roz, who was crouching beside Kettlestrom's severed head.

'It's done, Roz. It's over. Let's get the hell out of here.'

'Sure thing, Nick.' Roz rose to her feet, gathering up Kettlestrom's head in her hands as vital evidence.

'Did *he* have any final words to say?' asked Nick, nodding to the head of the former director of Stalkford's FBI Office.

'He actually apologised to me, Nick. For making an attempt on my life. He said he was promoting me to be head of Stalkford's FBI Office, and that I should start work immediately. He said I could hold him entirely responsible for all that had happened. Then he said he couldn't feel his waders . . . and that was it.'

'Too bad, Roz. I guess you have another load of blood cells to separate,' said Nick, looking around at the surrounding remains. 'And no fresh recruits to assist you.'

'That's okay, Nick,' said Roz, reaching for her police hat, which had been tucked inside her ballgown for safety. 'I'm not afraid of hard work. And this way, as head of Stalkford's FBI Office – and potentially police commissioner, if I play my cards right – I can at least liaise properly with you and help coordinate a combined effort to stop these persistent supernatural eruptions you keep having. So it's all worked out well in the end.'

'Almost,' said Nick, handing over Capello's head to Roz, who promptly popped it inside a paper bag as evidence. '*Almost* . . .'

'Nick?' asked Roz gently, sensing Nick's personal pain oozing out of him. 'I presume all this was one of those "alternative endings" you'd been contemplating, without Kettlestrom himself being remotely aware of it. Am I right?'

'Another sound deduction, Roz. Naturally, I kept the whole thing to myself, letting Kettlestrom believe he was planning it all. Unfortunately, no matter how much I crunched the numbers, there was no scenario I could think of that would spare Capello's life. Or avoid all these obliterated police cadet wannabes.'

Roz placed an understanding hand on Nick's shoulder as they headed through the main doors, leaving the mansion's mass of mangled remains far behind.

'What will you do now?' she asked, as Nick led her towards the mansion's car park, where his Honda Civic stood idling. 'I seem to recall you have some divorce proceedings to discuss with Jacinta.'

'All in good time, Roz,' replied Nick mournfully. 'Right now, I'm going back to bed.'

Later, looking up at the moon and weeping for his deboned buddy, Nick saw the skull one final time.

Only it was different now, Nick thought. Softer, almost. Like the one in that old Scotch Tape video advert.

It winked at him.

And, at long last, Nick slept.

THE BLACK STEEPLE

CHAPTER ONE

'You've crossed my last straw, Jacinta,' snapped Nick Steen, and by God he meant it. If his soon-to-be ex-wife said one more thing about Duncan's brain, he'd yank his aforesaid metaphorical last straw back from under her metaphorical-yet-still-simultaneously-literal feet and eject her on to the neighbouring hillside. Not that she'd go willingly, Nick knew. First he'd have to endure yet another verbal slanging match, until Jacinta finally became so enraged that she'd announce *she* was leaving *him* and wrench open the car door herself. At which point Nick would floor it all the way to their country retreat and finally give Duncan his rusks.

Except Nick knew he couldn't do it. For as much as he and Jacinta might each loathe the very ground the other stood upon, he believed, deep down, that a man couldn't just abandon his once-betrothed in the middle of a craggy, seemingly abandoned valley and expect her to wander it alone, even if she *had* penned a scathing review of his last book. And as far as sombre, eerie mountainous passes went, this one was particularly ominous.

Not only that, but even if Nick *could* summon up enough inner resolve to force his wife out of the car, he was well aware that Jacinta would inevitably turn up at their lodgings anyway at around 11pm, having strapped herself to some passing biker, and then there'd be yet another pointless late-night altercation to linger interminably alongside all those other pointless early-morning, midday, mid-afternoon, late-afternoon, early-evening and mid-evening altercations. And that would mean Nick wouldn't even get a chance to plan out his new novel, let alone put pen to paper. Besides, who was Nick kidding, anyway? Duncan ate cats now, he recalled, grimly. Not rusks.

'Why can't I just feed him one?' said Jacinta, dragging out a mewling stray from her handbag.

Nick glanced up to watch Duncan drooling in the baby seat behind, specially converted to accommodate infants in the six-feet-tall, 180-pound weight bracket. From here, his son resembled a wheel of Camembert with teeth, but Nick had to remind himself that *everything* appeared larger in the rear-view mirror.

'Because he's not meant to eat cats. He's supposed to be on a rusk and milk diet to reduce his meat-protein intake. And I don't want bits of feline all over the upholstery.'

'He's not a baby anymore, mister *writer*,' snapped Jacinta, who no longer called Nick Nick. 'He's got to move on to meat someday.'

'He *has* moved on to meat,' Nick snapped back. 'He eats cats, dogs and occasionally horses. That's one of the reasons we're moving, remember? Because the neighbours were beginning to suspect.'

'They can buy other pets.'

'They *did* buy other pets. If you remember, Duncan ate *those* pets as well.'

If he was expecting another retort, it didn't come.

THE BLACK STEEPLE

At last, Nick thought, relieved. *I've won a round. I've actually won a round.*

'Furthermore,' he continued, striking while his personal iron was temporarily hot, 'he *is* a baby, still. A mere three months old, according to the birth certificate.'

Nick couldn't prove whether that document was genuine, of course. For neither he nor Jacinta had been present at its signing. The paperwork had simply appeared, alongside Duncan himself, in their spare room one afternoon early in March. Neither of them remembered birthing Duncan physically. Certainly not conceiving him. For there had been no mutual attempts to conceive anything between them for years. Nor had there been any mutual attempts to *prevent* conceiving anything between them, for that matter.

And yet the family photo album proved congress of some kind must have happened at some point in the recent past. For the evidence was there, listed and dated accurately in both Nick and Jacinta's handwriting. Snapshots of life during Jacinta's pregnancy, assorted hospital visits, and ultimately Duncan's birth itself and those initial terrifying coddlings. Yet neither Nick, nor Jacinta, retained any memory whatsoever of the events themselves.

Until, late one night, he'd finally realised what had happened.

'Go on,' Nick said, sensing Jacinta was heading there again. 'Out with it.'

And lo, it began. How this entire thing was Nick's fault. How Duncan had emerged as a result of Nick's imagination coming to life after he'd gone and slept with a sentient cursed typewriter three years before. How that leaking imagination had somehow morphed itself into the form of Duncan, a character from Nick's novel *The Stalkwich Blasphemy*: a crazed man-child with multiple head stitchings who'd been conceived after an unholy union twixt woman and Cosmic Outer God – that very woman, now that parts of the novel were coming alive, being none other than Nick's own wife, Jacinta. How Duncan was somehow, and without Jacinta's prior knowledge or consent, the fruit of her own overactive passion for some vast interstellar force of eldritch Chaos, summoned and conjured on to this earthly plane via unholy sacrificial rites committed by a deranged and murderous religious sect previously confined to the pages of Nick's novel. How she regarded Nick as being personally responsible for her having given supposed birth to a cosmic freak that may or may not be part demon, and who passed stools so large no nappy on earth could hope to contain the merest fraction of their contents.

'Well, like it or not, Jacinta, that's the hand we've been dealt,' snapped Nick.

'By *you*!' she retorted, wildly. 'The hand *you* dealt us. You and your sordid writings. And I suppose I should be grateful that my brain's retained no memory whatsoever of Duncan's conception or birth, if the passages in your book are anything to go by.'

'My novels are well respected, Jacinta,' said Nick, with an air of calm he wasn't remotely feeling. 'Even the wholly unacceptable bits. Which is why the esteemed Baron Rochlain himself has invited me up here to the remote desert town of Silth as writer-in-residence, in case you'd forgotten. So that I can finally get some peace and quiet to write, without having to stop every five minutes to go pacify some distraught neighbour about their wolfhound's missing head.'

'And you think Duncan's going to leave the pets in Silth alone?'

No, thought Nick.

He didn't think that was going to happen for one moment. But if he could somehow educate, or at the very least train, Duncan to observe the established routines and mores of polite Society, then perhaps his lumbering man-child might still stand a chance of becoming an upstanding member of the Stalkford community. For hadn't Nick protected and guided Duncan's progress so far? Hadn't he been the one to fend off the endless jibes and barbs that a cruel and judgemental Society had already flung Duncan's way?

And where the heck had Duncan's real father been through all of this? Up above in some outer cosmic galaxy somewhere, partying with other Cosmic Gods, waiting to be summoned down on to our earthly plane once again to impregnate some other unsuspecting drug-crazed counter-culture floozy. And all the while, Nick was at the paternal coalface, dipping Duncan's feed in fresh milk and attempting to change his nappies single-handed. Plus mopping up numerous spills, which increasingly included pieces of badger.

But Nick didn't care about all that. He loved Duncan with all his heart, and was more than happy to clear up his son's unsuspecting victims. Because, damn it, Nick Steen was Duncan's *real* father. Nick was the one who'd conceived him *intellectually*. And Nick had just as much right over Duncan's future wellbeing as any blasphemous force of Un-Nature. If it ever came down to some aeon-spanning interstellar paternity suit, Nick vowed, he'd be lawyered up and ready.

'He'll leave the Silth pets alone if you feed him those damned rusks I gave you, Jacinta, instead of lobbing some poor stray into his cot and letting them fight it out. We're supposed to be teaching Duncan manners. The more you keep tossing him live prey, the worse he gets. When he becomes all frenzied up like that, he hardly knows what he's doing.'

'You said it,' huffed Jacinta.

'What's that supposed to mean?'

'You know full well what that means. All those stitches on his head? He's simple, that's what he is.'

Damn it if she hadn't just crossed Nick's last straw *again*. But he wouldn't slam the car's brakes on just yet. No, Nick was going to have *his* say this time.

'Let me tell you about those head stitches,' he began. 'Because each one of those head stitches tells a story.'

'Not the bloody head-stitch story again,' gasped Jacinta, lighting up a cigarette.

Nick immediately snatched it from her hand and tossed it out of the window. 'No fumes, Jacinta. We have a child in the car.'

'We have a *demon* in the car, you mean.'

'We don't know that he's a demon.'

'Of course he's a fucking demon.'

'You conceived Duncan by coupling with an *Elder Cosmic God*, Jacinta. Not Satan himself. There's a big difference.'

'Like what?'

'Well, for one, the seed of each deity is distinct. Satan's is apparently hot, like lava, while that of a Cosmic God is luminescent and ejects outwards in myriad phantasmagorical colours.'

'Just tell me about the goddamn stitches,' said Jacinta, sighing. 'Even though I've heard it all before. *This* stitch was caused by "Society"; *that* stitch was caused by "Wider Society" …'

'And the stitch next to that one was caused by "The Authorities",' continued Nick, pointing them out individually in the rear-view mirror while Duncan grinned back at him, blowing raspberries. 'That stitch to the left of it was caused by Stalkford City Council. The one next but one to that was caused by our Local Education Authority … The big one across his forehead was the fault of Stalkford City Reserve Teaching Pool – and both stitches on his cheeks were kids on the estate.'

'Are you going to go through all eighty-eight stitches?'

'Eighty-*nine*. He got another one last night scaling Stalkford Cathedral, remember? Which you could have prevented if you'd just kept an eye on his cot.'

'I have a life too, you know!' cried Jacinta, yelling at him again. 'I didn't ask to give birth to a cosmic demon. It's only because you have such a sick mind that we're in this bloody situation.'

True, Nick's mind *was* a bit sick, he had to admit. But it *had* to be,

THE BLACK STEEPLE

damn it. How else could he create such visionary — and oft queasily erotic — horror fiction? And that was the answer to all their problems, ultimately. For Nick now felt that his writing alone was the key to ending the pervasive horror of his literary horror incarnating itself as real-life horror. Once Nick was settled in Silth, with a fresh novel under his belt, he felt sure that, somehow, he'd be able to assuage these escaping demons of his mind; to convince them once more that there was more fun — more *terror* — to be had on the printed page, where Nick would no longer be hellbent on fighting them off each day.

And with the kindly support of his new benefactor, the esteemed Baron Rochlain, Nick could finally bring peace to Stalkford again. He could eradicate the real-life horrors by trapping them once more between the pages of a brand-new book. He could turn the horrendous supernatural events of the past three years into a bestselling volume that would ultimately serve as his psychic demons' eternal prison. A Tome of Terror: that was how Nick saw it. And maybe that could even be its title: *Nick Steen's Terror Tome*.* Then, with all the acclaim he'd get from its publication, and for fending off the imminent threat of supernatural Armageddon, Nick could spend his future years caring for Duncan, guiding his surrogate son away from the path of evil and down the one leading straight into his neighbour's garden.

And if those demons refused to return to the printed page? If the unleashed hordes of Nick's imagination once again insisted on escaping from that dimension-portal inside his head? Well, at least he'd have Duncan by his side to fight them off: a vastly overgrown Cosmic God-in-waiting, who might snuff out any number of supernatural entities with a simple flex of his oversized mitts. As long as Nick could nurture Duncan's unholy potential and direct his son's

---

* Heh heh heh. GM

powerful and borderline uncontrollable energy solely against those supernatural assailants currently waging war on Stalkford's citizens, rather than said energy being used against the citizens themselves, plus their pets, things should hopefully work out fine at long last.

Nick blinked suddenly, as a flash of movement in the surrounding hills caught his eye. He'd noticed something similar a few minutes earlier, he recalled. A dart of red in the distant hills, almost like a moving figure. As though some unknown watcher had peered out briefly from behind a rock, or rushed from one concealed ridge to another.

Perhaps these hills were inhabited after all, despite the letter Baron Rochlain had sent him the week before, specifically warning Nick to fill up the car's petrol tank and pack a couple of spare jerry cans, as there were 'no inhabited establishments anywhere along the abandoned valley'. Surely, despite the Baron's warning, there were *some* people around.

And yet there was something uniquely strange about that vivid flash of scarlet red. It was an odd colour to have glimpsed this far out in a lonely stretch of desolate grey hills and craggy, blackened rock. Perhaps it was a slaughtered sheep or something like that, Nick wondered, idly.

Slaughtered ... Now, why had he chosen that particular word?

'Are we nearly there yet?' said Jacinta. She was asking for Duncan, Nick realised, articulating what his man-child might be asking if he could talk instead of just moaning and grunting in the back of the car like an itchy gorilla.

Actually, that was unfair. For although Duncan's vocal abilities lagged some way behind his physical development, and he couldn't yet articulate anything in the region of a rudimentary sentence, his son did know a smattering of individual words. Namely 'cat', 'dead' and 'kill'.

'We'll be at the house very soon,' said Nick. 'No thanks to you,

Jacinta, I might add. It's a good job I packed those spare jerry cans or we'd have run out of petrol trying to find the main road again.'

'That's not my fault,' Jacinta spat at him. 'Duncan shat on the map, remember?'

'The map *you* wedged underneath him in order to contain the flow.'

'At *your* insistence because you wanted to protect your upholstery.'

'Exactly. From the contents of Duncan's droppings, because *you'd* forgotten to pack his changing mats.'

'Because *you* hadn't given me enough time to …'

'Enough, already,' rasped Nick, aware from a globule of sputum striking the rear-view mirror that Duncan was becoming distressed. 'It's okay, champ,' he cooed reassuringly, smiling at the son that wasn't technically his, even though technically he was. 'We'll soon be there, buddy.'

'Buddy' was Nick's preferred term of affection now, given that 'Little Man' sounded rather like a direct insult.

But Nick's soothings, for once, had no effect. Instead, Duncan remained in a state of distress, staring wildly up at the passing hills through the car's windows.

'What's up with him?' said Jacinta. 'Is he gearing up for another plop?'

'I don't think so,' said Nick, worried about the threat of ploppage but not convinced it was their most immediate problem. 'It's something else. And it's not us constantly bickering, either. That usually makes him scream and chew his hands. No, this is something different.'

Nick turned his head to the right, looking out in the direction in which Duncan appeared to be scowling. Then he called back gently over his shoulder to the man-baby sitting behind him. 'What is it, champ? What do you see?'

Duncan continued to moan and babble incoherently, kicking his legs out one by one so that they hammered violently against the rear of Nick's seat.

'No kicking, buddy,' said Nick, worried Duncan's movements might send them careening across the road into a ditch.

'Maybe he saw a wild cat,' said Jacinta.

'Maybe,' said Nick, still looking out through the driver's-side window. He could only do so in short bursts, needing to keep his eyes on the road ahead at the same time, but he wondered if Duncan had also glimpsed what he himself had been glimpsing. As he glanced up into the hills again, he thought he caught another flash of red far up in the craggy heights. Only this time on Duncan's side of the road. It *was* a figure, Nick decided. He felt sure of it now. A figure in a red *hood* . . .

Then Nick's man-child screamed.

'Duncan!' yelled Nick, glancing back in alarm at his oversized toddler. 'Duncan, are you okay?'

But Duncan was more than okay, Nick saw. In fact, he was perfectly happy. Evidently, the scream had been one of apparent joy. For Duncan was now kicking his legs excitedly in the air while clapping his massive hands with glee.

And waving.

Waving up at the hills as they passed by.

Waving to whoever was up there.

CHAPTER TWO

The house stood alone and isolated in the heart of the rocky valley, eight miles south of Silth. As Nick finally swung his Honda Civic into its rough, boulder-strewn driveway, he was surprised to find no car there other than his own.

'You said the Baron was going to meet us here,' Jacinta hissed.

'The Baron's a busy man,' Nick countered, slowing the car outside the front door of what looked to him like a glorified barn. Though he hated to admit it, his wife was right. The Baron *had* said he'd be here to welcome them. Maybe he'd hitchhiked, thought Nick. Scratch that. Barons didn't hitchhike. So maybe he got a taxi instead? Scratch that, too. Barons travelled via chauffeur, not lowly cabbies with a perpetual axe to grind. Scratch that thrice. Barons instructed their chauffeurs to stick around, engine idling, with neither thought nor care for expended petrol.

Scratch it all to hell, Nick concluded. The Baron *wasn't* here.

'Help me get Duncan out,' Nick said tersely, opening the driver's-side door. 'And watch for any stray stools.'

He looked up at the house as he stepped outside, hoping the interior of the cabin might prove slightly more impressive than its exterior. At the very top of the building, he identified a boarded-up window.

'There's loft space, at any rate,' he said.

'That looks perfect for Duncan,' said Jacinta, following Nick's gaze. 'We can find a strong padlock in town.'

'I told you before, Jacinta,' Nick snapped at her. 'We are not locking Duncan up. He'll sleep on the same floor as you and I, and we'll feed him rusks and milk until Society learns he is one of us, and only very occasionally mauls innocent vertebrates.'

Jacinta tutted audibly, muttering to herself as Nick opened the rear door on the driver's side and yanked out Duncan's bags. These were mostly filled with Duncan's droppings, and consequently were as heavy as sandbags. One by one, Nick dragged them over to the edge of the drive and began erecting a makeshift mound. In the morning, he'd cover the small mountain with petrol and burn the lot, making sure to wait for a strong southerly downwind.

Returning to the car, he saw that Jacinta was still in the front seat, filing her nails.

'Where's Duncan?' said Nick urgently, noticing that his son was no longer inside the car.

'I let him out.'

Nick froze, completely stunned. 'You let him *out?*'

'To stretch his legs. They're over four-feet long now, you know.'

Jeez, thought Nick. They'd only been three-foot eight when they'd set out that morning.

'But who needs padlocks?' Jacinta added, smirking, as she continued to file her nails.

They were back to that, then. Nick doing his level best to integrate his dangerous and unpredictable son of a Cosmic God into Wider Society while his resentful wife sniped and nit-picked over details at the sideline – whereupon Nick would then hurl back his own volley of retaliatory nit-pickings until Jacinta inevitably responded again in kind. An endless war of perpetual nit-pickery. It was like 'Nam all over again. And Nick had now had enough.

'You do realise he'll go out there and maul all the wildlife?'

'What wildlife?' said Jacinta. 'We're in the middle of a barren, rocky wasteland.'

THE BLACK STEEPLE

That was true, Nick had to admit. If he'd known the supposed countryside surrounding Silth was going to be quite as starkly arid and ominously threatening, he might have turned down the Baron's invitation and moved to the coast instead. At least out there by the sea, Duncan could have gorged violently to his heart's content on fish and assorted marine life, instead of domestic animals. But out here in this wasteland, at least, there was hopefully limited damage his son could do. Duncan might bring back the tube of a snake or some sand lizard's legs, but there were hardly herds of sheep or cows milling around that he could start blindly goring.

Or so Nick hoped. For he hadn't taken Duncan into town as yet. And Nick knew that at some point, he'd have to do just that if his son stood any chance of being accepted as a fully functioning member of Society. Admittedly, a Society that had proved merely cruel and judgemental as far as Nick's son of a Cosmic God was concerned. A Society that instinctively ostracised the misunderstood 'other' in their midst and regarded Duncan as a viable threat to its supposed system of law and order. A Society that viewed his natural faecal droppings as a public health hazard unable to be disposed of via normal household waste, meaning Nick had to deliver sacks of them to his local disposal plant via industrial tipper, *at his own personal expense.* A Society that had turned on Duncan at every single step of his abnormally swift physical development, and now held him legally liable for a spate of pet maulings, despite the fact that he retained no memory of said maulings, and for whom, as a legal minor, the laws of this country *did not apply.*

But Society didn't care about that. Society would change its laws, if it had to. Society would purge the outsider from its midst.

But not on Nick Steen's watch.

No way, José. Whoever José was.

For though Nick realised he was now sounding like some damned liberal, the type of being he would ordinarily mock, jeer and finally hurl heavy objects at, this was about *Duncan.*

As far as his son of an Elder Cosmic God was concerned, Society itself would have to change. Society would have to learn that even the cursed hellspawn of an Elder God had feelings, too. Admittedly, those feelings were largely feral and geared towards indiscriminate acts of aggression against unsuspecting members of the animal kingdom. And Nick knew, deep down, that those feelings would only intensify as his son grew older and, Nick presumed, larger.

But with Nick's help – and maybe, ultimately, some form of industrial cage in which he might be displayed to members of the public for a modest sum – Duncan's primal raging could hopefully be contained, softened and ultimately made profitable, given all Nick's hard rearing over the years. And if all else failed, Nick had an alternative plan up his sleeve: one that involved Duncan being trained by the army to do battle against the escaping demons of Nick's mind. Then Society would know his son served a useful purpose, however uncontrollable his initial primal rages might be.

All of which meant Nick had to keep Duncan on the straight and narrow.

'There he is,' said Nick, observing the man-child sitting amid a pile of rocks at the side of the house, which to all intents and purposes constituted their backyard. As he watched, he suddenly realised what Duncan was in the process of doing. 'No, Duncan!' roared Nick. 'No!'

But it was too late. As soon as Duncan heard Nick's cry, he started crawling forward on all fours, leaving in his wake a stool the size of a ten-pin bowling ball.

'My damned back,' said Nick, dragging the dropping over to the mighty shit-mound half an hour later, once he'd managed to secure Duncan safely inside the cabin. He'd flame the pile later that evening, he decided, concerned at how vast it had already grown and beginning to worry that it might topple over in the night and crush them all to death while they slept. Leaving one of the jerry cans beside the teetering dung mountain, he reflected upon his new lodgings.

Jacinta had claimed the best room for herself, naturally, leaving Nick to choose between the small room next to it or the second of the cabin's larger bedrooms. Nick chose the former as his personal kip zone and writing study, electing to move Duncan's cot into the latter. His son's bedroom was already on the snug side, Nick soon realised, yet he figured he could ultimately knock down a wall or two if necessary and fit Duncan's feet in that way.

But that was work for tomorrow. Now, with Duncan napping after an impromptu meal of rusk and snake, Nick finally had a few minutes to himself.

Moving away from the towering shite-mound to avoid the toxic gases it was already emitting, Nick found himself becoming increasingly curious about the neighbouring countryside. Who or what exactly was that strange red figure both he and Duncan had glimpsed up in the hills on the journey out here?

Intent upon getting his bearings, Nick wandered over to a small rise situated a short distance ahead, beyond the trail leading up from the main valley road.

Climbing to the top of the ridge, Nick's eyes were met with a dusty expanse of sandy, rock-strewn wasteland. Screwing his eyes tight, Nick stared out towards the far end of the valley, and identified the desert-town settlement of Silth, several miles distant. Turning his attention to the opposing side of the valley, Nick took in the vast sweep of the surrounding mountain range. He was hoping, he realised now, to gain another glimpse of that mysterious, red-hooded figure.

Why was Nick feeling so troubled by what he'd seen out there in the hills? Was it because Duncan had seen it, too, perhaps? Was Nick instinctively bristling because he sensed some kind of threat to his son? If so, Nick welcomed that feeling. It was clear as crystal that

Duncan's biological father wasn't going to help one bit if his son's safety was at stake; it would be up to Nick alone to protect Duncan from his many enemies. For Shri-Chiluba-thu-hulahaarrckh (so named in Nick's *The Stalkwich Blasphemy*) had abandoned his son at birth and left Nick alone to pick up the pieces. And if Shri-Chiluba-thu-hulahaarrckh deigned to return to this mortal plane one day and demand immediate access to his son? Well, Nick would fight that too. Initially via a polite 'cease and desist' letter, then using conventional warheads.

But that was a long way off, Nick figured. Right now, he was in charge of Duncan's welfare, and that meant eternal vigilance.

At the very moment at which that thought entered his mind, Nick's eyes were drawn to something else he could see in the valley below him. Something he hadn't noticed before, despite having just run his eyes across the entire stony expanse.

Perhaps it had previously been obscured by the clouds of greyish dust whirling around the plain below, whipped up by harsh, turbulent winds blowing in from the craggy mountain peaks beyond. But what Nick could now see on the valley floor, situated some distance from the main road, was a building.

Nick shielded his eyes from the westering sun, straining to make out what looked to him like the steeple of a solitary wooden church.

But this was the steeple of a solitary wooden church unlike any other steeple of a solitary wooden church Nick had ever known. For this particular steeple of a solitary wooden church was painted entirely in black. So black that Nick knew instinctively, without quite knowing why, that this was nothing less than the Black Steeple itself.

The name captured the building perfectly, Nick decided: a phrase not only referring to the blackness of the steeple, but somehow also incorporating the rest of the church, which Nick saw was constructed largely from wooden boards, themselves painted in black also, but less striking visually than the essential blackness of the main black steeple. Hence Black Steeple as a blanket term.

The Black Steeple then, Nick decided. Heretoforth it would be known under that name alone. No more. No less.

The Black Steeple.

The Black Steeple.

<u>The Black Steeple.</u>

But who painted a steeple black? And the church under it, for that matter? What kind of crackpot religion did such a thing?

Nick began to feel an uncanny sense of foreboding about this eerie-looking place of worship, and as he pondered his own questions, a huge cloud of dust whipped up in front of the distant church, once more obscuring it from view.

The only way he'd get answers to his questions, Nick knew, was to go down and investigate. He looked at his watch, noting he still had an hour or two until his official welcome luncheon at the Baron's manor in outer Silth. He could afford a quick break – and, frankly, would welcome the time away from Jacinta – so he made his way over the crest of the ridge and ventured down into the valley itself, passing between scarred boulders and several stunted, lifeless trees.

As Nick reached the plain below and waited for the dust cloud to dissipate, he felt a strange crackling in the air around him, as if a coming storm were about to break. And as the cloud of whipped-up sand particles finally settled, Nick saw that things were no longer quite as they'd seemed mere moments before.

For the Black Steeple was no more.

It had vanished. Completely disappeared from sight, as though the entire building had somehow become airborne on the raging winds and ascended into the sky above.

In its place stood nothing. Nothing at all but stones and dust. The same flat, rocky plain Nick had seen when he'd first gazed out across this blank, featureless country.

Feeling a sudden chill in his bones, Nick tightened the collar of his brown leather blouson and made his way back to the house.

★

Where Duncan was up on the roof, clambering, Nick noticed with mounting horror, across the perilous sloping slates towards an unsuspecting pigeon.

'For God's sake, Jacinta, why weren't you watching him?'

'I was watching him,' said Jacinta, sunning herself on a swiftly erected lounge bed. 'Then I stopped watching him.'

'Why the hell did you do that?' yelled Nick.

'Because I was making a fucking cocktail!' Jacinta yelled back, nursing what looked to Nick like a triple piña colada, served in one of his own metal goblets.

'You were supposed to be making his rusks.'

But castigation was pointless, Nick realised, for Jacinta was already nose-deep in her next magazine.

'Down, Duncan!' yelled Nick, calling up to his son. 'Come down now. Bad Duncan. Naughty Duncan.'

It was useless. How could a three-month-old man-giant know what Nick meant? The kid could barely understand basic phrases, let alone instructions to descend a precarious slanting roof. As far as Nick was aware, the only instructions Duncan had even a vague understanding of were 'Leave that cat alone' and 'Not inside the bath, Duncan.'

'Leave that pigeon be!' cried Nick, hoping Duncan would understand at least half of the sentence. But it was useless. Duncan had no idea what 'pigeon' meant. Only that he could potentially grab the thing and pluck it bald before chewing off its head.

Nick watched, helpless, as Duncan continued to crawl towards the unsuspecting bird. Anticipating a sight he had no remote desire to witness, Nick braced himself for the imminent mangling – but all of a sudden the bird took flight, flapping down from the roof towards the ground below.

Immediately, Duncan followed it, scrambling towards the edge of the roof.

'No, Duncan!' yelled Nick. 'Stay! Stay!'

But it was too late. With an innocent and wholly unsuspecting grin on his face, Duncan grunted with glee as his massive hands lost what little grip they had on the furthest rooftiles. In a split second, the forward momentum of his oversized body propelled Nick's son outwards, toppling him over the roof's edge into open air. Then the force of Earth's gravity yanked the colossal frame downward, and he hurtled head-first to the ground.

Nick closed his eyes.

When the sickening thud finally ceased echoing across the valley plain, Nick summoned enough courage to look again. Incredibly, Duncan was now sitting on his behind, chewing merrily on the wrenched neck-stump of the mangled pigeon.

'Thanks for the help,' said Nick to Jacinta, accentuating the sarcasm of his tone for greater emphasis, knowing his wife was largely inured to Nick's many ironic jibes.

'He'll live,' she said, and the horror of it was that Nick knew Jacinta was right. For very little physical injury – not least multiple head wounds from falling off various buildings – appeared to affect Duncan's wellbeing at all. Nick's son was, he had to admit, what common parlance frequently described as a 'unit' of a man-baby. One that would soon grow into a unit of a swollen adult, before eventually transforming into a unit of a vast cosmic deity. For now, though, all Duncan required in order to continue his day was one more stitch.

'This one,' Nick said, glaring meaningfully at Jacinta half an hour later while sewing Duncan's head back together in the kitchen, 'was caused by neglect. Specifically, the neglect of Jacinta Steen, Duncan's biological mother.'

'Thus spake Duncan's *non-biological* father,' quipped Jacinta, hitting back at Nick, right where it hurt.

'Get him dressed,' said Nick, his mind choosing to ignore Jacinta while preparing itself for the task of rolling another giant shit-sphere out to the towering turd-pyre. 'We're expected at the Baron's Masonic Lodge by two. And tomorrow, *you* can flame Duncan's droppings.'

Only Nick knew already that she wouldn't. For the toxic mound outside their front door was fast becoming a symbol of their fractured family dynamic: one that already hung by the thinnest of threads as Nick struggled to co-habit with Jacinta and provide Duncan with some half-arsed sense of domestic stability. One that might suddenly collapse and destroy them all overnight, unless Nick continued to battle daily with the mound's festering airborne bacteria.

He reached into a nearby cupboard and removed Duncan's blazer.

'Steam it, will you? His bow-tie's in my suitcase.'

CHAPTER THREE

'Welcome to Silth Lodge, Mister Steen,' said Baron Rochlain, handing Nick a glass of sherry. 'I trust your drive here was amicable?'

No, it was not, thought Nick. For, as usual, he and Jacinta had fought like tigers the entire journey.

But before he could say as much, the Baron's eyes turned immediately from his to rest instead upon Jacinta's own. 'And a special welcome to *Missus* Steen, I presume?' The drink Rochlain offered her was exactly the same size as Nick's, even though *he* was the guest of honour. 'May your time here,' added Rochlain, eyes still trained on Jacinta, 'prove a fruitful experience for us *all*.'

Nick nodded politely, even though he hated his own creativity being compared to that of others. Particularly Jacinta, who was only really 'creative' in the realm of make-up and nails. He examined the Baron more closely. The man was taller than he was, Nick noted, even if Nick himself was really, *really* tall. Rochlain was thinner, too, despite Nick also being extremely thin. (Nick was almost paper-thin, in fact, while at the same time being compact and broadly muscular as well. Plus sinewy.)

'Thanks,' Nick replied, 'though I should warn you that we're about to divorce, and we both get increasingly aggressive on drink.' He handed both glasses back to the Baron untouched, noting as he did so that Rochlain's hairline was receding, meaning the man was no immediate threat to Nick's virility and would most likely fail to attract Jacinta were she to somehow wrestle her glass back from the

Baron's hands, neck it in one and pounce hungrily on their host in an attempt to embarrass Nick publicly, as she was wont to do of late.

Yet on closer inspection, Nick saw that any initial perceived loss of follicle depth on Rochlain's head was negated almost entirely by his sternly contoured widow's peak and lean, angular, almost hawkish features. These gave the man a distinct air of quiet confidence and command, accentuated by the dark-blue velvet smoking jacket and floral, damson-coloured ascot tie he was wearing. Rochlain might yet prove a threat, Nick decided. He'd have to watch Jacinta like a hawk.

'I see you dressed for the occasion,' said the Baron, smiling. 'How splendid.'

Nick had indeed dressed for the occasion, electing to sport his black leather dinner suit with bootlace tie, silver steer-skull belt buckle plus stirruped cowboy boots. The outfit might no longer possess the power to attract Jacinta, but it would no doubt prove smoking hot to any passing female guest Nick might potentially corner if he deemed her sufficiently attractive. But as things currently stood, there appeared to be no one else at this reception besides the Baron himself. Whose eyes, Nick noted to his chagrin, were still all over Jacinta.

Clearly the Baron had been referring to *Jacinta's* costume, which, Nick now saw, though he hadn't personally sensed its effect for years, was both deliberately and effectively raunchy. Tall, hot-pink velvet shoulder pads and a cerise power-skirt, with black lace tights and killer heels. Plus a thick smear of red lipstick to complete the desired effect. No wonder the Baron was hooked. Nick watched as his wife grabbed both sherries from Rochlain's hands and necked them together.

'Another,' she said, directing the word at Rochlain as if it were an order.

THE BLACK STEEPLE

'Of course, my dear,' said Rochlain, moving past an antique bookcase behind them towards a neighbouring drinks cabinet, upon which stood several bottles of assorted spirits and nibbles already prepared. Nick noticed then that the entire room was lined with books, most of them ancient and evidently extremely rare, if the Baron's padlocked glass panels were anything to go by. Most of the volumes appeared to deal with esoteric subjects, such as divination, necromancy and Gef the talking mongoose – or man-weasel, to use the correct scientific term. Yet among this vast library of occult texts, Nick failed to spot any of his own works. Which was odd, he thought, considering he'd been invited here by the Baron expressly on the strength of his horror fiction. Perhaps Rochlain kept those particular tomes in a secure, fully alarmed and temperature-controlled environment, like Nick did.

The Baron handed Jacinta two more sherries, then reached down to open a small concealed freezer compartment in the lower half of the drinks cabinet.

'And how about an ice lolly for your son?' He drew out a multi-coloured popsicle and handed it up to Duncan, who immediately reached down and slapped it from his hand. 'A charming young man,' said the Baron. 'Already the talk of the town.'

Nick bristled. What the hell did he mean, '*Already the talk of the town*'? Had Society been spreading cruel rumours about his son all the way up here? Was Stalkford City Council's sinister reach so long it had somehow penetrated this remote and dusty desert town of Silth?

Nick realised he'd only known Rochlain for twenty seconds, yet already had no idea where precisely he stood with the guy. After all, Nick was supposedly the Baron's esteemed guest, but Rochlain hadn't yet deigned to discuss Nick's work, already seemed to be making moves on Jacinta, and was potentially feigning politeness regarding the reputation of Nick's beloved yet wholly unpredictable son. Sure, that could have something to do with Duncan having ripped the heads off two of Rochlain's Dobermanns in the driveway outside, but the remaining three had managed to escape, albeit without their hind legs.

And hadn't Nick intervened immediately with a muslin cloth doused in lion's urine to frighten Duncan away? Was the Baron *really* still upset about an entirely innocent mauling?

'As I said before,' Nick said, attempting to smooth things over, 'he's teething right now. Well, *fanging*, to be more precise.'

Rochlain gazed upwards, attempting to examine what could only truthfully be described as Duncan's jaws.

'Smile, Duncan,' said Nick. 'Smile for Uncle Rochlain.'

'Smile, my child,' said Rochlain, trying to tickle Duncan on the chin.

'I wouldn't do that,' warned Nick, but Duncan's mouth had already parted in a broad grin, exposing several long and pointed incisors, each over three inches in length and razor-sharp. A tank's worth of dribble flowed out over the Baron's hand.

'My, my, you *are* a big lad, aren't you?' said Rochlain, parting Duncan's mouth wider with both hands to expose a second row of fangs growing in immediately behind the first.

Like the teeth of a shark, thought Nick. *Only bigger.*

Megalodon Mouth, that's what Society would start calling him. Jaws Gob, maybe. Or Poseidon Breath. Those *bastards*. Damn it, why hadn't Nick noticed that second row of fangs before now?

I know why, he thought. *Because it's Jacinta who's meant to have been cleaning Duncan's teeth each day, that's why. While I flame all the droppings.*

No doubt extracting flaps of shredded flesh and fur from between her son's fangs somehow interfered with Jacinta's busy nail-filing schedule. Meaning Nick would have to do that job as well now. And frankly, cleaning Duncan's fangs meant Nick would also have to increase his private insurance premiums in readiness for the inevitable day when Duncan accidentally bit down on his writing hands.

'I do *love* your ascot, Baron,' said Jacinta, squeezing herself in front of Duncan and planting both hands on the Baron's arm.

Jeez, thought Nick. *She's already put away four sherries and is practically brimming. Plus, she's left me holding the man-baby again*, he reflected bitterly.

Sickened by his wife's blatant hands-on-arm business, which had already progressed to a hands-playfully-squeezing-aforesaid-arm business, Nick looked around, hoping to mingle with the other arriving guests. Then, as soon as he could offload Duncan elsewhere, he could finally begin circulating and spinning his boot-spurs provocatively in the direction of some awestruck female.

But there *were* no other arriving guests. No awestruck females. Nick's drinks reception, if you could even call it that, was a total no-show.

The strange sense of uncertainty nagging at Nick's vitals grew steadily worse. Now that he came to think of it, not only was his welcome party as newly appointed writer-in-residence completely unattended, but the Baron's Lodge was about the only significant building they'd passed on their way through Silth. The rest of the houses were either drab, single-storey bungalows or ramshackle lean-tos. If the town of Silth could sport such a refined and graceful historical building as the Baron's Masonic Lodge, then where were the rest of the town's aristocratic gentry housed? For Silth itself looked like the end of the earth. Run-down, isolated, and – if Nick's suspicions about that cruel rumour mill already targeting Duncan were true – simmering with brooding hostility.

For Nick couldn't count the number of malevolent stares they'd received from furtive-looking townsfolk peering out from behind shuttered blinds and parted curtains as he'd driven Jacinta and Duncan through town. People seemed to be watching them continuously from shopfronts and alleyways as they drove by. And there was one particular figure that had *truly* unnerved Nick, he recalled now. A dark figure whom Nick had glimpsed standing stock-still by the side of the road, watching his progress. An eerie figure who appeared to be wearing what looked to Nick like a red monk's habit, the face concealed from view beneath a long, scarlet hood . . .

Nick froze.

A scarlet hood – like the one he'd seen in the hills . . .

'Another sherry, Mister Steen?' asked Baron Rochlain, approaching Nick to proffer a fresh glass. Jacinta was on the floor now, clinging to the Baron's legs.

'Thanks, but I'm driving,' said Nick, watching as Jacinta reached up from the ground to grab the glass from Rochlain's hand before Nick even had a chance to finish his sentence. 'I think we'd better go, Jacinta,' said Nick. 'I have work to do.'

'Which reminds me,' said Rochlain, reaching inside his jacket to produce a small parcel from his inner pocket. 'Please accept this welcoming gift from the Masonic Order of Silth.'

Nick took the package from his host's hand and tore open its wrapping. Inside was what looked to Nick like the hoof of some long-dead animal.

A *cloven* hoof.

'A lucky goat's foot,' said Rochlain, smiling strangely at Nick.

Nick had heard of a lucky rabbit's foot before, but never a lucky *goat's* foot.

'What's so lucky about it?'

'Take it home with you, Mister Steen, and you'll find out.'

Nick sensed a strange iciness in the Baron's tone, and a sharp sliver of fear ran down his spine. For some reason unknown to Nick's conscious mind, the cloven hoof he was now holding in his hand was *frightening* him. It might well prove lucky for some, Nick figured, but he suspected that that particular someone was not going to be him. For the thing, he

THE BLACK STEEPLE

suspected, was a charm of some kind. A form of superstitious trinket used by country folk in remote and largely backwards villages. Maybe a *love* charm ... Maybe the Baron was intending the hoof to work its magic on *Jacinta* instead, and was hoping Nick would place it, completely unawares, in the middle of their family home.

'Thanks, but no thanks, Baron,' Nick said, handing the goat's foot back to his host. 'I couldn't possibly accept such a generous gift.'

'I insist, Mister Steen,' said the Baron. 'We in the town of Silth are extremely proud to have such an esteemed author residing with us. We *all* feel that only the luckiest goat's foot this town possesses would be fitting for an esteemed author such as yourself.'

Nick looked around the room again. Who was this '*all*' Rochlain was referring to? It was still just the Baron standing here, as far as Nick could make out.

'You keep a lot of goats' feet here in Silth, do you?' asked Nick, wondering why a cultured man like the Baron would see fit to dabble in superstitious folklore.

'Goats are a man's best friend, Mister Steen.'

'I think you mean "dogs".'

'I do not mean "dogs",' said the Baron, a sudden edge in his voice. 'A dog will eat its dead owner, will it not?'

'A goat will eat its *live* owner,' Nick rejoindered.

'You have much to learn about goats, Mister Steen,' said the Baron, icily, taking back the hoof from Nick's hand. '*Much.*'

'Anyway,' said Nick, moving things on. 'I don't need luck to write. All I require is right up here.' He pointed to his own head, which had to stand in for his brain, given he couldn't quite reach in that far.

'I'm disappointed, Mister Steen,' said the Baron, his expression still cold despite his smile. 'If I wasn't such a huge fan of your writings, I might venture to say I've been insulted.'

Great, thought Nick. *Not only has my oversized son of an Elder God decapitated my benefactor's Dobermanns, but my drunken wife's come on to* him and necked all his booze, and now I've gone and metaphorically crapped in his charitable hands by rejecting his offer of a lucky goat's foot.

Yet Nick's instincts at self-preservation wouldn't relent. Something about that goat's cloven hoof, the oddness of the locals, that run-down town with a mysterious figure in a red hood, the eerie vision of a disappearing Black Steeple, and – yes, Nick had to admit it – Baron Rochlain himself, were all combining to unnerve him.

Maybe he should head back to Stalkford in the morning. Surely it was better to fend off complaints from multiple pet-less neighbours than endure more of this creeping strangeness. After all, Nick had a novel to write, wherever he chose to write it, and Duncan's nappies weren't going to change and burn to a merciful crisp by themselves.

But, some inner instinct told him, it wouldn't do to upset the Baron right now.

'Let's say I'd prefer to accept your gift as an incentive, Baron. A means to spur me on to greater heights. Then, when my book is complete,' Nick said, 'and you and the Masonic Order of Silth are happy with the result, I will gladly accept your lucky goat's foot.'

The Baron's smile turned warm again. 'Succinctly and quite intelligently put, Mister Steen. Not to mention honourable. Please consider any hint of supposed insult I may have detected in your rejection to be an ephemeral mirage that is now wholly absent.'

I think that means he's accepted my apology, thought Nick, breathing a sigh of relief. But if Nick had to dream up excuses each time he wanted to keep on the Baron's good side, he was going to have his work cut out, what with Jacinta's boozy flirtations and Duncan's inveterate head-ripping of the local wildlife.

'Come on, Jacinta, it's time to go,' said Nick, prising his wife's hands from the Baron's arse. Once he'd succeeded in extricating Rochlain from Jacinta's advances, he did the same with Duncan, who was currently growling and attempting to crawl towards Rochlain's three remaining largely legless Dobermanns.

THE BLACK STEEPLE

'Good luck with the writing, Mister Steen,' said the Baron, as Nick forced his family outside and back into his idling Honda Civic. 'I look forward to reading your work.'

'Thank you, Baron,' said Nick, pulling away at last and accelerating at some speed along the street. Yet before his car had quite driven out of sight, Nick glanced into his rear-view mirror and saw several sleek-looking black limousines immediately pulling up alongside the Baron's Lodge.

Nick braked and immediately swung the car around. So there *were* other guests arriving, after all. As he drove back past the lodge once more in the direction of the valley road beyond, he looked out through the passenger window, noting that there were now more than fifteen vehicles parked in the mansion's inner courtyard, with various well-dressed couples being welcomed in by the smiling Baron.

As Nick's car passed by, the Baron appeared to glance up in his direction. And as Nick peered at his rear-view mirror, he saw a wall of curious faces staring back at him as the Baron's guests turned as one to *watch* . . .

CHAPTER FOUR

Nick slammed on the brakes *again*.

'Last straw crossed, Jacinta. Now get out and walk.'

Nick's wife willingly obliged, the car being only ten yards from the front door of their cabin.

By the time Nick had parked up and prised Duncan's legs free of his man-baby seat, Jacinta was already inside on the sofa, nursing a mug of cocoa while brushing the hairs of an object Nick immediately recognised.

'Where did you get that?' he asked.

'It was a present,' she replied.

So Nick *had* been right about the Baron, after all. And when Rochlain had failed to convince Nick to take home the love charm intended for his wife, he'd evidently elected to cut to the chase and surreptitiously hand the lucky goat's foot directly to Jacinta.

'From him, is it?' asked Nick, pointedly.

'No. It's *for* him.'

'A present *for* Baron Rochlain?'

That couldn't be right, surely? The Baron and Jacinta, both gifting each other lucky goat's feet that were in reality potent supernatural love charms. What gave?

'I meant to hand it to him before we left. He's been so kind to us,' Jacinta continued. 'Gifting us this house for the entire summer. I thought the least I could do was give him a small present.'

So it was '*I could*' now. Not '*we could*'.

THE BLACK STEEPLE

Those charms must be pretty damn potent, thought Nick.

No wonder both she and the Baron had fallen in lust the second they'd met, if they'd both been carrying *those* in their pocket-slash-cleavage. Luckily, Jacinta had been too wasted to pass hers on.

Yet why was her charm an *identical* goat's hoof? Nick had presumed it to be a local tradition, peculiar to Silth alone. So why was Jacinta, who'd been living with Nick in Stalkford for the best part of a decade, suddenly party to the strange and unfamiliar folkloric customs of some far-off desert town?

Clearly there were more hidden depths to Jacinta's personality than even Nick had suspected. And he'd suspected *three*.

He stormed out of the lounge, slamming the door behind him. Seconds later, the door reopened against him and slammed the other way, tit-for-tat against his back.

Fine. He'd cook dinner for himself, then. After all, he'd done it once before, even if Jacinta couldn't remember the occasion, despite him pointing it out repeatedly.

After his fourth attempt, Nick washed up the dishes, fed Duncan some raw beefsteak on a rusk, then gave his son a nice warm hosing before bed.

At midnight, an exhausted Nick finally finished drying out the bathroom and surrounding corridors, then went in to kiss Duncan goodnight. That was merely a turn of phrase, of course, for Duncan was well beyond paternal kisses now. Handshakes, too. The best Nick could manage of late was to pet him gently while he was busy digesting something, and hope the sudden movement didn't rattle him too much.

He was just about to read Duncan one of his own early slasher novels before bed when he remembered he had a father's job to do first.

'Look, champ,' he said, gently but firmly. 'You can't just go around biting the heads off Dobermann pinschers.'

At the mention of that word, Duncan began to snarl. Then Nick realised it was just another fang coming through.

He tipped a sachet of Teethas between Duncan's jaws, relaxing his son slightly, then carried on. 'What's worse, though, Duncan, is what happened at the petrol station this morning. You can't drink fuel, okay, champ? And you definitely can't chew the arms of the attendant who's only trying to douse spreading flames. Understand me, kiddo?'

Nick waited. And continued to wait. Hell, he'd wait all night if he had to. He'd make sure Duncan nodded back at him, however long it took. Make sure he learned to understand the difference between wrong and *really* wrong. Because if Nick had any chance of taming this beast-child before it reached monsterhood, he had to put in the time now.

But by 3am, Duncan still hadn't nodded. In fact, he was fast asleep and causing the very foundations of the cabin to quake and vibrate with each raucous, otherworldly snore.

Nick gave up, deciding to head to bed himself. As he passed along the corridor and entered his study, he shut the door firmly and locked himself in. The last thing he wanted was Jacinta stumbling around drunk during the night and mistaking him for Rochlain.

As he yanked open the pull-out bed, Nick saw a strange crimson glow coming through a small gap in his curtains. Dousing the lights (not literally – they were electric), Nick crossed over to the window and pulled the curtains slightly apart. The reddish gleam appeared to be radiating from beyond the elevated rocky ridge he'd stood upon earlier that day. The area where he'd glimpsed his strange vision of the Black Steeple.

Intrigued, Nick made his way downstairs and wandered out into the house's front yard. The night was thick and black, lit only by the eerie crimson luminescence coming from beyond the ridge.

THE BLACK STEEPLE

Making his way past the mound of teetering excrement, which Nick had been unable to burn as planned owing to him waiting in vain for Duncan's nod and which he was now convinced was beginning to sway, he crossed the roadway leading up from the valley and walked over rough ground towards the elevated ridge. Ascending the steep incline to its very top, Nick looked out once more on to the great, rocky wasteland beyond, and beheld a terrifying sight.

For there before him stood once more the distant, imposing edifice of the Black Steeple – but this time, the building was lit up by the glow of a flaming pyre, burning fiercely in front of it. And the Black Steeple was not alone. Around the flames, Nick glimpsed hints of apparent movement. Removing a pair of binoculars from his dressing-gown pocket, Nick held them up to his eyes and focused the lenses on the scene below. There, dancing before the walls of the Black Steeple and around the flaming pyre itself, were a group of hooded figures. All of them were dressed in long red capes, and were totally unidentifiable as individuals, owing to a range of strange, eerie masks they wore in front of their natural faces.

Masks depicting creatures Nick barely recognised. Demonic countenances so horrific, so blasphemous, that even Nick's occasionally questionable morals were sorely affronted.

A ritual, Nick realised. *A Satanic rite. Some form of unholy Black Mass.*

Yet the reality was far worse. For as Nick watched, the door of the blackened church behind the dancing throng suddenly opened, swinging aside to reveal another six sinister hooded figures sporting obscene codpieces.

Six figures in black and purple robes . . .

Nick felt a wave of panic rising from within. For those six hooded figures who had now emerged from the Black Steeple itself carried in their arms a long medieval serving platter, upon which lay a prostrate, as yet unidentifiable figure.

A sacrifice! thought Nick, in sudden panic.

He was about to witness a human sacrifice ...

Thrusting the binoculars back into his dressing-gown pocket, Nick ran down the rocky slope in front of him, yanking out the .44 Magnum revolver he'd got for his forty-fourth birthday from his other dressing-gown pocket. As Nick moved closer to the sinister ceremony, he decided he would use the gun's loaded bullets on the six main platter-carriers. Once those were dealt with, he would scoop up the victim in his arms, taking care to respect and preserve the woman's dignity, given she was more than likely a scantily clad, semi-naked female. Then he'd high-tail it the hell out of there to a quiet bar somewhere for a relaxing debrief over dinner, followed by a nightclub and potential late-night 'coffee'.

As Nick tore through rows of stunted, leafless trees, the distant glow from the fire ahead of him suddenly began to fade. And as he stepped out on to a ghostly, barren plain, he realised that the Black Steeple had once more completely vanished.

He shook his head, confused. There was no longer any sign of it at all. No building, no flaming pyre, no occult worshippers, no chance to shoot anyone.

No scantily clad, semi-naked female ...

What the hell is going on here in Silth? Nick asked himself – then decided he'd practically given himself the answer.

Hell was going on here in Silth, he realised, grimly.

Hell, quite literally, on earth.

*

By the time Nick got back from the police station the following morning, Jacinta was on the telephone, cooing provocatively into the mouthpiece like she'd done with him that one night they'd courted. She was also stroking her precious goat's foot.

'Give me that,' he snapped, yanking the phone from her hand. 'Who is it?' he barked into the receiver, even though he already knew the answer.

'Good morning, Mister Steen,' said the Baron, jovially. 'I was just calling to say hello and ask if everything is okay up at the house? Unfortunately, we've had some complaints here about missing pets.'

Nick already knew about that. It was all the police sergeant in Silth had been interested in discussing.

'We're fine,' said Nick, ignoring that element of the Baron's sentence. 'Except I witnessed something wholly strange and unexplainable here last night.'

'Oh, really?' replied the Baron, a note of mock-surprise in his voice. 'Of what nature?'

'Un-nature,' said Nick, then told him about the Black Steeple and the apparent human sacrifice he'd glimpsed. And about how the police sergeant in Silth hadn't believed a word Nick had told him when he'd driven there first thing this morning. Instead, the sergeant had displayed unnecessarily threatening behaviour towards Duncan.

Meanwhile, Jacinta sat sniggering on the sofa.

'And you say the desk sergeant didn't believe you?' the Baron asked.

'He said there's no Black Steeple there. Nor has there ever been a Black Steeple there, as far as he knows.'

'Well, there you have it, Mister Steen. I'm sure it's simply down to your overactive authorial imagination. You did say it's been leaking out.'

No, Nick hadn't said that at all. In fact, he'd deliberately refrained from mentioning anything to do with his leaking interdimensional brain-portal, for fear that the Masonic Order of Silth might somehow see fit to change their minds about inviting him here on a surprise sabbatical and elect instead to cancel his lucrative fellowship grant.

So how did the Baron know about Nick's leaking brain? Surely few people read newspapers in a dead-end town like this, so far from Stalkford. It was highly unlikely that news of Nick's affliction had spread this far south.

Then again, the Baron certainly knew enough about Nick's books, or he wouldn't have invited him up here in the first place. He wouldn't have sent that emissary from the Masonic Order of Silth to contact Nick personally in Stalkford and hand him a huge wad of money in exchange for moving to Silth and writing his next book in a state of idyllic seclusion and total comfort. However the information had come to him, Baron Rochlain evidently knew more about Nick's life than he'd initially let on.

Then Nick twigged, turning to glare darkly at Jacinta, who was still sniggering. She winked and blew him a sarcastic kiss.

'The sergeant said the Black Steeple has never been there, "*as far as he knows*",' Nick said, turning his attention back to the Baron. 'Which doesn't mean it *isn't* there.'

'Except that it *actually* isn't there,' countered Rochlain.

'Except that it actually *was* there,' countered Nick, countering the Baron's initial counter.

'Until it actually *wasn't* there again,' double-countered the Baron, re-countering Nick's initial countering.

'Until it actually *was* there again,' Nick double-countered against the Baron's previous double-countering.

'Until it ultimately *wasn't* there again,' thrice-countered the Baron against Nick's own double-counter.

Nick sighed inwardly, realising he didn't possess a thrice-counter to triple-counter back. And a good job too, he decided. For he and the Baron were getting close to a countering war – and Nick was already embroiled in an endless war of nit-pickery with Jacinta. What with all that was going on between the three of them, including the looming threat of an imminent destructive love triangle, there was no way Nick could commit troops to a second front. That way risked both the Nitpickalypse, and potential Countergeddon.

'You must forgive my obstinacy, Mister Steen, but you see, Sergeant Stack does sterling work for our town. It's largely due to him that Silth is entirely free of crime.'

'That's an understatement,' said Nick. 'The arsehole attempted to clawprint Duncan. Luckily, they couldn't hold him down.'

'I presume they took his whisker patterns instead?'

'I think there are more pressing issues than a few missing pets, frankly.'

'Such as?'

'Such as the potential existence of a satanic coven in the town's midst, conducting a ritual Black Mass involving actual human sacrifice.'

'As I say, an escaping figment of your imagination, Mister Steen. And I'm sure you're familiar with the law that states that without evidence of a body, there can legally exist no case of murder?'

Nick didn't like the cut of this man's jib. Not only had Rochlain been more than likely exchanging increasingly saucy phone calls with Jacinta as their respective goat's feet went to work, but there was also something else about him that Nick didn't trust. The Baron might present a suave and sophisticated gentlemanly exterior, but Nick was beginning to suspect there was something more sinister going on beneath the man's blazer-and-ascot exterior. In fact, Nick felt increasingly convinced that the Baron knew far more about this sinister Black Steeple and apparent human sacrifice than he was letting on.

'*I'll* find the body, then,' said Nick.

'As you wish, Mister Steen. But I wouldn't spend too long on that. God forbid this bizarre obsession with a disappearing Black Steeple should threaten to interfere with your writing schedule. We in Silth are all looking forward to reading your latest horrotic masterpiece. That is, after all, the *reason you're here*.'

Again, that edge in the Baron's tone. As though he wished to remind Nick that he was here solely on the Baron's time and dime. And the more Nick thought about that, the more absurd the notion of him being a financial benefactor of Nick's work became. For the mental vision of the esteemed Baron Rochlain poring over Nick's books, particularly the brazenly horrotic sections, was one Nick hadn't paused to think about up until now. Yet the more Nick did think about it, the weirder that vision began to look.

Unless the Baron wasn't quite as squeaky clean as he liked to present himself as being? Maybe there was a side to Rochlain's personality that he preferred to keep hidden. After all, hadn't his personal library been filled to the brim with ancient, occult texts? Maybe he hadn't wanted *Nick* up here in Silth at all. Maybe all he'd really wanted was to be closer to Nick's *wife*.

'I should warn you now, Baron,' said Nick, playing dumb for now. 'My writing's pretty strong stuff. You'd need a stiff drink or two to get through the racier sections, believe me.'

'Fear not, Mister Steen,' laughed the Baron from the other end of the phone. 'I'm far more worldly wise than you could possibly imagine.'

'Whatever, Baron,' said Nick. 'Gotta go.' He slammed the phone back into its cradle – not because he'd had enough of Rochlain, particularly, and not because he wished instead to castigate Jacinta for getting all hot and saucy with his new employer at ten-thirty on a weekday morning.

No, Nick had just caught sight of another snake-tube on his front porch.

CHAPTER FIVE

'Repeat after me, champ,' said Nick, addressing Duncan in the car's rear-view mirror. '*No. Kill. Snake.*'

'*Kill,*' growled Duncan, beaming.

'Not quite, kiddo. Listen again. *No. Kill. Snake.*'

'*Kill!*'

Duncan's feet slammed into the back of Nick's seat, thrusting his own feet hard against the accelerator pedal.

Nick immediately applied the brake, but knew deep down that it was only a matter of weeks before Duncan ended up killing them both, accidentally or otherwise. Nick *had* to calm his son's wilder instincts, or Society would be on them in a flash, threatening to lock Duncan away in some high-security containment facility, ideally on its own island.

'Listen, champ. I accept that rusks are beyond you now. But if I don't curb all this mindless head-wrenching of yours, it'll be us little people next. And then that big frightening cage I've been talking about will appear. Then the news cameras, and the tanks, and multiple air strikes – and before you know it, you'll be stuck at the top of the Post Office Tower with the Red Arrows making formation kamikaze runs at you above a whooping crowd.'

Duncan emitted a terrifying sound that Nick suspected was a laugh, but which still had the raw potential to burst the human eardrum. Then he kicked the back of the seat again. Nick fought to control the car's sudden acceleration, swerving wildly to avoid the approaching crash barrier before bringing the car back to a normal speed once more. Maybe he should avoid educating Duncan inside a moving vehicle.

As Nick swung the Civic left towards the main valley road, he slammed his brakes on again.

There, in the middle of the road, stood the scarlet-hooded figure.

That eerie stranger Nick had glimpsed before, clothed in its red, monk-like cassock.

The Watcher in the Hills . . .

As Nick manoeuvred his vehicle around the figure, it turned with him, the hood drawn so far over its head that any facial features remained completely concealed under the dark, scarlet folds. As Nick glanced back through his rear-view mirror, he caught sight of the figure still staring after him, motionless as a brick.

Watching.

Who is that? wondered Nick, his mind already considering the grim possibility that the mysterious Watcher was somehow involved with the human sacrifice he'd witnessed the previous evening. The satanic ritual Baron Rochlain had insisted was merely a figment of Nick's overactive authorial imagination.

Well, Nick would see about that. As the figure retreated into the far distance, Nick felt more resolved than ever to investigate personally the mysterious events of the night before, with or without the help of Sergeant Stack. First he'd attempt to unearth some trace of evidence on the valley plain that might prove what he'd seen the previous night was real. Then he'd go looking for the Watcher himself, and find out from him – or her, or *it* – what exactly was going on here in Silth.

Nick put his foot down through the valley road, confident that Duncan was now safely asleep in the seat behind him, having gorged himself comatose on a wild coyote Nick had accidentally clipped on the small side road leading down from the cabin.

THE BLACK STEEPLE

He'd initially considered walking to the site, with Duncan in tow, across the ridge he'd climbed the night before. But seeing as his son now routinely ate through his own chains, Nick suspected he might not be able to control Duncan if he suddenly lurched towards a passing bear or cougar.

But the weight of Duncan's droppings were now slowing down the car. Nick considered pulling over to scoop them out, but didn't want to risk waking his son again. Grimly, he began the exhausting task of breathing through his mouth alone. For one word, and one word *only*, came to mind when Nick dared, as a means of mental distraction, to describe the smell of Duncan's stools.

Unholy.

Pushing that thought from his mind, Nick spied the distant ridge overlooking the valley plain to his right and followed the rough track leading out to the scene of last night's vision – if, indeed, a vision was what the thing had been.

Parking the car beside a clump of large boulders, Nick left Duncan inside to sleep off his feed, then wandered across the rocky ground towards the apparent location of last night's flaming pyre.

Nick felt a cold chill as he reached the scene of the apparent sacrifice. Yet no matter how much he might wish to prove the Baron wrong, Nick realised this sudden sense of fear might still only be an impression brought about by his brooding subconscious. Keeping an open mind, he bent down to examine the ground where he'd spied those hooded worshippers dancing, searching for any trace of the sacrificial ceremony he'd witnessed the previous evening.

But there was nothing there. Nick combed the entire area, but found not a single trace of ash, embers or human blood.

It was as if the whole thing had never even happened.

Perhap I'm going crazy, thought Nick. *Perhap I'm imagining things that just aren't there, like Rochlain said. Or mayhap they were there, but were mere shreds of my authorial imagination flowing free, also like Rochlain said.*

If that was true, Nick reflected, perchance that was a good thing? The fact that these visions were appearing, then *dis*appearing? Surely their subsequent vanishment meant Nick's instincts had been correct. That his visions at long last were telling Nick that they *preferred* to disappear, after all. That they wished to return to the confines of the printed page, as Nick intended.

Which meant that maybe Nick's plan was working. The horrors unleashed by his authorial brain were finally giving up the literal ghost. Nick's desire to write another novel, regardless of the chaos he'd inadvertently been unleashing around him over the last few years, was now, somehow, forcing those demons of his mind back into the brain that had spawned them. Maybe the Black Steeple, and its terrifying scarlet-caped worshippers, were figments of Nick's imagination that his conscious mind had subsequently forced *back* to wherever they'd first come from. Perhaps his mind had made them appear, then disappear, as his natural resilience fought to purge these incarnated horrors from the face of Stalkford.

Yeah, that *had* to be it. And as long as Nick found no body or trace of the sacrifice he'd seen about to take place on the steps of the sinister Black Steeple, then most likely it signified he really *was* winning the war against his escaping imagination.

He grinned to himself. He'd found it, at long last. A way to close the portal in his brain, to confine its horrors permanently to the world of humble paper.

Now Nick would be able to vanquish these demons by himself, without enlisting any help from Duncan. Sure, he might need to let Jacinta have her wicked way with Baron Rochlain for a bit longer while Nick got his initial rough draft done, but their divorce would soon be through, and Nick always had his spurs and boots should he fancy a brief, meaningless dalliance of his own.

THE BLACK STEEPLE

He breathed a sigh of relief, gazed out one last time across the vast expanse of grey dust and rubble in front of him – and then saw it.

A dark stain on the ground.

Slowly, Nick walked over to it, then leaned down to examine the strange mark. It was rusty in colour.

Blood, Nick realised. *Dried blood.*

He rose to his feet again, then caught sight of something else. A shard of crumbling, black rock ahead of him, sticking up at an angle from the stony ground.

Nick crossed over to the jagged protuberance, bending down again to examine what it might be.

A *step*.

A *black step*.

Exactly like the one Nick had seen leading up to the door of the supposedly imaginary Black Steeple ...

Desperate to disprove his mounting suspicions, Nick looked up again to see if he could locate any more evidence that something solid had once stood here.

And saw it, half-buried in the ground.

'A pulpit,' Nick muttered to himself, having made his way over to the object.

An upturned pulpit. A pulpit that had been turned upside down and painted entirely in black ...

'The Devil's pulpit?' Nick wondered, aloud. Or something more sinister?*

Nick carefully examined the upturned, blackened pulpit, then noticed a small black book lying near its far end. Cautiously, Nick lifted the book in his hands and opened it.

---

* Though there are few things more sinister than the Devil's pulpit, there *are*, nonetheless, a few. Par example, the Devil's Washbowl, which is not a washbowl as such, but instead a workspace used largely for food preparation in Hell's Kitchen, though more often utilised by assistant chefs as a conventional toilet. GM

He felt another chill pass through his body as his eyes met with row upon row of strange runic symbols, penned in what looked to his eyes like human blood. And as Nick examined them further, a second icy chill coursed down his spine as a small black object dropped from the book's opened pages into his palm.

A key.

A small, *black* key.

As he held the small black key in his hand, Nick's peripheral vision caught sight of a strange object lying half-hidden in the rocks up ahead.

From where Nick was standing, it looked, bizarrely, like some sort of strongbox. Upon reaching it, his suspicions were confirmed: that was indeed what it was. Some sort of *strongbox.*

But what was some sort of strongbox doing out here in the middle of an abandoned, rock-strewn valley? Some sort of strongbox that, like the other objects Nick had recently discovered, was painted entirely *black*. A black sort of strongbox, which bore, Nick discovered, as he narrowed his eyes in an attempt to make out a strange yet solid physical protrusion upon one of its sides . . .

. . . a *padlock*.

A padlock *made entirely from black.*

Nick took the small black key he'd found inside the black book next to the black pulpit near the black step, and placed it into the black padlock he'd found on some sort of black strongbox, and twisted it sideways.

He heard a click.

Nervously, Nick snapped open the padlock, lifted the lid and discovered, within . . .

A roll of black parchment.

Carefully, Nick lifted out the roll of black parchment and held it up to the light. Dimly, on its blackened pages, Nick could just discern what looked to him like yet more eerie runic symbols hidden below.

THE BLACK STEEPLE

All entirely impenetrable to Nick's mind, save for one single word. A name, Nick realised. A name eerily like his own.

'HARLAND STEEN'

'Harland Steen,' he repeated, aloud.

Then, as if repeating 'Harland Steen' aloud had somehow summoned it, he witnessed a sudden, terrifying, apocalyptic vision.

On the floor of the valley plain before him there now stood, once more, that familiar vision of the sinister Black Steeple. In front of its opened doors danced the same ring of masked, hooded worshippers, chanting their sinister refrain. Yet now Nick could also see a group of men tied together in front of the worshippers, bound to each other's bodies on the makeshift funeral pyre.

Preparing to burn.

Nick cast his eyes over the doomed victims. An army of protesting men in cotton clothes and wide-brimmed hats, squirming and raging helplessly against their hooded oppressors. Seventeenth-century Puritans, he realised. Zealous in life and courageous in death.

And the hooded worshippers themselves? Nothing less, Nick realised, than the forces of Darkest Evil. Forces of Darkest Evil that were preparing to destroy – for all time – the forces of Lightest Good . . .

'No!' Nick screamed as the hooded worshippers reached forward with their flaming torches and lit the pyre of Puritans. He screamed as the men went up in flame. He screamed at this horrifying vision of a world where Evil reigned, triumphant.

And as Nick screamed, he saw one of the roasting Puritans slowly lift his head, the man's features gradually coming into view from beneath his wide-brimmed capotain, to fix the helpless writer with a terrifying glare.

For the face of the Puritan holy man staring back at him, as flames licked higher and higher around his tethered body, was *Nick's own* . . .

As the terrifying vision was obscured suddenly by the wall of raging flames, Nick realised his ears were in fact now hearing something other than his own screaming, as he'd personally stopped screaming a second or two earlier so that he could catch his breath before continuing to scream his existing scream. But that second section of Nick's scream never came. For the fresh scream that had effectively interrupted Nick's initial scream, even though technically it had already been screaming alongside Nick's own pre-existing scream, was the scream of something else entirely. And as the apocalyptic vision Nick had just witnessed faded away and became nothing more threatening than a lonely valley plain, Nick realised the particular scream he was still hearing was coming from the vicinity of his own car.

'*Duncan!*' Nick yelled, running back over to his vehicle – whose doors, he saw now, were all hanging open.

'I'm coming, kiddo! Daddy's coming!'

But it wasn't Duncan who was screaming.

The scream was coming from the freshly-disembodied-but-still-alive head of a semi-digested puma.

'Thank goodness,' gasped Nick, attempting to extract its thrashing lower half from the vice-like grip of Duncan's mouth.

But if there was any reality at all to the macabre vision he'd just witnessed, Nick suspected that very soon, there might be no goodness left *in the entire world* . . .

CHAPTER SIX

Wow, an alluring librarian, pondered Nick to himself, still hardly believing one existed. How he'd like to get shushed by *her*. As he walked over to the reception desk at Silth's local library, he barely noticed that for the first time in his life, he hadn't gone straight to the shelves to see if they were stocking his own books, and if not, why not. Instead, he was making an automatic beeline for this bewitching brunette in spectacles, while thanking the Lord he had a reason for interrupting her day that didn't involve castigating the entire branch for failing to file his complete works by year of publication.

'Hello, miss,' he said, upon reaching the desk.

'Hello back,' she replied, stamping a late return without looking up at him.

Jeez, thought Nick. Was this female librarian for real?

'I wonder if you can help me?' he asked.

'Maybe I can, maybe I can't,' the female librarian replied, finally lifting her eyes from the book stamp to pierce Nick's own gaze with what he immediately identified as a borderline sultry glare.

'Maybe you *will*,' said Nick, testing the water.

'Maybe I *won't*,' she parroted back, effectively telling Nick the water into which he was dipping his metaphorical toe was *smoking hot*.

He took a deep breath, taking her in. Early thirties, he guessed, with long auburn-coloured hair tied up at the back. Several stray strands hung loose down one cheek, and her face appeared flushed with hard work. Nick loved that. Like she'd been working up a proper sweat stamping books and hadn't had time to re-scrunch.

'I'm trying to research an historical figure who may or may not have once lived in Silth.'

'How exciting,' she said, leaning herself – or, more specifically, parts of herself – over the counter. Nick couldn't tell if she was speaking sarcastically or not, and, frankly, he didn't much care.

True, the request wasn't that exciting, even to Nick. But he had to find out who Harland Steen was, and if that meant enduring this woman's alluringly sarcastic jibes for an hour or so, that was more than okay with him.

'Oh, it's exciting,' he confirmed, even though he knew it technically wasn't.

'Good,' the librarian said, finally relaxing the hard glare on her face into what looked to Nick like a hint of dreamy obsession. 'Because I *love* exciting things,' she added, murmuring the words breathily through full, cherry-red-lipsticked lips.

Easy, tiger, thought Nick. *Keep your mind on the job.*

'That's good to hear,' he said. 'The guy's name is Harland Steen.'

Abruptly, the female librarian's face lunged towards his, her features suddenly so close to Nick's own that he could see his own reflection in the lenses of her spectacles.

Thank God *he* was looking smoking hot, too.

But as suddenly as she'd lunged towards him, the female librarian had rebounded backwards, having merely employed the edge of her desk for bodily purchase.

And before Nick had a chance to mourn the loss of their close physical proximity, the female librarian had used that purchase to reverse away from the desk and swing herself out from behind the main reception area to slip one arm around his waist.

'You don't mind?' she said, looking up at him while squeezing herself closer to his manly chest.

'Not if you don't.'

'I don't mind at all. In fact, I wouldn't remotely object if you clasped my body rather tightly against your own.'

'Seriously?'

'It's my job as head librarian. I don't want a poor stranger getting lost in my big, unexplored library.'

'I guess not,' he said. After all, Nick *was* a stranger in town, and maybe it made sense for her to clasp a newcomer physically close to her, even if the library itself was essentially just the one room.

'You guessed right, Mister *Nick Steen.*'

Ah, then she knew who he was. Which explained why she was coming on to him so strongly. For with the newfound fame Silth would soon be acquiring as a creative haven for the historic forging of Nick's latest horror masterpiece, one that would single-handedly confine the escaping horrors of his mind back into the trusty confines of the printed page, the town's female librarian would no doubt become hugely respected throughout Silth as one of Nick's closest champions, and a fellow saviour of Mankind by association. No wonder she had the female hots for him.

'Harland Steen was one of Silth's founding forefathers,' she began, leading Nick across the room to the library's nearby microfilm reader. 'A seventeenth-century Puritan firebrand who dedicated his life to battling Satan and his demonic hordes.'

'Yeah, that's the guy,' said Nick, daring to squeeze her closer to him another inch or two, nevertheless mindful that it might potentially send them both sprawling together across the library floor.

Not that getting tangled up with this woman amid a pile of Nick's horrotic works would necessarily be a *bad* thing . . .

'We have a collection of historical town documents gathered conveniently together on this roll of microfilm,' she said, reaching into her tight roll-neck sweater to pull out a necklace buried in what Nick hoped were particularly soft folds beneath. As Nick watched, the female librarian tugged sensually on the chain, drawing it up through the gap between her two assets to reveal, at length, a spool of neatly labelled microfilm.

'We'll have to part our bodies now,' she whispered, staring deeply into Nick's eyes before releasing her grasp on his waist.

'Sure thing,' replied Nick, half-whispering his own phrase. Then he sat himself down in the chair before the microfilm reader, where he would no longer have to keep hiding his excitement.

Damn it, why couldn't Jacinta have been a sultry, sensual female librarian like this sultry, sensual female librarian? As the smoking-hot focus of his current primal lustings loaded up the microfilm reader with that lucky spool of film she'd just removed — a spool of film that was probably still warm — Nick cast his mind back to his and Jacinta's single courting day.

It didn't remotely compare.

'This direction spools the film down,' said the female librarian, twisting the machine's spooling knob sideways. 'And this direction spools it up. See?'

Nick watched as she twisted the knob in front of him sideways with her hand, then twisted it back in the other direction again. Left to right, then right to left, then left to right again, followed unexpectedly by another right to left and a third left to right. Which would, on the microfilm reader screen, Nick knew, result in an upward-downward motion. Specifically up, then down, then up, then down, then up again.

'And *this* movement,' she said, leaning down to whisper the words softly into his ear, 'spools it *all the way round.*'

Slowly, she twisted the microfilm reader knob around in a circular motion, then made a bigger circle, then twisted it left to right again, then right to left, and so on and so forth — which, on the microfilm reader itself, Nick realised again, meant up and down and round and round and up and down and round and round and up and down and up and down and up and down.

Nick realised she was behind him now, reaching round with her other hand to grasp a similar-looking knob situated on the left-hand side of the machine.

Nick watched, helpless, as she used her left hand to pump the spool leftward, then rightward, then all around, and round again, and round again, getting faster, and faster, and even faster, and faster still.

Now Nick's eyes were caught between her right hand and her left hand, transfixed by both sets of painted nails twisting this way and that, moving the knobs left and right (up and down on the screen, remember), then right and left (on the screen still, down then up), and left and right (up then down on the same screen), then all around (on the screen a dizzying sideways motion across a range of printed matter, followed by yet more up-and-down motions before a dizzying sideways motion in the opposite direction), moving faster and faster and faster and faster (represented on the microfilm screen as a continuous physical 'pumping' for information), as the female librarian continued to whisper softly into his ear, until ...

'I get the hang of it now, thanks,' said Nick, lifting the female librarian's hands from both knobs, before gripping on to them himself for dear life.

'It's quite simple, really,' she murmured, close by. 'Just let me know if you need any help.'

And with that, she walked away from him, back to the reception desk. Dammit, Nick felt exhausted. And somehow used. As he turned his head to watch her go, he caught sight of her peering back over her shoulder at him as she went, a mischievous twinkle in her eyes.

Dammit, this little honey-bee could *sting*.

'You're going in the wrong direction,' Nick called out, realising that she was still looking back at him and was about to walk into a wall.

Turning around sharply, the female librarian corrected her angle of approach and finally slipped back behind the reception desk, where she once again commenced the hard stamping of some late returns.

What the hell was happening, Nick wondered. He'd only known this woman for two minutes, and already he was absolutely smitten with her. And she him, by all accounts.

Just cool it for now, buddy, Nick thought to himself. *You're a married man. For a week or so, at any rate. Then, once Jacinta's divorce papers are finally settled, you and the female librarian can go at it like jackhammers on a soon-to-be-dualled carriageway. That way Jacinta won't be able to cite 'cheatering' for extra points.*

Nick breathed in deeply, forcing his mind to return to the task at hand. Right now he needed to focus his energies on this microfilm reader in front of him, and figure out exactly what the hell was going on here in Silth with all these strange visions of a Black Steeple and an apocalyptic battle between the Forces of Good and Evil he'd been having.

Slowly, methodically, Nick ran his eyes over the enlarged newspaper clippings on the screen in front of him, scrolling through numerous local newspaper stories about roadworks changes on the main valley pass, local school sports day competitions, amateur dramatic society feuds, the usual birth and death announcements. All that boring life crap Nick tried his hardest to avoid when forced to endure existence amid 'polite' society. The occasional snap of a prize-winning cow caught his eye, particularly one that had evidently been born with three heads and seven legs, but generally the contents of Silth's local rag was all much of a muchness. He had to dig deeper, he realised, so elected to play it bold and scroll backward in time immediately, all the way to 1647.

THE BLACK STEEPLE

After three hours,* Nick finally had it. There, in the bottom left-hand corner of page four of the *Silth Evening Gazette*, practically hidden away between neighbouring woodcuts of yet another deformed cow and some geese flying upside down, watched by a farmer standing on his head, was the story Nick had been looking for.

FINAL BATTLE LOFT
Good 0 - Evil 6

Nick ran his eyes over the ensuing article, remembering to substitute the letter 's' for every printed 'f', the most compelling evidence yet put forward by scientists that people in the past were stupid.

Goody Wimpole writef - On thif eighteenth day of June in the fixteen-thoufand and forty feventh year of our former Lord, did two-fcore brotherf pure and noble make battle with feven-fcore Magicianf black on the blfaphemouf ftepf of Fatan's curfed Black Fteeple, and were there roundly beaten by the fatanic forcef of the moft cruell and finifter Canon LeRoche. Thif final conflagration being itfelth a fcheduled rematch of yon previouf Final Battle twixt the Forcef of Light and Darkneff, that didft refulteth in a draw. Thif itfelth hadft neceffitateth both teamf to fecure frefh figningf, fome fent from the Vatican itfelf at the moft holieft requeft of Pope

---

* I'm skipping ahead here, as it was mainly just endless microfilm spooling, and there's a strict 40,000 word limit for this tale. GM

GARTH MARENGHI

Ʃimon the ſecond, along wyth a propoſed name change that waſ ſeverely oppoſed by the moſt holieſt of our Puritan forefatherſ on behalf of hiſ glorbiouſ Brethren, whoſe ſacred name iſ, nay waſ...

Nick scrolled the microfilm onward to the next page, and almost jumped out of his seat. For there, facing him, was the face of the very person he'd been looking for. And, despite the inevitable flecks and scratches of intervening centuries, Nick realised the old adage was true. The camera never lied. Here, in front of Nick's very eyes, sporting the same priestly cotton clothes and wide-brimmed capotain he'd glimpsed in his recent vision, lay the mirror image of his own features. A rare, seventeenth-century sepia-tinted photograph of Harland Steen himself.

'He's exactly like me,' said Nick, aloud.

'*SSH!*' shushed the female librarian from her nearby desk.

Nick turned, immediately turned on by her stern vocal castigation. As the female librarian's scowl softened somewhat, realising it was Nick himself who'd spoken, she once again stepped out from behind reception and walked sultrily over the library floor towards him, moving like it was a damned catwalk.

'Found everything you need?'

'I think so,' said Nick.

'I do mean *everything* ...' she whispered softly in his ear, having moved herself back round behind him, her hands poised once more over both twirling knobs. Immediately, Nick rose to his feet and turned to face her, not wishing to risk another physical demonstration of the microfilm reader, in case they accidentally deleted all records or ended up breaking the machine.

But they were damned close, Nick realised. A mere half-inch lay between his lips and her pouting ones.

THE BLACK STEEPLE

'Well, maybe not *everything*,' Nick replied, now only a quarter-inch away from those pouting lips of hers. 'Because there are one or two *other* things I need.'

'And what other things are those?' she murmured, lips parting slightly to form an enigmatic smile like the Mona Lisa's – but one that was far more attractive, frankly.

'Good question,' Nick replied, stalling for time. As hot as he was, it wouldn't be good to be seen going at it with a female librarian in public, he figured. They couldn't do it right here, right now, on top of the microfilm reader, for example. Not only did Nick not wish to be held liable for potential repairs, but he also might need to use the microfilm reader again at some point soon while looking up further information pertinent to his investigation of the mysterious supernatural goings-on currently going on supernaturally in Silth.*

'Well, if it's something you *really* need,' said the female librarian, quartering another quarter-inch towards him (essentially one-sixteenth of an inch), 'I'm sure you'll find it *right here*.'

He felt her hand move towards his body, and prayed he could somehow hold things together. Then, by some miracle, he realised she was simply lifting a book for him to look at.

'It's *The Big Bumper Book of Black Magic*, which includes an entire section on the Ancient War Between Good and Evil – or Darkness and Light, as it was previously known. I believe it goes into some detail about Harland Steen and his Holy Brethren.'

'Holy Brethren?'

'That's what they called themselves. The Brethren, for short. Brother Harland didn't believe in using two words when one would suffice.'

'"The Holy Brethren" is three words,' Nick said, correcting her. '"The Brethren" is two.'

---

* He didn't, as it turns out, but he doesn't know that right now. GM

Nick knew he was being petty, but he fervently disagreed with Harland Steen on that one. In his book (not his actual books), books demanded full explanation throughout, employing multiple words to describe whatever it was that was being described in order to avoid any hint of potential ambiguity creeping into the story's meaning. If a writer wished to say, 'Yea, some do say 'twas the thrashing purple-skinned demon that twists victim's nipples, which are known throughout all of Stalkford as the purple nurples,' then they should just say that. No way should they write, ''Twas the Purple Nurpler' and expect readers to know what the hell they meant. One might just as easily be referring to a cocktail or a fresh strain of STD.

'You really are a fantastic wordsmith,' said the fully corrected female librarian sheepishly.

'Thanks ...' Nick smiled, taking the book from her hand and attempting to add her name before realising he hadn't yet asked her what it was. But then, she hadn't bothered to tell him it, either, so he figured they were quits on that score.

'I wondered whether you might like to meet me for a drink later this evening?' she asked, coquettishly.

Of course I would, Nick thought. *A drink and whatever else she might wish to proffer.*

But Nick couldn't, he knew. For he had Duncan to consider.

'I can't this evening,' he said. 'I have to look after Duncan, my adopted borderline-feral man-child.'

'Oh yes, Duncan,' the female librarian said. 'I've heard that people in your home town were being extremely cruel to him.'

'And you should hear what Society said as well,' Nick replied, immediately wanting to tell her how Stalkford City Council had banned Duncan from all the county's zoos until their missing macaws and gazelles had time to repopulate. But he knew he'd need a stiff drink inside him to tell her *that* one.

THE BLACK STEEPLE

'Well, I just want you to know, Nick Steen, that I disagree *fervently* with those people,' she said, staring deeply into the author's eyes. 'Anything those people say about poor Duncan, you can guarantee I'm *fervently* opposed to.'

'Thanks,' said Nick, hardly believing his luck that he'd bumped into an attractive woman who used 'fervently' twice in the same paragraph, even though that was, grammatically speaking, inelegant. As he was reflecting upon whether to tell her that and suggest he start educating her, an old man passing behind on his way to the newspaper section barged into the female librarian, thrusting her forcefully into Nick's arms.

They were now 0.2cm apart from each other's lips, i.e. two millimetres. As she leaned in that extra two millimetres towards him, Nick prepared to throw caution to the wind at long last, and commence some immediate frottage.

Then tore himself away, for he felt *other* eyes upon him. Nick could sense that somehow, somewhere, he was in the process of being *watched*.

'Another night, female librarian,' he said, gently easing himself away from her.

'My name is Samantha.'

'Another night, Samantha the female librarian.'

'You can call me Sam, if you like.'

'I actually prefer Samantha, the female librarian.'

'Whatever you prefer.'

'Another night then, hot legs. I promise.'

As she turned her body aside coyly to let him pass, Nick headed back over towards the library's main door, clutching *The Big Bumper Book of Black Magic* in his hands. As he did so, he experienced once more that eerie, uncanny feeling he'd had just now. That sense of being *watched* ...

Which is when Nick saw the figure in the shadowy recess beyond the far table where the old man was now sitting.

A figure dressed in a scarlet hooded robe.

The Watcher . . .

Nick paused mid-step, wondering whether to confront the figure who'd been following him since he'd first set foot in Silth.

Later, Nick decided, aware that Duncan would soon be needing his evening feed. And besides, right now Nick wanted to go somewhere else and think about Samantha the female librarian.

CHAPTER SEVEN

Having thought particularly long and hard about Samantha the female librarian, Nick arrived back late. He went into the lodge and checked in on Duncan, who was sleeping soundly, albeit caked with tufts of fur and animal bones. Dammit, couldn't Jacinta at least give the kid a bib? Nick scraped up the lifeless remains of an unlucky stray and tossed it on the fire, then tiptoed back along the corridor to his own room. As he was about to enter it, he overheard Jacinta speaking with someone on the telephone next door. Cautiously, he leaned his ear against her bedroom wall and listened in.

She was flirting with the Baron again, if the words 'my naughty Rochey Wochey' were anything to go by. Nick considered leaving them both to it, then elected to stick around for a while longer and see if he could overhear potential evidence against Jacinta that he might be able to use in their imminent divorce proceedings.

'All in good time, Rochey Wochey, all in good time,' Jacinta continued. Nick struggling not to vomit openly on the corridor floor. 'Remember, good things come to those who wait ...'

What the hell were they both waiting for? Nick didn't care what they did, now that he had access to Samantha the female librarian and the microfilm reader.

'Of course I've tried it on ...'

Wait a minute, though, thought Nick, starting to fume. *Sleeping with my wife is one thing. But sending her fruity negligees is beyond the pale.*

'Of course it fits ... you guessed my size *exactly* ... Well, it's a *little* tight ... in *certain* areas ... But I don't think you'll mind that, when you see what I look like in it ... My little *Rochey Wochey.*'

Jacinta began to laugh in that way she used to do when Nick had just received his latest advance. The sound sickened him now, especially as it was directed at Baron Rochlain instead of him, the man who'd evidently lied about inviting Nick up here, when it was clearly only Jacinta he'd been interested in all along.

Dammit, she was purring now. Purring like a cat. This *was* sick. True, Nick had purred with Jacinta himself, in the past. Got inside a matching cat costume and lapped up bowlfuls of milk together before scrapping with his love-rival (Tony Corbet, orthopaedic consultant, also catted up) to win Jacinta's affections. But if she thought Nick was going back to that phase of their relationship, and was somehow hoping he and the Baron would suit up in some back alley and slash at each other while mewling, she had another thing coming. Nick had dignity now. The only way *that* was going to happen would be if Jacinta coughed up for some stag horns and hired a couple of extras to be their collective rear-ends. Then he'd happily go at the Baron just for fun.

She was purring louder now. And *hissing* ... Hissing and purring, like an alley cat on heat, scratching and pawing at a heavily-maned mate. Yet Nick could hear words in between those hisses, too. Words he didn't quite understand. He listened harder, pressing his ear so close to Jacinta's door that he knew he risked a weevil crawling in if he wasn't careful.

Then he realised what kind of words he was hearing. For Jacinta was speaking in *Latin*. But no ordinary Latin, Nick suspected. No, this was *medieval* Latin. But no ordinary medieval Latin, either, Nick realised yet again. Oh no. For Jacinta was speaking medieval Latin *backwards* ... Not just backwards, though, Nick realised thricely, listening even harder against the door. Jacinta was speaking medieval Latin backwards, and *upside down*.

THE BLACK STEEPLE

The Devil's Latin ...

That could mean only one thing, Nick knew. Jacinta had evidently gone mad while he was away from the house, sought immediate psychiatric help from a doctor in Silth who'd placed her in a hypnotic trance and regressed her back to a former life, thereby uncovering a hitherto deeply repressed split-personality residing somewhere within her brain. Either that or she was practising for a television quiz show. One like *Mastermind*, say, with her chosen specialist subject being archaic occult languages – for which she was displaying, Nick had to admit, a precocious linguistic fecundity.

Two possible explanations. Unless, Nick thought suddenly, Jacinta was now a witch.

And, given that Nick suspected the town of Silth might well be harbouring some dark occult secrets surrounding the existence of a potential satanic coven in its midst – a coven that possibly may or may not be connected to an ancient order of Black Magicians who once fought and won a titanic Final Battle against the Forces of Evil and also Darkness – there was a strong likelihood that Jacinta had deliberately gone the way of the Wicca while he'd been out.

Three possible explanations, then. With the fourth being that Jacinta had not in fact turned into a witch while Nick had been out, but had *already been a witch for some time* ...

That made most sense, he figured. After all, his wife had theoretically already coupled with a Cosmic Outer God, according to the escaping events of Nick's book, *The Stalkwich Blasphemy*. And in that book, if Nick recalled correctly, the novel's female protagonist had been manipulated and prepared for her satanic conception ritual by a demonic cult of sex-crazed witches and warlocks wearing dark robes and little else. Ultimately, Nick's female protagonist (whose name he couldn't remember) had been initiated into the cult herself. So why wouldn't Jacinta have been initiated, too, if the novel itself had somehow come to life?

It might also explain Jacinta possessing her own lucky goat's foot. The one she claimed to have brought along with her as her own gift to the Baron. The love charm Nick assumed she'd gifted in return for Rochlain's own, both of which were evidently working like dreams. But what if they weren't supernatural love charms at all? What if it was just the one goat's foot that Rochlain had initially intended to offload on to Nick, but which Nick had refused to accept, causing the Baron to somehow pass it on to Jacinta without Nick seeing? And what if the goat's foot wasn't intended to arouse Jacinta's latent passion for Rochlain at all, but to achieve some other unknown sinister purpose instead?

It could all be some dark design intended for Nick alone, that the Baron hoped to achieve by enlisting the aid of Nick's wife. Was Jacinta herself part of this ominous satanic conspiracy?

As if to fan the flames of Nick's swiftly raging suspicions, Jacinta went back to snarling and hissing down the phone to the Baron.

Nick had had enough. Easing his ear away from the wooden panel, he removed the small weevil that had crawled in despite his best efforts to prevent it and wrenched open Jacinta's door.

Too late. His wife had already placed the phone back on its cradle and was busy painting her nails.

'Who the hell were you talking to in backwards, upside-down, medieval Latin, Jacinta? And I do mean "who the *hell*".'

'That was just a crossed line,' Jacinta replied, nonchalantly. 'Someone in the Vatican, I think.'

Damn it, if his wife didn't have an answer for everything. And, Nick had to admit, a crossed line with someone phoning from the Vatican itself was highly plausible.

'Oh, you found my weevil,' Jacinta said, rising from the bed to take the small insect from Nick's hand.

'You *know* this weevil?' Nick said, incredulous.

'Of course I do. He's my pet weevil. I call him Rochey Wochey.'

THE BLACK STEEPLE

That was highly plausible, too. But Nick couldn't help thinking that he was being played here. For, if he remembered correctly, the weevil had crawled into his ear while Jacinta was still on the phone. So if she'd been talking specifically to the weevil itself, surely she'd have noticed that it had crawled out of sight through a hole in the door and into Nick's ear while she'd been speaking to it, and would have realised it was no longer listening to her at all. And, Nick knew from bitter experience, Jacinta would *never* have stood for anyone not listening to her.

Unless the weevil's diminutive size meant that she'd lost sight of the creature quite naturally and had continued to speak to it regardless. Dammit, Nick just couldn't be sure. And he guessed Jacinta knew that too. But one thing *was* certain. Jacinta owned a pet weevil she'd never once told him about. A pet weevil Nick now suspected was nothing less than a *witch's familiar* . . .

'Well, I'm not paying for the weevil's feed as well,' said Nick. 'If you want that thing nourished, *you* go get a job.'

'What are you blathering on about?' Jacinta said, scornful. 'It gets all its sustenance from me.'

What the hell? Was Jacinta somehow telling Nick, in so many words, that his own wife *suckled a weevil*?

'I share my food with it,' she said, deliberately confusing the issue *again*. The only way Nick could be sure about this potential wife-based weevil-suckling would be to see whether Jacinta bore the Weevil's Mark somewhere on her naked body. And his chances of locating that were nigh-on impossible.

Jacinta knew *that* too, he realised. Dammit, she was playing him, alright. Toying with him. Needling at him like the damned weevil itself, which had so nearly penetrated the inside of his own brain just moments before.

'Fancy a cat scratch, for old time's sake?' Jacinta murmured coyly, rolling her body across the bed in his direction.

'No way, Jacinta. I'm off to work,' Nick replied coldly, turning abruptly in the direction of the door. After all, his novel wouldn't write itself. Then, just as suddenly, he turned back to face her. 'What happened to that lucky goat's foot of yours?' he asked.

If the thing was a love potion, and *had* been intended for him, then it certainly wasn't working with Jacinta.

'Oh, I gave that to the Baron,' she said, rolling back over the bed to gaze yearningly at the phone.

'Have a fun night,' Nick said, and left.

★

He spent the rest of the evening absorbing *The Big Bumper Book of Black Magic* that Samantha the female librarian had lent him back at the library. For if his own novel *The Stalkwich Blasphemy* had indeed escaped into reality, then perhaps he could write another story based around that and the current strange events going on in Silth, which would then bring the unfolding real-life events to a happy conclusion where Good ultimately triumphed over Evil. Maybe by researching what had happened here in Silth more fully, Nick could somehow beat those visions back into his head, trapping them once again on the printed page.

And *The Big Bumper Book of Black Magic* was indeed full of juicy plot potential. As Samantha the female librarian had advised, there was an entire section devoted to Silth and the historic Final Battle fought by Harland Steen and his Puritanical Brethren against the Forces of Evil and Darkness. According to *The Big Bumper Book of Black Magic*, Nick's likely ancestor, Harland Steen, had formed a Holy Brethren to wage war against a dark, satanic order dedicated to the worship of the Hornéd One, ruled by a former lapsed priest known to his followers as Canon LeRoche.

A stab of recognition pierced Nick's memory. Didn't that name sound ever so slightly like the name *Baron Rochlain*?

THE BLACK STEEPLE

It did, Nick decided. So what were the chances that a God-fearing Puritan firebrand from Stalkford's distant past shared the self-same surname as Nick's own, when, at the very same time, Steen's arch-rival, a satanic Black Magician known as Canon LeRoche, *also* shared a near-identical name with that of Baron Rochlain, Nick's *own* immediate love-rival?

Something didn't add up. Despite things beginning to add up.

Something strange was going on here in Silth, as Nick had suspected for some time now (and which doesn't really bear repeating from this point on). Something to do with both a satanic coven conducting human sacrifices that Nick periodically glimpsed taking place before the steps of a terrifying Black Steeple, and the apparent history of the town itself, whose historic forefathers bore eerily similar names to its modern-day inhabitants, who were themselves acting in ways that might suggest they were an intrinsic part of a still-existent coven.

Nick read on. Luckily, someone in the past, evidently one of Harland's Brethren, had seen fit to take down minutes from a key meeting that had taken place several days prior to the Brethren setting out for battle against LeRoche's demonic hordes. Nick read through them, noting with relief that someone slightly cleverer than the usual seventeenth-century simpleton had changed all the erroneous 'F's back to 'S's, meaning it was so much easier to understand:

And lo, Brother Devlin Sayeth unto Steen, 'Penny for your thoughts, Harland Steen?'

And Harland Steen spake thus:

'Canon LeRoche is a SATANIST, and his clergymen a secret order of Black Magicians. We must form a Brethren, known from this day forth as THE BRETHREN, charged by God with bringing Light into Darkness. Order unto Chaos. Together we must standeth. Together we must fighteth. Together we must ventureth forth-eth into Siltheth, the Kingdom of Shadow, and purgeth Darkest Evil from the aforesaideth land. Plus all goats that we findeth.'

'Goats?' speaketh uppeth Brother Devlin. 'For what reason must we destroyeth all goats?'

'Becauseth Goats doth nibbleth my Capotain, Brother Devlin. They are the Devil's herd ...'

Nick shuddered. Then *that* explained Nick's most recent vision. Harland Steen had formed his Brethren to wage a Holy War against the satanic forces of Canon LeRoche, and had been burned to death in the process.

For Evil, according to *The Big Bumper Book of Black Magic*, had ultimately triumphed.

And if that was true, Nick realised, Ultimate Evil must still be kicking around somewhere, right here in Silth. Meaning it was more imperative than ever for Nick to find it.

It didn't take long.

For, as Nick was mulling over these very thoughts, a familiar orange glow appeared through a gap in his drawn curtains. Coming again, he suspected, from the distant valley plain beyond the house. The exact same spot where Nick had previously witnessed those eerie visions of the Black Steeple.

Then he heard chanting.

Another human sacrifice!

Nick tossed *The Big Bumper Book of Black Magic* on to his duvet and raced from the room, pausing briefly to check in on Duncan, concerned in case his son was becoming disturbed by the frightening noises coming through the windows.

But Duncan was no longer in his room ...

'Duncan?' Nick yelled out loud. '*Duncan!*'

Hell, Duncan must have snuck out on his own again. On the very night that a human sacrifice was taking place in their own backyard!

And Nick knew all too well that if Duncan accidentally stumbled upon a secret occult ceremony, there was no telling what this order of Black Magicians might do to him. No doubt they'd be pissed off at the interruption, for one thing. But they'd also know that their illegal activities had been discovered, and any hope Nick had of exposing a satanic conspiracy would be ruined forever as the group immediately went into hiding.

Nick had to move fast. Racing along the corridor of the cabin, he hammered his fist on Jacinta's door.

'Wake up, Jacinta! Duncan's got out again, plus there's a human sacrifice going on outside!'

He didn't catch her reply, if there had even been one, and had to hope she'd wake groggily from sleep and see the glow of the flames herself. Right now, Nick had to locate his son.

But Duncan was nowhere to be found. The backyard of the house was empty, and out here in the dead of night, the sound of chanting was growing even louder.

Nick tried not to panic. But he knew that if Duncan had escaped from the house, he would have heard the chanting, too, and wandered over to the site in his dumb innocence to see what all the commotion was about.

Nick ran past the teetering shite-mound that he still hadn't found time to flame, noting that Jacinta had done nothing whatsoever about igniting the damned thing herself. Too bad if it fell over in the night and crushed her to death. At least he and Duncan would be out.

But not yet safe, he reflected, grimly. *Not by a long shot.*

Propelling himself up the side of the rocky ridge, he looked out anxiously over the valley plain.

There, lit up once again by that giant flaming pyre, stood the Black Steeple. And before it, chanting as one around the flames in their satanic circle, danced the same hooded worshippers.

Nick raced down the far side of the ridge through stunted, blackened trees towards the valley floor, whipping out the binoculars from his dressing-gown pocket once again.

As he struggled to focus the lenses, Nick heard a terrifying sound. That chanting he was hearing, those strange sounds this secret coven were uttering as they danced around that distant flaming pyre – it was *Latin*, Nick realised. *Medieval Latin*. But not only that. These worshippers were chanting it *backwards*. Backwards ... *and upside down*.

Nick's worst suspicions were confirmed. As he finally settled the focus on the binoculars' lenses, he saw, emerging from the door of the Black Steeple itself, the same gathering of black-and-purple-robed priests, bearing a human sacrifice-to-be upon a vast metal platter. Yet there were more of them this time, Nick noticed. Many more. As many as twenty coven priests, struggling to support the weight of the figure they'd tied, still struggling against its bonds, on top of the metal plate.

A figure, Nick saw now, that was not a scantily clad woman as he'd previously suspected, but instead a gigantic man-baby.

Duncan!

They were going to sacrifice Duncan!

Frantically, Nick scanned the faces of the robed and hooded worshippers. But it was useless – their identities were completely concealed by those masks and their heavy satanic hoods. Except for one figure, that was, who stepped outside the dancing throng for a brief moment and drew back, almost deliberately, the hood covering her head.

Yes, it was indeed a *her*, Nick confirmed. And a truly evil *her* at that. For the woman facing outwards now, directing her gaze almost deliberately in his direction, as if she knew Nick himself must be out there watching ...

... was *Jacinta*.

THE BLACK STEEPLE

'Bang out of order!' Nick yelled. And, dammit, it was. Nick's own wife sacrificing the life of her hellspawn son to appease some devilish sect so that she could shack up with its chief satanic priest.

Well, not on Nick Steen's watch.

With adrenaline coursing through his veins, Nick sprinted forwards across the plain, yanking his .44 revolver from his other dressing-gown pocket and immediately snapping off a barrelful of rounds in the direction of the satanic clan.

But as he neared them, preparing to tear each priest a new one, he suddenly found he was punching and kicking at nothing but air.

For the priests, the Black Steeple, the blazing pyre, Jacinta herself, and Nick's beloved Duncan, were no more.

They'd vanished as one. Completely, into thin air.

Had it been merely another vision? Nick was relieved to think that the worst horror he could possibly have imagined might well have passed just as suddenly as it had appeared, in the manner of a bad nightmare.

But the horror *wasn't* over. Because when Nick got back to the house moments later, Duncan's room was still empty.

And Jacinta, like her missing son, was nowhere to be found.

CHAPTER EIGHT

Luckily, the female librarian known as Samantha was working late.

'I need that goddamn drink,' was all Nick had to say, and before he knew it they were both going at it like pile-drivers on a dual carriageway halfway along the horrotica aisle.

It was like no nookie Nick had ever known: him reading passages from his books aloud while Samantha shushed him loudly and firmly between chapters. Dammit, this was Nick Steen's kink. What kind of sick pervert read out loud in a public library?

Nick Steen did, that's who.

'*I said, ssh!*' bellowed Samantha. 'Or I'll rescind your library membership.'

'Fine! Then rescind it, Samantha,' Nick howled ecstatically between thrusts. 'Because I'm only going to read out loud in your library again, despite your strict instruction expressly forbidding me from doing so. If you wish me to stop reading out loud in your library, then I suggest you rebuke me even more sternly than before.'

And damn it, if this bespectacled she-castigator didn't do just that, shushing Nick over and over as he defiantly selected novel after novel from a nearby shelf, beginning with his splatterpunk classic *The Slaughterton Hacksaw Mangling*, before moving on immediately to his horrotic folk-horror masterpiece *Streaky Cock-a-Leekie*. But as Nick commenced reading aloud from this particular tome, Samantha abandoned the mere shushing of Nick and instead asset-batted the book clean out of his hands before issuing him with a major fine.

The sternly reprimanded author bellowed in ecstasy, for this erotic bodily slam-to over a blatant infraction of the library's official regulations was so wrong it *had* to be right.

'Now treat me like your microfilm reader,' Nick rasped, and immediately Samantha was all over his bodily mechanics, spooling his personal reels upwards, downwards, sideways and all around.

'Wait,' panted Samantha, spooling him in the opposite direction, 'I think I might have finally found what it is that I'm looking for.'

'Negative, Samantha,' Nick panted back. 'You need to keep spooling. Because what you're searching for is currently still hidden away somewhere.'

Samantha spooled him some more. 'I can feel I'm getting near it, though,' she gasped.

'No, you're on the wrong page, Samantha the female librarian,' panted Nick, beginning to feel dizzy from all the spooling. 'So you'd best keep spooling.'

'I must be getting close now,' hollered Samantha, as she spooled Nick even more firmly than before.

'Negative, you're looking at the wrong information entirely,' sighed Nick, wondering whether they might actually have to plump for a different document reel in around twenty minutes or so.

'I *know* this is the right one,' growled the librarian, huskily. 'Hold on tight, Nick, because I'm going to start spooling you like there's no tomorrow.'

'Then spool me, Samantha,' yelled Nick. 'Spool me like you've never spooled before.'

'I'm getting closer now,' Samantha panted five minutes later.

'To be honest, you're still some way off,' Nick gasped, starting to worry about the pains in his chest. 'Just keep spooling at your leisure and I'm sure you'll stumble on the right page eventually.'

'What about if I do *this*?' Samantha said unexpectedly, inserting a fresh spool of film into Nick's metaphorical slot-tray without warning.

'That's the ticket!' Nick howled, his enjoyment topped only by a final prolonged vocal shushing from Samantha.

Moments later, they were slowly declamping themselves, lighting each other's cigarettes and retracting Nick's fourth fine.

'If I find you reading out loud in my horrotica aisle again, Mister Steen,' warned Samantha, breathily, 'I may have to consider banning you from my library *permanently*.'

'I don't think you'd do that,' said Nick, winking playfully at her.

The female librarian rolled back on top of him. 'Wouldn't I?'

Two further intense microfilm searches later, one of them abandoned midway through, they were once again lighting cigarettes, Nick now having accrued multiple bans, with several of his books removed from the shelves and placed oh-so-teasingly on the nearby 'for sale' trolley. He was currently still a library member, but only just.

'I needed that, you hot fox,' said Nick.

'Me too,' Samantha said. 'It gets so dull out here, all alone in this small, backward town.'

'With respect, that's *your* problem,' said Nick. 'I was in the middle of telling you about *my* problem.'

'Sorry, Nick,' Samantha whispered, kissing his world-weary cheek tenderly. 'That was rude of me. I should have remembered that now we're both physically spent, the time for dominating your supposed free will in a public library is over. Go ahead. Tell me about *your* problem.'

'It's technically problem*s*, so may take a while.'

'I promise I won't shush you.'

'That's what I wanted to hear – until later on, maybe,' Nick quipped, winking playfully at her again and wondering if they might be able to squeeze in one more go on his metaphorical microfilm

THE BLACK STEEPLE

reader before heading home. But it was important to get things off his chest, he decided. Samantha was currently the only person in Silth he could potentially trust, and although Nick generally relied on his own head to solve his problems, he'd once heard someone say that two heads were better than one. And for that reason, Nick elected to tell Samantha everything.

He told her about his ailing marriage to Jacinta, and Society's cruel mistreatment of their son of a Cosmic God Duncan; he told her of Baron Rochlain's invitation for Nick to reside here in Silth while writing his new book, which Nick had hoped might seal up once and for all the demons currently escaping from the interior of his own head. He explained the strange and sudden appearance of the mysterious Black Steeple he'd glimpsed upon arriving here in Silth. He described the self-same Steeple's mysterious subsequent disappearance, followed by its strange and sudden second appearance, this time sporting signs of an apparent human sacrifice taking place on the very steps of the mysterious Black Steeple itself, glimpsed briefly before the mysterious Black Steeple's second subsequent disappearance.

He detailed his strange discovery of the actual remains of the previously disappeared Black Steeple prior to its third mysterious reappearance and subsequent additional disappearance (the very same Black Steeple now sporting signs of the apparent sacrifice of Nick's very own son of a Cosmic God Duncan), which themselves revealed physical evidence of the historic defeat of seventeenth-century Puritan firebrand Harland Steen, whom Nick suspected was an actual family ancestor, owing to Nick possessing an uncanny physical likeness to the photograph of Harland Steen that he'd located in the microfilm reader earlier on that very day. He told her about Harland Steen's historic involvement in a climactic Final Battle between the Forces of both Good and Evil, ending in a draw that necessitated a second Final Battle fought 'twixt the Forces of Light and Darkness, resulting ultimately in the deaths of Harland Steen and his religious Brethren, known to their followers simply as The Brethren. He explained his wife Jacinta's burgeoning love affair with the mysterious Baron Rochlain and possible joining of a satanic coven that may or may not be led by her chosen paramour. He spoke of the strange lucky goats' feet that may or may not be supernatural love charms; of Duncan's regrettable but wholly understandable proclivity for biting the heads off animals; and of the strange and mysterious abduction of both Jacinta and the aforesaid adopted son of a Cosmic God Duncan by the self-same satanic coven Nick had mentioned earlier, which occurred shortly before the fourth mysterious reappearance and additional subsequent disappearance of the aforesaid mysterious Black Steeple, which Nick didn't actually learn about until both during and after its aforesaid additional subsequent disappearance.

'To be honest, Samantha, I feel like I'm going out of my mind.'

'My poor Nicky Wick.' Samantha purred, stroking him like a big, soft lion.

'Hands off. That really irritates. The thing is, Samantha, I have no idea where Duncan is right now. He may well be dead, for all I know. I think that's unlikely, given he's the swiftly expanding son of a cosmic entity, but you never know. That demonic coven I uncovered looked like they knew exactly what they were doing.'

Samantha, who by this stage had strapped her asset-pack back on, reached in and removed a small bottle of pills from its cleavage canyon.

'Here,' she said, handing them over. 'Take a few of these.'

Nick sized up the bottle of small red capsules in his hands. 'What are they?'

'Anti-madness pills,' said Samantha. 'They'll cure you of all these hallucinations you've been suffering from. I'm convinced you're imagining all this, Nick, and that Duncan has simply wandered off again, as Duncan is wont to do.'

THE BLACK STEEPLE

Maybe she's right, Nick thought. *Maybe I am going mad.*

And wandering off was probably exactly what Duncan had gone and wonted to have done.

'I was saving those anti-madness pills for myself,' continued Samantha, 'but I don't think I'll be needing them anymore, Nick. For I'm no longer going mad all alone out here in this remote desert town of Silth. Because I've finally found what I've been yearning for. Right here, halfway up the horrotica aisle.'

'Me too,' said Nick. And now that he'd gotten to know Samantha more fully, he was tempted to suggest they move on to the actual microfilm reader for future sessions, sensing that together they might soon be approaching that fabled sexually ecstatic mystical state known only as Horroticavana. As long as no over-exuberant arse-shunt broke either of the two spooling knobs.

'Why don't you take one of those anti-madness pills right now?' Samantha said, twisting the top from the pill bottle beside him and selecting one of the red capsules between her fingernails. She leaned forward, dangling it close to Nick's lips. 'Just one little anti-madness pill,' she said, 'and all my little Nicky Wick's worries will be over. *For ever.*'

Why not? thought Nick.

Maybe by taking the anti-madness pill as Samantha advised, he'd at least stop worrying about them both arse-breaking the microfilm reader. That would allow him to concentrate his full mental energies on finding Duncan.

As Nick took the tablet in his hands and prepared to swallow it whole, he suddenly caught sight of a strange figure watching him from the far side of the library.

'That old man from earlier,' Nick said, shoving Samantha from his lap and rising to his feet. 'How dare you sit there in the dark, spying on our private throes of public passion!'

But as Nick strode towards the figure, he realised it wasn't the old man at all. For this particular figure, Nick now observed, was wearing a dark robe, its head concealed almost entirely under the folds of a heavy scarlet hood.

'*The Watcher . . .*' said Nick, deciding to *officially* name the mysterious figure who'd been watching him ever since he'd arrived here in Silth, having referred to him unofficially as 'the Watcher' numerous times. Then he realised this was the one element of his experiences in Silth that he'd neglected to tell Samantha anything about. Why exactly he'd neglected to tell her, Nick wasn't sure. But whatever subconscious reasoning his mind had independently arrived at, Nick had taken about all the damned watching he was prepared to endure.

'Who the hell are you?' he yelled, pulling on his black leather blouson.

The stranger's sleeves rose slowly upwards, exposing human hands within, which then pulled back its hood.

A thick mane of wavy black hair revealed itself, perfectly coiffured. The face below appeared somewhat weathered, yet strangely youthful for what Nick now knew to be an extremely elderly man. For he'd seen that very same face before.

'My name,' the figure intoned, in a deep and fruity tone, 'is Brother Devlin.'

'*Brother Devlin . . .*' Nick repeated, speaking the name aloud, but less fruitily than Devlin himself had just done. 'You're one of the priests from that strange, mysterious vision I had of a Final Battle 'twixt Light and Darkness . . . One of the Brethren who fought alongside Harland Steen *over three hundred years ago.*'

'The same,' said Devlin. 'And we need to talk, you and I.'

Too right we need to talk, thought Nick. *About how the hell a three-hundred-year-old man wanders around like he's still in his mid-forties — and, furthermore, gets his kicks from spying on two young lovers in the throes of erotic microfilm-reader-related passion.*

'*Alone,*' Devlin added.

THE BLACK STEEPLE

Nick called back over his shoulder, his eyes still trained on the seemingly time-defying priest. 'Samantha, can you make yourself scarce, please? We're discussing men's business.'

'But I work here, Nick,' Samantha replied.

Dammit, thought Nick. *She's right.*

Samantha *did* work here.

'Fine,' said Nick, forced to think on his feet. 'Then *we'll* go somewhere instead.'

And with that, he and Devlin went somewhere instead.

CHAPTER NINE

'I am a Wanderer,' boomed Devlin, sitting beside Nick in adjoining confessional boxes. Although this wasn't technically a confession, Nick knew that in here there would be fewer potential prying eyes listening in.

'Then you're not the Watcher after all?'

'I *am* the Watcher.'

'But you're also the Wanderer?' said Nick, attempting to clarify a conversation that had already become confusing.

'I am not the Wanderer. I am a Wanderer.'

Nick was still confused. 'Run that past me again.'

'I am not *the* Wanderer. I am *a* Wanderer.'

'Right ... And you're also a Watcher?'

'I am *not* a Watcher. I am *the* Watcher.'

'So you're *the* Watcher and *a* Wanderer?'

'Correct. Not *a* Watcher or *the* Wanderer. I am *a* Wanderer and *the* Watcher.'

'*The* Watcher, plus *a* Wanderer,' said Nick. 'And not the other way round.'

'Correct.'

'So, what *is* a wanderer?'

'*Wanderer*. The "W" is capitalised.'

Nick sighed, correcting himself. 'So, what *is* a Wanderer?'

'A Wanderer doth Wander the Earth, cursed never to die. Thusly I Wander ... yet also I *watch*.'

THE BLACK STEEPLE

'I'd personally argue that you're more of a Watcher than a Wanderer,' said Nick, grimly aware that this hooded man had been secretly observing everything Nick had been doing since he arrived here in Silth, including all that physical horrotica-play with Samantha and the microfilm reader.

'It's *the* Watcher,' corrected Devlin, again.

'Whatever.' Nick wasn't even sure he could trust this guy. After all, Devlin looked just like one of those Black Magicians he'd glimpsed in those strange and terrifying visions he'd been having. The ones dancing madly around the sinister Black Steeple in their red robes. 'And you say you were cursed?'

Brother Devlin's voice grew sterner in tone, as if angered still by some unresolved, centuries-old slight. 'By that most foul and dreaded demon-incarnate, Canon LeRoche. 'Tis he who placed this curse upon my soul, to Wander for all eternity through This Bursted Earth.'

This Bursted Earth ... Now that was a repeated phrase Nick could get behind. For was it not uncannily accurate, with the Earth itself all bursted now, ever since that day Nick's brain had also been bursted? And hadn't Nick's bursted brain in turn altered and bursted the very fabric of a pre-Bursted Earth? And yet Devlin seemed to be speaking of a Bursted Earth *before* Nick's time. A pre-existing, pre-Bursted-Earth, Bursted Earth. Perhaps that, too, was merely a symptom of Nick's own personal Bursted Earth come to terrifying life. A former fictional fragment of Nick's own Earth Burstings that, having bursted out into the Earth via Nick's bursting brain, had itself created an earlier Earth Bursting previously only existing as a fictitious Bursted Earth that had subsequently been incarnated as a real-life Bursted Earth, now bursted in the past and existing separately as some strange historical future echo of Nick's own current Bursted Earth. Specifically, *This* Bursted Earth.

Whatever the reality was, Nick decided to make a note of the phrase, should he ever choose to publish an account of his experiences one day in the far future, or potentially in some other plane of reality.*

'It all began with my Dabbling,' Devlin began.

'Your Dabbling?'

'My Dabbling in the Dark Arts. I was a Dark Arts Dabbler.'

'I thought you were one of the Brethren?'

'That came later. Before then, I Dabbled.'

'Can I just double-check that all these "Dabbles" are capitalised?'

'They are indeed.'

'Fine. Please continue.'

''Twas a convent of nuns out on a daytrip to see our new pulpit. You know how it goes. A vat of vestry wine, the odd joke about the world turn'd upside down, then my cassock doth turn'd upside down, and her habit, too. Before I knew it, my path to corruption, and hers, was assured. Thus, did I Dabble.

''Twas Harland Steen who finally saved me from my damnéd Dabbling. He who personally plucked me forth from Satan's flaps.'

Nick considered asking Devlin to elaborate, then decided otherwise. 'And Harland was my ancestor, right?'

'*Is* your ancestor.'

'*Is?*' repeated Nick, confused again. What was Devlin implying? That Harland Steen was somehow still alive?

'All will be revealed in time. Know for now that I fought alongside Harland Steen through both Holy Wars. And was with him at The End.'

'That bit where you all got burned?' said Nick, recalling his sinister vision.

Devlin nodded solemnly. 'We had marched out as one upon that morn to do battle with the Hordes of Satan on the very steps of his

---

* Which you, the reader, are currently living in. I, meanwhile, am inhabiting seven more. GM

THE BLACK STEEPLE

earthly Kingdom. That castle of shadow, the Black Steeple itself, where Dark Arts are practised, more foul and corrupt than any earthly magic.'

'Except for Paul Daniels, maybe,' quipped Nick, even though he knew the joke didn't completely work. For Paul Daniels' magic wasn't technically *foul*, as such. Merely infuriating. Largely because of Paul Daniels' imposing and relentlessly aggravating personality, but also because the miniature Yorkshireman stuck largely to basic card tricks and mere sleight of hand. Nick himself preferred to watch women in bikinis being sawn in two or folded into five sections via multi-flapped glitter-covered boxes – that was proper magic. Or some bouffanted mesmerist starting to drown while struggling to extricate himself from multiple padlocks in a suspended flooded tank. That kind of magic Nick had time for. But Paul Daniels? No fucking way.

'After many trials and tribulations,' continued Devlin, ignoring Nick's on-reflection-absolutely-hilarious Paul Daniels quip, 'we fought to the death upon those dreaded black steps. Until finally, with both defeat and victory poised in the balance, my dreaded Dabbling returned.'

'You mean you Dabbled *again*?'

'I am afraid so. At the very moment Harland Steen was preparing to floor Canon LeRoche with a right frontal jab, having first feinted with his left. It was then that I received a whisper in my right ear from someone calling himself the Dark One. Instructing me to put temptation in Harland Steen's way. And thusly compelled, I found myself summoning three devilish female harlots from the outer rings of Hell to tempt Harland Steen from his appointed task and lure him towards a bodily and spiritual *transgression* . . .'

Nick smiled to himself. Then his holier-than-thou relative had in reality been as much of a hot-blooded, sexually potent virile male as Nick was.

'And did he succumb?' Nick asked, playfully.

'In mind, if not in body. As Harland's thoughts became temporarily impure, distracting him from the task at hand, his mortal frame, and that of his loyal Brethren, were overcome by LeRoche's forces and burned alive at the stake upon the steps of that accursèd Black Steeple. Thus did both the Forces of Evil and Darkness triumph. And the Final, *Final* Battle was lost. For my part in bringing about Harland Steen's destruction, I was spared my own eternal damnation in Hell and granted eternal existence on this mortal plane instead. Cursed to Wander This Bursted Earth for millennia to come, alone and friendless, dressed in the scarlet robes of my Dabbling days to remind me of my sins.'

Insane, thought Nick. *This man's insane.*

'Just now you said Harland Steen *is* my ancestor, rather than *was* my ancestor. How come, if he was burned at the stake?'

'Though his mind succumbed to the advances of those summoned harlots, his mortal body stood firm.'

'I'll bet it did.'

'And for that reason alone, Harland Steen's soul was not cast into Hell, like those of his fellow Brethren, but instead transported by God to the Land of Eternal Lady Limbo, where it hath doth resideth ever since. There, Harland Steen hath been battling constant temptation, with those same three harlots I doth summoned.'

'I can think of *worse* problems,' Nick quipped, wondering how centuries of isolation in the Land of Eternal Lady Limbo could possibly be deemed some sort of punishment. Then he swiftly buried the thought. Jeez, what was wrong with him today? He ought to be obsessed with the search for his missing son of a Cosmic Elder God, yet in the short space of time since Duncan had vanished, Nick had already chalked up three microfilm sessions with Samantha, plus multiple shushing bouts, and was currently fixating himself on the horrotic connotations of his distant ancestor's moral plight in the Eternal Land of Lady Limbo.

THE BLACK STEEPLE

'Those "worse problems" now lie before us, Nick Steen. For with Harland out of the way, the Forces of Evil and Darkness continue to reign triumphant.'

'Meaning, I presume, that Silth has been run by his evil coven of followers ever since?'

'Wrong. By LeRoche *himself.*'

'By LeRoche *himself*? But surely the guy's long dead?'

Devlin shook his head. 'He is a Wanderer, like myself. For centuries, Canon LeRoche has used the blood and souls of innocent mortals to rejuvenate his ageing body.'

'*Baron Rochlain* . . .' stammered Nick, once again struck by the similarity in those names . . .

'The same,' Devlin replied, confirming Nick's suspicion. 'He and Canon LeRoche are as one.'

'You mean they're the same man?'

Devlin nodded, grimly. 'Yet they will not be a *man* for much longer.'

What the hell was going on here? thought Nick. Things were getting crazier by the sentence.

'Not be a man?'

'Not be *remotely* a man. For Canon LeRoche, also Baron Rochlain, intends to turn himself into . . .'

'Into what?' gasped Nick, hardly able to contain his mounting fear.

'The Goat of Silth.'

'*The Goat of Silth*?'

'The Goat of Silth.'

'What's the Goat of Silth?'

'It's a Goat,' explained Devlin, 'of Silth. The head of the Dark One's blasphemous herd. A terrifying sex-crazed Man-Goat that gorges on millet and bits of people's clothing until the End of Time. No longer will LeRoche require souls of innocents to feed his immortality, for he will soon rule the town of Silth *forever*. As a demonic Goat.'

Finally, things were starting to make terrifying sense. That strange goat's foot Rochlain had attempted to give him. And the second goat's foot Jacinta had told Nick she was gifting the Baron in return. Perhaps they were not simple love charms, but rather more powerful totems of some crazed religious cult devoted to turning their demonic leader into a massive, randy goat.

'I must be going mad,' said Nick, his sanity no longer quite capable of taking in all these mysterious witchy shenanigans. 'Yeah, maybe I've flipped. I'd best take some of Samantha's anti-madness pills, after all.'

Nick removed the bottle from his blouson pocket, twisted off the lid and tipped a handful of bright red capsules into his waiting palm.

'Wait!' snapped Devlin, thrusting his arm through the veil of gauze separating them to grip Nick's own.

That motion, and the sudden realisation that Devlin had just violated the sacred anonymity of the confessional box, had just saved Nick's life.

'Hand me that bottle,' said Devlin.

Nick obliged, transferring Samantha's pill jar to him through the confessional hatch.

'Look,' said Devlin, peeling off the bottle's label. As the one marked '*Anti-Madness Pills*' fell away, Nick's eyes took in a second label concealed beneath it. One that bore an entirely different name.

'*Instant Death Pills*,' read Nick, aloud.

'Manufactured,' said Devlin, scratching away a splotch of congealed blood to uncover the pharmacy address, 'at Baron Rochlain's very own Masonic Lodge.'

'*Demonic* Lodge, you mean,' quipped Nick.

Devlin laughed loudly, then immediately fell silent. 'Samantha the female librarian is one of *them*, Nick,' he said at length. 'One of the devilish coven now ruling Silth.' He extended a pointed finger towards Nick's chest. 'That lucky goat's foot in your breast pocket . . .'

THE BLACK STEEPLE

'There's no lucky goat's foot in my breast pocket,' huffed Nick emphatically.

'Oh, yes there is. *There!*'

Nick reached up to where Devlin was pointing and felt around inside his breast pocket. Sure enough, he felt a small object buried inside. Drawing it out, he shook his head in total disbelief.

He was looking at a hairy goat's foot.

'I had no idea,' he gasped, incredulous.

'Placed there by your wife Jacinta, no doubt, in order to bring you and Samantha the female librarian together.'

'Believe me, I wouldn't need a goat's foot for that.'

'But Samantha did. Did you not think it strange that a woman in her early thirties would throw herself at you, a heavy meat-eater in your late forties, the moment you entered a public library? Even though she was part of a conspiracy to destroy you, she would naturally have required an extremely potent aphrodisiac. The goat's foot, I'm afraid, was working on *her.*'

'Bullshit,' said Nick. No one needed a goat's foot to get the hots for Nick Steen, goddammit. Samantha was human, after all. Even if she *was* admittedly a human who was now potentially barely human.

'That's how LeRoche brought you both together, Nick. No doubt your wife concocted some story that the goat's foot was hers.'

'She did indeed,' muttered Nick, shamefaced. 'And she must have placed it in my breast pocket when I wasn't looking.'

Suddenly, it hit Nick like a sledgehammer blow. *The weevil* ... Rochey Wochey, Jacinta's suckling weevil. The damned thing must have popped the goat's foot into his breast pocket when Nick wasn't looking, before crawling back up into his ear.

But wait – hadn't the weevil crawled in *after* he'd met Samantha for the first time? Unless it had crawled in once before, of course. Maybe when Nick had been out, dragging Duncan's droppings over to the shite-mound. Maybe the weevil had tucked it inside a fresh shirt, knowing Nick would soon be removing yet another shite-stained one.

'I watched the whole thing play out before me from my shadowy corner in the library,' continued Devlin. 'You've been taken for a fool, Nick Steen. If you had consumed just one of those "instant death" pills ... Well, I don't have to tell you what would have happened to you.'

'What would have happened?' asked Nick.

Devlin glared at him.

'Just kidding,' Nick said, grinning from ear to ear. 'Thanks for saving my life, Devlin.'

'I wouldn't thank me quite yet, Nick. For our task is far from over. Remember, you can't trust *anyone* in Silth.'

Nick breathed a sigh of relief as Devlin tipped the contents of Samantha's pill jar on to the floor. Thanks to the five-second rule, they were no longer edible.

'Not least Jacinta,' said Nick. 'I guess she's been part of this coven for a while. That pinned effigy of me I found inside her sewing basket that one time I attempted to sew on a button. Then the Baron's unexpected invitation. All an elaborate ruse to get me up here. But why me, Devlin? Why do they want *me* dead?'

'In order for Baron Rochlain to turn himself into the Goat of Silth, he requires a human sacrifice.'

'Fine, then I'll just go back to Stalkford.'

'Not you, Nick Steen,' Devlin said. 'He needs the blood of one that hath consumed the entrails of a thousand wild animals.'

Duncan! thought Nick, suddenly panicking. *That's why they're after Duncan!*

'That's why they're after Duncan!' Nick yelled, suddenly frightened.

'Precisely. And, as Duncan's protector,' continued Devlin, 'as well as Harland Steen's living descendant, you alone can prevent your son's sacrifice and Canon LeRoche turning himself into the dreaded Goat of Silth. That is why they attempted to destroy you first. But now that you have escaped Samantha's instant death pills, they will move faster than ever to eradicate Duncan before you can intervene again.'

'But they've already *got* Duncan!' gasped Nick.

'That is why we must act *immediately*.'

'And do what, Devlin?'

'*Dabble*,' replied Devlin sombrely.

'Dabble? You mean . . . Dabble in the Dark Arts?'

Devlin leaned his head in towards the mesh separating him from Nick's booth. 'We must fuse your mind and soul.'

'Fuse?' replied Nick, aware that the word 'fuse' meant to 'merge', 'mingle', 'intermingle', 'join', 'blend', 'amalgamate', 'unite', 'synthesise' and 'compound', plus some more words meaning the same thing. 'Fuse them with what?'

'Another mind and soul,' Devlin continued. 'The mind and soul . . . of *Harland Steen*.'

CHAPTER TEN

'I believe it's down here,' said Devlin, as the two men descended a broken stairwell towards the lower crypt of a crumbling, disused church. 'Yes, this is the place.'

Together, they stepped into a darkened room. The crypt interior was small and cramped, lit by numerous black candles and upturned religious artefacts. In the middle of its cracked paved flooring, daubed in white paint across the broken tiles, was a five-pointed star within a circle.

'And you're absolutely sure this is a church?' said Nick.

'It's a deconsecrated chapel built around the same time as the Black Steeple,' explained Devlin. 'Known to the locals as "the Bad Chapel". It was originally going to be the scene of the original Final Battle between Good and Evil, but underwent some unexpected renovations after a blood leak, and both parties agreed the Black Steeple was more suitable for a climactic confrontation between warring religious ideologies.'

'So the Bad Chapel was ultimately let go?'

'The Hellflame Club used it occasionally for some minor diabolical Dabbling in the eighteenth century, but with no major spiritual altercations to speak of since then, it's fallen into a state of disrepair. But it is perfect for our purpose.'

'Which is?' asked Nick, somewhat wary of conducting any form of minor Dabbling in such a confined space. For if it came to punching up a demon or two, Nick's flexibility might well be severely restricted. And firing his gun off in a church, no matter how deconsecrated it might be, was a non-starter as far as Nick was concerned, given that the bullets might easily shatter the original stained-glass windows, which Nick had no intention of paying to replace.

'You must stand in the centre of the starred circle before you, so that we may transfer Harland Steen's soul into your own. Fuse them, so that your combined strengths can once more triumph against the Forces of Evil, Darkness and Chaos.'

'And Dabbling can do all that?'

'Indeed it can, for it will part the planes of existence and pluck out your ancestor from the Eternal Land of Lady Limbo.'

'What if he won't come?' Nick asked, concerned Harland might elect to stay in Limbo with his harlots. That's what Nick would choose to do, after all. If the alternative was rejoining battle with a bunch of goat-worshipping arseholes in capes, Nick would plump for the scantily clad rest-and-relaxation option every time.

'He will come. For it is either that or endure a never-ending battle against bodily temptation.'

'And what if he succumbs before we can reach him?' Nick was genuinely concerned. He couldn't believe *anyone* could hold off that long.

'If that happens, then Chaos will rule the Earth. The planes of reality will shut, and Harland Steen ...'

'Will finally get his end away?'

'The opposite. Should Harland succumb to bodily temptation, the Dark One will isolate him in an oubliette of eternal torment, and those harlots of his will instead transform into *harpies*.'

Sexy harpies wouldn't be so bad, surely? thought Nick.

After all, they could at least hover above your body and place less weight on your kidneys. Though on the other hand, they might well have devil-heads. Plus fangs, which would rule out at least one option.

'It is all a matter of time,' said Devlin.

A matter of time, repeated Nick, internally. Precisely what he'd been noticing a lot of, here in Silth. A matter of *time*. Or *shifting* time, to be more precise. Black Steeples and Black Magic rituals materialising and then dematerialising, before his very eyes.

'There's one thing I don't understand,' Nick said. 'Why does the Black Steeple keep appearing and disappearing? One minute it's visible, the next it's not visible – as opposed to *in*visible, if you catch my drift.'

'I do indeed catch your drift,' said Devlin. 'And the answer lies in the outcome of that last titanic Final Battle fought between the Forces of Light and Darkness.'

'You mean the Final, *Final* Battle?'

'Correct. The Final Battle after the initial Final Battle fought 'twixt the Forces of Good and Evil. For as I have described previously, that second Final Battle wasn't fully resolved in LeRoche's favour, with neither Light nor Darkness ultimately triumphing. As Harland Steen's soul continues to linger in the Eternal Land of Lady Limbo, so the presence of the Black Steeple itself hangs likewise in the balance, appearing then reappearing according to the fluctuating powers of the converging planes of Time. By undertaking the dark ritual before us, we will do two things. The first is gain access ourselves to the gates of the Eternal Land of Lady Limbo in order to rescue the soul of Harland Steen. The second is to tip the hand of balance in favour of LeRoche's forces once more, and fix the planes of Time in favour of the powers of Darkness, Evil and Chaos.'

'Isn't that dangerous?' asked Nick. 'Tipping the hand of balance in favour of LeRoche, Darkness, Evil and Chaos? Given we ultimately want to tip things in favour of Light, Goodness and Order?'

'Apocalyptic. But it is the only way we can ensure these forces share a mutual plane on which to fight. By Dabbling thus, we will freeze the planes of Time so that the Black Steeple stands once more before us. That way, we can ensure that the apocalyptic third Final Battle between the forces of Order and Chaos, plus the previous ones, can be refought.

'Only this time we will possess the combined strengths of *two* Steens on our side. Both Harland Steen and *Nick* Steen. Together, we will then destroy the Black Steeple utterly, along with Canon LeRoche and his demonic army of Chaos. For once our Dabbling ceremony is complete, the planes of Time will no longer be free to fluctuate.'

'Meaning whatever we summon up now will be here permanently?'

'Precisely. The Final, Final, *Final* Battle will be the last. There will not be a fourth.'

No Final, Final, Final, Final Battle, thought Nick, grimly.

Then this really was the final, final, *final* showdown.

'What about our Armies of Light, Good and Order, though?' asked Nick, warily. 'There'll only be three of us.'

Devlin smiled, indulgently. 'Fear not, my son. Once Harland Steen's soul hath been liberated, the spirits of his ghostly Brethren will appear alongside him. To fight with us, as Warriors of Light . . .'

Nick sighed. 'Then I guess it's almost time to permanently kiss goodbye to all earthly delights,' he said, mournfully.

'Fear not again, my son,' said Devlin, a mischievous glint in his eye. 'For Dabbling doth provide its own share of horrotic delights . . .'

And with that, he shoved Nick, blindly, into the circle.

★

'Do exactly as I say,' said Devlin.

Nick winced inwardly. He loathed doing what other people said, avoiding it as a rule. Sure, he'd reluctantly indulge instructions from a policeman, within reason. But a female policeman? No way. Nick hated authority in whatever form it took, preferring to get by in life on his terms alone.

And yet he had Duncan to think of now. And given that Nick had already stepped halfway over to the dark side himself, he'd have to accept that at this point in time, Devlin was in sole charge of freeing Nick's soul from the clutches of Baron Rochlain (Canon LeRoche in alternative form). But as soon as the good half of his soul had been fused with the good half of Harland Steen's soul, things would hopefully get back to normal and he, Nick Steen, with his long-dead ancestor merged fully inside him, could once more take charge of proceedings.

'Do what you have to, Devlin. But once I'm fused, I'm doing what the hell *I* need to do to rescue Duncan.'

'Keep *still*,' said Devlin, lighting a number of black candles within the edges of the circle, forming what Nick gradually perceived to be an internal pentagram. 'Do not step out of the circle.'

'It's more like a pentagram now.'

'Then do not step out of the pentagram that was recently a circle.'

'Why not?'

'Because you'll explode in a fucking hell-ball, that's why.'

'Ten-four,' said Nick. 'As long as that's the reason, and not just because you said so.'

As Devlin finished lighting the final black candle, the former priest began muttering some strange, mystical words. *Medieval Latin*, Nick realised, with a sense of familiar trepidation. He was speaking it backwards *and* upside down, just as Nick had feared he would. Yet there was a further element to it this time, Nick sensed. A quality he hadn't heard before when Jacinta had been speaking her own form of ancient Black Magic. For not only were these words of Devlin's spoken backwards and upside down, but they were also being spoken *widdershins* ... And if Nick knew anything at all about directions of flow, widdershins was the most evil of all possible directions. It was why those who followed the ways of Darkness were said to have taken the 'left-hand path'. Or *Satan's Way*. Counter-clockwise, in other words. An unholy direction. The *Devil's Direction*.

The direction of . . .

. . . *Widdershins*.

As soon as Devlin had muttered the first of his widdershinnsian phrases, the flames at the end of each candle flared suddenly and violently, burning taller and more fully. As Nick watched, they began to change colour, assuming stranger, more unnatural shades of red, blue, green and purple, plus some sort of see-through. And as the flames licked and danced in myriad hallucinatory shifting shapes and colours before Nick's goggling orbs, the music began.

A strange mixture of Gregorian chanting (again, backwards, upside down and widdershins) mixed with acid rock from the late sixties, Nick thought, replete with fuzz, phase and wah-wah pedal effects, off-beat drum rhythms and swirls of psychedelic organ.

As Nick looked and listened, his senses transfixed by the tall flames flickering around him, rising higher and higher towards the chapel ceiling, he began to perceive strange shapes moving within them.

Tall, hooded shapes shimmered back and forth, bearing strange black goblets in their hands. Some appeared to be squeezing blood into the goblets from what looked to Nick like pulsing chicken breasts. Then Nick thought he saw a satyr-like figure, blowing on a pipe – the pipe in question being the pipe of another satyr-like figure standing immediately to his right, who was in turn blowing the other satyr's pipe. Nick shuddered, blinking his eyes to rid himself of the sickening vision, but when he opened them again, things had got even worse. Now he saw what looked like a giant toad with its head coming out of its own arse, which appeared at the same time to belong to some form of multi-uddered cow. This collection of udders (thirty or more) were so apparently plentiful, they were being suckled by a multitude of what looked to Nick like tiny matchstick men.

As Nick blinked again, bleary-eyed beneath the strange hallucinatory glow of the phantasmagorical candle flames, he saw that some of the suckling figures were not in fact matchstick men, but tiny human effigies, their small woollen bodies pierced from head to toe with thick clusters of cruel-looking pins. To his horror, Nick recognised his own form among them. The same miniature effigy of himself he'd found in Jacinta's sewing basket. Nick watched in horror as this tiny cotton doppelgänger craned its neck upwards towards the multi-uddered cow and suckled greedily from what Nick presumed must be a metaphorical representation of the Dark One in half-toad, half-cow form.

'No!' yelled Nick. 'Devlin! Show me no more.'

'Keep your eyes open!' snapped Devlin. 'Or the planes of Time will not converge!'

Jeez, Nick would have to endure more of this. More of his pinned woollen effigy drinking from the tingling teats of a titanic toad-heifer. All he wanted to do was run screaming from this crazed pentagram that had formerly been a circle.

'Behold!' roared Devlin suddenly, as another strange vision began to supplant the former, appearing before Nick's eyes amid the swirling wall of multi-coloured flame.

Three figures, Nick counted, and as the heady psychedelic music swelled more sensually, Nick found his body doing likewise. For he finally began to recognise what, or rather who, were slowly manifesting themselves inside the flames.

In a matter of moments, three scantily clad females stood before Nick, dancing sensually – nay, *horrotically* – to the pulse of the swelling music. Displaying their bodily wares boldly. *Provocatively*. Beckoning Nick to step forward, towards them. Enticing him into the flames, so that all might be conjoined in what Nick presumed, and hoped, might be an immediate physical slam-dunk.

Instinctively, Nick took a step forward.

THE BLACK STEEPLE

'Stay where you are!' barked Devlin from somewhere Nick could no longer see. 'Do not step beyond the circle!'

'Pentagram!' Nick yelled, snapping himself out of his mental stupor.

Stepping back the inch or so he'd already traversed in his instinctive race towards the three sirens, Nick realised that Devlin's vocal error had probably just saved his life, rescuing him from what he now realised were those same three temptresses who had been besieging his dead ancestor endlessly day and night in that terrible Eternal Land of Lady Limbo.

For these were Harland's Harlots.

And as that name flashed once again through Nick's mind, the three women before him began to sing breathily, alluringly, their bodies swaying in perfect time with the swirling, psychedelic soundtrack, drawing Nick in once more through a provocative display of horrotic dancing. Transfixed by their voluptuous hip-swaying and evident vocal talents, Nick's imagination began to soar. To dream.

To *dare*.

For Nick sensed musical potential here. In another world, another time, he might have become their manager, he knew. He could already foresee in his mind's eye a lucrative career for the alluring trio: a glittering clutch of Grammy-winning albums, with Nick's shrewd management skills and own personal magnetism leading them to ever-more dazzling career heights, until inevitably they entered their child-rearing years and Nick would be forced to cast the net wide if he hoped to continue marketing the band, sacking them gradually, one by one, so as to preserve some form of perceived continuity before arriving once more at a fully rejuvenated, apparently ever-youthful line-up, which would once again score hit after musical hit and continue to line Nick's pockets, and semi-occasionally theirs.

But this thought, Nick knew, snapping himself out of his distracting reverie, was merely another bewitching wile from the minds of that mind-possessing trio in front of him. They were seeding the notion of vast global musical domination in Nick's fragile mind in an attempt to tempt him once more towards the edge of the pentagram that had formerly been a circle, which was all that stood between Nick and the eternal damnation of his soul.

And if he did that, if he stepped outside the pentagram that Devlin still insisted was a circle, he'd be stone-cold dead, his soul forever languishing in the eternal fiery armpits of Hell.

No way. No way was Nick Steen going to let the temptations of a sultry demonic all-female vocal group lure him towards his inevitable doom.

And it was Nick Steen deciding that, he vowed inwardly. Not Devlin, who no doubt liked to think he was keeping Nick's soul back from the very brink of Hell himself. No, Devlin could go do one, frankly. Nick Steen was in charge here. Nick Steen was in charge of his *own* destiny.

And then his eyes caught sight of a fourth woman.

Samantha.

Except this wasn't Samantha as Nick had known her. This was Samantha with her horrotic qualities maxed to the full. For while she appeared largely identical to before, with her eyes behind those stern librarian spectacles frowning back at Nick admonishingly as always, he noticed that the heavy return stamp she'd always kept in her left hand was missing. In its place was a pile of Nick's own most critically acclaimed bestsellers. And, one by one, she was lifting them up and tossing them over her shoulder into the fires of Hell beyond, shaking her head disapprovingly as she did so.

'No!' yelled Nick. 'Leave my oeuvre alone!'

'SSH!' shushed Samantha, placing a stern finger over her lips before ripping up the remaining books in her hand, tearing the pages from their spines and tossing them aside as their contents sparked and crackled with infernal flames. As Nick watched his life's work go up in smoke, he could resist no longer.

'You *vixen*!' he yelled, throwing himself towards the edge of Devlin's erroneously named circle that was still a pentagram.

'No, you fool!' cried Devlin. 'Step back!'

But it was too late. Nick's body was charging blindly towards the object of his lust. For despite Samantha trying to kill him with those instant death pills, Nick still had the hots for this castigating librarian. To be frank, he couldn't wait to get back to her and that microfilm reader.

For he was putty in Samantha's hands, like he'd once been putty in the hands of Jacinta when she'd first wrestled him from the Harley-Davidson he'd been trying out in that motorcycle showroom, even though he couldn't actually ride one. Jacinta could ride one, of course, being the showroom's female boss, and had subsequently ridden Nick that entire night, shifting all his gears from one to five, explaining that for the purposes of love play, Nick was her five-speed Sportster model rather than the six-speed transmission version featured on all models since 2007 that largely only improved fuel efficiency.

That relationship had ultimately turned sour, but this one wouldn't, Nick vowed. For if he could somehow find it in himself to forgive Samantha for attempting to end his life, he felt sure they could get over this thorny patch and get back to business in the horrotica isle.

'Resist!' yelled Devlin from somewhere distant, though Nick could no longer remember quite where, or who, Devlin was. Or what the hell he was doing here himself, except diving forwards blindly to incur once again the disapproving wrath of that noise-silencing, fine-issuing, book-remaindering Library Mistress.

'Shush me!' hollered Nick, loudly. 'Shush me, Samantha!'

And at that very moment, a hand shot forward through the surrounding wall of flame, forcing Nick's body back into the pentagram within a circle. A hand that remained firmly against his chest, preventing Nick from propelling himself any further forwards.

A hand that wasn't Samantha's hand.

A hand that was a *man's* hand.

Thick, gnarled and strong, just like Nick's own.

A hand whose arm, Nick saw, was draped in the brown folds of a cotton robe.

And as the arm continued to materialise before Nick's very eyes, so too materialised the rest of its body. As Nick watched, the flames dancing before his eyes began to flicker, then die. A hooded form stepped into the pentagram.

Another Watcher? Nick wondered, perceiving a figure closely resembling that of Devlin's own, before his true features had been revealed. And, like that previous stranger, this figure now reached up with both hands to draw back the drooping folds of its overhanging hood, to reveal beneath it a black, wide-brimmed capotain.

A face like thunder itself peered out at Nick from below the hat's rim. A face Nick knew well.

The face of *Harland Steen*.

'Thy work is done, Brother Devlin,' the face spake. Then the hand on Nick's chest lifted suddenly as the Puritan cast off his brown robe, revealing a plain cotton suit beneath.

'A moment more, Brother Harland,' said Devlin, speaking from somewhere nearby. 'Now behold . . . thy loyal Brethren.'

A second or two passed, then the flames of each black candle snuffed out as one, leaving a rising cloud of black smoke that gradually dissipated towards the ceiling.

'Where?' said Nick. He couldn't see any of the so-called Brethren.

'Sorry, there seems to be a problem,' said Devlin. 'It looks like the Brethren didn't make it, after all.'

THE BLACK STEEPLE

'What?' said Nick. 'Then how the hell are we supposed to—'

'I give the orders,' snapped Harland Steen, his eyes fixed on Nick's own, scrutinising his double's features in the way Nick himself had previously studied those of his ancestor.

'Thy soul is *corrupt*,' said Harland Steen, sneering with contempt at his earthly descendant.

'Yet thou hath saved him from damnation, Brother,' said Devlin, bowing solemnly. 'Praise be to Brother Harland.'

'Praise be to me, Brother Devlin,' Harland Steen replied.

And stepped into Nick's body.

CHAPTER ELEVEN

Instantaneously, Nick felt a second personality enter his own. He flexed his nerves, then his muscle tendons, before concluding that he essentially felt the same, save for a hitherto unheard inner voice raging at him whenever a carnal thought entered his mind. He also felt the urge to say 'thee', 'thou' and 'hadst' a lot, plus 'fart crackers', which is apparently a seventeenth-century phrase for 'breeches'.

At least, Nick thought with relief, he wasn't possessed.

'Thou art now possess'd,' the voice said to him, this time through what had once been Nick's own mouth. Evidently this second personality, which had only just intruded, had shifted inside him to become the more dominant personality. 'By the spirit of Goodness, Light and Eternal Order.'

Harland was taking charge of his body, Nick realised, suddenly aware of what talking in tongues must feel like. He decided two sentences were quite enough.

'Wait a cotton-picking minute,' Nick replied, speaking to himself. 'I'm in charge of this body.'

'Thou art not,' the other voice immediately countered, likewise, through Nick's mouth. 'Thou hast lain and sported with a witchy woman, and therefore hath surrendered thy bodily authority to me.'

'Bullshit,' said Nick, attempting to stick his fingers in his own ears in an attempt to claw out the invading spirit. But it was useless. The hands at the ends of Nick's arms instead reached further upwards, past his ears, to adjust the brim of the wide-brimmed black capotain he now appeared to be wearing.

Somehow, Nick's physical body had been fused, like his mind, with the incarnation of his dead ancestor, Harland Steen. And Nick was no longer even in part control of his own bodily functions. Apparently, these now belonged to the spirit of his usurping ancestor. Nick's body and mind were effectively trapped within the body and mind of Harland Steen, and there was bugger all he could do about it.

'There's been some sort of mistake, Devlin!' yelled Nick. 'I'm trapped in here and can't move my body.'

But Devlin couldn't hear him. For Nick's words appeared to be imprisoned somewhere inside his fused mind, and only Harland himself seemed able to comprehend them.

'Speaketh not the words "bugger all",' snapped Harland. 'For they art obscene.'

'I didn't speak them, I *thought* them,' replied Nick, internally. 'But I do admit they are obscene.'

'Then thinketh them not,' barked Harland. 'Lest you feel the touch of my rod.'

'Excuse me?' said Nick. 'Now who's being obscene?'

'*Blasphemy!*' yelled Harland. 'I speak of my rod and staff, those holy guides in mine pilgrimage through the valley of death, and thou speaketh of thy Devil's horn!'

'My mistake,' said Nick, backing down for now. Jeez, this guy was a real whack job.

'Good work, Brother Devlin,' said Harland, turning his attention back to the waiting Wanderer. 'Thou hath taken the righteous path from thy eternal punishment.'

'I pray so, Brother Harland,' said Devlin, nodding. 'God willing, I shall Wander this earth no longer.'

'You *rat*,' barked Nick, trying his hardest to direct his words through what he had to accept was now, to all intents and purposes,

Harland's mouth. 'You didn't care what happened to me at all, did you? You just wanted to bring an end to your own constant Wandering. Boy, when you said "trust nobody", you weren't joking, were you? Because I certainly can't trust you.'

Useless. Devlin hadn't heard a word.

'Silence, Heathen!' snapped Harland, slapping himself hard across the face. The Harland part of Nick's body appeared to relish the pain, while those physical nerve endings still attached to Nick himself winced visibly at the sudden flash of self-inflicted punishment.

'What the hell was that for?' Nick yelled, inside.

'For thy castigation of Brother Devlin's holy work. For he is the most righteous and holy of us all, mine own company excepted. We are *the Brethren*, sir, and you would do well to mark it. For, as one, we shall journey forth to do battle with the Armies of Eternal Chaos. And thou wilt join us, or sit at the back of thy mind and keep quiet.'

'What Brethren? There's just three of us. And I'm in this for Duncan,' added Nick. 'No one else.'

But Harland was already ignoring him, busy instead shaking the hand of Devlin, whom he hadn't spoken with for more than three hundred years. Nick watched as the eternal Wanderer cracked open a packet of leavened bread and bit the cork from a bottle of vestry red. Harland himself refused to partake, Nick noted, seemingly ill at ease with the prevailing mood of jovial camaraderie.

Nick realised he needed to get the measure of this lunatic before he could find a way out of his body. He had to figure out what made him tick, before exploiting any apparent weakness he might find. Because even though he needed to be fused with Harland in order for them to defeat the satanic coven of Canon LeRoche, there was no way Nick could go on living like this beyond a couple of days or so. Every single time he tried to get his brain to think of Samantha, for example, which he'd been doing for a few moments now, his mind suddenly filled itself instead with images of tranquil lakes, summer meadows and golden chalices in a clear-blue sky. Evidently this was how Harland had fended off the temptations of those three dancing harlots across the centuries.

But wait, thought Nick, struggling once again to conjure up the picture of Samantha in his mind. Maybe there was hope yet, if he could somehow work with whatever purified bilge Harland's own brain was currently feeding him.

As Nick drew upon his memories of the microfilm reader session in an effort to pollute the tranquil scene currently filling his mind's eye, he began to perceive a small figure in the golden rays of that distant summer meadow. And though it was still some distance away, Nick could see, even from this neighbouring field, that it was a *shapely* figure. Was it – *could* it be – Samantha?

Yes! Yes, it was definitely Samantha, the female librarian. There she was again, Nick saw, forcing her physical image to appear more fully within the purified set-dressing of his newly chastened mind's eye. Yes, there she was, lying on a vast haystack, *in flagrante*, beckoning to Nick once more with that stern, castigating finger of hers.

Then Harland punched his own body in the balls.

'Thou art mistaken, sir!' the Puritan snapped, as Nick's inner voice screamed in pain. 'Thou seest nothing in thy mind's eye but the finest, purest heavenly field on God's earth. And don't thou forget it.'

'Forgive me, Brother Harland,' croaked Nick, figuring he'd better start sucking up to the guy after all. And he could kiss all thoughts of a brief hay-roll with Samantha goodbye, too, because he certainly wouldn't be trying *that* again.

'Brother Harland,' said Devlin, coughing politely into his hand. 'We *do* have a titanic and climactic Final Battle between Order and Chaos to fight.'

'We do indeed, Brother Devlin,' said Harland, and then turned to address the empty space behind them. 'My Brethren, we face today perhaps the greatest trial we hath ever faced. Far greater than that which hath plagued me for three hundred years in the Eternal Land of Lady Limbo.'

The guy's genuinely mad, thought Nick. *The Brethren aren't even here.*

All that time resisting the advances of harlots in the Eternal Land of Lady Limbo must have fried his ancestor's brain. For now that their minds and souls were fully fused, Nick was able to reach mentally into Harland's brain and access some of his ancestor's memories. And he had to give Harland credit, for there was no way Nick himself could have resisted the temptations posed by those three harlots over the previous three centuries. What they couldn't do with a seventeenth-century millstone collar . . .

'Aargh!' Nick yelled, as Harland punched himself in the balls a second time.

'As thou may or may not be aware,' said Harland, continuing to address the non-existent Brethren, 'Canon LeRoche hath assumed another form since last we battled. He now goeth by the name of Baron Rochlain, and doth lure a great number of worshippers into his unholy trip.'

Trip. The collective name for goats, Nick noted, trying to ignore the pain in his balls. He'd learned the word having once had to look it up as research for part of a book he'd been writing.*

'His plan, I fear,' said Devlin, interjecting, 'is far worse than anything we hath faced before, Brother Harland.'

Sombrely, Devlin produced a small book from the folds of his robe and handed it to his leader. It was the very book Nick had previously discovered half-buried in the valley plain amid the ancient ruins of the Black Steeple. The one that was entirely black.

'*Diabolis Maleficus Catastrophicus*,' said Harland, reading out loud the book's title. 'The most evil book ever penned.'

---

* Specifically, a book almost exactly like this book. GM

THE BLACK STEEPLE

As Harland parted its leaves, Nick caught sight of its dedication page. 'For Mother ...' he said, within himself.

'Be silent,' snapped Harland, turning the page.

'Someone's drawn a cock on that beetle,' added Nick, wondering whether Devlin might have picked up this particular copy from the library instead.

'That is Adnophall, Chief Dung Beetle of Hell,' Harland replied, haughtily. The Puritan continued to read inwardly for a few moments, then spoke again. His voice was sterner now, far graver than before. 'Brethren, it is as I feared. Baron Rochlain, the latest bodily incarnation of Canon LeRoche, intendeth to turn his corporeal form into ... *the Goat of Silth*.'

'We knew that already,' said Nick, from inside his head. 'Devlin told me before he told you.'

'I am addressing my loyal Brethren,' said Harland.

'You're not, actually.'

'Brother Devlin,' said Harland, a look of exasperation on his face. 'Be there some way to extinguish this soul of my descendant, now that mine own hath been liberated from the Eternal Land of Lady Limbo?'

'I'm afraid not, Brother Harland,' replied Devlin. 'For now, we must keep the two of you fused, or thy soul will once more return to the Eternal Land of Lady Limbo before the Final, Final, Final Battle is won.'

'I'd be happy to go in his place,' said Nick, from inside himself. Frankly, he was starting to get bored and fed up with being trapped within the soul-fused body of a seventeenth-century Puritan firebrand, and fancied spending a bit of downtime with Harland's Harlots, after which he could always moot the idea of managing their long-term singing careers.

'Never,' said Harland, reading Nick's mind. 'My moral compunction will not allow it.'

Damned prude, thought Nick, hardly believing this was his own ancestor. He realised sexual repression must run in his family, otherwise he'd never have commenced a career in horror writing himself. But to hear such a staid and conformist worldview emerging from the mouth of his own body made Nick want to run about snorting like a randy Man-Goat himself.

'Alas, he is too far gone, Brother Devlin,' said Harland, still listening in on Nick's thoughts. 'Let us pray we may yet save his own soul from eternal damnation.'

'Whatever,' huffed Nick, beginning to suspect Hell might not be such a bad place to retire to after all.

'Now that the planes of Time have been aligned, my Brethren,' Harland continued, 'we have one final chance to defeat our enemy before Canon LeRoche's transformation takes place. We few, we unhappy few, have been charged by God Himself to do battle with the Dark One's army one final time. For today, my humble Brethren, the Final, Final, *Final* Battle doth await us.'

'Amen,' intoned Devlin, head bowed solemnly in the direction of his leader.

'Then let us depart at once,' announced Harland. 'Upward, Brethren soldiers, upward. Upward, and onward!'

'Upward, then outward, surely?' Nick said, mindful there was a door they'd all have to go through first in order to exit the Bad Chapel. 'Then onward, after that.'

Harland yanked the holy rod from his belt and held it aloft, over his own balls.

'Or just upward, like you say,' Nick added.

★

An hour later they stood on the rocky verge of the great valley plain on the outskirts of Silth. Some distance beyond, maybe three days' walk or more from where they currently stood, there loomed – if the planes of Time had indeed converged permanently as Devlin had promised – the Black Steeple itself.

'It'll take us thirty minutes by car,' said Nick.

'What is this "car"?' replied Harland.

Nick attempted to explain, then immediately gave up. For Harland wasn't listening to him. And Devlin, who did know what a car was and might have informed Harland, evidently preferred to do more Wandering.

'We must move swiftly,' Harland continued. 'Before Canon LeRoche can sacrifice this ... *Duncan*.'

'Like I say, a car will get us there in half an hour.'

'Brethren,' announced Harland, again addressing no one. 'Our voyage begins here, on this windswept valley plain.'

As if to confirm the truth of his words, a powerful breeze swept upwards and over their heads.

'Most of you will remember Brother Devlin,' Harland continued. 'It is he who will be looking after our lunchboxes, and distributing the weapons.'

At Harland's signal, Devlin reached into a sack and drew forth what looked to Nick's eyes like a piece of cheap jewellery.

'Step forward, Brother Marmon,' said Harland, holding out the glittering object to an imaginary member of the Brethren, before releasing it into his non-existent hand. Nick watched the object drop to the valley floor, where it shattered instantly. 'To you I entrust the Eye of Horus, which may be used to deflect the powers of Darkness, though I do stress the word "may".'

Is this guy serious? thought Nick.

Did Harland really believe someone had just taken some jumped-up cracker toy from his hands, with which he was supposedly going to battle a deadly coven of Black Magicians?

'Step forward, Brother Cadney,' continued Harland, clicking his fingers and signalling for Devlin to reach inside the sack once more.

'Into your hands I discharge these Holy Wafers, which may each be fanned in the face of God's enemies. Though go easy, as they do tend to crumble.'

Devlin handed out the wafers and released them into a passing breeze, whereupon they immediately disintegrated.

'You can't fight a coven with wafers!' cried Nick. 'And you need someone to hold them, for a start.'

'Brother Devlin,' said Harland again, snapping his fingers, impatiently.

The former Wanderer removed a third object from the sack and handed it over.

'To you,' said Harland, handing the object immediately back to Devlin, 'I bequeath this phial of Holy Water, to be flung across the path of LeRoche's demonic hordes.'

Devlin took the phial in his hands, examining it warily.

'Listen to me, Harland,' said Nick, piping up from within again. 'Holy Water ain't gonna cut mustard in twenty-first century Stalkford. In my pocket, there's a *gun*. A .44 Magnum.'

'Silence!' snapped Harland. 'Alternatively, Brother Devlin, you may swap the phial of Holy Water for this pouch of herbs. These,' he said, drawing them out of the sack himself, 'will emit a scent guaranteed to enrage, or cause to sneeze readily, the legions of Darkness.'

Devlin took the pouch in his hands, weighing it up against the phial of Holy Water. Then he sniffed it.

'Mint, mainly,' said Harland. 'Though you *may* add rosemary.'

'Your crackpot religious paraphernalia isn't gonna work,' snapped Nick. Dammit, if he didn't somehow find a way to pipe up so Devlin could hear him as well, they were all gonna get minced. 'Time's moved on, Harland. To fight a war these days, you need to have guns, knives, and ideally a flamethrower or two.'

'What madness dost thou speak of now?' yelled Harland aloud in response. 'Be silent!'

THE BLACK STEEPLE

'There is a *gun* in my pocket,' said Nick, furious now. 'Take the gun out and fire it.'

'Gun?' said Harland, apparently confused. 'What is this "gun" you keep speaking of?'

'The long, hard thing in my trouser pocket.'

'*Demon!*' cried Harland, punching himself a third time in the balls.

Gasping, Nick elected to abandon his plan. But if he didn't find some way to quit Harland's body by the time they arrived at the steps of the Black Steeple, things were going to get extremely messy.

Devlin coughed, politely. 'I believe your descendant doth owneth a "gun".'

By some miracle, Nick realised Devlin must himself have noticed the weapon in his pocket. So there *was* still a chance, he figured. A slim one, but if Devlin could somehow convince Harland to hand over Nick's gun, they'd at least stand some chance of defeating LeRoche's army.

'Give Devlin my gun,' yelled Nick, his internal voice now croaky from all the ball-bashing he'd endured.

'Never!' his ancestor bellowed, directing his anger at Devlin, too, this time. 'And this constant bickering is shameful. Canst thou not see that the forces of Chaos are already moving among us? Turning Brether against Brether? Recall ye now that we are the Brethren, charged with vanquishing Evil through Good, Darkness through Light, Chaos through Order. Together we must stand. Together we must fight. Together we must go forth into the Kingdom of Shadow and purge Darkest Evil from the land. And we must do it *now*, for Time doth marcheth on.'

Before Harland could take his first step across the wasteland, Nick seized his final chance.

'Have you heard of the word "bus"?'

CHAPTER TWELVE

Harland eventually accepted Devlin's definition of a 'bus', but by the time he'd accepted that a wagon that was able to move without horses *did* exist, and had led the non-existent Brethren back into town to board the '613' Valley Flyer, it became increasingly obvious to Nick that the vehicle was in the local garage for a reason, and wasn't going to get them past the outskirts of Silth, let alone across the valley plain. In fact, it broke down at exactly the same spot where they'd been standing more than three hours earlier.

'The work of the Dark One,' said Harland. 'Everyone off!'

'LeRoche is directing his dark magic against us, Brother Harland,' said Devlin, keying the vehicle's ignition repeatedly in vain as the group of imaginary Brethren herded out, apparently grumbling.

Maybe they *were* real after all, thought Nick. Maybe Harland's Warriors of Light did exist, but were far too light and ethereal to be seen by the human eye, and had no ability whatsoever to clutch physical objects. In which case, they'd be useless in a fight.

''Twas LeRoche who flooded this engine,' Devlin continued. 'And hired out the town's only accessible minibus to the deanery of Little Hormead on *this very day*.'

'*It begins . . .*' intoned Harland, ominously.

Together, the three men, one of them housed inside another, exited the bus themselves and began walking once again across the valley plain.

'We are now three hours behind,' snapped Harland, moodily.

THE BLACK STEEPLE

'Look, why not just *try out* my gun?' asked Nick, hoping the upcoming long walk over rocky ground might prove too boring, even for a joy-despising Puritan.

'No one needeth a *gun*,' Harland snapped, again.

This is madness, thought Nick.

Harland and Devlin had no idea what they were getting into. Because if Nick Steen routinely carried a gun, then the chances were strong that LeRoche's followers would also routinely carry guns. Especially as LeRoche himself, who was also Baron Rochlain, was a Wanderer like Devlin, and thus fully cognisant of recent historical developments in gunpowder technology. 'Recent' as in having occurred during the last three hundred years or so.

'The map,' said Harland, clicking his fingers again.

Devlin removed a piece of parchment from his robe and handed it over. Upon it were various details, scrawled in charcoal.

'It looketh like we need to cross that cow field yonder,' Harland said, pointing to an area of slightly darker-looking rocks ahead of them, 'then journey up yonderer pathway, t'ward the heart of Clowper's Wood.'

''Tis a haunted wood,' warned Devlin. 'Full of dark sprites and sinister brownies. And the last time I Wandered thither, there was a discarded toilet seat.'

'Yet Clowper's Wood is a shortcut we *must* take. For beyond its furthest edge standeth the plain of the Black Steeple,' intoned Harland.

'Apparently the Society of Black Churches have done it up rather nicely,' said Devlin, rolling up the map and placing it back inside his scarlet robe. 'Repainted the transept walls in satanic Black, added a couple of sex chairs to the main crypt. Plus they also breed their own chickens for daily sacrifice.'

As Devlin was talking, Harland gripped his arm suddenly. '*Look,*' he whispered.

'Good God,' Devlin replied, his own eyes taking in the terrifying sight immediately ahead. 'What in hell's name are they?'

'*Goats*,' said Harland. 'A field of goats. LeRoche is trying to frighten us, Brother Devlin. He wants us to turn back.'

'They're just goats,' said Nick, from within. 'You walk through them.'

'True, we must go forward, my Brethren.'

'*Forward?*' Devlin cried. 'Through the *goats?* We'll be nibbled to shreds.'

'We have no choice,' barked Harland sternly. 'If we wish to make up time and reach Clowper's Wood before sunset, then we *must* go forward. Through these goats.'

Thus, forward they went. And once they'd reconvened on the far side of the field, Devlin drew up a list of survivors.

'Only nine remain,' he concluded, glumly. 'The rest are missing, presumed dead.'

As Harland said a silent prayer, Nick decided he'd had enough. *Again.* 'No one got killed just now, Harland. The Brethren don't exist. All we did was walk through a field of goats.'

'LeRoche is whittling us down,' said Harland, ignoring him once again. 'Brether by Brether.'

Why won't Devlin say something? thought Nick. *It's as if he wants us to go to war without an army. Unless he's as insane as Harland. Why would he indulge the man's lunacy like this, if not?*

All three of them were going to be wiped out the second they took action against LeRoche's hordes. Unless Nick could somehow free that gun of his . . .

Devlin gasped suddenly in apparent pain, indicating a previously unseen tear in his robe.

'My leg! A goat doth bit me in the leg!' He winced. 'My thigh is exposed, Brother Steen. ''Tis a *sin!*'

Harland shook his head, disapprovingly, then made a religious sign with his right hand while uttering a small prayer. 'Thou ist forgiven, Brother Devlin.'

'What the hell?' cried Nick. 'There's no bite there. Not even a nibble. Devlin tore that damned hole himself!'

What was Devlin *thinking* of? Was this former Wanderer somehow so grateful to his newly unshackled leader for ending his aforesaid Wandering that he'd now succumbed to some kind of religious mania? Surely Devlin could see that there were no Brethren present, and that without a gun in their hands, there was no hope at all of them winning the forthcoming Final, Final, Final Battle.

'This is lunacy!' snapped Nick. 'Let me have control of my body again, Harland. Let me grab my gun.'

'Never!' barked Harland.

'Wait, you didn't let me finish. Let me grab my gun and I'll shoot that entire trip of goats myself.'

''S'Blood, Sir, what is this damned "gun" of which you keepeth speaketh?' cried Harland.

'You know what a gun is, Harland,' Nick said in an obsequious tone, electing to follow Devlin's example of placating his outer tyrant. 'They used them in the English Civil War, I believe.'

'Wrong, sir. Those were muskets, not guns. *That*,' Harland said, pointing to the bulky-looking bulge in Nick's trouser pocket, 'is no matchlock musket.'

'But,' said Nick, treading on yet more eggshells, 'a gun fires at a faster rate than any musket. You don't have to reload between shots.'

'You mean to say it requireth no lowering of a slow-burning match to yon priming pan via a trigger to fire the thing?'

'No, you just pinch the trigger itself and it shoots six times in a row.'

'*The Devil's work!*' yelled Harland. 'Thou hath consorted with the Dark One to work this foul machinery 'gainst the Armies of Light and Truth.'

'Devlin, will you just tell him what a damned gun is.'

But Devlin, Nick remembered, couldn't hear him.

'I will dispose of this magician's wand immediately!' bellowed Harland, yanking Nick's Magnum .44 from his own trouser pocket and hurling it away across the valley plain.

Nick watched it bounce behind a distant rock. 'You idiot!' he cried. 'How the hell are we gonna rescue Duncan now?'

'*Rescue* Duncan? Sir, I have no plan at all to *rescue* Duncan.'

'What do you mean?' Nick growled, inwardly.

'My intention, sir, is to *destroy* him.'

★

'Destroy Duncan?' Nick repeated for the fortieth time. 'But why?'

Still Harland ignored him. This was insane, thought Nick. Why wouldn't his ancestor tell him the reason why he intended to *kill* Duncan in order to prevent Canon LeRoche sacrificing Nick's son of an Elder Cosmic God in order to turn himself into the dreaded Goat of Silth, instead of merely *rescuing* Duncan and thereby foiling Canon LeRoche's aforesaid plans to sacrifice Nick's son of an Elder Cosmic God and thereby turn himself into the dreaded Goat of Silth anyway?

'Can you hear it?' said Harland, still ignoring Nick as they began to make camp in a clearing in the middle of Clowper's Wood. It was almost midnight, with the Witching Hour but a few hours away, and a strange religious chanting had commenced, borne on the wind from some far distance.

'Hear what?' asked Devlin, concealing his phial of Holy Water behind a nearby rock in case some phantom member of the Brethren attempted to steal it from his robe pockets during the night.

''Tis the Augmented Fourth,' said Harland. 'Also known as the Devil's Chord.'

'What's the Devil's Chord?' asked Devlin.

'The Evil Interval.'

'What's the Evil Interval?' asked Devlin, again.

'A chromatic scale omitting the perfect fifth and highlighting instead the diminished fifth.'

'Which means?' enquired Devlin, none the wiser.

'Dissonance ...' replied Harland. 'The language, of course, is Enochian.'

'What's Enochi—' began Devlin, then decided against unleashing a litany of further queries.

'Brother Devlin,' Harland continued. 'Unpack the bags, draw a pentagram in the middle of this clearing, place five white candles at each point, and five horseshoes behind those. Fill five silver cups with water and herbs, set those in the valley of the star, and chalk two thick circles in the ground within, the inner approximately seven feet wide to connect the valley of each star, the outer fifteen feet wide to connect all the points. Then,' he continued, handing Devlin a small scroll marked in charcoal, 'chalk the following Cabalistic formulae and signs of the Zodiac 'twixt both circles and ensure you leave sufficient room for a communal toilet. Then go brew the tea.'

'As you wish, Brother Harland,' said Devlin, Wandering off.

'We must sleep if we can,' said Harland, 'to preserve our strength for the Final, Final, *Final* Battle.'

Yet sleep proved impossible. For although Harland went out like a light, Nick himself remained wide awake. Why were Steen and Devlin intending to destroy Duncan, as well as Canon LeRoche? Surely Duncan was the victim here? For Nick's son was the one they intended to sacrifice so that Baron Rochlain could turn himself into the Goat of Silth. Damn it, Nick was sick of Society continually picking on his son. He had to find some way of extracting himself from Harland's body so that he could go to Duncan's rescue. Or was it Harland he had to extract from Nick's body? He just couldn't tell anymore. For the two had appeared to fuse physically as well as mentally, and if Nick couldn't somehow divide them up again tout suite, this forthcoming Final, Final, *Final* Battle was going to be a total wipeout.

He gazed around the silent camp, noting that Devlin, who'd volunteered for the first watch, was already asleep on the job. *Damn*, thought Nick. They were now totally defenceless in the middle of a haunted wood.

'Harland,' he whispered, trying to rouse his ancestor's sleeping body. 'Wake up!'

But it was useless. Harland was sleeping the sleep of the pure, and no amount of barking in his inner ear from deeper within his inner ear was going to change that.

Then Nick began to hear another sound, coming from within the pentacle itself. It was Devlin, Nick realised. Muttering to himself while he slept. Moaning some nonsensical gibberish, Nick presumed.

Or *was* it gibberish? Perhaps, as Devlin had once been a Dabbler in the Dark Arts himself, he was subconsciously relating some form of Devilish Incantation?

'No ... No ...' muttered Devlin, his body rolling to and fro, perilously close to the edge of the protective pentagram. '*Diabolis departum ... soonaspossum ...*'

Devlin looked like he was indeed in the throes of some internal religious battle of his own, brought about by some dark spirit invading the camp from the surrounding trees. Evidently Devlin was fighting off the clutches of some approaching wood demon.

Then Nick heard another sound emerging from between the nearby branches. The sound of leaves and twigs crunching underfoot.

Then he saw it.

Or rather, saw *her*.

'Hi, Nicky Wick,' said Samantha, gazing alluringly at him from the edge of the nearby trees. 'Time for another go on the microfilm reader?'

THE BLACK STEEPLE

'There's no microfilm reader here, Samantha,' said Nick, aware that her sudden appearance must be a hallucination of some kind. 'We're in the middle of a haunted wood.'

'Oh, but there is, Nick,' Samantha said, slipping her black turtleneck sweater downwards, over her left shoulder. Hell, she wasn't even concerned about stretching the elastic. No way could this be a *real* woman.

No, this thing was a demon, thought Nick. A demon sent here to tempt him. To make him step unwittingly past the protective border of that Cabalistic pentagram Devlin had erected, even though he was currently trapped inside a body controlled by Harland Steen.

'Step unwittingly past the protective border of this Cabalistic pentagram,' said Samantha, throatily. 'I promise you'll like what you see.'

She was beckoning him forward now, Nick saw. Beckoning him towards her exposed shoulder with that extended castigating librarian's index finger of hers, the one on her other hand still stretching back her roll-neck provocatively.

'Devlin!' hissed Nick, across the pentagram. 'Devlin, help me.'

But it was useless. Devlin couldn't hear him. For only Harland could hear Nick Steen, and he was well out of it. And Nick could feel himself succumbing to Samantha's seductive luring. Before he knew fully what he was doing, Nick found his body rising from the ground.

'That's it, Nick,' said Samantha. 'Come here, to me. We can do it on some ferns.'

Was this him, Nick wondered? How could he be moving his body when Harland Steen had control of his limbs?

But right now, Nick didn't care who was controlling his body. Because Nick Steen had never done it on some ferns before, although he'd always wanted to. The thought of he and Samantha slamming their bodies back and forth over some mossy woodland surface until they'd ground down the ferns sufficiently to feel the cold, hard touch of a bare wooden log on their backbutts was the stuff of sheer, primal ecstasy — provided there were no red ants in the vicinity.

The ultimate thrill, of course, would be if he and Samantha could somehow generate flame under the outdoor grinding of their collective haunches. For that was an erotic thrill known only to the distant cavemen and women of the Palaeolithic era, whose frantic outdoor couplings had thus created the miracle of fire, and secured the survival of our human race, though such carnal knowledge was now deemed lost.

Perhaps he and Samantha could create fire together ... And if they could do that ...

Nick was suddenly struck with an idea. Why, if they could do that, then Nick would have his own weapon he could fight with!

Some *fire*!

'I'm coming right for you, hot legs,' yelled Nick, striding towards the far edge of the pentagram. He had no idea whether Samantha could hear him, but he shouted out loud anyway. 'Let's burn fern.'

No one was stopping him, Nick realised. Were both Devlin and Harland somehow still asleep?

But Nick no longer cared. Any second now, he and Samantha would be diving into some shrubbery in an attempt to produce a natural element.

Yet as Nick prepared to launch himself across the border of the pentagram into Samantha's waiting arms, he found his body pausing suddenly at the precipice. Then, instead of clutching some soft flesh between his hands, Nick sensed his arms being raised, palms upwards, by forces unknown, to rebuff the threat of encroaching evil.

'Back, *witch*!' yelled Harland Steen, now fully in control of Nick's body again and thrusting Nick's influence back down inside himself. 'Away with ye, bawdy temptress!'

All at once, Samantha screamed like a banshee and sprang off into the trees.

THE BLACK STEEPLE

'You *fool*,' snapped Harland, addressing, Nick presumed, himself, given he was the only other member of the Brethren currently awake. 'You almost succumbed to the clutches of the Dark One.'

That was true, Nick conceded. Yet had he been the only one? Because as far as Nick could recall, he'd had no ability to move his own limbs since Harland's spirit had first entered his body. And he was pretty sure that ability would be nigh-on impossible to get back until their souls were permanently defused. Had it been because Harland was asleep that Nick had been able to retake control of his body?

Or had something else occurred?

A suspicion began to grow, deep inside his own mind. Perhaps Harland had not been quite as asleep as Nick had initially suspected? Maybe it was Harland *himself* who had walked his own body towards the waiting Samantha?

And if that was true – if Nick's ancestor, who'd fought off the temptations of three Harland's Harlots for more than three hundred years, had somehow found himself unable to resist the advances of the most horrotic lady Nick had ever encountered, even for just a moment or two before his misguided sense of Puritan morality had ultimately prevailed – then Nick had at last found Harland Steen's weak spot.

His ancestor had the hots for Samantha, too.

'Up!' yelled Harland suddenly, as if attempting to break into Nick's train of thought. 'Everyone up!'

And as Devlin rose groggily to his feet, Harland's voice deepened as he roused his non-existent followers to action.

'The Sabbat is upon us, my Brethren. The Witching Hour is at hand. Let us march . . . *to the Black Steeple!*'

CHAPTER THIRTEEN

Raising his head tentatively over the side of the ridge, Nick – through the eyes still controlled entirely by Harland Steen – saw them. Around thirty figures in scarlet hooded capes, arms raised in supplication towards the dark edifice towering above them.

'Behold, my Brethren, the Black Steeple ...' intoned Harland, solemnly. 'In a matter of moments, Canon LeRoche will appear down there, below us.' He turned his words inwards and addressed Nick privately. 'As well as thy captive son, Duncan. Whom I shall also kill.'

'Harland, I beg you,' said Nick. 'Please spare my son of an Elder Cosmic God. You have no idea what Society's done to him over the last few weeks. He's really had a tough time, what with people accusing him of mauling their pets when he's already moved on to wild beasts. Society ought to cut him some slack. I'm asking you – *imploring* you, Harland. Spare Duncan's life. After all, he is your own step-flesh and blood.'

'*Blasphemy!*' snarled Harland. 'Now ye will join these sinners on the flaming pyre, as soon as I canst pluck you from my insides.'

'But why kill Duncan to prevent LeRoche turning himself into the Goat of Silth, when we can *rescue* Duncan and *still* stop LeRoche from turning himself into the Goat of Silth? It doesn't make sense.'

'Because Duncan's soul is not to be sacrificed – at all.'

'Not to be sacrificed?' Nick repeated, incredulous. 'At all?'

'Fool. Dost thou still not understand? Duncan's soul – and *body* – are to be *fused* with LeRoche's own, turning them *both* into the Goat of Silth.'

Nick could hardly believe his inner ears (housed within his outer ears). So the plan wasn't to sacrifice Duncan at all, but to *fuse* his body and soul with LeRoche's – exactly as Nick's body and soul had been fused with Harland's. And if Nick's current predicament was an indication of what might then follow, Duncan would be trapped inside his own fused body, but with LeRoche's mind at the helm, controlling his physical movements.

The prospect was *terrifying*.

'As long as thy son of an Elder Cosmic God breathes,' said Harland, 'so too doth breathe the damnéd soul of the Goat-in-Waiting.'

'By which I presume you mean the pre-manifested Goat of Silth?'

'Correct. But with thy son of an Elder God completely destroyed, we shall move on unopposed to battle with LeRoche.' Harland turned and began addressing the gathered imaginary Puritans. 'Within the hour, Brethren, the powers of Evil, Darkness and Chaos shall be forever vanquished from the land.'

Not if I can help it, Nick vowed.

But the truth was, he couldn't help it. For what powers did Nick possess, trapped inside a body controlled by a seventeenth-century Puritan forefather with a perpetual holy axe to grind? No powers, that's what. Meaning there was nothing whatsoever he could do to intervene in the forthcoming confrontation between powerful cosmic forces.

And, morally speaking, what right did Nick have to intervene anyway? Should he really be even contemplating trying to allow the powers of Evil, Darkness and Chaos a chance to become the Goat of Silth, merely to protect the temporary life of a son who wasn't technically his, and who, if he grew much bigger, was going to end up as a destructive, all-powerful Cosmic God anyway? Did Nick really have the right to prevent the defeat of those aforesaid forces by the Armies of Good, Light and Order?

Yet this was *Duncan*, dammit. Shouldn't Nick, as Duncan's guardian, do everything in his power to protect him? Nick's insides writhed with angst, and he listened helplessly as Harland turned to Devlin, who was crouching beside him on the ridge.

'Thou must lead the assault, Brother Devlin.'

'Why must I?'

'Because thou *must*. Now, hast thou remembered thy phial of Holy Water?'

Devlin checked the pocket of his robe. 'I have it, but I'm not sure it's going to go round all of them.'

'Fear not. We also possess that pouch of herbs.'

'Ah, yes. The pouch of herbs.'

'If either of you two knobs had grabbed my gun instead of hurling it away across the valley plain,' roared Nick from inside, 'we might have stood some chance of beating these arseholes. As it stands, this is a suicide mission.'

Again, only Harland heard this, and – again – he ignored Nick.

Nick couldn't quite believe it, but he realised he was now attempting to convince Harland and Devlin to abandon the upcoming assault. For that seemed to Nick to be the only sure way of saving Duncan's life. Also, frankly, he was furious about being physically frozen. Nick didn't personally mind dying in a Final, Final, *Final* Battle against the forces of Chaos, but he wanted the chance to flex his own limbs and mix it physically with these Black Magicians who'd stolen his beloved Duncan.

But whatever way Nick crunched the numbers, saving Duncan's life increasingly felt like a lost cause. Even if his son of an Elder Cosmic God managed to mistake Harland's body for Nick's own, it would only make a volatile situation worse. For should Duncan run to Harland, mistaking him for Nick, then Canon LeRoche – in the

THE BLACK STEEPLE

form of Baron Rochlain – would be close behind him, making a beeline for the Brethren's leader. And if that happened, there was a high chance Duncan would get caught in the ensuing crossfire. What, precisely, that crossfire would consist of wasn't yet known to Nick. But he felt sure that even if these Black Magicians weren't using guns per se, they would certainly possess a large stock of knitting needles and sewing pins in that unholy armoury of theirs. And if these were somehow propelled by the forces of dark magic, there might well be some serious resultant injuries requiring the use of Elastoplast and antiseptic cream, neither of which the Brethren were carrying, not realising they'd since been invented.

One thing was certain: whatever weapons Rochlain's followers *did* possess would surely trounce anything wielded or propelled by the dangerously out-of-touch and non-existent Brethren. And if Harland and Devlin ended up losing this Final, Final, *Final* Battle, and Rochlain succeeded in fusing his body and soul with Duncan's own, turning himself into the terrifying Goat of Silth, then they'd all be stomped or nibbled to death within the next half an hour.

There were no good options, thought Nick, staring down at the satanic ceremony unfolding below. The coven of worshippers had now joined arms and were dancing in a ring around the flaming pyre Nick had foreseen in his earlier visions. On the steps of the Black Steeple behind them stood Baron-Rochlain-slash-Canon-LeRoche, his black hooded robe festooned with sewn-on runic symbols.

If Nick could have only reached into his blouson pocket for his spare pair of binoculars, he might have been able to discern precisely who was taking part in the mass ritual below, but there was no way he was going to convince Harland there were now pieces of glass that could make you see things up close.

He had a pretty good idea, anyway. Jacinta, certainly, would be down there, along with all those townsfolk Nick had seen arriving at the Baron's Masonic Lodge the one time he'd been over there. And each one of them would no doubt have some kind of voodoo pin or curved and ornately handled dagger concealed surreptitiously about their person.

'I'm gonna say this one more time, Harland,' Nick warned, hoping against hope that he could somehow convince the soul of his distant ancestor to listen to him. 'You *have* to give me back control of my body, or this is going to be a massacre. You can't fight demons with wafers anymore. You need long-range artillery. Let me take over this mortal frame and we might stand *some* chance of winning this battle.'

'And grant thee freedom to *rescue* thy cursed son? No way.'

As if to emphasise the point, Harland reached down and punched his own body in the balls again.

'*Arsehole* . . .' spluttered Nick, doubling up in indescribable pain.

'That's quite enough of thee,' said Harland, straightening his body again, leaving Nick to wince agonisingly inside. 'Brethren,' he continued, standing on the edge of the ridge to address his phantom followers. 'The ceremony is about to commence. This be the day. This be the hour. The commencement of the Final, Final, *Final* Battle. Today, we purgeth this world of Evil, Darkness and Chaos. We shall not waver until every Black Magician on the plain below lieth dead, and the Black Steeple collapseth to ruin. But before we doth charge, may I first say a few words . . .'

Good Lord, thought Nick.

'When I first formed this Brethren,' Harland continued, 'all those centuries ago, I possessed only a cassock and a dream. Then I realised that I didn't need that cassock after all, for it was too big and too Papist, and thus I spake to myself—'

'CHARGE!' cried Devlin, and with that, the Wanderer leaped over the top of the ridge and flew down the hill's edge towards the ring of waiting Black Magicians.

'Devlin! *I* am the leader of this Brethren!' yelled Harland, leaping over the top of the ridge after him.

THE BLACK STEEPLE

Through Harland's eyes, Nick watched in awe as he suddenly caught sight of a pale, ghostly line charging through the trees behind Devlin. A host of balding, overweight men in long robes, transparent and vaguely glowing.

So the Brethren are real after all, thought Nick, as he watched the Warriors of Light continue to run downwards, occasionally tripping over on the hems of their phantom robes. As they neared the line of worshippers dancing about the ring, the ghostly Brethren began wafting wafers before them and swinging liturgical scents hither and thither.

Then, as they converged upon the line of Black Magicians, LeRoche's followers broke formation and launched themselves into the fray. Priest against Puritan, robe against robe.

Amid the sprawling chaos of hurled sandals and swinging candles, Nick caught sight of Devlin, foolishly using up his entire phial of Holy Water in a vain effort to douse the roaring pyre. Then Nick's sight was cut off as a group of marauding Black Magicians made a beeline for himself and Harland.

Nick sensed a hurled sewing needle pass mere inches from his head as Harland drew a wooden goblet from his pocket and held it up in the face of the approaching coven. Nick recognised the face of Sergeant Stack, to whom he'd reported the satanic ceremony the previous morning. Now the man was clothed in a long red robe and muttering in Latin – backwards, upside down and widdershins – while wielding what looked to Nick's eyes like a lethal safety pin.

'Begone,' yelled Harland, still holding forth his goblet, but it had little to no effect on the approaching wall of Black Magicians, just as Nick had suspected.

Then the devil-sheriff, now joined by three more hooded worshippers – whom Nick immediately identified as Steve Davis, Dennis Taylor and Ray Reardon – produced something else from his pocket: a small knitted doll with what looked like a wide-brimmed hat attached to its tiny head. An effigy of Harland Steen himself...

Nick felt a mild twinge in his gut and sensed himself fall to the floor. This time, he didn't immediately get up again. For Harland, too, was down, Nick realised, and gasping for air like Nick. The pain in their collective stomach from the thrusted needle was really starting to smart.

'And this is why you need a *gun*,' cried Nick savagely. 'I could have plugged that arsehole long before he got us with that safety pin. And now those three are gonna start potting our balls.'

'Demon!' yelled Harland, hurling himself up from the ground and towards the town's sheriff, whom Nick saw was preparing to tear the head entirely from the small cotton doll. Nick wondered whether his own life might be spared, given his current body essentially possessed two heads. But then he decided that, as his own head was effectively concealed inside Harland's, ripping off the main head from the cotton effigy would most likely kill them both.

This was the moment of death, then, Nick realised. And he hadn't even had a chance to punch anyone. What a waste.

But then suddenly, between him and the sheriff, there strode a ghostly yet vaguely overweight figure. One of the Phantom Brethren, Nick realised, who'd evidently abandoned his pouch of herbs in favour of a boxing stance.

As the transparent priest swung his fist right through Sergeant Stack's body, the devil-sheriff erupted with laughter, inadvertently lowering his hand – the hand containing the small doll. At once, Harland sprang forward, wrestling the doll from the sergeant's grasp, and immediately began the long and arduous process of depinning it. As he did so, Nick felt his ancestor kick out with their shared leg, aiming it straight at the sheriff's balls and sending the Black Magician flying backwards.

Then a nearby voice shouted, 'Catch!' and Nick felt Harland's head turn to see another ghostly Warrior of Light, similarly balding and overweight, hurl a flaming torch in the direction of the ghostly boxing priest. He'd evidently lit it from the flaming pyre, Nick realised — and he'd hurled it too soon, for if he'd only paused for a moment to think about what he was doing, he might have foreseen that his ghostly Brether would be ill-prepared for such an unexpected curve-ball, and might blindly catch hold of the wrong end with his hand.

As the ghostly Brethren-boxer did precisely that, the hurled flame caught immediately on his phantasmagorical robe, and he went up like a firework.

'Leave them to it!' yelled Harland, springing off into the terrifying whirlwind of this Final, Final, *Final* Battle.

Nick watched helplessly as the ghostly Brethren fought in vain against the swarm of marauding Dark Priests. Some of the Brethren, offset by sudden sneezing fits brought about by wafting frankincense, were cut down where they floated, while others tripped on their robes, becoming trapped within the suffocating folds before rolling, unsuspecting, into the heart of the flaming pyre. Others, Nick saw, punched out uselessly, their ghostly fists unable to connect with anything corporeal, and were subsequently bludgeoned.

It was a massacre.

Meanwhile, Harland Steen strode past his dying Warriors of Light across the plane of Time, making his way towards the steps of the Black Steeple itself. There, Nick now saw, a cowering figure crouched, caught in the iron grasp of the satanic ritual's Dark Master of Proceedings, Canon LeRoche himself.

Duncan!

Helplessly, Nick cried out Duncan's name. And in a moment that seemed to Nick like a miracle, he saw his surrogate son's head turn suddenly in his direction. A great, clumsy grin spread across Duncan's confused features as his paternal saviour strode towards him.

'Duncan!' yelled Nick, suddenly realising that Duncan probably hadn't heard his own voice at all. For Duncan, Nick knew, was mistakenly assuming that Harland's *face* was Nick's own. He thought that his own father had come to rescue him from the clutches of these satanic warlocks. 'It's not me, Duncan!' Nick yelled out in vain. 'Run away!'

But Duncan couldn't run away, Nick realised. For Baron Rochlain, Canon LeRoche himself, no less, had chained Duncan's hands and feet to the metal platter on which he was now sitting.

'Silence!' yelled Harland, cutting off Nick's thoughts. 'Thy son must die!'

'Wrong!' cried Canon LeRoche, who was also Baron Rochlain, but was now dressed up like Canon LeRoche again. '*Thou* must die!'

Holding up his free hand, which Nick now saw was glowing like a purple ball of fire, the Dark Master of Ceremonies was preparing to cast some form of fiery spell at them.

Harland held up his wooden goblet once more, as if to ward off the threat of approaching Evil.

But Canon LeRoche merely laughed. 'Toys and trinkets,' the Baron scoffed. 'They are no match against the mighty powers of the Dark Lord of Time!'

'Presumably that's you?' asked Nick from within, slightly unsure, as the Baron's sentence hadn't technically specified to whom the sentence was referring.

'Of course it is he,' cried Harland, the man's forward stride never wavering. 'But not for much longer!'

With that, Harland stopped holding the wooden goblet aloft in his hand and hurled it instead, straight into the grinning head of Canon LeRoche.

Nick winced as a dull thunk sounded, followed by a hissed utterance of the word 'Bastard!'

As the Baron fell backwards, clutching his bruised forehead, Nick found his body striding forwards again, only now he was moving towards Duncan.

THE BLACK STEEPLE

'Run, Duncan!' cried Nick, realising with horror what was in Harland's mind.

'Dadda!' cried Duncan, smiling. But Nick knew that he hadn't been heard, and that Duncan was inadvertently saying 'Dadda' to the face of Harland Steen.

'Run, Duncan! This man means to kill you!'

Nick watched as Duncan's smile softened slightly. As if he could detect, somewhere deep down, that something wasn't normal about this man who looked exactly like his sworn protector. Had he somehow heard Nick's words, deep within his proto-cosmic God mind? But all hint of apparent confusion soon vanished as Harland stepped closer to the unsuspecting man-child, reaching into Nick's pocket to produce not a stray cat, as Duncan evidently expected, but something else entirely.

Nick shuddered.

For there, in his own hand, drawn from his own pocket, was his *gun*.

The gun he'd thought had been hurled away.

The Magnum .44 – which Harland Steen himself was now aiming directly at Duncan's head . . .

CHAPTER FOURTEEN

'Hey, that's *my* gun!' said Nick, hardly able to believe his eyes.

Devlin must have retrieved Nick's piece from the valley floor when neither Harland nor he were looking. But how had it come into Harland's possession without Nick noticing?

'Correct,' said Harland. 'Devlin handed it back to me when your mind was distracted by that comely book-harlot.'

Not just my *mind*, thought Nick. But even with his recently acquired knowledge of Harland's private lust, he was still powerless. For the Baron was still down, rubbing his forehead, while Duncan clapped his massive mitts with glee at what he evidently presumed to be some sort of toy. Perhaps, in his excitement, Duncan might be persuaded to wrestle the weapon from Harland's hands. But it was already too late for that, Nick realised.

Harland's finger was already squeezing on the trigger of the revolver, preparing to send a .44 slug on a direct flight path into the unsuspecting, heavily stitched forehead of the obliviously grinning man-child.

Until, seemingly out of nowhere, another hand lurched forward and snatched Harland's own, lifting his entire arm upwards, sending the exploding bullet high into the sky.

''*S'blood!*' snapped a struggling Harland, desperate to find out who'd shaken his killer grasp.

Nick sensed who the person was before Harland had even lain their eyes on her. For there, barely contained within the shapely folds of her scarlet robe, stood Samantha.

THE BLACK STEEPLE

'Nice gun,' she murmured, still clasping Harland's wrist.

'Back, temptress!' Harland hissed, but Nick could feel no real attempt by his ancestor to wrestle his arm free from Samantha's grip.

'Let *me* have a go on your big gun,' she cooed, throatily. And even if Harland still wasn't *entirely* sure what a real gun was, he definitely understood the metaphorical meaning in this instance. In mere seconds, the massive weapon was in *Samantha's* hands. And then, even merer seconds later, it was in the hands of LeRoche – to whom she'd just thrown it.

'What hast I done?' bemoaned Harland to himself.

'Only what any right-thinking male would have done in your position,' said Nick, relieved that Duncan's life had been saved – for now. 'You're human after all, Harland. Like the rest of us.'

And even though Samantha the female librarian was ultimately working for Baron Rochlain (aka Canon LeRoche), and was part of the town's satanic coven, *and* had tried to kill Nick by replacing the label on a bottle of instant death pills to make it look like they were anti-madness pills instead, Nick couldn't help but appreciate the fact that his recent horrotica-aisle paramour had just saved Duncan's life. Nick allowed himself just a brief moment of rose-tinted nostalgia, recalling with bittersweet, almost melancholy, fondness their joint physical slamming against the library's metaphorical microfilm equipment.

'She got to me, too, Harland. *Cherchez la femme.* Which is French for: "It's not our fault, it's theirs."'

'Come on, Harly Warly,' Samantha purred. 'Limbo time's over now. Let's get physical.'

'No, no . . .' mumbled Harland, muttering to himself. 'It canst not be . . . It canst not be . . .'

'But ist is, Harland, ist is . . .' murmured Samantha in his ear. Nick knew this was merely a cunning ploy to seduce his distant ancestor, but it still felt pretty good to him. Meaning he did absolutely nothing to prevent Harland straying from his moral path in the hope that he might also, if only vicariously, get it on with Samantha once again.

As Harland allowed his wide-brimmed capotain to be lifted from his head by Samantha's slenderly curvaceous arms, and his clothing to be stripped, garment by humble garment, Nick felt a sense of relief at last that he was powerless to intervene. For there was no way he could stay Harland's hand from those imminent physical pleasures awaiting him. No way at all.

Oh well, thought Nick, smiling inwardly and preparing himself for yet another round of horrotic pleasure as Harland reached their arms forwards to remove the rest of Samantha's robe.

Then he heard the sound of Nick's gun click closely beside their heads.

'Enough foreplay,' said Baron LeRoche into Nick and Harland's other ear, as Samantha stepped back from their fused bodies. 'Tie him up.'

Nick sensed rougher hands grabbing his body then, and realised, when Harland finally summoned strength enough to look around them, that the Phantom Brethren were no more. Before them now stood row upon row of scarlet-robed worshippers. The amassed members of LeRoche's satanic coven, once again chanting their backwards, upside-down, widdershins Latin. In horror, Nick realised that the Final, Final, *Final* Battle had been decided, after centuries of stalemate. And Victory had been awarded to Darkness, Evil and ultimate Chaos.

As the Baron stepped forwards to address Nick and Harland directly, a cruel smile spread over his thin, angular features. 'Come with me, children, to my Black Steeple,' he said, even though Nick and Harland weren't remotely children. 'It is time for your evisceration by the *Goat of Silth*.'

★

THE BLACK STEEPLE

They were bound lengthways upon a satanic altar. Nick knew it was a satanic one because there were bits of dried chewing gum rubbing against his arse cheeks.

The Black Steeple itself was quite impressive, even if the features themselves were somewhat hard to distinguish, given the entirety of the interior was painted black. Nick could hear a few of the coven stumbling over each other's feet as they filed in from outside to take their places beside the pews, which had been placed upside-down.

Behind Harland and Nick – also hard to distinguish, seeing as they, being tied to a satanic altar, were essentially looking at everything sideways up – stood Canon LeRoche himself. Next to him, meanwhile, still chained to his arm and playing with a dead dingo someone had thrown him as a distraction, sat Duncan.

'They're going to fuse them,' said Nick, needlessly, as it had been Harland who'd told him that particular piece of information in the first place. 'They're going to fuse their souls and turn LeRoche – and *Duncan* – into the Goat of Silth.'

Nick expected Harland to express an opinion on the matter, but for once his ancestor was silent. Probably paralysed by his own lustful urgings, Nick figured.

'I wish she'd grabbed my other gun,' Harland said, at length. 'My personal matchlock musket. I wish she'd gripped my priming pan and slowly sparked my tinderbox.'

'This isn't the time, Harland,' Nick said. 'We have to figure out a way of getting out of here. We have to free Duncan and somehow escape the Black Steeple to fight another day.'

'I wish she'd poured gunpowder right down my barrel and stuffed me with her scouring stick.'

'Harland!'

'She can dip her burning match cord into my gunpowder pan and blow me sky-high any day.'

It was useless. Harland's mind was gone. Three centuries of battling harlots in the Eternal Land of Lady Limbo and a saucy come-on from Samantha had finally taken its toll.

Nick could hardly blame his ancestor for losing the moral high ground. But if Harland was way out of it now, then *Nick* had to have control of their body.

'Listen, Harland,' said Nick. 'Give me control of our mortal frame. You've had control up till now, and look where it's gotten us. Now I'm pretty decent with the ladies, and I stand a much better chance of charming Samantha than you do. After all, we did it on a metaphorical microfilm reader multiple times, and were about to move on to the real thing.'

'You've *coupled* with Samantha?'

'Technically, she coupled with me.'

'Then you will couple no more. Samantha is *mine*, damn ye. So abandon all hope of controlling this body, youngling.'

Before Nick could protest, the cacophonous sounds of the Black Steeple's tuneless organ piped out loudly in the darkness. The dark ceremony was at long last underway.

Nick watched helplessly as a flash of purple light illuminated the interior of the Black Steeple, followed by a huge puff of black smoke. Above, Baron Rochlain, now Canon LeRoche incarnate, started to chant in medieval backwards upside-down widdershins Latin. Nick could understand what was being said a little better now, given he was upside down himself, meaning that part of the language was therefore comprehensible. He still couldn't comprehend the backwards or widdershins bits, but Nick was grateful for that, as the little he *could* interpret included an instruction to suck out the insides of a boiling frog from the wrong end.

All at once, Nick realised that the demonic sounds of the detuned pipe organ had somehow acquired a backing band, again playing that late-sixties psychedelic rock Nick had previously heard when Devlin had performed a not dissimilar ritual upon himself.

THE BLACK STEEPLE

And look where that got us, Nick reflected bitterly. Instead of successfully fusing souls with Harland Steen in order to locate and rescue his son of an Elder God Duncan, the entire thing had been a total washout. Harland had wanted nothing to do with Nick at all, and had instead been determined only to destroy Duncan with impunity, before succumbing to the horrotic wiles of Nick's former paramour.

At that very thought, Nick heard the sound of female singing. Then, through the strange multicoloured smoke and hallucinatory candlelight of the church's swaying lanterns, he perceived the lithe, sensual forms of Harland's Harlots, once again materialising from the Eternal Land of Lady Limbo to dance alluringly around the forms of Duncan and LeRoche.

'Sweet Mother,' said Harland, to himself. 'Yon three, *again.*'

'Forget them, Harland,' replied Nick. 'That time's past.'

'Come hither, dear ladies,' cried Harland. 'I hath elected at long last to succumb to thy temptations.'

But Harland's Harlots ignored him now, instead moving even closer to the Canon-Baron, as if anticipating the primal force of Chaos he was soon to unleash upon his own person.

'But soft,' said Harland. 'They doth abandon me ...'

'That's right, Harland,' said Nick. 'Now that you've succumbed to temptation, they've moved on to the teasing part.'

'The *teasing* part?'

'You're putty in their hands, Harland,' Nick explained. 'No amount of wilful desire will make the least bit of difference now. They lured you in, hook, line and sinker. Like Samantha lured me. And now that the Final, Final, *Final* Battle has been lost, only physical and psychological torments await us.'

And something far worse, Nick added, to himself. For already he could see that the Baron's features were shifting, stretching strangely across his cheekbones, the flesh pulsating grotesquely. Around him,

Harland's Harlots continued to sing and dance in provocative fashion. Then, in a shower of sudden sparks, a large purple hula-hoop of light appeared, spinning in circles around both the Canon-Baron and the captive Duncan, while a large blanket of multicoloured dry ice spread out across the floor of the building.

Nick heard the voices of the coven members chanting behind him. Saw, upside down, their hooded heads sway as one from side to side as the main part of the bizarre satanic ceremony commenced.

The Fusing of the Souls . . .

Nick suddenly saw that Duncan was now standing on the Canon-Baron's shoulders. Or was it the other way round? (I don't mean Baron-Canon). Nick was no longer quite able to remember if he was still lying on the upturned altar or not. Was it him who was upside down, or was the altar itself now the right way up? For the geography of Nick's surroundings was changing, and he wondered if he'd been drugged. Then all that had been black suddenly went red, as if the Black Steeple had been somehow dipped into the blood and fire of Hell itself. And with that shift in hue came a swelling crescendo from the pipe organ and psychedelic backing band, as Harland's Harlots appeared to lift Duncan up and over LeRoche's head, before lowering his body once more towards the Baron.

Then they were holding nothing at all, and the room around Nick was spinning. Spinning so wildly that he could no longer tell if he was lying down or standing up. And he only continued to spin, faster and faster, at immense, insane speed. Or was it the Black Steeple itself spinning? Nick could hear Duncan yelling from somewhere – or was that a burst of manic laughter? Nick didn't know.

When the room, or his own mind, had finally stopped spinning, and Nick had managed to fight off the sickening sense of nausea as his mind's senses slowly returned to normal, he finally saw where Duncan was.

Or didn't see, to be exact.

THE BLACK STEEPLE

Because Duncan was no longer at Baron LeRoche's side. And Baron LeRoche was no longer at Duncan's side, either.

Instead, looming where both had previously been standing, was a monstrous, snorting thing with red fur and hooves.

The Goat of Silth.

And Duncan, Nick realised, was somewhere inside it.

CHAPTER FIFTEEN

An ear-shredding bleating filled the air, drowning out the accompanying psychedelic soundtrack. Then the giant monstrosity that was the Goat of Silth charged and clattered itself madly about the interior of the Black Steeple like a wild goat, only one that was massive, with bits of dark magician and Elder Cosmic God fused inside it. The creature, if that's what this thing was (Nick thought it qualified far more strongly as a monster, but hesitated to call it that as the thing was partly formed from parts of his surrogate son – who was, admittedly, intrinsically part-monster) was going stir crazy. Smashing against walls and columns with its horns, occasionally impaling any nearby follower who failed to leap out of its crazed path of destruction.

And with each jarring slam of its body against the foundations of the Black Steeple, the floor below rumbled deeply as the entire building shook. Blocks of black masonry dislodged themselves from the arched ceiling and fell upon unsuspecting coven members.

Then the demon commenced stamping its hooves at insane speed on the stone floor, shattering the tiles beneath it as if they consisted of nothing more solid than a crumbling fortune cookie – only a fortune cookie that was entirely flat to start with, which admittedly is not the norm for a fortune cookie, as they are generally round, if not vaguely spherical. In fact, Kendal Mint Cake is the better analogy here. So: the Goat of Silth was shattering the tiles below its hooves as though they consisted of nothing more

THE BLACK STEEPLE

solid than a crumbling slab of Kendal Mint Cake – but a slab of Kendal Mint Cake that was black in hue, and not the usual icy white, as a white Kendal Mint Cake would more appropriately suit the description of a demonic Man-Goat destroying the floor tiles of a *non-deconsecrated* church, i.e. one that was still consecrated and therefore holy, i.e. a normal one that isn't black and is instead some sort of pale grey.

But there was no more time to think of slabs of crumbling Kendal Mint Cake, for Nick saw that the Goat of Silth was starting to eat its followers, kicking them high into the air with its hindlegs and impaling them on its horns, before shaking its big Goat-of-Silth head violently to dislodge them, and then nibbling violently on their mangled particulars.

'No, Duncan!' cried Nick. Not because he felt any shred of sympathy for these doomed Black Magicians. As far as Nick was concerned, the Goat of Silth could nibble their collective arses from their elbows, and then some. But Nick knew that once this devil had consumed its fill of mindless subservients, the Goat of Silth would most likely move on to him, too, followed by Harland (technically, it would eat them at the same time, but Nick was the more important of the two, so came first), and then the whole of Stalkford. Then, no doubt, the world. Then the universe. Then the outer reaches of the known universe. Then possibly a black hole would eat *it*, and the Goat of Silth would return to our known galaxy in another plane of Time and start eating us all over again.

Nick *had* to get through to Duncan somehow.

'Duncan!' he yelled. 'Listen to me!'

But Duncan, in whichever part of the Goat of Silth he was currently residing, wasn't listening. Instead, whichever of the Goat's two fused souls – LeRoche's or Duncan's – was in charge of bodily functions in the monster's lower-half, was currently emitting droppings the size of double-decker buses from its rear end. Nick suspected this particular part of the Man-Goat was probably under Duncan's jurisdiction, so directed his appeals there.

'Duncan!' shouted Nick, aiming his voice at the Man-Goat's backside, trying hard to avoid its kicking feet. 'I know you're up there, champ. I know you're excited because you no longer have to wear nappies and can pass industrial-sized stools to your heart's content, but I need you to listen to me.'

All that met Nick's ears immediately after he'd uttered that sentence was a colossal passing of fetid air from betwixt the Man-Goat's haunches, followed by the passing of yet another mountainous stool. But Nick persisted.

'Listen to me, Duncan. You *have* to get out of there. They're using you, kiddo. Like Society's used you your entire life. Over three months of ridicule, cruel jibes and patronising smiles about your so-called ultra-violent tendencies. And now they're laughing at you *again*, Duncan. They're laughing now, but soon they'll be crying. Everyone in Stalkford will be crying, Dunky. Because Baron Rochlain is using you to destroy the entire world. Exploiting you – that's a big word, isn't it? It's actually another word for "using you" or "making you do things". Anyway, Baron Rochlain means to exploit you for his nefarious satanic purposes, champ, which in my book is even worse than exploiting you for financial gain.

'Because, as you know, buddy, I've raised that matter between us before –and I believe, if your grunting meant "yes", that exploiting you is only morally acceptable as long as you're also recompensed financially. And that is something I'd like to discuss with you again once this whole thing is over and that strong cage I keep mentioning has been constructed, in which you can be displayed publicly for a fee. But believe me, Baron Rochlain only wants you to stomp entire cities to the ground with those thundering hooves of yours, Duncan – with no thought of who's gonna clear it all up, least of all the droppings. And there won't be anyone left alive to do that, Duncan. Don't you understand me? LeRoche wants a world peopled only by a stomping, frothing Man-Goat charging through piles of rubble and teetering mounds of its own effluence. But I'm here to save you from all that, Duncan. Daddy's here to free you from the arse-end of this colossal Man-Goat.'

But how exactly *could* he free Duncan? Nick was still trapped inside a body physically controlled by his ancestor, Harland Steen.

Or was he?

For, without realising it, Nick had just been speaking to Duncan through his own mouth. Something had changed, Nick realised. Something had given him the ability to move his own lips, at last. And that's when he heard the whimpering.

The whimpering deep inside his own head. The whimpering of a dispirited, horrotica-deprived Harland Steen.

'No good times for me . . . No sweet caresses . . . No man-musket firings . . .'

Evidently, Harland's self-control had waned to such an extent that he had inadvertently passed juridsiction of his own head to Nick. That was something, at least, but all Nick could do currently was move his mouth. And even were he able to somehow bite a way into Duncan via an alternative route of entrance, he still needed control of his own body to get him there.

Plus, both he and Harland were still tied up.

Suddenly, there was a terrible ripping sound, followed by a shower of blood bursting from the Goat of Silth's left shoulder, as if a titanic boil had suddenly burst.

The Goat of Silth brayed and bleated, clattering madly and slamming its hooves hard against the upturned altar upon which Nick lay, dislodging its legs and tipping the entire structure downward at one end. Suddenly, Nick was upright, but still at an angle. Yet from here, he could finally see the full horror unfolding before him. As the Goat of Silth continued to ram its followers, impaling them on its devilish horns, Nick could see a dark shape sprouting through a rent in the Man-Goat's shoulder, where previously a vast zit had appeared to explode. This dark shape looked to be a head of some kind. A head covered in what looked to Nick like *stitches* ...

Nick could hardly believe his eyes. *Duncan!*

'Dadda!' yelled Duncan, looking around wildly from a hole in the demon's body as the Goat of Silth continued to pound its feet madly around the collapsing interior of the Black Steeple.

'That's right, kiddo!' yelled Nick. 'It's me! Your surrogate daddy. Not your real daddy, who apparently resides in some far-off dimension in a remote corner of the outer cosmos, but the daddy who actually clothed you, bathed you, taught you to kill rats with your bare hands as long as you promised to avoid domestic pets. *That* daddy.'

'Dadda!' shrieked Duncan again, reaching through the hole in the Man-Goat's shoulder in an effort to make his way over to Nick.

'Thattaboy, champ!' Nick yelled, struggling to be heard above the demonic bleating, psychedelic pipe organ and constant wailing from Harland's Harlots, whose close harmonies were getting even better with practice.

'You've got to climb out of there, Duncan. You have to de-fuse your soul from that of Baron Rochlain, and foil the evil machinations of the sinister Canon LeRoche – who is, incidentally, the same person as the Baron, only in different skin now. But I'll explain all that to you when you're a bit older. For now, you have to prevent the Baron from destroying Stalkford and letting Chaos take charge. You have to force your way out of there.'

But as Nick uttered those words, the Goat of Silth roared wildly, snorting and stamping its feet, then rounded on him. As it stomped towards him, Duncan's head, which was still sticking out of the Goat of Silth's shoulder, was in turn forced to face in a different direction – away from Nick.

THE BLACK STEEPLE

With Duncan's attention now distracted by a screaming worshipper, Nick prepared himself for the worst as the Goat of Silth dipped its vast head towards its chest and shuffled backwards a step or two, getting ready to ram Nick with its horns.

'Listen to my voice, Duncan!' yelled Nick as loudly as he could. 'Do you really want to stay inside the Goat of Silth, doing giant plops all your life? Let me tell you now, the days of hunting domestic pets and wild animals will be over. It'll be millet only for you, Duncan. Nothing but millet and occasional scraps of cloth nibbled from the cardigans of passers-by. Because Rochlain's going to nibble all the good stuff for himself, Duncan. All the meat on those mangled victims will be his alone. You'll get the arse-end, Duncan. The leftover scraps. And instead of getting bigger and growing into the vast son of a Cosmic Elder God you were destined to be, you'll shrink inside this manic Man-Goat and eventually pass out accidentally with one of your own droppings. Think about that, Duncan. The Baron will have you spending the next millennia producing goat's cheese, which no normal person likes. And you'll never see either of your two daddies again.'

That was all Nick could do. For he could already see steam snorting from the Goat of Silth's nostrils as the monstrous form thumped and hammered its hooves at incredible speed once again upon the ground. Then, emitting one last terrifying demonic bleat, the Goat of Silth charged at Nick.

Yet before it could impale him upon its approaching horns, the demon suddenly leaped upwards, leaping right over the upturned altar upon which Nick lay helpless and immobile.

Then a terrifying howl filled the room as the few remaining Black Magicians began to shriek, clamouring at the doors of the Black Steeple in a desperate attempt to escape. As they fled past him, Nick heard the appalling sound of two unseen demonic beasts slashing, clawing and tearing at each other's flesh, roaring and shrieking like two stop-motion dinosaurs.

As one of the fleeing worshippers smashed into the altar as he passed, knocking the altar – and Nick – over on to one side, the author finally saw what was making all that terrifying noise.

It was a scene of gruesome body horror glimpsed until now only in the pages of Nick's most horrifying prose. Yet here it was, in the literal flesh.

Duncan, now almost fully grown as a Cosmic God-in-waiting, was tearing his way through a vast rent in the Man-Goat's back, squeezing its body out of shape as the Goat of Silth slashed backwards with its horns in an attempt to spear Duncan from behind – but to no avail. For though Rochlain's soul was doing its very best to prevent the rupture of its goat-like frame, Duncan was having none of it. The threat of being fed on millet alone had done the trick, bringing into sharp and sudden focus the severity of his predicament.

As the beasts continued to maul and slash at each other's bodies, Nick felt a sudden movement close by. His hand, which had somehow come loose from its bonds with the sudden shifting of the upturned altar, was now, inexplicably, moving towards something he could see lying on the floor nearby.

His revolver ...

The gun must have been dropped by LeRoche as his terrifying bodily transformation began. But now it was back in Nick's hand. Had he somehow acquired control over his physical body at last? Nick tried flexing his muscles, to no avail. It was *Harland Steen's* hand reaching for the gun. Not his own. Evidently, his ancestor was still in control of Nick's physical functions, and was now aiming Nick's revolver at the two battling demons.

'The Goat of Silth ...' yelled Nick, desperately. 'Take out the Goat of Silth!'

THE BLACK STEEPLE

For Nick knew that if the Goat of Silth's body was plugged, Duncan would probably find it easier to crawl out of the rest of its back.

But the gun in Harland's hand appeared to drift sideways from the Baron's goat-like form, its barrel aiming instead at the emerging monstrous man-child.

'Duncan shalt die!' barked Harland. 'For then the Goat of Silth shalt die also. And Evil, Darkness and Chaos shalt trouble this land no more!'

As Harland prepared to open fire, there was a sudden mighty rending of flesh, splattering everyone in the Black Steeple with a shower of unidentified innards.

As Harland's arm wiped desperately at his eyes to clear them of dripping gristle, Nick saw that the end had come at last. Duncan had finally forced himself out of the Goat of Silth's shoulder, discarding the demon's hairy carcass behind him like an unwanted duffle coat. The hideous clattering and bleating had stopped.

Duncan was free.

'Dadda,' Duncan said, proudly, unaware that Dadda, or at least Dadda's body, which was controlled by the soul of his ancient ancestor, was still intent upon killing him.

And before Nick even had a chance to cry out a warning to his son, Harland swung the gun once more towards Duncan's unknowing head.

'Duncan!' Nick screamed out loud in slow motion. And as the long, protracted scream eventually stopped, Nick saw that he had been granted a further moment's grace. For Harland Steen had opened fire in the only way he knew: by reaching into Nick's pocket for a piece of taper he could light, alongside a pouch of gunpowder, neither of which were there.

'Where is thy gunpowder pouch?' Harland shrieked, scrabbling about desperately inside Nick's pockets. 'Quickly, man!'

Nick had to act fast. Harland's hand had already located Nick's box of bullets, and though he was currently trying to light each one individually with a nearby candlestick, Nick knew he only had precious seconds before Harland picked up on Nick's own thoughts and worked out the correct way of loading the weapon. And this time there would be no Samantha nearby to interfere with Harland's aim.

'Duncan!' cried Nick. 'I'm trapped inside this body, just like you were. My soul was *also* fused. This man is trying to kill you.'

But Duncan only smiled, moving towards Nick with a familiar, loving grin.

'Duncan, listen to me! This man is going to *kill* you.'

'Silence!' snapped Harland, opening the revolver's barrel. 'Ah, I see how 'tis done ...'

As Harland began sliding the bullets in one by one, Nick tried one final time to appeal to his son.

'Listen, Duncan. Dadda would never harm you, but this man will. Take the gun from his hand, Duncan. Grab the gun!'

And the gun *was* grabbable now, Nick realised in horror. For Harland had snapped the barrel shut and was aiming it once more at Duncan's head.

'Dadda!' squealed Duncan.

'Eat the gun, Duncan!' cried Nick.

Then Harland really did open fire.

As the gun's barrel exploded, Duncan's eyes blinked. A look of blank confusion crossed his gnarled features as the bullet passed straight through one of his stitches, embedding itself deep in his forehead. As the wounded beast's expression changed to a profound look of hurt, followed by one of distrust, then, almost inevitably, a look of primal rage, Nick prepared himself for what was to come.

As Duncan roared wildly at him like a furious lion, Nick did his best to prevent an imminent act of patricide.

'No, Duncan! Don't do it!'

But Duncan did it.

Slashing with his claws, Duncan bit off Nick's hand, swallowing the gun in one gulp. Then his son of an Elder Cosmic God reached down, yanked Nick's body from the altar, and stuffed the entirety of his father's head between his jaws.

Nick did his best to shield himself from what he knew was to come, sucking what remained of his trapped soul and body downwards into Harland's outer body and soul as Duncan clamped down hard and, with an excited shriek, chewed off Nick's head.

At once, Nick found himself in a tunnel, with a bright light visible at the far end, beckoning him upwards. Was this death? Was this finality? Had he been chewed and decapitated by his own surrogate son?

Slowly, Nick found himself moving towards the light. For if this was death, then surely all the hurt must finally be over, he figured. All the pain. All the sorrow. All the questionable grammatical judgements he'd had to put up with over the years from Roz Bloom, his erstwhile editor. All Jacinta's nagging. All of that was done with. And Nick was free to travel towards the light and gaze down upon Duncan and that daughter he had somewhere, to monitor their fates from above.

Bracing himself, Nick thrust his body upwards, towards the light ...

... and emerged through the stump of Harland Steen's severed neck.

'Dadda!' cried Duncan, grinning again, his anger and rage instantly quelled by the new toy he'd discovered. For Duncan had suddenly found a good Dadda, emerging from the severed neck of his *bad* Dadda.

As if unwrapping a favourite Christmas present, Duncan's fangs tore open what remained of Harland Steen's eviscerated body, rescuing Nick's soul from the clutches of his now permanently deceased ancestor.

'Come on, champ,' said Nick, hugging his massive man-child close to him. 'Let's go grab a Wimpy.'

*

As Nick climbed back up the ridge with Duncan, he saw flames coming from the burning shite-mound beyond. Had Jacinta finally performed her own share of parental duties before setting out for the sacrifice of her own son, perchance? Nick seriously doubted it. Perhaps the towering turd-pyre had caught fire by itself, burning up slowly from the impacted offal inside it? Either way, when Nick finally reached the top of the ridge, he saw his car parked immediately below it. A sitting duck.

'Quickly, Duncan, before it collapses,' said Nick, rushing over to his vehicle. Strapping Duncan immediately into his man-child seat, Nick slid his own body in behind the steering wheel, then paused for a moment.

Hadn't he left his car parked outside the library after he'd first done it with Samantha, then gone and Wandered elsewhere with Devlin?

So how, and why, was his car here now?

And once Nick had finally realised how odd that was, it was too late to do anything about it.

Because the car was already surrounded.

'Come out of there, Duncan,' said a voice, which Nick recognised immediately as Devlin's. So Devlin hadn't died in the Final, Final, *Final* Battle then.

Neither had Jacinta, who Nick now saw was standing beside him, still dressed in her red robe, with a flaming torch in one hand and that pet weevil of hers in the other.

THE BLACK STEEPLE

Nor had Samantha perished, for that matter. For she, too, was standing on Devlin's other side – far too close to his body for Nick's liking.

Behind him, Duncan bit through his safety straps and kicked his way out, through the passenger-side door. Nick watched as he bounded across the bonnet of the car and joined the demonic trio standing out in front. Nick wondered if he might do the same, then saw that any attempt by him to escape from the car was doomed. For the hooded members of what he now realised was Devlin's own satanic coven stood about the car in a vast circle, their elevated hands waving flaming torches aloft.

To his right, Steve Davis, Dennis Taylor and Ray Reardon stood in front of Nick's empty jerry cans, chalking their cues.

'I said trust *nobody*, Nick,' said Devlin, smiling evilly, the former Wanderer-slash-Watcher's face lit up devilishly by the car's beaming headlamps.

Soon it would be lit up by something far brighter.

And *hotter*.

'Now, instead of Canon LeRoche, *I* will fuse *my* soul with Duncan. Now *I* will become the Goat of Silth.'

'You damned Dark Arts Dabbler,' yelled Nick. But he knew, deep down, there was no escaping from *this* trap.

He watched as Samantha and Jacinta began to dance horrifically and horrotically together on either side of Devlin, while the other members of his coven yanked down on chains Nick now saw had been connected to the giant, flaming shite-mountain.

And as the teetering mass-turd began to topple forwards, preparing to crush and incinerate Nick's portable coffin, he glimpsed the cruel, leering faces of Devlin's Dabblers staring in at him.

Nick keyed the ignition in vain.

They'd thought of everything.

'Duncan!' Nick yelled out in fear as the first of the flaming turds slammed straight through the Civic's roof, inches from his head.

Nick's crushed gearstick erupted into flames.

'*Champ!*'

But Duncan didn't hear him. For Duncan was with his new family now.

Waiting for his dinner to cook.

SPECIMEN

(The Spinewood Intruderings)

CHAPTER ONE

My arse wouldn't quit. And for once, the raging fire jolting me from sleep wasn't a figment of my latest nightmare.* No, this particular inferno, which had just snapped me awake at the wheel of my car, was coming from *below*.

I'd been on this lonely mountain road for three hours now, with no sign of a lay-by, and my anus hadn't let up once. What had begun as a persistent itching north of the perineum (I'm still taking about my anus), deep within the dark folds of my leathered colon, swiftly tore at my passage walls like a spreading bushfire, burning me up in the closed cabin of my Ford Taurus and threatening to induce an involuntary bout of violent hip-twisting that, were I to indulge a

---

* i.e. the climactic denouement of the previous story, *The Black Steeple*. Yes, that entire tale was another of Steen's ongoing nightmares – and no, you can't have a refund. GM

frantic urge to claw at the source right now, might throw me instantly over the precipice of this perilous mountain pass.

True, there'd been no other cars in sight since I'd set out from the ski lodge earlier this evening, but sod's luck still ruled in a post-brain-leak world,* and the chances were strong that the second I braked hard in the road, hoisted my rump rightward and jammed one driving hand up my beleaguered crevice, some moonlight racer would pull up behind me, start hammering his horn, then swing past the right side of my car while copping a stunned eyeful.

My personal dignity couldn't allow that. For I was (and still am) Nick Steen, esteemed paperback horror author, condemned by my own acts of literary hubris† following a self-destructive sadomasochistic sex-fling with a cursed Chinese typewriter to wander a world monstered with the living figments of my own imagination. And if that sounds like the blurb from one of my own paperback horror novels, that's because it is, only one that I haven't published yet, owing to me still living the damned thing out for real in the immediate here and now.

Maybe one day I'd be able to put this whole 'monsters escaping from my own head' experience down on paper, like my terrifying paperbacks of old. Maybe one day all the real-life horrors I'd been battling for the last three years, currently marauding their way through Stalkford and outer Stalkford like a troop of randy gibbons, gibbering and gesticulating with their ginger-hued genitals in the general direction of the human genus, would feel like nothing more tangible than Ed Poe's feted 'dream within a dream' (albeit one that was technically a dream *without* a dream).

But first I'd have to deal with these damned piles.

---

* See the events of *Garth Marenghi's TerrorTome* and *Garth Marenghi's Incarcerat*, in which the imaginative content of Nick Steen's head spill out. For the slower-witted among you, there will be a further in-text recap shortly. GM

† This is that in-text recap I was talking about. GM

SPECIMEN

I fought to relax both shanks, knowing that in a matter of hours I'd be back in Stalkford. And then the small matter of raging haemorrhoids would pale into insignificance against the far thornier issue of confronting my soon-to-be-ex-wife, Jacinta, at our former home, in an effort to decide what to do with our daughter, Meredith. Specifically, to establish which one of us now owned her outright, and was ultimately responsible for her mounting psychiatric bills.

Frankly, with the amount of money Jacinta had just put away from her own damned book deal, my feeling was she could front all of Meredith's stress-related expenses herself, and then some. Especially given that in the process of doing so, she and Fibbford would no doubt happen upon some revolutionary new regression-therapy system, to be marketed subsequently and exclusively through their newly incorporated joint publishing company.

I smiled ruefully, recalling my own dealings with the infamous Dr Fibbford. He and I had worked together on one of my own books a few years back. A rare non-fiction work, for which Fibbford had employed his self-patented and still-highly-secret Fibbertronics System, the world's first foolproof, fail-safe, lie-detector deflector. It had been crucial to the work in question: namely a colossal ruse I'd successfully spun, with the help of the Fibbertronics System's ability to confirm an outright lie as undeniable truth, about me having been abducted on numerous occasions throughout my life by alien visitors.

That book, *Comminglement*, had become an instant multi-million-copy bestseller, but unfortunately Fibbford and I had parted ways soon after when he temporarily switched off his Fibbertronics System and immediately saw through my persistent attempts to attribute non-payment of his invoice to a variety of non-existent extenuating circumstances.

We still kept in touch, though. Mainly because Fibbford's co-ownership of Jacinta's rival bestseller meant his presence was required at various lawyers' meetings concerning the proposed disposal of our respective assets. Yet things were decidedly frosty between us. And, to be frank, I had the distinct impression the pair of them were conducting some sort of secret torrid affair behind my back.

But being unable to disprove Fibbford's constant denials without exposing the existence of his top-secret Fibbertronics System (which would put me in breach of contract and immediately cast doubt on the 'authenticity' of my own infamous abduction story), I was forced to remain silent about my suspicions.

As if to mock my plight, a sharp, sudden stab in my rectal cavern shot me forward against the steering wheel. As my '95 Ford Taurus swerved dangerously close to the edge of the mountain path, I yanked back violently on the wheel. My route home, after all, was along one of the most dangerous highways in outer Stalkford: a thin path running across the top of a vast mountain range, which passed between two adjacent mountain ranges, resulting in a sheer drop to oblivion on either side.

With the inevitable aftershock in my colonic passage immediately kicking in, I sensed the car fighting to right itself, each tremor from my aggravated pile-cluster rocketing through my nerve endings like demonic fireflies whirling above a raging inferno.

What the hell was up with me down there? This was like no other pile problem I'd ever encountered – and I say that as someone who's hosted numerous clutches over the years, having been weaned on a high-protein red-meat diet since the cradle. And though as a result my adult sack-seed was without doubt the strongest and purest in all of Stalkford, perennially flowering haemorrhoids were its inevitable downside. Yet I'd never faced an onslaught of piles so crippling that I'd been forced to consider trying chicken for once.

Until now.

As my car finally resumed its former position in the road, I craned my neck over the steering wheel in an attempt to distract my mind

SPECIMEN

from the persistent burning below. Seeking respite in the distant heavens, I glanced upwards through the windscreen into the vast night sky above, glimpsing what promised to be a gibbous yet strangely full-looking moon emerging from behind a lone wisp of cloud. A lone wisp of cloud that was the only wisp of cloud visible in the entirety of the starry heavens (hence *lone* wisp of cloud).

But no sooner had I taken in the marvellous aerial vista than my rectum roared anew, re-roaring again almost immediately, before roaring even more violently a third time. And as it roared, re-roared and re-re-roared, my lower region began to convulse, thrusting me forward again and slamming my forehead hard against the car's windshield.

As the vehicle careened once more towards the edge of the passing precipice, I yanked on the steering wheel hard, forcing my car back across the road – before realising at the last second that I was now perilously close to the *opposite* edge of the passing precipice.

Jesus, was this pile somehow *alive*? The damned thing seemed to have a mind of its own. Was it trying to *kill* me? I realised I'd have to pull over soon and scratch like hell, or risk being sent to a premature fiery grave over the edge of the mountain pass.

But before I could even think of applying the vehicle's brakes, my damned rectum whipped up a fresh whirlwind inside, lurching me sideways, forcing the car into a lethal spin. I whirled helplessly in circles as the mountain range beyond each window blurred dizzyingly with the revolving motion of my spinning vehicle. This was it, I realised. This was the end. There was no way my Ford Taurus could stay in the central lane without flying outwards, over one of the two nearby edges. I braced for the inevitable drop, consoling myself that at least the hellish itching would stop imminently.

Then felt nothing.

Nothing at all.

Only stillness.

And silence.
Silence and stillness.
Stillness.
And silence.
Was I falling?
Was this eerie hush a silent precursor to my final moment?
A deceptive quietude before my imminent death?
Was it?
Was it?
I waited.
Still the silence.
Still the stillness.
Was I *still* falling?
Was I *still* still falling?
Curious, I opened the car door an inch or so and looked out.
I was still in the road.

Swinging the door open wider to confirm I hadn't left the perilous mountain path at all, I waited for the dizziness still swirling in my brain to fade, then stepped out. Taking stock of my surroundings, I saw that there were no lights situated along this lonely stretch of road – merely the beams shining forth from my car's headlamps. The place, nevertheless, appeared to be lit by a vague, eerie light. I shivered, feeling strangely exposed. A cold feeling of isolation crept over me, before realisation dawned that the weird source of illumination was coming from somewhere *above*.

The moon, I remembered. Coming out from behind that lone wisp of cloud ...

Yet before I could look up once more into the night sky, I felt another movement in my anus. No longer the sharp sting of my waspish piles, however. No, this was a different sensation. Like a dull throb coming from somewhere deep inside me. Like the slow pulse of some distant heartbeat.

SPECIMEN

I found myself counting along with its persistent drumming, tapping the side of my leg with one forefinger as the light reflected from the snowy mountain peaks began to shimmer and flicker with the self-same beating of my pulsing crap-pipe.

Suddenly, my senses sharpened. How could reflections of light on a distant mountain top match the rhythmic beat of an anal spasm?

Incredulous, and with a sense of mounting fear, I looked up into the night sky above, searching once more for that lone wisp of cloud from behind which had begun to emerge the trace of a gibbous moon.

But there was no gibbous moon.

For the object that *was* emerging from behind that lone wisp of cloud was something entirely different. Something that looked to me like a giant spinning Catherine wheel. But a giant spinning Catherine wheel that wasn't remotely a giant spinning Catherine wheel. For the object I saw, far above, was nothing less than a multi-coloured ball of revolving lights.

And as I watched, the ball – or balls – of revolving lights continued to spin and hover silently in the air far above, flickering brightly in the black heavens, shimmering and pulsating in the night sky.

I watched them, mesmerised, as the eerie lights gleamed and glowed and sparkled in time with the slow and steady beating of my seemingly sentient back passage.

And it was at that precise moment that I realised I'd seen them somewhere *before* . . .

CHAPTER TWO

Fibbford: Now, tell me what's happening.

Steen: It's gone again ... Behind that lone wisp of cloud ... No, wait! ... There it is! Coming out from behind that lone wisp of cloud ... It's right above me, now ... High up in the sky ... Like some giant Catherine wheel ... And yet not remotely a giant Catherine wheel ...

Fibbford: Describe the object in more detail. But lose the Catherine wheel stuff.

Steen: Like ... balls of light ... A cluster of balls ... Like a bunch of spinning, fluorescent grapes ...

Fibbford: Is that one object or several objects?

Steen: I can't tell ... It feels like ... they're watching me.

Fibbford: I'll put down 'several objects'.

    (pen scratch)

Steen: I'm scared, Fibbford.

SPECIMEN

Fibbford: Who else is there with you, beside these objects?

Steen: No one ... Just me ... All alone on this perilous mountain road-slash-pass ...

(grows agitated)

Fibbford: Relax, Mister Steen. You are in my office, reliving your experience from the safety of my brand-new Highlander leather sofa. I have regressed you by means of hypnosis to the night of your abduction. You are quite safe. What are the objects doing now?

Steen: To be fair, I think it is just the one object.

Fibbford: What's the object doing now?

Steen: No, hold on ... There is more than one object, I think. Yeah, I'd say it's definitely several objects.

Fibbford: Let's call them lights.

(pen scratch)

What are the lights doing now?

Steen: Shimmering ... I can see it shimmering!

Fibbford: You can see *them* shimmering.

Steen: Them. Sorry. I can see *them* shimmering. Dammit! Dammit!

Fibbford: What's happening?

Steen: I'm getting back inside my Ford Taurus. I've got to get out of here! Got to get away. To run, i.e. drive off. I'm petrified . . .

Fibbford: Do you think you might wet yourself?

Steen: No . . . I'm currently totally dry down there.

Fibbford: Like I say, this is a brand-new Highlander leather sofa. Where are the objects now?

Steen: Object. I think it is actually just the one object.

Fibbford: (pen scratch)

Where is the object now?

Steen: Don't know . . . I'm speeding . . . Speeding along this perilous mountain road-slash-pass . . . Got to get away . . . Before . . . Before . . . Oh, God . . . There! . . . In my rear-view mirror! It's . . . they're . . .

(pause)

Fibbford: Is it 'they're' or 'it's'?

Steen: It's . . . No, they're . . . following me! The light or lights is or are following me! Oh, God! Oh God, it's or they're getting closer! I . . . I . . .

Fibbford: Please, my Highlander leather sofa . . .

(Indistinguishable fumbling. Tape recording ends)

– Comminglement *by Nicholas Steen (with Dr Dave Fibbford)*

SPECIMEN

Convincing, on the whole. Especially the sofa part. We'd put that in for effect, and Fibbford had even claimed a second couch on his policy allowance (though hadn't gifted it to me). I dreaded to think what the insurance guys would have said if they could have heard our laughter when Fibbford pressed stop on that tape recorder ...

I smiled at the memory, looking up at the night sky far above, now empty again. For whatever had been up there seconds before appeared to have vanished.

A feeling of relief washed over me; I'd been completely convinced, for the briefest of moments, that I'd just seen the exact same multi-coloured balls of light I'd allegedly witnessed in that entirely fictional account of my alien abduction.

Still unnerved, I concentrated my gaze on that lone wisp of cloud high overhead, eerily similar to the one I'd imagined years earlier. I strained my eyes to peer through it. Dared whatever might be hiding in there, mid-wisp, to come out again and reveal itself.

But nothing emerged.

Probably a case of the meat sweats then, I figured, making my way back to the car. That mildly feverish feeling I got after eating half-cooked pork too close to the bone. Sure, I'd since learned the art of patience in cooking, but persistent cravings for seared animal flesh still meant that I occasionally gorged before meat was remotely cooked, and the hog roll I'd skewered at the ski lodge's 'roast your own' joint before setting out had been no exception. Frankly, neither chop had even made it to the roll.

True, I'd built up a resistance to chronic food poisoning over the years, those microbes still thriving in the half-cooked meat merely adding to the high levels of potency swelling in my own personal seed-sack. It was just too bad Jacinta and I were no longer in the business of rearing calves together. For Meredith had been our only brood,* and though she had evidently inherited a great deal of my raging testosterone levels, picking fights with her contemporaries from her first day in nursery, I'd been hoping that Jacinta and I might have given her at least one sibling to join the daily fray.

Maybe if we'd embarked upon one last physical set-to before splitting up for good, our frenzied body-bout might have produced, in its wake, a stout triplet of stunning prime-stock human proto-bullocks.

But it was not to be. Our marriage was over, and the messy issue of divorce would be rearing its sorry head again the moment I got back into Stalkford. I figured the sooner we could call time on our relationship altogether – handing ownership of Meredith over to Jacinta, ideally – the better. For rich and potent seed like mine was wasted if it couldn't be free to rear. It was time for Nick Steen's littlest hobo to move on. By which I mean *biggest* hobo.

As I stooped to get back in the car, I realised my anal throbbings had ceased. Whatever had been aggravating me down below, causing me to spin towards a fiery death over the side of a mountain precipice five minutes before, had now completely abated. As though it had never been there at all.

Like those lights in the sky . . .

Unnerved, I swung myself back into the Taurus and keyed the ignition. Comforted by the warm red glow coming from the dashboard lights, I put the vehicle in gear and turned the car around, heading off once more along the lonely mountain road towards Stalkford.

As I put my foot down, I reached over to switch on the radio. I was hoping to catch Danny Matterland, Stalkford's almost-famous perennial late-night shock jock. I was craving some barely human

---

* With the exception of Duncan in the second story featured in this book – which, if you haven't read before this one, frankly makes you a freak. And yet Duncan in that tale is an imaginary child, the story itself being a mere dream, and if that now constitutes a massive spoiler for those reading this current story first, tough shit. You freak. GM

SPECIMEN

company on this final stretch of road, and what could be better than an hour or two listening in to Matterland's incorrigible anti-establishment take on all manner of controversial topics, not least his thoughts on unfair divorce settlements, a topic he invariably tackled via a sequence of comically exaggerated 'extreme' scenarios, with a powerful range of wacky voices. These had been of immense comfort to me of late, and no doubt to all those other guys phoning in from their cars or friend's sofas at every hour of the night.

Yet before I could squeeze finger and thumb around the radio dial, the thing switched on by itself. A sudden burst of harsh static pierced my eardrums as I began to twist the dial left and right, wincing at the abrasive sound. But all that seemed to come through the car's speakers, from station to station, was a cacophonous storm of white noise.

Then, as suddenly as it had turned on, the thing switched itself off. But that wasn't *all* that had switched off. For the comforting red glow from the car's dashboard had also vanished, I noticed, along with the gentle hum of the engine. Evidently, my Taurus had lost all power, and was now slowing to a halt.

As the vehicle's wheels finally stilled, I keyed the ignition repeatedly in vain, hammering the steering wheel with my fists as the engine continued to fail.

Damn it! I was alone out here *again* ...

Then I felt it. That pattern of vague, intermittent thumps, quickly building in pace to form a regular, unnerving rhythm. The arse-tremors were back, for that's what I now knew them to be. And they were coming once more from the depths of my colonic passage: a steady pulse of itching pile-thunder, counting time like the steady beating of a human heart.

Or was that a sonar beep? For the distant throbbing from my rectum now sounded vaguely mechanical to my ears. Yet my arse wasn't underwater, as far as I could tell. A radar blip, then, given I was physically thousands of miles above sea level? But why would a radar beep be coming from my colonic tunnel? It sounded crazy, but I couldn't shake the feeling that this slow yet systematic beating from my piles was a *signal* of some kind, reaching outward through my shank flaps, past the confines of the Ford Taurus and into the world beyond.

Or should that be *the sky above* . . . ?

I recalled again the strange reflection of those pulsing lights I'd glimpsed on the nearby mountain tops; visual echoes of the eerie, multicoloured object I thought I'd seen floating and rotating in the sky far above. Reflections that had matched perfectly the timed beatings of my very own bum drum.

With a gnawing stab of terror firing through my vitals (itself separate from the persistent pile pain), I wound down my window and craned my neck out to look up at the sky.

And there it was again. Far above, separating itself once more from that lone wisp of floating cloud.

A jiggling cluster of multicoloured light-balls, whirling and revolving in bizarre motion; changing shape, stretching and contorting themselves into outrageous angles, before resuming their original form again to become what looked like . . .

Damn, it was no good. I couldn't tell *what* the thing was. And it had already changed shape again. At one point I thought it looked like a shimmering cow bell, but then it turned into something resembling a giant slinky. And then a curvaceous barfly with a killer perm, though it could have been my imagination doing that.

As I watched these bizarre transformations of light occurring in the sky far above, the only thing I was able to confirm about the object's appearance was that its shifting displays of light were indeed pulsing and pulsating in perfect time with my private anal throbbings.

How could I explain that? Unless I considered the terrifying notion that the two were somehow *connected*. That the beating of my

SPECIMEN

lower sphincter was in some inexplicable way a sort of signal to whatever this thing in the sky was.

I thought again of my book, *Comminglement*. And my supposed alien abduction. Surely everything in that book was mere fantasy, only masquerading as undeniable truth? A tale of cosmic abduction manufactured as a sure-fire bestseller, with Dr Dave Fibbford's revolutionary Fibbertronics lie-detector-deflecting system transforming my blatant detected lies into irrefutable truth?

Surely it was all merely the product of my authorial imagination?

Except that that very authorial imagination, I recalled with sudden trepidation, was now *alive*. No longer confined to my head alone, since that fateful day I'd slept with a cursed typewriter and sold my soul to Type-Face, Lord of the Prolix. That dreaded day of infamy when a portal to another dimension had opened inside my brain, releasing whatever cosmic or homebound horrors my imagination could dream up into the real world. Horrors including, I now suspected, my own 'true-life' account of supposed alien abduction ...

As I looked up at the distant cluster of lights, I realised they were now moving away at speed from that lone wisp of cloud. Towards *me* ...

I ducked my head back inside the car and keyed the ignition again. Useless. The engine was still dead. The radio, too, I discovered, trying once again to tune in to *Matter's Matters* with Danny Matterland.

Then I felt the ground shift under me. Terrified, I clutched the steering wheel tightly in both hands as the entire car was lifted upwards, away from the ground ...

I glanced through the driver's-side window again and saw the nearby mountain peaks sinking lower in the frame.

I was ascending into the sky ... In disbelief, I leaned out again and looked up once more into the dazzling kaleidoscope of shifting, multicoloured lights. Shielding my eyes against the blinding illuminations, I began to perceive a strange shape forming itself within the whirling fluorescence. An object of some kind, its exterior shell flat like a circular sheet of metal, but one that formed and reformed itself over and over into myriad twisting shapes and sizes, before resuming its former flat, cigar-shaped frame.

A craft of some kind, I realised.

A *spaceship!*

Then, amid the chaotic patterns of light, I thought I saw a round hole appear in one side, exposing what looked to me like a dark, black interior. A window, perhaps? And through that window, if that's what the thing was, I saw something more. Something sickly blue in colour. An oval shape resembling a bald, grey head with black, diamond-shaped slits for eyes.

A face . . .

A terrible, sickly face I'd glimpsed once before, in my mind's eye late one night on my way over to Fibbford's office. The face of an interstellar being I'd falsely claimed had abducted me on a similar stretch of lonely mountain road.

And now the thing was staring back at me for *real*. From the apparent window of a *genuine* flying saucer.

In a sudden fit of shrieking, mind-numbing terror, I thrust both fists into my mouth in an attempt to stifle my screaming.

For my mind had just recalled something else. Recalled what, in a short amount of time, this creature in the spaceship would do to me.

CHAPTER THREE

Fibbford: And that's the last thing you remember?

Steen: Until I woke up on the road to Stalkford.

Fibbford: What time was that?

Steen: The clock on the dashboard of my Ford Taurus said 3.57am.

Fibbford: And you'd last looked at the clock on the dashboard of your Ford Taurus at . . .?

Steen: 3.56am.

Fibbford But you cannot account for the time in between?

Steen: I have no memory of that time at all.

Fibbford: Meaning you've somehow lost an entire minute of your life.

Steen: An entire minute I can't remember. An entire minute I'll never get back. An entire minute I have no memory of whatsoever . . .

(breaks down in tears)

Fibbford: Here ...

(hands tissue)

Steen: I don't need one.

Fibbford: I think you'll find you're crying.

Steen: Oh yeah, right ...

(takes tissue and blows nose)

Fibbford: An entire minute of missing time ...

(sound of lunging)

Steen: What the hell happened to me in that entire missing minute, Doc? How come I can't remember anything at all about that aforementioned entire minute?

Fibbford: Remove your hands from my lapels, please. To answer that question, Mister Steen, I must regress you via hypnosis, in order to ascertain precisely what occurred on that fateful night, in that terrifying entire-minute window.

Steen: Sure thing.

Fibbford: One question, first. Have you definitely been to the toilet?

– Comminglement *by Nicholas Steen*
(with Dr Dave Fibbford)

SPECIMEN

Unfortunately, whatever had occurred in the entirely fictional one-minute window I'd written about so glibly in that fictional account of alleged alien abduction was now about to occur for real. Except that the process itself wouldn't take a mere minute. Because, by some hideous warping of time and space, which my fictional alien abductors were theoretically able to manipulate, I knew that this single Earth minute would in fact consist of forty-eight hours of traumatic bodily interference in an alternate temporal dimension. An elaborate intimate body probe, which was due to commence imminently if I didn't find some way of getting back down to Earth in record time from my floating Ford Taurus.

I turned my eyes from the multicoloured craft above and looked down instead. My eyes, still dazzled by the light, struggled to make out anything in the darkness below. But I saw enough to know that the mountain road was no longer directly below me, and the car in which I now hung, suspended in mid-air, had somehow begun to drift. In which direction, I couldn't tell. If we'd been veering to the right, below me would theoretically lie a shallow valley – a natural crevice at the base of the mountain range through which ran the Wyrm Lake River.

But if we'd drifted leftward, then below me would lie instead the dark, primeval forest of Spinewood.

Perceiving what looked like some sparkling reflections far below, I prayed it was the river, kicked open the car door and jumped ...

I felt the cold, paralysing rush of upthrust winds as I began to plummet, bracing myself for the harsh plunge into icy water. But in seconds, I found myself crashing instead through a cushioning canopy of collapsing foliage.

Meaning I'd hit the forest, after all. As the soft branches of Spinewood's musky-smelling pines broke under my hurtling haunches, my downward descent gradually slowed until at long last I found myself collapsing on to an incline of earthy ground littered with cones and soft pine needles.

GARTH MARENGHI

As I clambered to my feet, a colossal roar sounded from above as a large object followed me down, nosediving through the trees above my head. Lightning-fast, I leaped to one side, watching helplessly as my Taurus – or what remained of it – thundered hard against the steep incline, then barrelled at increasing speed down the sloping hillside, crashing through breaking foliage before landing with an audible thump somewhere further down.

I ran after it, hoping I might be able to salvage the catalytic converter, at least (which had been replaced at huge personal expense after a recent MOT, and which the garage appointed by my insurance company following the incident would not allow me to retain, even though the vehicle is still technically one's property until one elects to sell it to said company).*

My route through the forest was partly lit by beams of multicoloured light projecting downward from the terrifying alien craft overhead. I ducked and weaved as these beams flitted and darted through the surrounding branches, until at long last I caught sight of my crushed car, smoking and steaming beside what looked like a disused wooden shack.

---

* I would add that this company (and yes, this plot detail is based on a real-life shunt) also claimed that the converter itself was damaged, despite the shunt in question occurring at the opposite end of the vehicle, and furthermore would not accept an independent assessment by a team of private investigators plus a physics teacher I'd already hired, the costs of which the insurance company would not allow me to include as legitimate expenses incurred by the accident, and for which I am now ultimately out of pocket. Bottom line is that I now drive an inferior make of car with a worn catalytic converter through no fault of my own, and am currently involved in two separate cases at the small claims court for non-payment of service, despite said team of private investigators and physics teacher being ultimately not called upon to make their professional assessment in a court of law and for whom sixteen nights of essential and detailed preparatory work is therefore not relevant or refundable. Essentially, if you get involved in an accident two weeks after paying more than £6,000 for a new catalytic converter, you can kiss goodbye to that catalytic converter, even if said catalytic converter is still *entirely functional*. Including the details of this dispute in a printed work such as this is my only legal recourse and serves as a warning to Humanity. GM

SPECIMEN

I laughed out loud. I couldn't believe my luck. For the shack was my property! Of all the places to end up, my battered Ford Taurus had parked itself, however roughly, in the grounds of my own private writing cabin in the woods beneath the Spinal Mountains. My own secret writer's retreat: a haven to which I frequently escaped whenever I needed to concentrate on work and/or avoid my family.

I walked straight past my ruined vehicle, electing to remove the catalytic converter at a more convenient time, and made my way towards the front door of the cabin, extracting the key to the shack from my trouser pocket.

As I did so, the lights from the craft above passed by, slowly edging away into the distance, leaving me, and the surrounding woodland, in complete darkness.

I unlocked the cabin door and went in.

The place was a tip, but that was normal for a writer's private domain. Especially an author like me, who specialised in horror and – of late – true-life, fully-lie-deflected paranormal alien abduction accounts.

I kicked aside an empty pizza box and made my way over the pine-effect flooring to my writing desk. I checked the time on my watch, grabbed the phone receiver from its cradle and dialled our house number in Stalkford. Though it was approaching four in the morning, I figured Meredith would be awake with anxiety again.

I was right.

'I said get *lost*, creep!'

'Hi, Meredith. It's Dad.'

'Dad!'

'Has that nuisance caller been bothering you again?'

'The *fifth* time! He keeps calling when I'm alone in the house.'

'Like I said last time, Meredith, it's just the late-night prowler from my slasher novel *Ring Ring*—'

'I know, but—'

'Wait, let me finish. From my slasher novel *Ring Ring, Ring Ring, Ring Ring, Ring Ring, Ring Ring, Ring Ring*. And also the sequel, *Ring Ring, Ring Ring, Ring Ring, Ring Ring, Ring Ring Again.*'

'Where the hell have you been, Dad?'

'I went skiing.'

'For half a year?'

'Meredith, I've been fighting the escaping figments of my imagination for *three years*. I deserved a holiday, and it was your mother's responsibility to inform you I was going on a six-month hiatus. I can't personally live with her anymore, as you know. So I duly faxed her to fax you that I'd be incommunicado for several months, which she evidently failed to do. Hence you being wrongly irked at me for being left completely alone with the late-night prowler from my novel *Ring Ring, Ring Ring, Ring*—'

'Dad, call the *police!*' she snapped, interrupting me before I'd been able to finish the full title *again*.

I realised it was time for some tough love. 'Listen, Meredith, you're old enough now to take on some responsibility yourself. *You* need to call the police. Not me.'

'Please, Dad. Just call them.'

'No can do, kiddo. If I call them, I'll start yacking with the sergeant and we'll waste precious time before we even think of getting round to rescuing you. If *you* call them, they'll admittedly not believe you for a few hours, but, *crucially*, the prowler won't be able to call you once while you're on the line. Meaning genuine respite from the horror during which you can gather strength and/or have a comfort break. It's not difficult, is it?'

'But who *is* he?' my daughter gasped, her voice wavering.

'If I'm honest, Meredith, I don't actually remember. You have to understand, I wrote that book a *very* long time ago, when things were different and my attitude towards women wasn't as respectful or understanding as it is now. But I'm sure he'll make himself known to you at some point soon. Probably via the door to the cellar, or through your bedroom window when you're just starting to drift off. So you'd best be on your guard.'

'You don't care about me anymore.'

'Meredith, I'm bloody *swamped* at the moment, okay?'

I was getting angry, I realised, but my daughter simply had no idea how stressful things were for me with all these denizens of my fevered brain becoming increasingly incarnate.

'I'm at war with the demons of my own mind, remember? I have to do battle with said demons twenty-four-seven, while at the same time sorting out this bloody separation settlement with your mother, *plus* I have to do my VAT. By the way, where *is* your mother?'

'She shacked up last month with that bloody hypnotherapist of hers. Dr—'

'Fibbford,' I said, my voice growing suddenly hoarse as the man's name deigned to part my lips. So Jacinta had finally moved in with the good doctor, had she? I could have guessed as much. After all, with his assistance she'd roundly trounced my own book sales with her rival account of nocturnal alien abduction, *Jacinta's Cosmic Journey*. A book that was an obvious fantasy, frankly. Nothing more convincing than an erotic wish-fulfilment saga detailing my ex-wife's supposed abduction from bed by some interstellar Venetian stallion who supposedly took her on an all-expenses-paid-for cosmic cruise around the universe in an attempt to get her to bear his race of telepathically gifted star-children.

But with Fibbford's infamous Fibbertronics System masking her own fabricated account under a cloak of irrefutable scientific 'proof', aided and abetted by a steamy promotional photoshoot to boot, she'd left my own alien abduction account in the proverbial dust.

'Typical. I'm meant to be meeting her at the house later today to discuss your future,' I said.

But Meredith wasn't listening.

'He's coming in, Dad! I can hear someone downstairs!'

'Meredith, will you calm down? Things will be fine for a while yet. First he needs to sing some creepy nursery rhymes from a distant room, then he has to follow that with a few cryptic messages daubed on the walls in red lipstick. If he's only just through the cellar door, you still have until midnight tomorrow, probably, by which point I'll be there to decapitate him.'

'*Will* you?'

She had a point. I might not be there at all if that eerie spacecraft in the sky made another appearance. Naturally, in an ideal world I wanted to be there to save my daughter from the crazed psychopaths of my own imagination, but my busy schedule currently included fending off an onslaught of grey-skinned alien entities, so something had to give.

'Listen, kiddo,' I said, trying to calm her down, 'I'm having to keep myself hidden at the moment. I'm currently stuck in my writing cabin in Spinewood.'

'But Dad, *I need you!*'

That hurt. Deep inside, like an arrow piercing my heart. My darling daughter, pleading desperately for help from her beloved father – at the *precise* moment I had far worse troubles of my own to deal with. How selfish could she be?

'I'd say you could come out here,' I explained, 'but if memory serves, that prowler of yours has a tendency to follow his victims, wherever they hide. Plus, there's a strong chance the crazed hillbilly from my novel *The Spinewood Axe Massacre* might also make an appearance, so it's probably best you stay there.'

'I hate you!' Meredith screamed, then hung up on me.

Normally, those words would smart, but I'd heard them a lot lately, to be honest, and had developed a fairly tough skin as far as my daughter's primal rage was concerned. Hopefully several courses of psychotherapy would sort all that out, if I could somehow convince

SPECIMEN

Jacinta to pay for them out of her recent multi-million-pound three-book deal.

I quickly dialled Flint Rustin, the local police sergeant in Stalkford, cut his yacking off at the source and instructed him to send over a patrol car to scare off Meredith's prowler in exchange for a free book. That would at least buy her – and me – some time until the following day. Although, the way things were going, I wasn't sure I'd make it home by then, either.

For there was something about the way in which the spacecraft – if that's what the thing truly was* – had focused on me so intensely for the last hour or so that convinced me I hadn't yet seen the last of it. And this imitation log cabin of mine, while it had served as a refuge for me on many occasions in the past, somehow didn't feel as cosy as I remembered.

Partly that was because I loathed paying utility bills, and generally kept the place in total darkness, which also helped fuel my imagination. But something about those creeping shadows forming among the deep wood-effect recesses around me were starting to give me the proverbial jitters.

I placed the phone receiver back on its cradle and made my way over to the main window, where it was comparatively light. But that itself was eerie, because there shouldn't have been any light at all out there in the deep, dark woods of the Spinal Mountains. Catching sight of something flickering strangely through the curtains, I pulled back the drape an inch or so, widening my view of the woodland beyond.

And saw that it was back.

---

* It was. GM

CHAPTER FOUR

Steen: I see a strange light ... outside ... in the woods ...

Fibbford: Where are you now?

Steen: In the cabin ... I can't sleep ... need pizza ...

Fibbford: Describe it.

Steen: Large box, half-empty, two separate side-orders of chicken wings.

Fibbford: I mean the light.

Steen: Oh, right ... Wait ... Something's wrong ...

Fibbford: What is it?

Steen: I ordered half Hawaiian with Tex Mex plus extra chillies, and a large Meat Meltdown. They forgot the Meat Meltdown.

Fibbford: Concentrate on the light. What do you see?

Steen: Hard to tell through the trees ... Flickering ... Something spinning ... like a large Catherine wheel ... And yet it isn't remotely a Catherine wheel ... Descending now ... Through the trees ...

SPECIMEN

from the sky above me . . . Those lights . . . Shining like fireflies . . . It's landing . . . The thing is landing! . . . The thing that looks like a giant Catherine wheel, but that isn't remotely a Catherine wheel is landing . . .

Fibbford: Remember, I have a bucket right here . . .

Steen: It's opening up . . . The lights are going crazy . . . I can see . . . I can see something coming out . . . Something that looks like something*s*, i.e. the plural of 'something' . . .

Fibbford: What are these . . . somethings?

Steen: Things . . . Beings . . . Small grey beings . . . Swarming from those revolving lights . . . Like ants . . .

Fibbford: But *not* actual *ants*?

Steen: No. Actual ants would be nigh-on impossible to spot from this distance.

Fibbford: Describe them in detail.

Steen: Thin . . . Grey . . . Bald heads . . . Like human spermatozoa – but with arms and legs.

Fibbford: Where are they now?

Steen: Coming . . . Coming towards me!

Fibbford: An alternative phrase, please.

GARTH MARENGHI

Steen: *Heading towards me! Heading this way! Help! Someone, help! I'm all alone out here! Help!*

(panicked fumbling)

Fibbford: *The bucket, man ...*

— Comminglement *by Nicholas Steen (with Dr Dave Fibbford)*

And they really *were* heading this way. For though my account of a second attempted abduction from the safety and security of my own writing cabin had been entirely fictional in the pages of *Comminglement*, it was reality now. For out here in the woods, before my very eyes, *precisely* as I'd described it before Fibbford's self-patented Fibbertronics lie-detector-deflecting system, the cluster of spinning multicoloured lights had returned.

I watched, terror-struck, as the craft descended through the trees, then hovered above the muddy earth about seventy feet from my cabin. Scarcely able to believe my eyes, I watched helplessly as a metallic gangplank slid from one side of the craft, precisely as I'd imagined it doing all those years before.

Then, as I knew they would do, the alien beings emerged.

A terrifying army of shrivelled, hairless forms. Grey-skinned, as I'd pictured them in my mind's eye, with bald heads and black, diamond-shaped eyes.

They started darting like tiny insects across the underbrush towards me.

Despite my fear, I found myself unable to turn and run. Instead, I stood stock-still by the window, my whole body frozen with terror. Maybe they hadn't seen me at all, and were merely interested in the exterior of the cabin itself, which consisted largely of steel-based faux log sidings requiring little in the way of re-staining, repainting

SPECIMEN

or re-sealing, thus saving thousands on regular maintenance with a thirty-year guarantee against rot. Maybe evidence of a hot deal had somehow piqued their interest, and any moment now they'd be returning to their craft, carrying with them a faux log or two to compare favourably with genuine tree samples inside their advanced-tech interstellar laboratory.

Who was I kidding? These beings were after *me*, not my rustic-effect summerhouse cabin with old-wood surface detail, plus standard-feature high-quality tongue-and-groove panelling.

At once I felt the adrenaline rush through my body, and realised I could now move again. But where could I run *to*? My forty-five-year all-meat diet meant fleeing back uphill might pose a problem. While I might possess the necessary muscular strength, speed would be an issue, and I could soon find myself overtaken by this marauding alien horde.

What if I could fight my way around the side of the house somehow, and escape that way, dodging those lights ahead of me by slipping under my battered car, then rolling sideways into the trees again, once the swarm had passed by?

I turned from the window to face the darkness of the cabin's interior, lit partly now by those lights shining through from the spacecraft outside. Shimmering, rainbow-hued reflections danced over the log-effect wallpaper, peppered with the darting silhouettes of those advancing beings.

Then something materialised in front of me. A long, grey form, squeezing itself slowly out of the hole of my disused fireplace (I'd installed a central-heating system, which, while more expensive, required no wood-splitting). As I watched, helpless, a cruel-looking head rose upwards from the grate, coal-black eyes blinking at me inquisitively from its protruding, snake-like neck. It was one of the beings, only larger than those I'd glimpsed outside, and it was reaching out for me from the cabin's chimney stack like some terrifying giant mamba.

Then, from a small orifice beneath those black, fathomless eyes, where a nose might have sat, the thing emitted a sharp puff of black, acrid gas, like some demonic and poisonous devil-fart.

I bolted.

*

I wasn't sure where I had bolted to, exactly. I only recalled that I'd instinctively grabbed an old pair of pants from the floor to mask my nose from the alien's acrid blast, then catapulted myself through the rear door of the cabin and out into the trees.

Coming to my senses again, I immediately hurled myself around the side of the cabin, dived upon the ground, then crawled forward at pace beneath my battered Taurus. As I lay there, panting, in the darkness, my ears caught the sound of shattering glass, followed by the rush of skittering, pattering feet as those alien lifeforms swarmed into the cabin in search of me.

Realising I couldn't stay hidden for much longer, I rolled sideways, emerging from beneath the car and straight into the neighbouring bushes. Scrabbling at speed down a small ravine, I leaped to my feet and pelted myself through the trees as fast as I could, away from the cabin and that terrifying cluster of multicoloured lights still spinning and shimmering in the neighbouring trees.

I flew blindly through the forest, somehow still unhampered by the encroaching darkness that should have been surrounding me. Then I realised that the source of light illuminating the path ahead was the spacecraft again, closing in behind me and evidently in fast pursuit, zipping through the trees on either side of my fleeing body. It was like a cat playing with a doomed mouse before sinking its fangs into the tiring flesh, or a troubled child plucking the wings from a captured fly before being sent, quite rightly, to an institution.

SPECIMEN

I dashed madly through the foliage, cutting my limbs on surrounding branches, soaking myself in fetid pools of swampish filth as I struggled desperately to outrun the alien craft tailing me relentlessly through the trees. At long last, I sensed another light somewhere up ahead, one that seemed to shine in an entirely different way from those otherworldly bulbs currently directing their rays at my fleeing body. A man-made light, perhaps. Sensing freedom, I made a beeline straight for it. As the light ahead of me grew steadily clearer, I saw that it was, in fact, two lights.

Headlights!

Bursting through the thinning treeline in front of me, I plunged into the centre of a lonely country road, too late to hail the articulated lorry already passing me by. I cried out in vain, then sprawled, exhausted, on the cold tarmac. Gasping for breath, I forced myself to my feet again, aware that I had to continue running if I were to have any hope of escape. But it was useless. I was physically spent, and a sitting duck for my pursuing alien abductors.

Then I saw it, not thirty metres down the road. A *third* set of lights. Not from the spacecraft this time, nor the headlights of some passing truck, but the comforting, reassuring gleam of a neon sign. The warm, inviting glow of Paul Ball's All-Night Diner.

It was a place I knew well, having sought it out numerous times as an alternative writing venue whenever my imitation log-cabin retreat became a claustrophobic anathema to the spirit of creativity – or whenever I'd run out of pizza. Rising to my feet with renewed vigour, I staggered towards the distant glow. If I could hide out here until morning, then those alien pursuers behind me would inevitably disperse, losing all trace of me amid the strong competing scents of other human bodies.

Hardly believing my good fortune, I yanked open the door of Paul Ball's All-Night Diner and stepped inside.

CHAPTER FIVE

As I did so, a familiar wave of inquisitive stares rose as one from above mugs of steaming coffee and fried all-night breakfasts, as the diner's lonely clientele looked up from their meals to scrutinise this new, bedraggled stranger in their midst. I watched their customary expressions of bored self-absorption grow increasingly suspicious, but that was normal when entering Paul Ball's diner, and not the thing that was bothering me.

For there was something else present, besides the usual air of underlying hostility. Something terribly wrong. At first I couldn't put my finger on it, but once the nagging thought had taken root, it seemed so glaringly obvious that I was surprised it hadn't struck me the second I entered the diner, as opposed to two seconds later.

Like I say, I'd frequented Paul Ball's establishment numerous times over the years; had supped scalding coffee and chewed gristly bacon baps there for as long as I could remember. But never, in all my years of lonesome self-pitying rumination in the greased interior of that late-night fried-food dive, had I ever seen a single woman. (Apart from, I should say, the weathered yet overly friendly and not unattractive waitress, Phyllis, who no doubt moonlighted after-hours as a topless dancer so she could put enough food on the table for her large gaggle of starving, semi-related chicklings.)

What normally greeted one upon entering Paul Ball's diner was a steamy cafeteria filled with single men hunched over separate tables, poring over crumpled newspapers and failed football-pool results

SPECIMEN

amid a pile of brimming ashtrays. The usual vision of middle-aged males mulling moodily over the tattered fragments of their broken lives.

But today was different. Although the men were there as always, dotted around the diner and staring up gruffly from their gelatinous fried eggs, others were sitting with them now. Companions, they seemed to be at first glance, though that word could hardly be associated with a greased-up den like this. Guardians, perhaps. Or sentries, maybe. No, those words didn't quite capture the true horror of the situation. Prison wardens ... That felt more like it. For accompanying this forgotten army of failed, world-weary male warriors, were the stiff, austere and imposing presences of their aggrieved other halves.

I glanced over them, catching sight of Biff Fudge's wife, Madge, whom I'd only ever spoken to previously during a road-rage incident in which we'd both shrieked insults about each other's weight. And there, beside Ian Haggard, was his wife of eleven years, Meryl, who was anything *but* haggard, and who only ever dined at high-class restaurants while Ian sat alone at this very diner.

In the booth opposite him sat Old Man Gristler, who had been a full-time wood-chopper in his youth, but who now brewed moonshine and poached poultry for profit. He had somehow seen fit to invite his previously bedbound sister from Dankton all the way up to Spinewood to accompany him for his customary all-night chowdown on non-specific meat offcuts.

All of them were staring at me. Every lonely, world-weary male I'd ever known to ingest ('eat' is the wrong word) at this establishment, along with their hitherto unseen female companions. Then a voice called out from behind the counter.

'Close that fucking door.'

Jolted out of my thoughts, I turned and did as the voice had commanded. Then I stepped further into the room, moving through that sea of unnerving, watchful expressions, which continued to glare in my direction as I passed.

I took up my usual position at the counter. 'No need to swear,' I said to the weathered, middle-aged waitress whom I imagine also moonlighted as a topless dancer after-hours.

'What the fuck do you want?' she asked, pouring me some coffee from a cloudy pot. I smiled – at least *she* was her usual self.

'Three fried eggs, four bacon rashers – not too stringy – three large sausages, three hash browns, a large glass of chilled orange juice and five toasts with butter, plus separate portions of jam and marmalade. Eggs have to be sunny-side up.'

'Your usual, then?'

'That's correct, Phyllis,' I said, winking at her. 'My usual.'

'Then say "usual" and stop wasting my fucking time.'

With that, Phyllis plopped a mid-sized dollop of cream in my coffee, despite knowing full well I only liked a large-sized dollop of cream, and wandered off along the counter to crack some eggs.

'Sunny-side up, remember,' I said, suspecting that Phyllis's mind wasn't quite on the job. Maybe she'd ballsed up her last lap dance, or something. But with all the stress I was going through myself, what with all those alien sperm-beings on my tail and my ongoing divorce settlement with Jacinta affecting sales of my fabricated alien-abduction story, I'd been expecting a bit of support, to be honest. After all, Paul Ball's diner prided itself on providing greased meat, angry banter and an occasional bawdy innuendo from whatever resident cheery wench was currently working overtime. Today, I realised, that simply wasn't happening.

'Where's Paul?' I asked, intending to make an official complaint on the sly and get Phyllis duly reprimanded, if not sacked. I liked Phyllis, but she really had put too little cream in my coffee. Then I remembered that the proprietor usually worked from home,

SPECIMEN

watching television or playing pool on the company-owned games table undergoing permanent repair in his front lounge.

'I'm back here,' said a voice coming from the kitchen area behind the counter. I looked up as a tired-looking man wearing an oily chef's apron wandered through the open door.

I should have recognised it was Paul immediately, but he no longer looked quite as furious as he normally did. In fact, he seemed depressed.

Phyllis tossed my eggs violently in the frying pan and flipped them sunny-side down.

'Do these,' she snapped, stepping away from the hob. Paul snapped suddenly to attention and took the waitress's place at the frying pan.

'Evening, Nick,' he said, manipulating the eggs with Phyllis's abandoned spatula.

I glanced back at the waitress. She was already sitting on a stool on the customer's side of the counter, flicking through a home furnishings catalogue while lighting up three cigarettes at once.

'What gives, Paul?' I whispered.

'It's her fag break,' said Paul, staring down intently at the frying eggs.

I edged myself back along the counter towards Phyllis, hoping to catch her attention.

'Hey,' I said.

She didn't 'hey' back.

'Thought I might mosey on down to the Raunch later,' I said, casually. 'If they're still doing their Giant Double-Jug special?'

I expected something, at least. Maybe not the usual exchange of whoop-inducing double-entendres we generally partook of on a rainy night, but a basic 'Don't you mean Giant Double-*Jugs*?' wouldn't have gone amiss.

'Do what you fucking well like,' said Phyllis. 'I'm going home.'

Something was deeply wrong here. If I didn't know better, I'd think Phyllis appeared to be upset about something. True, most women always were, but that didn't usually prevent this particular one from squeezing another doughnut sale or two out of some unsuspecting punter with a subtle wink or well-timed surreptitious shoulder-squeeze. No, something else had happened. Something that had overturned the delicate status quo of this male-heavy all-night fried-food restaurant.

And there was no way a man like Paul Ball would ever be performing menial work at his own establishment, confined to the kitchen area of all places, unless he'd somehow happened upon a distinctly sorry state of affairs.

I gasped, a sudden suspicion taking root.

Maybe Paul and Phyllis were now a *couple*... Maybe they'd realised they had more in common than simply sharing the letter 'P' at the beginning of their respective names. Maybe they'd realised that they both worked here at Paul Ball's diner, and wore similar aprons.

Meaning maybe they'd lost their minds entirely and got *married*...

I'd seen it happen to the best of men. Overnight, a complete recalibration of an entire relationship culminating in total surrender to the other half and her natural propensity for wrenching the balls clean off her supposed nearest and dearest. Like every other guy in here, this poor bastard was now well and truly hitched.

'Paul?' I whispered, sneaking back to his end of the counter. 'I think you've overdone those eggs.'

The thing that was previously professional fried-food operative Paul Ball continued to stare down blankly at the pan in front of him. My eggs were totally ruined. He'd evidently been chopping and flipping them without the faintest idea of what he was meant to be doing. The man was a wreck.

'Look, Paul,' I said, choosing my words carefully. Divorce was never an easy subject to bring up. 'I'm going through something similar,

SPECIMEN

buddy, but there *is* light at the end of the tunnel. Or so I'm told.' I leaned across the counter, trying to get him to look up from the pan. 'Look, you have to man up, Paul,' I said. 'Because this, I gotta say, is one sorry-arse display. Now, there's a good solicitor I can recommend, whom I admit *is* expensive, and is someone I *should* have employed instead of the shyster I actually ended up hiring at cut-rate. But if you—'

'Don't lean over the counter!' barked Phyllis, right behind me. I sensed a small pistol at my ear that I suspected she'd just drawn from the region of her brassiere.

'I'm not leaning,' I said, calmly and carefully.

'Good. Or I might think you're fucking stealing something,' she added.

'Sure thing, Phyllis,' I said, placatingly, withdrawing my head further across the counter, away from the region of Paul's own. 'I was just saying hi to Paul, that's all.'

But there was no way anyone could just say hi to Paul in his current state, I realised. For he was still standing in that same spot, sliding what was left of my eggs to and fro in the pan amid a cloud of rising smoke.

'Clear that up,' ordered Phyllis. Paul immediately obeyed, slouching over to the sink with the smoking pan. I heard a violent hiss as he doused the contents of the pan in his usual sink of yesterday's rancid water, and knew then that the prospect of a fried breakfast was literally off the table.

'Mind if I use your john?' I asked Phyllis, aware that I hadn't yet paid for my breakfast and so was not technically a paying customer, but hoping that my use of the word 'john' might appeal to her instinct for colourful phrasing.

She held out her hand, waiting. I duly filled it with a crumpled note, then made my way across the diner, past the rows of still-staring loners and their glaring spouses, towards the toilet area situated at the far side of the room.

Though my piles had temporarily cooled off, it seemed, I was all too aware that they might erupt again at any moment, and what with all the terror and confusion of my recent attempted alien abduction, I knew that my brain had most likely engaged some form of subconscious self-numbing procedure to dull and nullify the crazed itching I'd felt earlier. Best that I deal with it now, while there were some barely adequate facilities to hand.

I walked past the final dining booth, where Stew McCafferty – whom I'd last seen contemplating jumping from the Stalkford bypass, although I'd been too busy to try and convince him to do otherwise – sat alongside his steely looking wife, whose name I didn't know, having met her only seventeen times. She leaned her head forwards provocatively, daring me to address her husband, staring up at me coldly with that same icy indifference that had no doubt contributed to Stew's decision to step back from the ledge, thus avoiding far worse trouble in the afterlife when she'd eventually catch up with him, having lived a full and event-filled life of her own on his insurance pay-out.

I walked past her and entered the toilet area. The first cubicle was completely blocked, and the second was locked – no surprise in this place, where constipation was a frequent occupational hazard. Luckily, the third one was empty, so I opened the door and squeezed myself inside.

Locking the door behind me, I yanked a wad of paper from the plastic spool, wiped what I could from the seat, then perched myself over the central throne, pulling as many segments of paper from the holder as possible in anticipation of the frenzied clawing to come.

But as I set to in earnest, I was shocked to find that there was no blessed relief to be had whatsoever from scratching the terrible itch I'd felt earlier. For now there was no itch at all. No pain whatsoever. It was as if my cluster of piles had somehow completely vanished. As if the appearance of that strange bunch of revolving multicoloured lights I'd seen in the skies above me had caused them to retreat.

SPECIMEN

Had my piles, then, really been some kind of communicating device? Had they merely throbbed and pummelled my lower sphincter so that I'd come to an ultimate standstill on that very stretch of lonely mountain road? Had the presence of my persistent throbbing, beating in time with the steady pulse of those eerie overhead lights, been some form of signal?

Perhaps my piles, as crazy as it might sound, were some sort of tracking device?

Then I remembered something else I'd written in *Comminglement*. Recalled, in sudden horror, the small, almost irrelevant detail I'd dreamed up with Fibbford on that comfortable, brand-new Highlander leather sofa of his.

I remembered I'd invented the *implant*.

CHAPTER SIX

Fibbford: You say you have arse pain?

Steen: That's right, arse pain. Huge pain in my arse.

Fibbford: Are we talking rectal prolapse pain?

Steen: No. Just pile pain.

Fibbford: I was going to say. Rectal prolapse pain is something else. Like the goring of a hungry hound.

Steen: As I say, I think it's just piles.

Fibbford: And do these piles go away occasionally?

Steen: Intermittently.

Fibbford: And that has nothing to do with meat intake?

Steen: No. I'm always on the meat. Have been since birth.

Fibbford: So it says ... here in your medical notes ...

        (ruffles some paper)

SPECIMEN

According to this, you have excellent seed.

Steen: So they say. But yes, I do.

Fibbford: Maybe that's what they were after.

Steen: Who?

Fibbford: These . . . visitors.

Steen: You think these alien abductors are after my seed?

Fibbford: Perhaps they wish to create a new race of super-powered alien beings. You say these abductors of yours were small, thin and grey in colour . . . Wan, shall we say?

Steen: They were indeed wan.

Fibbford: Then maybe they're seeking the seed of some strong and fertile human buck. I suggest these piles of yours were some form of rectal probe, implanted in your back passage to assess the quality of your seed and possibly track your position across the cosmos from their vast alien mothership.

Steen: That makes sense.

Fibbford: I think your seed must be very strong indeed.

Steen: It is, Doctor. Indeed, it is.

– Comminglement *by Nicholas Steen (with Dr Dave Fibbford)*

My seed. That's what they'd been after when they took me up in their spaceship and did those terrible yet strangely exciting invasive things to me. They'd sought my seed to sire a race of super alien beings so they could wage war against rival star systems up there in outer Betelgeuse, or wherever Fibbford had looked up as the place most suitable for an untraceable intergalactic war to take place.

But that had all been complete nonsense, dreamed up by the pair of us as a way of hoodwinking Joe and Jill Public into parting with their hard-earned cash for a vicarious taste of what it might be like to become sexually desirable to an entire race of complete strangers and taken on an all-expenses-paid trip around the wonders of the cosmos from the lonely discomfort of their own homes.

But now, bizarrely, those very horrors of my imagination were suddenly free to roam the skies above us. And those very alien beings who'd never actually abducted me for real, were now hell-bent on abducting me for real.

For my *seed*.

I stared down at my drooping man-hammer. Hard to think that this humble sausage of mine harboured the genes that might settle some aeons-long intergalactic calamity between once-powerful alien races.

But then, no one else I knew had ever been weaned on an all-meat diet. So there was no telling how potent my seed had become, especially now that my unleashed imagination was running free. For if monsters of my own design were now able to roam the living world, why not my other creative juices, too?

And it *did* look larger than before, now that I gave the matter some thought. It was hard to see exactly in the dim light of this cramped cubicle, but it seemed to me as if the girth had expanded suddenly while I was sitting here in the dark, contemplating the ultimate cosmic purpose of my loins.

SPECIMEN

In fact, the more I stared at my winky, the more potent it looked, seemingly rising upwards from the gloom of the toilet bowl beneath. Was it a trick of the light, I wondered? Or was I somehow excited by the thought of my own otherworldly virility? So much so that nature was even now readying my troops, preparing a vast gland army for some future interstellar conquest?

Then a hand that wasn't mine grabbed my balls.

I yelled out, grasping wildly at the wall for a light switch to illuminate my unseen assailant – but I could no longer rise from the seat.

Whatever had clutched my man-marbles was gripping on for dear life, forcing me to lower my haunches back down upon the rim.

Then the hand began to tug.

I felt both shanks dip suddenly as whatever lingered below me in that deep, dank toilet went to work on dragging me in.

I grasped the edge of the seat with both hands as my mystery grabber yanked and yanked at my nether regions, slowly, inexorably, pulling me further into the pan.

The pain in my thigh-globes was excruciating now, sending agonising tremors upwards through my kidnapped meat and two.

I had no idea whether there was enough room for my whole body to be sucked physically into the sewage outlet of Paul Ball's diner, but whatever was currently residing down there among the tangled network of pipes was giving that possibility its best shot.

Feeling my lower half drop, I found myself being sucked suddenly downwards, deeper into the pan. I knew it would be useless to cry for help. In his current state, Paul Ball would probably just burn some more eggs, while Phyllis would inevitably stuff me further down the outlet with a ragged mop, or prevent me from getting back up by waving that pistol of hers in my face.

Grasping wildly behind me with one hand while clinging on for dear life with the other, I fought to locate the position of the flush handle.

Alas, I couldn't feel one, which irked me greatly, as that meant this particular toilet either had one of those unreliable push-down buttons on the top of the cistern lid, split in two so that you could select either a hard or soft flush – the latter of which would be completely useless to me in my current position – or some chained flushing handle hanging to my left, no doubt somewhere that would either a) be impossible for me to reach from my current position half-buried in the pan, or b) require much harder yanking, which, likewise, was currently impossible for me to achieve, me being situated half in and half out of the toilet.

With no other option left, I reached up behind me with my free hand, feeling myself twisting lower into the bowl with the sheer force exerted upon my gonads by the mystery grabber beneath. With little strength left on that side of my body to force myself upwards, I realised I had mere seconds left until I sank entirely.

With a titanic yell, I thrust my raised arm as far as I could in the direction of the cistern lid, grasping about wildly on its china surface with my fingers for any sign of a flush button ...

... and found it!

I yelled out in triumph and fought wildly to assess, by touch alone, the nature of the button's surface.

My heart immediately sank again, for it was the dreaded *double* button. And if I pressed down on the wrong half, I might succeed only in initiating a soft flush, which would fail to provide enough power to suck out whatever was clasping my privates from below.

As if reading my mind, the thing gave another sharp tug, almost tearing me hook, line and sinker from the edge of the toilet rim. I clasped my fingernails to the edge of the plastic flush button, aware that one more yank from this pan-based attacker might well shear them off completely from my clutching fingers.

In sheer terror, I emitted a sudden involuntary burst of gas from my thwapping buttock-flaps. Yet instead of embarrassment, I felt a giddy sense of elation, praying that the unholy funk now billowing from my rear end might somehow disrupt the attentions of my unknown assailant, much like a squid fires disruptive plumes of body ink at a film crew forcing it to fight with dosed-up basking sharks. I felt a slight yet noticeable weakening of the thing's grip as it struggled wildly with the killer mist descending around it.

This was all the signal I needed, and with a flash of victorious rage, I yelled out loud once more for increased strength and thrust my fist downwards again, slamming a knuckle on *both* halves of the flush button.

An immense roar burst from the cistern as water rushed into the interior of the pan, drowning my attacker amid the sudden deluge.

At once, its grip on me weakened, and as the cold rush of flush fluid lubricated my trapped flesh, I returned my free hand to the edge of the toilet seat and heaved myself upwards, launching my body on to the cubicle floor as whatever lay trapped amid the whirling chaos of the sudden waterfall behind howled and screamed in what sounded to me like an alien tongue.

I pulled up my trousers, fastened the belt and stepped forwards cautiously to peer over the rim of my recent battleground.

The thing inside the pan was a hand. But a hand like nothing else I'd ever seen: grey in hue with a queasy, rubbery texture, and only three fingers, which bore mauve circular suckers at their ends. As I stared in disbelief at what had been groping me, the fingers rose from the pan once more as the flowing water subsided, reaching out in my direction.

For the flush hadn't destroyed the thing, I realised. Merely stunned it. The alien hand was itself attached to a long, grey arm that was now rising, by degrees, from the flush-hole itself. Yet there was little time to imagine what form of extra-terrestrial life this strange limb might belong to, for the strange sucking pads had, by now, risen clear of the water and were readying themselves for a fresh assault.

As they advanced in my direction, I backed away towards the cubicle door, noticing now what looked like individual faces on the surface of each sucker. Faces that looked very much like those of the beings I'd seen emerge from the craft outside my cabin, and of that hideous snake-like monstrosity that had crept out of my fireplace.

Three sets of familiar, black, diamond-shaped eyes blinked in unison at me, then began to snake in and around themselves as the fingers on the end of that grey-fleshed interstellar toilet tendril dipped, curled and twisted themselves to form an unmistakeable single-digit 'sit and swivel' symbol.

But before I could utter the words, 'And fuck you too,' the hand shot into the air, propelled by a long, grey arm now rushing from the toilet basin at speed. I caught a brief glimpse of the fingers contracting above me to form what looked like a pummelling fist, then cowered against the wall as the mighty alien hand smashed through the ceiling of the cubicle, ripping the timber planking from the roof of Paul Ball's diner and exposing the night sky above me.

At the same time, the wall I was leaning against collapsed backwards and the toilet exploded, showering me in chunks of shattered china and stagnant cistern water.

Then the rest of the roof gave way, collapsing around me as the outer walls of the diner also crumbled. Whatever it was that had still only partly emerged from the toilet pipe now suddenly shot upwards from the sewage pipe, moving so fast that I was unable to make out its true form, before vanishing into the blackness of the sky above.

I looked around me, expecting to find the remains of Paul Ball's customers dashed like smashed lemmings against the smoking rubble of his ruined diner.

But instead, I saw only the wives. They stood before me in a neat row, seemingly untouched and unhurt. Phyllis stood in the very centre of the row, piercing me with that cold, terrifying stare she'd recently developed.

SPECIMEN

Hadn't they seen that terrifying alien thing emerge from the pipe outlet? Weren't these other halves aware that Paul Ball's diner had just collapsed in an explosion of flying rubble and pulped sausage meat?

Then I realised they were more than aware. For, as one, this strange, silent assembly of other halves lifted their heads in unison and gazed out into the depths of space. I followed their line of sight and saw, high above us, that familiar cluster of strangely revolving, multicoloured lights. And, as each of the former wives of Paul Ball's recently living customers raised their hands skywards, pointing towards the distant spacecraft, I realised they must be communicating telepathically with whatever extra-terrestrial intelligence was hovering above them.

With a growing sense of doom, I watched as their hands at last dropped in unison towards the ground once more – except they froze midway, so that the hands now pointed *outwards*, directly in front of them . . . *towards me*.

As the being that had once been Phyllis the jovial bar wench opened its mouth, the others did likewise, and for one terrifying moment I thought they were about to sing a hymn like those awful ladies' choirs on charity television appeals. Instead, the mouths uttered a different sound entirely.

One that chilled me to the very bone.

It was the terrifying, cacophonous shriek of mocking laughter.

Yes, those ex-wives of Paul Ball's exploded clientele were laughing at me. Mocking me. Ridiculing the fact that I was the last man standing in a bursted diner. And, for all I knew, the last man on Earth (although it later turned out that I wasn't – more on that anon).

No doubt these Gorgons were trying to stun me rigid before moving in for the kill, which I suspected wasn't going to be the kind of attack a trio of sexy gothic vampires swarming lustfully over some imprisoned real-estate salesman in a remote Transylvanian castle might attempt. So I took my chances and ran.

Sprinting across the rubble into the main parking lot, I saw to my horror that every vehicle parked there had been crushed flat by the collapsing walls of the destroyed diner. I glanced behind me again and saw that long line of possessed diner's wives moving as one towards me, fingers still pointing in my direction as their strange, alien-like laughter continued to reverberate from their hardly-human-anymore mouths.

Then I heard it, approaching from the far distance. The sound of a lorry's horn, no doubt alerting Paul Ball that another lonely male customer was en route, and wanted him to get the sausages on.

I had to warn whoever was heading here that Paul Ball's diner was no more; that what remained in its place was nothing less than a sinister alien presence infecting the wives of every lone male frequenting Ball's former establishment.

I ran out blindly into the road, attempting to flag down the approaching lorry. I had to get away from here. Had to escape the horrors behind me, and the horrors overhead (plus the additional horrors of being spattered with festering bog water).

As the driver of the lorry hammered loudly on his horn, warning me to get clear of the road, the terrifying wave of mocking laughter behind me swelled more loudly as those sinister other halves continued to mock and ridicule my feeble efforts to escape.

Knowing I had no other choice, I stood my ground in the glare of the truck's approaching lights, ignoring the slow yet relentless movement of those alien women approaching from behind. Either they would get me, or the truck itself would, but I no longer had any choice.

Then the miracle I'd been praying for arrived, as the truck driver at long last lost his nerve and slowed, swerving to avoid both myself and that row of pointing bints stepping out as one into the road. And

SPECIMEN

as he did so, I made a sprint for it, grabbed hold of a stray strip of canvas sack I'd noticed flapping wildly from the truck's right-hand side, then hoisted myself into the back of the passing vehicle.

Leaving, within seconds, the remains of Paul Ball's diner far behind me.

CHAPTER SEVEN

The truck rattled along the road at an insane pace, as if the small delay it had endured while slowing past the destroyed diner in order to avoid me had thrown it badly off schedule. As the vehicle continued its way along the mountainous woodland pass, I found myself rolling sideways in the dark with each sudden swerve, slamming up hard against a wall of firmly packed canvas-covered objects. My balls were still in agony, having been strangulated by that supersized alien entity emerging from a public U-bend, and I figured one more blast to my marbles might potentially render the entire area uninhabitable, inflicting incalculable damage on the integrity of my future seed.

As the truck swerved again, I rolled with it, my hands grasping in vain for some stiff or solid protuberance to grab on to. Once again, I was flung hard against whatever it was the truck was transporting, and as I attempted to push myself back from the canvas coverings, my fingers felt a distinct softening beneath the surface. Most likely these were perishable goods of some kind, I figured. Vegetables, maybe, or some other useless product.

Owing to the darkness of the surrounding woodland through which we were travelling, I had no means of confirming my suspicions. But it seemed to me that there were several oblong canvas-covered blocks arranged in rows within the truck, all of which became increasingly soft and mushy to the touch as I slammed repeatedly against them. Reaching out with both hands, I confirmed that there were no hard or sharp surfaces to be found upon any of

SPECIMEN

them. I guessed they were either giant-sized marrows, huge aubergines or massive courgettes of some kind. Possibly even gargantuan cucumbers or vast avocados. Whatever the nature of these titanic greens, this had to be a collection of the largest, mushiest prize-winning produce ever assembled in one place.

Maybe I was on my way to a farmers' market, where agricultural big knobs gathered to compare the size of their respective yams, but I doubted any single lord of the land could have grown such a collection of impressive field-born perishables single-handed.

And even if this oversized produce really was the product of a single straw-sucking Barley Mow, why would he risk transporting his entire load in one truck in the middle of the night?

I reached out again in the dark and felt along the oblong mass immediately to my left. The canvas sheet covering it was wet to the touch now, giving way even more deeply beneath the pressure of my palm. As I rubbed my hand across the top, I sensed a slight ridge upon its front surface. A thin, natural gulley that appeared to curve downwards, then upwards again, in a vaguely semicircular motion towards the object's opposing side.

I followed the line of the curve again with my finger, feeling the ridge come to an end at a position level with its starting point on the far side. Then I ran my palm over the space between the two points, feeling the surface level rise half a centimetre or so as I moved between the two positions.

Struggling to comprehend what this miniature 'hill' might constitute, I attempted to visualise the object as I'd been tracing it, and could think only that I'd been carving the shape of a large letter 'U' upon its as-yet-unidentified, pliant surface.

Rolling suddenly to the left with the truck's motion, I found myself thumping up against one of the objects positioned near the gap through which I'd first entered. Beneath the canvas covering, this, too, bore a similar U-shaped ridge along its front, as did two more objects that I felt as the truck braked suddenly and slid me violently towards the back side of the lorry's cabin.

Struggling to recall what kind of giant vegetable might contain such a unique and seemingly uniform indentation, I gradually became aware that the truck had stopped swaying.

We'd evidently entered a straight stretch of uninterrupted road, so I took immediate advantage of the lull in swerves and moved my hand once more along the object closest to me, angling my arm upwards this time, towards whatever lay positioned above that strange U-shaped rise on its front.

Suddenly, a passing street lamp illuminated the interior of the truck, and any excitement I might have felt at the realisation that we were now entering the outskirts of Stalkford was roundly quashed by the terrifying sight my eyes soon beheld, as I realised at long last what objects of horror I had unknowingly been travelling with (and inadvertently groping).

For here, lying beside me on the floor of the truck, piled up against other similar-looking forms like rows of genetically-flattened cucumbers, their motionless heads protruding from the canvas sheets in which they were wrapped, lay all the *men* of my road.

Here was the face of Postman Crawley, whose leg had been amputated last year after my Dobermann savaged him. Beside him lay what looked like the head of road-sweeper Jake Guzman, whose name I only knew because I'd once had to report him for urinating up the side of my Jenson Interceptor. And here, immediately to my left, lay the smooth, unmistakeable features of my former next-door neighbour Steve Hayman (one-time lead guitarist with Quorum).

All these men, I realised, practically vomiting with revulsion, were *bald*. Not only that, but there was not a single trace of stubble on their skin. Fearing the worst, I reached over and pulled the canvas sheet further down from its position above Steve Hayman's neck.

SPECIMEN

I gasped aloud, clamping one hand over my mouth to mask the noise. For Steve Hayman's chest was hairless all over, as if his entire body had been shaved. And yet here, too, was that strange, almost eerie, lack of stubble. Were Stalkford's men engaging in some sick mass-regime of all-over body waxing? Or was the true horror even more shocking than that? As my deepest fears took hold, I confirmed that the chests of those other bodies lying around me were similarly as smooth as silk. Together, these uncanny, hairless forms exuded an eerie quality, resembling newly constructed forms of freshly moulded putty. It was as if there had occurred some sudden and all-consuming, paralysing loss of identity in these men. Some change that had left these once-hairy, sweat-reeking warriors more featureless than a newly twisted Pritt Stick. What I was looking at in the murky shadow of that overnight delivery truck was a total lack of life-giving testosterone.

A dearth of *male seed*.

For each man – and hairy-chested men these barren husks had once been – now had the appearance of some sickly eunuch. A terrifying brood of rejected litter-runts, all lacking the spark and vitality of their rearing days.

Days when they'd routinely flee their wives and gather together in some cheap watering hole, throwing darts and sinking pints on late summer evenings while stuffing grab-bags of spiced crisps and dry-roasted peanuts into mouths and gullets, rueing the day they'd ever got hitched.

And now the glorious potential of their virile states had seemingly vanished, as if swamped under a tidal wave of petty grievances from their significant other halves. Repeated complaints about their apparent poor hygiene, slovenly behaviour, inability to listen and supposed rudeness towards apparently mutual friends.

I shivered as a further terrifying thought gripped me: one that had quietly emerged from a particularly dark and concealed inner recess of my mind. It was the nagging thought that these former men, these buddies of mine (not close buddies – more buddies-of-acquaintance) were, even now, in their exposed, hairless state, *not quite all they seemed*.

Reaching down again with my hand in a vain attempt to allay my suspicions, I ran one finger over the canvas where I'd previously felt those contours of an unspecified U-shaped ridge – and sensed, with a rising feeling of trepidation, that they all occurred in the area usually associated with the processes of human reproduction.

Steeling myself, I whipped back fully the canvas sheet covering Steve Hayman, and stifled my cry of abject horror. For there, before me, moulded into a perfect fattened 'U', was the smooth and featureless blank void of an Action Man penis.

By which I mean lack of penis. No ball bits. No sausage part. No happy sac to speak of. Merely a flat, arid flesh-desert of blank nothingness.

I tore frenziedly at the sheets covering the other bodies, yanking them free from those silent, immobile forms, revealing that they, too, were completely featureless in the downstairs department.

I was travelling in an apparent funeral cortège of emasculated former men . . .

But were these actually the men in question, or merely things that resembled them? Were these, in fact, cleverly constructed *clones*, intended to replace, over a period of time, the men of our town in a slow yet relentless programme of secret bodily substitution?

I thought back to Paul Ball in his diner, operating like some kind of half-arsed automaton. I knew he couldn't ordinarily cook for shit, but not once, when I'd spoken to him earlier, had he hawked up saliva and spat over his shoulder while frying my eggs, something he was wont to do whenever either of us organised an all-male barbecue.

If the 'Paul' that had been burning my eggs was in fact some form of alien replacement, like these strange vegetable-like pods lying beside me in the truck, then perhaps I still had time to find my

SPECIMEN

real-life buddies and save them. Maybe the invasion – if that's what this was* – was still in its early stages. Maybe I could, even now, with creatures pursuing me from every scientific dimension, save Stalkford from the threat of alien annihilation.

As I pondered possibilities that twenty-four hours earlier I'd have regarded as distinct *im*possibilities, I felt the truck slow as it pulled into a side street. I crawled over to the gap through which I'd first entered, and pulled back the loose flap of canvas covering the truck's canopy. I recognised the location immediately. We were in Wassock Street – only two bus stops away from my own house.

Scarcely believing my good fortune, I prepared to leap out as we drove past my former residence (soon to be Jacinta's property alone, no doubt, once we'd finalised the divorce paperwork) – then realised that the truck was pulling to a halt outside *that very building*. What the hell was a truck full of vegetablised de-groined men doing pulling up outside my own bricks and mortar?

I heard the doors of the truck's cab swing open, followed by two people clambering out, one on either side. So there were a pair of drivers up front, I realised, having assumed there would be just the one. As the sound of their footsteps passed along each side of the truck, I caught sight of their silhouettes against the floodlit canvas flaps.

There was no mistaking those slinky and sultry forms. These delivery drivers were *women*.

Incredulous, and fearing the worst, I scrambled to conceal those bodies I'd partly uncovered, then hid myself beneath one of the canvas sheets, aware that the lady drivers were making their way round towards the rear end of the vehicle.

Sensing a macabre purpose in this footbound diversion, I pressed myself up against the body of Adam Bone, a local plumber I'd never

---

* It was. GM

hire again, even if it turned out that he wasn't a bald and hairless vegetable. I was somewhat grateful now that the groin area against which I was pressed was flat as a pancake.

Seconds later, the rear flaps of the truck's canvas canopy were flung wide open. Between the resting, comatose heads of Dan Bartlett, our local locksmith (and yes, a partly reformed criminal) and Mickey Sparks, the town's resident Elvis impersonator, I watched those two delivery ladies climb up lithely and effortlessly into the truck's rear.

Though it pained me to say it, by the looks of things, these two strapping cab-lasses were giving their presumably male forebears, whose jobs they'd evidently replaced in this new, twisted, topsy-turvy alien world, a decent run for their money.

I kept myself as still as I could, affecting a similar vegetable-like demeanour, then watched, incredulous, as those two Trucktough Tinas, with scarcely a pant or grunt between them, *carried one of the groinless male husks outside* ...

Was I seeing things? Had my fevered, overactive escaping imagination finally turfed out the entire contents of my brain before my very eyes? Were these two Wheels'n'Heels employees actually doing manual work *competently* – and, apparently, *more efficiently* than their male counterparts?

No, it had to be some sort of illusion. Some form of visual trickery designed to catch me, and other other-halves like me, off our respective guards. But, try as I might to explain away this bizarre phenomenon, I couldn't help but accept the evidence of my own eyes. For before me, without any hint of a quibble or one single bawdy observation about the assemblage of naked male bodies lying prostrate before them, these two Dumper Darlings had calmly and quietly removed one of the groinless men from the silent gloom of an industrial delivery truck and transported him outside.

And the body in question, I realised, was none other than that of Steve Hayman, my very own next-door neighbour. Steve, by the way,

SPECIMEN

used to play guitar in The Haymakers before forming Quorum with Benny and Richie Resistance (plus Denny Thin on drums), and the one thing you *could* say about the latter band was that all four had demonstrably strong seed, if the subsequent name change from 'Quorum' to 'Plenum' over the ensuing months to reflect an increasing number of spouses enlisted as additional band members was anything to go by.

I watched as Steve's body departed in the arms of the two drivers, past my own front lawn and through the entrance gate of his own property.

What the hell were they doing, removing the bald and hairless body of my former next-door neighbour from a truck and depositing him at his own address?

I slid from my hiding place and crept across the floor of the truck for a better view, noticing one of the delivery women resting Steve's legs on one shoulder while she reached out with her free hand to ring the doorbell of his own house.

Instantly, as if the delivery had been expected and was running late, the door swung open to reveal Steve's luscious, practically ethereal and potentially part-plastic Scandinavian wife of twenty years, Astrid Hayman. She wasn't smiling, I noticed, which was unusual, as the only person in the entire world she'd previously refused to smile at was me.

But, thinking about it, I'd never seen Astrid interact with other women before now. The only time I'd actually met her to talk to was in the company of Steve and the gang on our way back from the pub, when I told her that, on the whole, they'd done a better job on her lips than Jacinta's.

Maybe women didn't smile at all in each other's company? Maybe all their conversations together were essentially a form of private conspiracy? Maybe this invasion had been coming for a *very* long time . . .

Without a word of greeting between them, the two Shipment Sheilas carried the body of groinless Steve Hayman past Astrid into his own house, and in that moment I seized my chance and leaped out of the truck on to the street outside.

I ducked my head so that I couldn't be spotted and vaulted over the hedgerow into my own front garden. Tucking myself up tight against a row of rose bushes, I craned my neck sideways and peered through the thorny branches to catch a glimpse, if I could, of what exactly was going on next door.

To my horror, the two curvy couriers were already stepping back out of the house, now with a *different* body in their arms. This one, however, was fully clothed, and still carrying the Fender '64 Telecaster he always slept with. For this was Steve Hayman himself. No longer the groinless version of Steve Hayman I'd seen being carried in from the truck. *This* Steve Hayman was the Steve Hayman I'd jammed with, collaborated with on musical adaptations of my work, barbecued alone with and yes, commiserated with numerous times over the collapse of my relationship with Jacinta. He'd even penned me a song I could sing in the bath when I was feeling strung out or hassled by my marital woes, with him doing the harmonies on a separate TDK cassette.

'Lover, Don't Break Me, Come Back Here and Make Me' was the title of the song, I recalled, and Steve had subsequently recorded it for the Recca label, with me on maracas for the main chorus. What a wonderful afternoon that had been, beating sticks for twenty minutes in his home studio while Astrid brought in rounds of coffee and doughnuts, then more rounds of coffee and doughnuts when I proved to her that the first batch wasn't remotely sufficient.

Now look at her, I reflected, watching her standing on the porch of Steve's house (yes, *Steve's* house, him having paid fifty-seven per cent of their initial deposit), coldly and callously sending her own

SPECIMEN

husband off in a drugged and evidently comatose state to whatever fate now awaited him, while a new groinless and compliant Steve Hayman doppelgänger was even now attending to his new duties, and no doubt preparing a tray of coffee and doughnuts for *her* instead ...

The full horror of what was now happening in Stalkford hit me like a brick. Whatever had been chasing after me from those revolving lights, pursuing me from my faux log cabin and through the woods, and grabbing me from a partly blocked U-bend, was just one part of a larger, and more terrifying, alien invasion. One that intended to replace every man in Stalkford with subservient simulations of their own selves, programmed to obey their now-dominant other halves without question or protest. No doubt with a list of chores as long as their hairless arms.

It was a mass takeover of human society that would uproot centuries of the status quo and turn all us males into ants, presumably. Husbands, fathers, fiancés and bits on the side; all would bow down to the New Order, working in chains like a prison gang, murmuring, 'Yes ma'am, no ma'am,' over and over like a mantra, before laying down our lives to serve the Queen Ant herself, bringing her, even in death, titbits and sweetmeats throughout the day as she feasted on our plucked and groin-extracted bodies.

It was a vision of hell so terrifying that even *my* mind couldn't have dreamed it up.

No, I thought, trying to calm myself at the terrifying implications. Something else was going on here. Something so grim and frightening that if I didn't find a way to stop it soon, there'd be little of Stalkford left to endanger with those escaped denizens of my *own* brain.

For the spirit of Stalkford would be already dead. The state of order upon which society rested would be long gone. The world as we knew it would have gone to hell in a proverbial handbasket, and nothing further that my mind could throw at it would make the slightest bit of difference.

There'd be no point in fighting anything anymore, for there'd be nothing worthwhile left to save. No hope. No meaning. No men.

Stalkford would belong ... *to the Ladies.*

CHAPTER EIGHT

I watched the pair return to the truck, one yanking the canvas flap back down over its rear while the other walked round to the front cabin. For a brief moment, the latter turned in my direction, staring intently up the garden path leading to my own front door. Seconds later, she was joined by her companion, who likewise paused to peer through my front gate, as if contemplating some unfinished business in the immediate vicinity. Then, as calmly as they'd arrived, these *uniformed* women turned together in perfect unison and got back inside the truck. Seconds later, I heard its engine fire up and watched as the vehicle drove off once more along the road.

When it had finally disappeared around a far corner, I raised my head and peered through the rose bush again, to see whether Astrid had gone back inside. Steve's front door was in the process of swinging shut, and through the latticed curtains of the adjacent front lounge I glimpsed the unholy sight of Steve Hayman's substitute already dusting at the front window ledges with an orange fluffer and rubbing away smears on the pane – smears that had been put there, no doubt, by the nose-tip of his coldly snitching, formally ingratiating yet eternally neighbour-snooping, husband-emasculating, authority-dobbing other half.

Look, I'm not a misogynistic. Never was. Never will be. I firmly believe that Man and Femme are almost equal. But there are certain qualities inherent to each species that cannot be replicated in the other. For example, ladies can't shred on the guitar like men can. I'm not saying ladies *can't* play guitar, because I saw Suzi Quatro play guitar on television one night (and, believe it or not, she actually played *bass*). What I *am* saying is that ladies can't *shred* on the guitar. They might well play fast, but they can't *shred*. And that's because pounding one's axe, in all senses of the word, is a uniquely male practice, and this can actually be proven by science. Let me explain.

Electric guitars operate via a magnetic field generated by bar magnets wrapped in coils of thin wire located below the strings, known to professional guitarists, or axemen, as 'pickups'. These 'pick up' individual magnetic signals created through vibrations in the strings above, which have themselves become magnetised by the central magnetic field flowing upwards, thus creating a small electric current. This current is then transferred via an electrical circuit to an amplifier, which subsequently transmits the signal onwards to a loudspeaker, which is how traditional 'rock' is created.

What the buyer's manual doesn't tell you is that each separate magnetic field generated by the guitar's string vibrations are themselves formed partly by vacillations in the axeman's fingers, which are in turn connected via a complex system of nerve tissues and neural pathways to the persistent electrical throbbing of his *testicles*.

Said testes create somewhere in the region of two to three hundred million spermatozoa per day, or approximately one thousand, five hundred per second (a figure which, in my own case, can be tripled). For the average male, however, around fifty to one hundred million sperm are created daily (and between eighty to three hundred million sperm set out upon each ejaculative journey), all of which are created via similar *coiled structures* known as seminiferous tubules.

Thus, mitochondria, that part of a cell which generates the energy powering the movement of each sperm, is produced via a system almost *identical* to that which powers the electric guitar. And while research in this particular field is still ongoing, it is now widely accepted in the scientific community at Stalkford Polytechnic that

SPECIMEN

the unique melodic rhythms of an axeman's shred are directly related to the continual pulsing of his daily sperm count, which may be increased or held back at will in direct proportion to the amount of time he chooses to spend pounding one particular axe over the other.

Essentially, this means that all the great guitar solos you have known and loved over the years are the direct result of a complex balance occurring between the physical constitution of the axeman in question, his technical proficiency on his chosen instrument, the electromagnetic make-up of the guitar in question, and how frequently or not he elects to channel his own physical pumping patterns into the wider electrical circuit created each time he picks up and pounds his personal axe.*

And to see Steve Hayman, formally lead guitarist of The Haymakers, forced to down tools (in all senses of the word) to pick up a fresh duster in some mocking parody of his natural calling was an affront to nature, in my opinion. I'm not saying he shouldn't or couldn't have dusted around the house occasionally – I'm simply saying that the existence of said house and said duster were a direct result of income earned and received from Steve's own guitar-playing. And maybe partly from Astrid's professional interior-design hobby.

Tearing my eyes from this nauseating spectacle, I crawled across my lawn towards the front door of my own house, conscious that if any of those other suspicious, malevolent other halves peering through curtains along the street saw me arriving home, they'd dob me in immediately to whatever alien authority might currently be residing within or without our current Earthbound dimension.

Arriving at the base of my front door, I reached up with one hand and rang the doorbell. I heard it chime inside, but there was no answer. I checked my watch. Even taking into account the one

---

* For a more detailed examination of this subject, see *It's Called Hard Rock for a Reason* by Dr Neil Pincer, with a joint foreword by the real Steve Hayman and myself. GM

minute of missing time I'd no doubt incurred during my initial sighting of the UFO, if the events of *Comminglement* were anything to go by, I was still arriving home at around 5.31am.

'Meredith!' I whispered, aware she was probably still avoiding her midnight prowler. 'Meredith! It's me! It's Dad!'

There was no answer, but I knew she had to be there. Most likely she was sitting on the stairs in the front hallway mere feet away from me, staring in horror at the red house phone through which that terrifying voice I'd dreamed up all those years before had been tormenting her, threatening to break in at any second.

'I'm not the late-night prowler,' I whispered, more loudly than before. 'It really is your dad speaking.'

Still no response. Aware that I couldn't afford to whisper any louder, for fear of being overheard by Astrid next door, I elected to play my trump card.

'I have some money for you.'

The door swung open to reveal Meredith, exhausted and bedraggled, standing on the entrance mat with a large steak knife in her hand.

'What are you doing down there?' she said, staring at me like I was some form of worm.

'I'll tell you in a moment,' I said, crawling in and kicking the door shut behind me. As I rose to my feet, I realised Meredith was still holding the knife out towards me.

'Cash,' she demanded.

I stuffed one hand into my pocket, pulled out a couple of fivers and handed them over.

'I'll assume this is because you're stressed out,' I said, manoeuvring the knife away from me. 'But, for once, Meredith, this isn't my fault.'

'Bullshit,' she replied, moving the knife back into position.

'Look, I'll admit that this late-night prowler of yours is indeed a figment of my own imagination let loose upon unsuspecting reality as a result of my leaking mind,' I said, trying to reassure her. 'But I would have been here hours ago if things hadn't gone tits-up elsewhere on my way back through the Spinal Mountains.'

The knife hadn't moved.

Sighing, I reached into my pocket again and dragged out a twenty-pound note. Meredith grabbed it from my hand and at long last lowered the blade.

'I can't explain everything that's happened, but for now just accept that I'm being pursued by a malevolent race of interstellar alien beings intent upon emasculating the entirety of Mankind – a plan that may or may not be partly assisted by key female collaborators on Earth, who, I'm afraid to say, will be publicly executed once the status quo is restored. And besides,' I added, remembering my other phone call from the night before, 'I called the sheriff about that prowler and he said he'd send a squad car over. Didn't he call round?'

'Someone in uniform turned up,' Meredith replied, 'but it wasn't a man.'

'It wasn't a man?' I repeated, startled at the implication of my daughter's words. 'You mean, it was a lady? A lady policeman?'

Dammit, had they gotten to Roz, too?

'Women are allowed to be police officers, Dad.'

'I'm not debating that now. I'm simply trying to establish whether this officer of the law was being impersonated by a lady. Specifically, Roz Bloom, my erstwhile editor.'

'I'm not sure it *was* a police officer. She looked more like an FBI agent. She was wearing a suit.'

'A *suit*?' I could barely hold myself together. How fast were these invaders – and Roz, specifically – moving? Only an hour and a half into their invasion of Earth, and they'd already begun wearing suits. Hell, what would any of us men have left to wear if *that* stalwart of male identity likewise became theirs? Soon they'd move on to balaclavas and combat slacks. Maybe even leather trousers (though, grudgingly, I would allow the latter).

'You say she looked like an FBI agent? What did she want?'

'She asked if *you* were at home.'

I shivered inwardly. So Roz herself must have got to Flint Rustin soon after I'd phoned him. That would explain how the aliens had been able to pinpoint my location in the cabin soon after our call – unless the intermittent signal from my throbbing piles had brought them there. Ultimately, it didn't really matter how they'd found me. The fact was that they'd already infiltrated the police department, and were now presumably in full charge of law and order throughout Stalkford.

It was merely a matter of time before they caught up with me again.

'Where's your mother?' I asked.

'I told you. She's gone to visit that hypnotherapist of hers.'

'He was *my* hypnotherapist first,' I snapped, still angered by Jacinta's theft of Fibbford, *my* psychiatric guru, in pursuit of her own rival bestselling account of alien abduction. And I couldn't help but think that, at this late hour, there was probably very little hypnotherapy going on. But was Fibbford *really* Jacinta's type? I would have thought his thin, curly hair and thick Dorset accent would have been an immediate turn-off, given her preference for swarthy Mediterranean types.

And with regard to his own interests, Fibbford *never* mixed business with pleasure. No, given that the publication of *Jacinta's Cosmic Journey* had made them both extremely – almost sickeningly – rich, there had to be some other reason for their apparent midnight conference.

'I'm heading over there now,' I said. 'Something's going on between those two, and I'm determined to find out what it is. Don't panic, they're not having an affair.'

SPECIMEN

'Can I come?' asked Meredith.

'No, I need you to stay here in the house and hide out until I return.'

'But Dad ...'

'It's too dangerous out there, Meredith,' I barked authoritatively. 'I can't say exactly why, but there's a strong likelihood that there are beings out there intent upon demasculating me physically and replacing my body with some sort of mindless, subservient automaton. I don't want you getting hurt in the process.'

In truth, I highly doubted those beings would do anything to harm Meredith at all, her being one of their own kind, but frankly I couldn't handle the constant moaning while I attempted to turn the tide of an interstellar invasion.

'I wouldn't mind you being a mindless, subservient automaton,' she said, confirming the wisdom of my decision.

'I'll bet you wouldn't,' I snapped, having just about had it up to here with all this emasculation-justification talk. It had to stop. And it had to stop now.

'You're staying right here, missy,' I said. 'Go hide in that airing closet under all the soft blankets and don't open the door to anyone. Unless it's me,' I added.

'But what about the night-caller?' she asked, suddenly nervous again. 'What about the late-night prowler?'

I picked up the knife and handed it back to her.

'Take this. There's also a handgun in the drawer of my writing desk,' I said. 'Plus a flame-thrower in my bedroom closet.'

I knew deep down that neither of those two things were actually there, but Meredith's face relaxed a bit, regardless. A necessary evil, I figured. Sometimes you had to tell a huge, largely incomprehensible white lie to be a good dad, I reflected. I just hoped, one day, that Meredith would appreciate all that I'd done for her.

'I'll be back soon, kiddo,' I said, kissing her forehead. 'Remember, go for the gut first, then hack like mad at the balls.'

And with that, I left my daughter in the hall, departed via the rear door of the house so as to avoid any prying female neighbours, and ran as fast as I could to the observatory.

CHAPTER NINE

It was getting towards sunset* as I made my way up the grassy hill towards Stalkford Observatory, which itself overlooked the main town and a large stretch of countryside beyond. This was where Fibbford had leased his new set of offices in order to conduct fresh experiments with his pioneering Fibbertronics System.

A crimson half-moon floated above me, bathed in a sea of pink swirling cloud. It rested, lounging almost, against a wide bed of glittering stars, sparkling and twinkling over the Earth like reflections of light bouncing from the surface of bubbles in some gigantic cosmic foam bath. An apt metaphor, I decided, as no doubt whatever intelligence now controlled the skies over Stalkford was somehow in league with that legion of terrifying female other halves I'd

---

* The apparent leap from morning to evening here, with Nick Steen having left his house only minutes before when it was only the break of day, is due to the controlling alien entities displaying increased mastery over time and space. To wit, they are now able to steal gaps of missing time numbered in hours rather than entire minutes. While this great leap in time may feel arbitrary to the less clever among you, it is in fact a well-considered and sophisticated act of literary design, effectively creating for you, the reader, a similar mood of disorientation and confusion to that experienced by Nick Steen and other alien abductees who frequently report disarming temporal phenomenon.

Furthermore, the resultant transition from the dawn of early morning to this forthcoming scene of star-speckled twilight, with rays of a westering sun spreading out across the heavens, helps invest the imminent conclusion of this tale with a certain atmospheric grandeur, and has nothing whatsoever to do with a lack of narrative planning on my part. GM

encountered, all of whom were no doubt currently ensconced in real-life bubble baths of their own while their respective degroined servants went to and fro at speed, refilling hot water as necessary, lighting more tealight candles and changing the TV channel when instructed, before heading out to the local late-night pharmacy for yet more bags of Epsom salt.

I looked up at that great half-moon in the sky and wondered if Mankind would ever find a way to strike back against these cold and quietly calculating, luxury-obsessed oppressors.

As if to quash my hopes even further, the dark silhouette of the approaching observatory dome slowly obscured the moon's surface as I drew closer, like a dark planet finally aligning as foretold by seers and prophets throughout the aeons, eclipsing the sun's (or in this case, the moon's) rays and casting our fragile world into the depths of eternal darkness. I emphasise the word 'like', as it *was* just an illusion caused by the shape of the observatory dome covering the illuminated moon, so I wasn't unduly panicked, fully expecting it to be a temporary obstruction.*

I climbed up the steps towards the main building, which itself consisted of various government research labs and scientific development facilities. I knew that Fibbford had had his eyes on a suite here for some time, and I guessed that with all the money he'd earned from collaborating with both myself and Jacinta, he'd at long last made his dream come true.

I was panting and sweaty as I ascended the final steps towards the main door of the observatory tower unit. An illuminated buzzer panel on the right listed various department numbers and names. I ran my finger down the list and pressed the one marked 'Fibbertronics, Inc.'

Almost immediately, a voice buzzed through the adjacent intercom.

'Fibbertronics Incorporated. State your business.'

---

* Which it was. GM

SPECIMEN

'It's Nick Steen,' I said, still breathless from my long ascent. 'I'm here to see Dave.'

'Here to see whom?'

'Dave.'

'Dave?'

'Dave Fibbford.'

'Dr David Fibbford?'

'Correct. Dr Dave Fibbford.'

'Dr David Fibbford?'

'Fine,' I sighed. 'Dr David Fibbford.'

'One moment.'

I'd have a word with Fibbford about that. One thing I couldn't stand was sanctimonious secretaries. Especially when it was *my* abduction tale that had pioneered the use of his hugely successful Fibbertronics System.

'Dr David Fibbford will see you now.'

As the voice from the intercom crackled into silence again, an electrical signal pinged audibly as the main doors slid apart, allowing me access to the building.

I stepped inside and looked around. I was standing at one end of a long, featureless grey hallway with what looked like a large ticking clock hung upon the far wall. Beneath the clock stood a reception desk, behind which sat a still and silent figure. It looked from this distance as if a shop mannequin had been posed there, perfectly arranged and dressed for work. For at this distance, there seemed to be not a breath of life about the figure. Presumably, this was the receptionist with whom I'd been speaking. Tentatively, I stepped forwards.

As I walked slowly down the hall towards her, a voice sounded from a set of hidden speakers situated somewhere overhead.

'Wipe your shoes on the mat provided,' it said. The voice was indeed that of the receptionist again, only it seemed even more cold and dispassionate now that I was inside the building itself.

Sighing to myself, I wiped both feet on the entrance mat and resumed my journey down the corridor, making my way towards the desk at the far end of the hallway. As I did so, my shoes began to click audibly on the panelled flooring, as though someone had attached metal heel plates to them without my knowledge. But a brief check of my undersole confirmed I was plate-free and that the phenomenon was created by something else entirely.

Similarly unnerving was my gradual realisation that, as I made my way forwards, the distant reception desk began to loom far larger in my sight than could be expected from a scientific viewpoint, as if the dimensions of the corridor were widening and distorting beyond all known laws of science, the further I traversed them.

The proportions of the desk, behind which sat the still strangely motionless receptionist, continued to expand as I drew nearer, until by the time I arrived before it, the surface towered over my head by around fifty feet or so, and the receptionist sitting behind it loomed over me like some titanic-sized Goliath in female secretary form.

I watched, increasingly unnerved, as her head leaned over the edge of the desk and she stared down at me through a pair of gigantic round, red-rimmed glasses. Her pale blue eyes loomed even larger through the glass lenses, like twin planets of swirling ocean, fixing me in their penetrative gaze.

'Relax,' said a voice, which bellowed loudly at me from above, echoing through my eardrums like the cosmic command of some vast, mythological deity. 'You are merely experiencing the temporary side-effects of Dr David Fibbford's latest experiment. The effect should wear off in time.'

I wasn't sure I believed her. While to my mind I was still of ordinary size, everything else in this strange, eerie corridor seemed to have grown exponentially, to the point where I now felt like a small child trapped in a world of terrifying female adults.

SPECIMEN

Was this really a side-effect of Fibbford's ongoing experiments with his infamous Fibbertronics System, or were those alien beings currently invading our planet in fact distorting the dimensions of time and space in order to make men like me feel deliberately small and helpless, sowing seeds of doubt and fear in our minds so that all thought of waging an act of protest was effectively disabled by our new-found status as middle-aged toddlers?

'You'll want the top floor,' bellowed the receptionist. Covering my ears against the resounding din, I made my way across the floor towards the elevator shaft, feeling those two massive eyes in those giant spectacle lenses following me all the way.

I called for a lift, and as soon as the elevator doors parted, I stepped inside and pressed the button for the top floor, which I presumed must be somewhere near the main observatory dome. As the doors began to swish shut, I caught sight of the receptionist's head, now the size of some swollen industrial balloon, dipping down to the level of the elevator to stare in at me as the doors slowly began to close.

Before the panels had fully sealed, one of her huge eyes winked at me, and as the lift began to rise with the slow yet steady shifting of the elevator cable, I tried my best to concentrate instead on what I was going to say to Fibbford.

I watched the each floor number illuminate on the panel as the elevator rose, until, with a sudden ping, it stopped moving and the door panels directly beside me opened.

I looked out into what was indeed the circular globe of the observatory's main viewing platform. The intersecting rows of concave roof panelling above were almost fully parted, allowing the entire sweeping vista of Stalkford's west-facing skyline to shine through.

From here I could see the entirety of the town stretched out below me as the glorious red sun continued to set in the distant west. Above my head, I could see the vast and endless distances of the outer cosmos stretching out into infinity, sparkling with millions and millions of brightly shining stars.

Lowering my gaze from this mind-melting, anxiety-inducing glimpse of a vast and distant cosmic infinity, I saw something else equally unnerving: the silhouette of a human figure sitting in a chair before the giant observation window. From the location of its apparent head sprang a mass of curling locks, spiralling upwards so wildly that they resembled nothing more than a vibrant nest of exploding metallic Slinkys.

'How nice of you to drop by, Mister Nick,' said a familiar voice, coming from the region of the thing's head. As it spoke, the locks of curling hair bobbed and reverberated with sudden movement. The voice I was hearing was disarmingly gentle, its accent pure Dorset.

I was in the presence of Dr Fibbford.

'Nice place you have here, Dave,' I said, striding forwards. As I did so, a row of lights flicked on overhead, revealing in full my former hypnotist and fellow publisher in crime.

'I prefer things dark when I'm communing with the outer cosmos,' he replied. 'And it's Dr Fibbford, by the way.'

'Dr Dave Fibbford,' I said, humouring him.

'Dr *David* Fibbford.'

I took a seat in the chair opposite him, which I presumed was reserved for his paying clients.

'Hope I'm not intruding on anything?'

'Not at all, Mister Nick. Now, if you could just connect yourself up to the main circuit board, please,' he said, his finger indicating a machine on the desk between us that looked to me like one of the strange, wired contraptions I'd seen stacked against the walls of Steve Hayman's home recording studio.

'Yes, a modular synth. I suppose it does resemble one in part,' said Fibbford, squinting hard at me through his customary pair of golden wire-rimmed, circular-framed Windsor spectacles. 'But I see you're

SPECIMEN

unable to comprehend the basic connection procedure for a standard twelve-hundred-watt digit flanger.'

'You're reading my mind?' I said, distracted by his evident new-found ability to tap in to my unspoken thoughts. I watched warily as Fibbford began attaching a number of multicoloured wires to the ends of my fingers.

'All in good time,' replied Fibbford, as he proceeded to slip each of my digits into its own individual metallic finger-sock.

'Suffice to say,' he continued, concentrating intently on the task of tightening, via a miniature screwdriver, various tiny bolts running along the side of each finger-sock, 'my patented Fibbertronics System of advanced lie detection deflection has moved on apace since our previous dalliance.'

'You're telling me,' I said, as Fibbford proceeded to plug me, via a range of rainbow-tinted stereo jacks attached to the ends of each enclosed finger, into the main central circuit board. This done, Fibbford smiled mischievously at me through those squinty eyes and flicked a separate switch on the machine's wooden lid. All at once, I felt a sharp, tingling sensation shoot through both wrists, racing rapidly upwards through my whole body. I didn't know what he'd plugged me into exactly, but I certainly felt connected.

'Now, let's talk business, shall we?'

'Where's my wife?' I asked.

'Oh, she's somewhere,' Fibbford said, already distracted again and fiddling with a range of brightly coloured knobs attached to a larger, more solid-looking machine on his right.

'She was supposed to meet me at my house to discuss our divorce settlement and ownership of our daughter.'

'That's right,' said Fibbford, placing one finger in his ear, as if attempting, momentarily, to block out the sound of my voice. I waited while he twiddled with various other knobs, watching his curly, bouncing tendrils of hair crackle and spark with what looked like rushing particles of electrical energy.

'Do you know you have pulses of sparking energy crackling through your hair curls?' I said.

Fibbford held up one finger against his lips, silencing me, then continued to fine-tune the balance levels between each of the waiting knobs. Finally, a large wave of multicoloured light soared through his hair tendrils before shooting off into the space over his head like a shimmering wave of miniature Northern Lights.

At the same time, I felt a pulsing sensation flow through my own system, like a throbbing wash of invasive energy entering my particulars. But instead of shooting back outwards and upwards, through my own hair, this counter-energy appeared to delve lower, deep into my body, soaring and scorching like a thrusted firebrand, scoring down into my loins, then up again, searching and seeking, until, at length, I began to feel the familiar rhythm of pain pounding in my lower half, centred deep within the hollow passage of my anal walls, as the familiar itching of my eternal pile-dance recommenced.

'What are you and my wife up to?' I gasped, already in a state of panic having realised I had no means of grabbing the table for balance or thrusting one mitt up my beleaguered crevice to alleviate the pain which these multicoloured wires attached to my finger-ends had cruelly brought about.

'Well as you know, Mister Nick,' said Fibbford, 'you and I made a pretty penny from our multi-million-copy bestselling account of your fabricated alien abduction.'

'Enough to buy you this plush office suite at the famous Stalkford Observatory, no less.'

'I do believe you're getting ahead of yourself,' said Fibbford, twisting a dial on another machine stacked against the left side of his chair. 'These offices were purchased with earnings from your *wife's* multi-million-copy bestselling account of her *own* fabricated alien abduction.'

SPECIMEN

Before I could pass comment on that, an even more intense burst of pain exploded in my rectal cavity, which I realised was now connected to the main electric circuit board on the desk between us.

'Leave off!' I cried, sounding, in my helpless state, like a desperate schoolboy from some distant, 1970s school-based children's drama.

'All in good time,' Fibbford said again, and I had the distinct feeling then that he was starting to enjoy this. 'You see, following those historic accounts of your respective unexplained UFO abductions, missing one-entire-minute time periods and suspected rectal alien implanting, I couldn't help but feel that such a ludicrous and implausible chain of paranormal events was only accepted by the paying public as a direct result of the pioneering lie-detector-deflecting technology of my patented Fibbertronics System.'

'Of course. That's why you and I used it in the first place,' I snapped. 'It was a scheme we hatched together at that Steve Hayman gig, remember? Me with my innate ability to hoodwink gullible readers with a rip-roaring tale of unfathomable horror, and you with your ability to confirm the truth of my so-called alien-abduction account with a fail-safe lie-detector-deflecting system you said you'd been developing in your spare time. A mechanical programme that not only detected lies, but deflected them as well, meaning we could, as you'd explained to me while we were propping up that beer tent together, having met previously by the urinals, and I quote, "in effect deflect and reject what we elect to detect".'

'Correct,' said Fibbford. 'Before selecting and perfecting the projecting of one's neglecting ...'

'To wit,' I continued, 'the subjecting, injecting and disrespecting of my erecting ...'

'By those who are inspecting,' concluded Fibbford.

'Excepting', I added, 'that I told you to scrap that entire rhyming section in your patent application, because no one takes a Dorset accent seriously, least of all when its relating whimsical ditties in an attempt to ingratiate yourself with the governing body of Her Majesty's patent office. That last-minute omission alone secured the patent, remember, which had been roundly rejected three times for that specific reason.'

'Nevertheless, Mister Nick,' Fibbford continued, 'it is wholly unlikely that anyone would have believed your ludicrous fictional account of alien abduction without the aid of Fibbertronics.'

'And why, no doubt, you subsequently welcomed my wife's rival account of her own alien abduction with open arms.'

'True, she did fling herself at me.'

'I'll bet she did.'

'But as you know, Mister Nick, I have no time for spontaneous amorous shenanigans, at least until my own life's work is complete.'

'Which is?'

'All in good time,' said Fibbford, who was now *really* starting to piss me off. 'You see,' he continued, 'following the publication of *Jacinta's Cosmic Journey*, your wife's account of alien abduction and interstellar cruising with a supposed cosmic Stud Lord—'

'Yeah, I read the blurb,' I said, interrupting him. 'Which is *all* I read.'

'—a book once more made entirely credulous through the pioneering and now fully patented method of my legally trademarked Fibbertronics System—'

'Whatever,' I interjected.

'—I was set up for life, and able to purchase this plush suite of scientific laboratories here at the famous Stalkford Observatory.'

'While Jacinta bought her own mansion outright in the prestigious Vampton Hills.'

'Yes, I know it well,' said Fibbford. I looked up at him sharply, detecting once again that familiar mischievous smirk emerging beneath those squinting, playful eyes.

'Do you, now?' I said, pointedly.

SPECIMEN

'Well, Nick, my life's work was *half* completed by that stage, and I did need a bit of a rest from all these Fibbertronicities. Not that I *got* much of a rest ...'

And with that barbed slight on my marital woes, Fibbford began tittering like a schoolboy. The laugh was high-pitched and like no other laugh I'd ever heard, consisting almost entirely of an uninterrupted row of single, high-pitched notes repeated in regular rhythm until a fresh intake of breath was required. As laughs went, Fibbford's was neither infectious nor remotely convincing. Yet it was designed, I knew, to threaten the very integrity of my seed.

'Ah, yes, your seed,' said Fibbford, once again reading my thoughts. 'As well as your other outpourings.'

'What do you mean?'

'Well, this brings me to the crux of things, Mister Nick,' Fibbford said, swivelling his chair around to look out once again at the evening sky. The sun on the horizon had almost set, and the crescent of the half-moon far above us, which I'd glimpsed on my way here, now shone brightly in the enveloping darkness of an all-consuming night sky.

'Specifically,' continued Fibbford, 'these eternal leanings of your own brain, brought about, I read, by some ill-advised bodily wrangling with a mechanical typewriting device.'

'That's correct,' I said, defiantly. 'And I'd advise you, man to man, not to get fresh with that Fibbertronics System of yours, either. These damn machines have minds of their own.'

'Fear not, Mister Nick. For now that you've conceived such a possibility in your mind's eye, I will resolutely avoid making any kind of move on the wiring sockets. You see ...'

He spun round slowly in his chair once more to face me, then realised that he'd spun the opposite way and his hairs were now tangled in the wires protruding from the nearby electrical units. Spinning round twice the other way to disentangle himself, he continued.

'The unleashing of your imagination into this mortal sphere,' he explained, leaning his head forward across the desk to meet my gaze once more through those small, round-rimmed spectacles of his, 'has shown me the glorious potential of Fibbertronics beyond mere deflection of basic fib-detection. Now that these lies and fabrications of yours, created in your mind's eye, are out in the open as fully fledged beings of brain and matter – now that the fictional constructs of your creative imagination are manifesting themselves as living beings – the scientifically proven fabrications of my Fibbertronics System seem tame by comparison. Almost primitive. For example, we were previously able to convince the unsuspecting reader that your claim to have received some form of alien implant in the region of your rectal passage was factually true. Yet now, with the current incarnation of your darkest thoughts, I'm able to produce irrefutable physical proof of your formerly spurious claims.'

'Proof?' I said, tersely.

He slipped a sheet of photographic paper across the desk towards me and turned it over so that I could see in full the grainy image reproduced on one side. It was an X-ray of someone's insides.

'*Your* insides, to be precise,' said Fibbford. 'For this is an X-rayed photographic image capturing a portion of your lower sphincter.'

'And what the hell's that?' I said, pointing to a small cube of solid white matter residing amid the usual contorted mess of my twisted inner workings.

'That, Mister Nick, is your implant. The one these fictional alien beings you previously dreamed up for profit have placed inside your body for real, so that they can track you across the galaxy and monitor far more than your intimate inner workings.'

'But what is it?' I repeated, aware that I was none the wiser.

Fibbford smiled enigmatically, his eyes screwing tightly together so that he resembled a self-satisfied mole.

'*A typewriter key.*'

CHAPTER TEN

'A *typewriter* key?' I repeated.

'The return key, to be precise.'

What the hell was a typewriter key doing inside my back passage? Specifically, a typewriter key I now recognised as having come from that ancient Chinese typing machine I'd purchased three years ago and had formed a physical relationship with. The self-same typewriter through which I'd inadvertently summoned the cosmic demon known as Type-Face, Lord of the Prolix. A creature whose head was partly formed from typebars and keytops, and who'd subsequently opened the hole to another dimension in the middle of my own head.

Was this some kind of sick cosmic joke at my expense? Was Type-Face himself somehow using this manifested alien implant in my rectum as a way of goading me from a distant cosmic realm; taunting me with the idea that he would, one day, return to Stalkford in order to claim my soul?

'Possibly,' said Fibbford, listening in. 'But your immediate problem's these aliens.'

'They're after my seed,' I said, fear once more taking hold.

'Wrong, Mister Nick,' said Fibbford. 'They already have your seed.'

'Already?' I gasped, incredulous.

'Those grey-skinned, skinny alien beings that chased you through the forest and into your woodland writing cabin? Those are your *children*, Mister Nick. Formed from seed already extracted from your personage during your previous alien abductions.'

'My *children*?'

'They were chasing after you because they wanted to play. They were shouting "Papa" at you. But you spurned them.'

'No!' I yelled out loud. 'Those things can't be mine! They were so withered and pasty-looking.'

'It would appear your seed isn't half as strong as you initially suspected, Mister Nick. In fact, I would go so far as to say that it's extremely weak seed indeed.'

I began to panic. With the advent of my escaping imagination, not only had it turned out that I'd been regularly abducted by an interstellar race of alien beings, but now it seemed the seed they'd been extracting to people their ailing species in some far-off galaxy was of weak and insipid quality.

That was hard enough to fathom, but if it was in any way true – if, somehow, my years of persistent and exclusive meat-eating had somehow backfired and bequeathed me the vitality of some formerly neutered steer – why were these beings still pursuing me? Maybe my alien kids did indeed wish to express some love and gratitude for their old pop – I got that – but that didn't explain why the entire town of Stalkford had been taken over by an army of sinister other halves who were already subjecting their hard-working male counterparts to lives of subservient serfdom.

Surely my seed wouldn't allow *that*?

'*Your* seed, no,' said Fibbford, chiming in again on my innermost thoughts. 'But your wife's is another matter entirely.'

'My wife produces seed?'

'Egg-shaped seeds, to be precise. From which sprout her *own* aliens. Which are also real.'

'My wife's aliens?'

'You forget, it was the publication of your book *Comminglement* that led to your wife dreaming up her own rival tale of alien abduction. An account that was, unfortunately, initially influenced and

SPECIMEN

inspired by your own imaginative outpourings. Hence the aliens in *her* book are also real now, arising as they have from the escaping creative juices of your own mind.'

'And you?' I asked then, fixing Fibbford with my own steely gaze. 'What are your plans now? Given that both our alien abductors exist for real. What's your interest in all this?'

'Like I say, Mister Nick,' Fibbford replied, 'the Fibbertronics System could now be perceived to be, in this post brain-leak world, nothing more than a rather quaint and redundant footnote in the annals of scientific progress.'

'Go on,' I said, dreading what Fibbford was about to impart, yet confident nonetheless that he was going to impart it.

'What I really want now, Mister Nick, is to have what you have. The ability to construct my own living fibs. Fibs that can be neither detected nor denied, but will instead proliferate globally and beyond. I want my Fibbertronics System to expand, extending beyond the boundaries of known science, creating fibs and lies and fabricated porkies that will reach out across the cosmic divide and convince the unsuspecting of their total veracity, wherever they may be. I want—'

'To rule reality,' I said.

'In a nutshell,' replied Fibbford. 'And by connecting you to my electrical motherboard via your fingers — a motherboard that itself connects via my hair tendrils to the minds of the ruling alien elite above us — I will thus extract the fabricative-incarnating faculties of your own brain and have them implanted, via the advanced surgical technology possessed by these extra-terrestrial beings, into my *own* brain.'

'And what if they disagree?' I snapped, anger rising. 'What if they want to implant the imagination-escaping element of my brain into *their* brains instead?'

'You forget, Mister Nick,' said Fibbford, relaxing back in his chair and flicking a small jolt of stray miniature lightning from one of his hair tendrils, 'these aliens are your wife's aliens. And your wife still owes me certain favours.'

'I see,' I replied, 'but wait until that alien Stud Lord of hers finds out about your bouts of recent frottage. Maybe he'll have something to say about that.'

'He might have done, when he was alive.'

'You mean he's . . .?'

'Not alive. That's right.'

'You mean . . .?'

'Dead. That's correct. And killed by Jacinta, no less. Well, her offspring, I should say . . .'

That word again. *Offspring*.

'What do you mean by her "offspring"?' I said.

But Fibbford didn't need to reply, for all at once, the true horror of the situation hit me like a brick. I couldn't have claimed to be shocked by the revelation that my ex-wife had done away with her own lover, but for him to be killed by her *offspring*? That was another matter. And, unless I was mistaken, Jacinta's 'offspring' meant only one thing. This invasion force of alien female entities, hell-bent on subjugating and demasculating Mankind for all time, were none other than Jacinta's personal brood of cosmic children.

At that moment, I looked up, despairing, and noticed something happening in the sky above my head. For the distant half-moon I'd glimpsed in the clouds beyond Fibbford's hair tendrils had now moved. Not geographically speaking. Instead, it appeared to have turned sideways, appearing now like a floating, lopsided, malevolent grin.

As I continued to watch it, the grin turned upside down, becoming instead a horizontal curve pointing earthward at each end. Then, slowly but surely, the curved object that was once a half-moon began to grow larger in the space between those retracted roof panels, expanding in size over our heads as the thing started to move closer towards us.

SPECIMEN

A familiar pulse began throbbing in the area of my rectum, and once more I glimpsed those pulsating, multicoloured lights revolving and reverberating along and around the rim of what I now realised was an advancing spacecraft!

'Look out!' I screamed aloud. 'It's coming!'

'I know,' said Fibbford, beaming cruelly at me through those damned round-framed spectacles of his. 'I've just summoned them.'

As the gleaming metallic rim of the gigantic flying saucer loomed over the roof of the observatory dome, the panels directly over my head also retracted, offering a full view of the vast spaceship hovering directly above.

Then Fibbford's hair began to spark and crackle anew, and as the horrendous tittering of his high-pitched laughter filled the airwaves surrounding me, I felt my body rise from the chair amid a sudden beam of blinding, electrical light that bound itself tightly around me.

Then, as had happened to me numerous times before (which I could now recall with grim and stark vividity) . . .

. . . I was abducted.

CHAPTER ELEVEN

I must have blacked out. For the next thing I recall, following the bright whiteness of that powerful enveloping light beam, was waking up on a flat, metallic surface. The metal finger-socks had vanished and I was now lying, completely naked, in the middle of a strange, featureless room. There were no walls at all, and I was still surrounded by that powerful white light, so I guess it was more of a limitless space than a room, to be honest. And it wasn't *entirely* featureless, either. For amid the cold, icy palette of this apparent nowhere zone, I saw, floating beside me, a small, circular tray.

I squinted, trying to make out any markings in the enveloping whiteness that might betray hints of a door or window. But I saw nothing. Just limitless white light. Nor was there a hanging light bulb of any kind, and yet the entire space continued to shine with a blinding luminescence akin to the Las Vegas Luxor Lamp – which, incidentally, is not worth a visit. It's just light.

As far as I knew, I appeared to be trapped alone in some form of unknown, hermetically sealed and self-illuminating oubliette.

I glanced over at the tray again and saw that it had changed its appearance. On it there now lay a row of strange, metallic implements. Each one consisted of a variety of sharp blades and needle points that appeared to point out from and into the tray's centre at strange geometric angles, defying all the known laws of science. One of them was a blade inside a needle, itself forming part of a larger needle which was in itself a blade, yet at the same time a needle,

SPECIMEN

surrounded by the same needle in another dimension of interlocking blades, that were also *not* interlocking.

How had they got there, I wondered? Who'd put them there? What were they there for? What was this place? Where was I? Plus variations on the above.

I started to pant with fear, my repressed abduction memories continuing to overwhelm me, despite them having started out as total lies that I'd recklessly spun without fear of any consequences. For this room, this illogical, limitless space, was nothing less than some kind of operating room.

An operating room situated on that strange multicoloured light cluster I'd seen in the sky that was actually a massive spaceship. An operating room I'd been in before, I now recalled. Many times, in fact. A surgical environment in which certain beings had used those very tools on the floating tray beside me in order to extract samples of my potent human seed. The self-same seed that Fibbford had told me was a weak and feeble strain – but I knew that to be a complete lie. No doubt he was already testing the prototype of his refined infamous Fibbertronics System to block all evidence of such blatant subterfuge by connecting me to the machine in such a way that anything he told me through it was immediately accepted by me as truth.

Well, he had a way to go yet, because I knew better. I knew that my seed was strong, dammit. I knew I was a human bullock, and that these unknown alien abductors of mine were hell-bent on extracting my seed so that they could people their distant race with strong and vigorous star-warriors to conduct and win a devastating interstellar war.

And as that's all it was, I had better simply lie back and enjoy the process, as I'd done so many times before. Hadn't I?

But suddenly, fear took hold of me again in this barren, featureless space, as I recalled that these beings only ever wanted my seed, and nothing more. Once abducted, they extracted what was required from me coldly and clinically. They weren't remotely interested in my looks, if I remembered rightly, or my rugged masculinity. And there was no physical coupling with some gorgeous female alien. It was a case of pure scientific experimentation.

I began to whimper quietly to myself, remembering the touch of those whirling, revolving interdimensional blades they were about to insert. And as I whimpered, still quietly so that no one else would hear, despite me being high up above the Earth in a hovering saucer, I began to sense another presence – another *intelligence* – in the room with me.

I screwed up my eyes in an attempt to block out the brightness, and discerned a terrifying form emerging from the light. A grey, hairless head appeared seemingly from nowhere, bobbing around on what looked to me like a long, snake-like neck. As it slid across the space towards me from that bank of enveloping whiteness, I perceived the sharp, black diamond-shaped eyes of my U-bend assailant, and knew now that there was no longer any avenue of escape for me.

The thing snaked and slithered into the space above my head, hovering there like some terrifying killer kite, while behind it entered, again from that cold, featureless bank of white light, what looked to me like a swarm of miniature beings. As they emerged from their respective dimension and crowded around me, I realised that these were the terrifying beings who'd disembarked from the landing spacecraft and pursued me through the trees of Spinewood.

They gathered around me in their multitude, staring at my body and poking their long, distorted fingers at my bits. In protest, I looked up again at the horrifying head floating above my own, pleading silently with whatever alien intelligence might be housed within its terrifying visage.

Like a miracle, the thing suddenly spoke.

SPECIMEN

Not literally, for this being had no mouth to speak of – or with. Instead, it seemed to be communicating with me telepathically, for waves of strange, ethereal speech began sounding deep inside my own brain, forming human words across the space between our communing minds – and evolving, by degrees, into the voice of John Virgo from BBC One's *Big Break*.

'Welcome,' it said.

'Good evening, John,' I said back, trying to sound ingratiating. I decided it was wisest to affect an air of confidence, or at least nonchalance. 'I do hope you won't be snookering me tonight?'

'Snookering?' the thing replied, without a trace of humour. But that was to be expected with a voice like that of John Virgo.

'Just a figure of speech,' I said, moving the conversation on, having realised that although I was able to interpret the voice in my head as that of John Virgo from BBC One's *Big Break*, the supreme alien intelligence manifesting itself above me probably didn't have access to UK mainstream TV, and would therefore have no idea what BBC One's *Big Break* was. Or, being an alien, perhaps it just feared Jim Davidson.

'What do you want from me?' I said.

'All in good time,' the thing replied, mimicking Fibbford's own oft-repeated phrase. Either the good doctor had already embedded himself so deeply within the social strata of this alien society that these beings were now copying his idiosyncratic Dorset turn of phrase, or the space creatures themselves were commingling so deeply with Fibbford's mind that they had begun stealing his own speech patterns and peculiar West Country patois.

Suddenly I sensed a commotion over by the implement tray. I turned my head and saw one of the grey aliens, taller than the others, attaching what looked like a surgical mask around its head. With the thing finally secured (on its chin, where its apparently missing mouth was actually located), the alien picked up what looked like a small sheet of glowing metal and walked over to my bed.

Turning the object over in its three-fingered hand, the alien indicated an array of strange symbols arranged in various rows on the sheet of metal, then pointed with its finger to a small dotted line at the bottom.

'Sign,' said the voice of John Virgo.

'What the hell am I signing?' I said, naturally suspicious after all my recent legal entanglements with Jacinta's lawyers.

'A consent form.'

'I.e. a legal waiver?' I countered.

'Correct,' said Virgo. 'In case you expire.'

'Under the anaesthetic, right?'

'Wrong. Under *no* anaesthetic.'

I guess it made sense from their perspective, but, speaking frankly, I would have liked to get my own solicitor to go over the small print before going under the knife.

But then these weren't conventional knives, I remembered, so my shyster lawyer would probably refuse anyway.

'Terms and conditions are non-negotiable,' said John Virgo, snaking down beside the outstretched sheet to nod his bald, grey head at the dotted line. 'You can just use your finger.'

I could hardly believe what I was not exactly hearing. Sign a glowing metallic sheet with just my *finger*?* Reaching out with my hand, I attempted to trace my signature along the dotted line with my finger alone. And there, before my very eyes, appeared physical evidence of my own handwriting materialising *as I wrote*, without a single ink cartridge having been attached to my scrawling digit.

'I can hardly believe it,' I gasped, audibly.

'And there are further wonders and scientific marvels where we come from,' said Virgo, snaking back up towards the ceiling now that the legal waiver had been attended to.

---

* Note that I conceived this tale long before the invention of touch-screen technology, hence this uncanny depiction of now rudimentary touch-screen interfacing is both terrifyingly prescient and uncannily accurate. GM

SPECIMEN

'Wait,' I said, erasing my signature miraculously with a separate digit end. 'That one went a bit weird. Let me redo it.'

I signed once again on the dotted line, but this time my signature looked even worse.

'Hold on, let me go back one more time,' I said.

But my third attempt was no better, and in fact now included small gaps in the signature itself that effectively split the words into three separate segments.

'It's just fucking nonsense now,' I said, becoming enraged.

'Just tick there,' said Virgo, snaking down to nod again at a small box-like symbol in the bottom right corner of the document, evidently suspecting I was playing for time.

Except that I wasn't. I was actually genuinely aggrieved that this bizarre alien technology, while technically impressive, was nevertheless unable to replicate exactly one's individual signature, and in fact appeared to be all too happy to accept a rough imitation of the original as a legally binding agreement – which, to my mind, created a potential legal minefield in the matter of personal identity, and in turn opened the floodgates to fraudsters and ethically questionable corporations who now had a version of my own signature that was completely unique, legally binding and yet *not my actual signature*.

Meaning that a rogue autograph could now be used without my knowledge to access personal information, complete private transactions in my own name and potentially order fast-food deliveries in the small hours at my personal expense, yet to a *different* address.

It was too horrendous to imagine.

Nevertheless, I ticked the box-shaped symbol with my finger, resigned to accepting whatever nefarious financial plans these beings might have in place to drain my numerous bank accounts, and remembered instead that a more immediate problem lay in the sharp implements to my right that were already in the hands of the tall alien beside me, who was moving them, all too quickly, towards my penis.

'If it's my seed you want,' I said, growing nervous, 'I can sort that for you, no problem. Just give me a bottle, two minutes and some private reading material, and I'll be on my way. But I do require solitude.'

Ignoring me, the group of small, shorter beings shuffled closer to the bed, their bald, grey-skinned heads and black diamond-shaped eyes blinking in apparent anticipation of the procedure about to take place.

'Are these my children?' I asked.

'No, these are students from our Medical Academy on Belgon 9,' said the voice of Virgo. 'Is it alright with you if they sit in on this particular procedure?'

Typical, I thought. *It would have to be my alien abduction they sat in on.*

But I couldn't really say no, I realised. After all, they had to learn how to implant things from *somewhere*.

'I guess it's fine,' I said, sensing any attempt at a protest would be instantly dismissed anyway.

'It would indeed,' said Virgo, and I realised that, as we were both communicating telepathically, he in turn, of course, had full access to all *my* internal thoughts.

Just then, the tall alien to my right clicked his three fingers (clicking, luckily, only requires two fingers, with the third digit serving as a cushion), and immediately the entire class of smaller-sized aliens attached masks to their respective chins. Then, when all were secured, the tall alien leaned down with a multi-bladed, fourth-dimensional Swiss Army knife in his hand and reached out once again in the direction of my penis.

I began to panic, sensing all of a sudden that the last thing this blade was designed for was extracting seed from one's sac and shaft. I don't know how exactly, but the sudden conviction grew in my mind that the only thing these whirring blades, which were slicing

SPECIMEN

in and out of each other like some deadly tesseract-fork of fourth-dimensional super-steel, were scientifically capable of was basic slicing and dicing.

And what these beings truly wanted from me, I began to suspect, was anything but a fresh sampling of Steen's superior seed-stock. No, these beings were intent on one thing, and one thing alone.

The severing of my shaft to its very wick.

No doubt they intended to preserve such a specimen inside a jar of alien pickle-juice somewhere, before conducting cruel and humiliating experiments upon it in some far-flung laboratory in a remote, distant galaxy. Like putting a hat on it and making it jump around with tiny electrical gonad-charges.

And that's when I began to scream.

CHAPTER TWELVE

'Relax,' said the voice of John Virgo, 'we only seek to extract more of your seed.'

But I didn't relax. Instead I continued to scream, for somehow I knew that the thing that was the voice of John Virgo inside my head was lying to me, and that the tools supposedly meant to extract my seed would instead be used to extract it *permanently*.

And then, as if to confirm my fear, those whirling blades in the three-fingered hand of that tall, grey-skinned alien began to glow and revolve at incredible speeds, flashing with multicoloured light reflected from whatever distant dimensions they were now passing through. And as they did so, the glaring whiteness of the room began to dissipate, its powerful rays transforming before my eyes into a rotating sphere of rainbow-coloured hues, whirling and spinning around me like a rotating globe. A globe of heavenly energy, in the centre of which lay I, alone now but for the voice of John Virgo in my head, calming me, reassuring me that they weren't about to lop off my manhood.

'I assure you, Nick, that you still have everything to play for. We are opening, for you alone, the doorway to another dimension . . .'

'Via those rotating dimension blades?' I queried, hoping against hope that he might actually be speaking the truth.

'Correct, Nick. Hence "dimension" blades.'

'And you're genuinely still after my seed?'

'Correct again. You're winning this round, Nick. Of that I can

SPECIMEN

assure you. And believe me, Nick, the process itself, on this occasion, will be quite painless ...'

As Virgo uttered those words in my head, a shape began to emerge from the swirling light display spinning at high speed around me, forming itself, by degrees, from the racing psychedelic backdrop, into what looked like a human form. But a human form beyond compare, curved and beautifully rounded. As the final configuration of matter separated smoothly from the mass of orbiting, kaleidoscopic patterns behind, I could finally confirm that the shape before me was a lady.

And *what* a lady. Though I could see only a silhouette at present, there was enough in the outline alone to convince me that what was materialising before me was nothing less than some sort of cosmic super-woman. A star-spangled vision of female bodily perfection.

As its smooth, rounded shapes moved slinkily in my direction, the still-silhouetted form of this unknown cosmic lady began to spark and smoulder before me, like glowing embers in a warm fireplace in the cosy faux log cabin of my mind, unlike the real one I'd never actually used – a fireplace before which lay a rug made from a white tiger I'd personally shot dead, plus a box of Thorntons chocolates at rest against a chilled bucket of ice-cold Strongbow.

Then, as the gleaming cosmic sparks crackling inside this heavenly female form finally subsided, the silhouette at last began to accrue the frontal hues and contours of a fully dimensional flesh-and-blood woman.

What stood before me at last was a naked Celestial Body, hotter than an imploding star (which itself is a miniature sun, and thus almost as hot), and more sensuously alluring than the 1976 Pirelli Calendar.

For this lady, like myself, was the epitome of bodily perfection. A veritable star-queen. No wonder the aliens had selected her as my breeding partner. For with my seed, and her nest, who knew what wondrous superior physical star-children might one day emerge from the tethering of our respective loins, then set out to rule the entire galaxy? Who could guess what perfectly formed brood of Cosmic Lions and Galactic Amazons might soon stomp all rival life-forms to death wherever they found them lurking? The potential for such heavenly physical perfection was beyond human comprehension, yet here it was, physically present before me.

Then, as the beautiful figure moved its head into the light, I finally saw who it was.

'Jacinta,' I hissed, under my breath.

'Don't hiss "Jacinta" under your breath, Nick,' said my ex-wife, stepping towards my bed and perching sexily on its far end.

'And where should I hiss it, then?' I said.

Jacinta swivelled from her sitting position, swinging one leg upwards, on to the bed, before inching herself forwards like a hungry cat, moving over my body.

'Whisper it into my ear, Nick ...' she said, huskily.

'No way,' I said, inching myself back against the headboard, which I realised didn't exist on this particular bed, and so I found myself falling backwards on to the non-existent floor as a result.

Yet before I could collapse, something cushioned my fall (I suspected it was John Virgo, whom I didn't really want present in such an intimate setting, to be honest) and before I knew it, I was back on the bed, with my beautiful, naked ex-wife crawling hungrily in my direction. Sensing Jacinta's hand was approaching a place it hadn't visited in years, I fought back the natural urge to forgive her immediately for all her apparent wrongs.

'What the hell are you doing here?' I said, trying to play for time. I needed to think. To reason logically with myself before happily throwing caution to the wind. 'You should be back at the house, waiting to discuss our divorce.'

'Forget about the divorce, Nick,' said Jacinta, hissing lustily at me like she'd never hissed lustily at me before (which was literally true,

SPECIMEN

Jacinta having never hissed lustily at me at all). 'We don't need to separate anymore. Together, you and I can rule the entire galaxy with our cosmic brood. So quit stalling, Nicky Boy. Let's make aliens.'

I waved her back, momentarily. 'What about Fibbford?' I said, admittedly keen on her proposal, yet aware there was all manner of unfinished business between us to resolve, which ideally should come before any wild and ill-advised act of physical congress – though I was increasingly caring less and less about said unfinished business in anticipation of the frantic bodily mauling I was about to receive.

'I only needed him to get my own book out,' she whispered, tracing a pattern of kisses down the side of my cheek and halfway down my neck.

'Look, Jacinta,' I said. 'Things have moved on a bit since then.'

'They're moving on now, alright,' she panted, moving herself even closer towards me.

'Fibbford wants to control the universe,' I said, focusing my mind on the job in hand. For if we were to let our respective guards down for one second, Fibbford would no doubt have us both destroyed while we were busy commingling, before taking over the entire universe for himself.

'I can handle *Fibbford*,' she whispered, deep inside my ear-hole. 'Like I'm about to handle you.'

'Like you handled that cosmic Star Lord, too?' I said, extracting her tongue from my eardrum; it was actually beginning to annoy me with what sounded like the constant lashing of a ship's rigging during a major storm.

'He got what he wanted,' whispered Jacinta, moving over to my other ear. 'Now come and get what *you* want.'

'Can you stop doing that to my ears?' I snapped, repositioning my own head in response. 'What about all these other halves of yours? This army of female beings taking over Stalkford and subjugating an entire occasional workforce of lonely and dispirited world-weary men?'

'I remember them,' purred Jacinta. 'Lonely, world-weary men ...'

'That's what I just said.'

'Have you been lonely and world-weary without me, Nick?'

I guessed I had, at that, but it had nothing to do with Jacinta's absence. It was the constant threat of my leaking brain that kept me up at night. I turned my attention back to the present, realising Jacinta still hadn't answered my question.

'You still haven't answered my question,' I said, shifting her weight from my lower intestines, which were permanently inflamed and apparently something I ought to keep a careful eye on. 'The one about the army of female beings taking over Stalkford.'

'Let's not talk about that right now,' she said, running her fingers affectionately through my brown, smoky topaz hair.

'No, let's, Jacinta,' I said. 'Or frankly, there'll be no hanky-panky.'

Her smooth, exploring fingers suddenly gripped my face lustily. 'They only want what I want, Nick. A human stud to bring home the bacon.'

'Fine,' I said, even though that didn't quite tally with the terrifying vision I'd witnessed in Paul Ball's diner, or the dark and creepy interior of that female-driven delivery truck.

But what the hell.

Surrendering to my morally questionable yet ultimately innate natural human lustings, I duly threw aforesaid caution to the wind.

'Then do it to me, babe.'

And with that, Jacinta went at me like a mad tigress on a felled antelope.

Marvelling at the speed with which a man could be ravished, we rolled left to right in a frenzied ecstasy of passion, until we fell completely off the invisible bed and were caught by John Virgo again – whom I told to get lost – before finding ourselves rolling once more across the invisible bed. On this, we continued to tussle physically, rolling over and over and over until we fell off it again and were caught a second time by John Virgo, whom I once more told to get lost.

Then, as we found ourselves wrestling on a bed of multicoloured bubbles, I became increasingly convinced that coupling with Jacinta could indeed seed an entire universe with our physically perfect, unconquerable offspring. And as we continued to hammer away at each other, I realised I need never fear again the escaping horrors of my own mind. For together, Jacinta and I, along with our mighty brood, would decimate Stalkford into a trillion atoms if we so wished, permanently destroying all traces of my escaping imagination, along with the human race itself, forcing whatever survivors remained into a system of cosmic prison-planets, upon which, as Star Gods, we would routinely detonate nuclear missiles and atom bombs, destroying all who stood in our way.

'Yes!' I screamed. 'I think that's a great plan!'

But suddenly, like a cold pail of water being thrown over two tussling alley cats, the reality of the situation hit me.

I was thinking like one of *them*.

Why was I doing that?

And then I *saw* why.

I was underneath.

Jacinta was *on top*.

That wasn't right. Never, in all our years of marriage, had I ever been *underneath*. I was strictly an 'on top' guy. Call me old-fashioned, but I preferred things done by the book.*

And Jacinta had never once complained. True, she'd attempted to bring up the matter with me numerous times, but I'd resolutely

---

* With the exception of typewriters, where all positions are, by their very nature, unconventional. GM

refused to discuss it, meaning we'd never technically disagreed about the situation.

But things were different now. For this was a *commingling*, I remembered. A physical union engineered by alien intelligences far superior to Mankind's own. Intelligences now attuned to the earth-shattering changes wrought by an increasingly dominant race of Cosmic Ladies.

My world had literally turned upside down.

'Now, hold on a minute,' I said, as Jacinta grabbed me by the shaft, laughing maniacally against the wall of colours still swirling about us.

'I have it!' she screamed. 'At last, I have the world in my grasp!'

And with that, the whirling room suddenly turned to white again, and I saw that beside me there stood once more that tall alien with his attendant group of medical students. He appeared exactly as he had before, with that nightmarish range of dimension-cutting blades clutched in one hand.

A roar of laughter erupted over my head. I looked up in terror and caught sight again of that terrible, grey-skinned, diamond-eyed being on a snake-like neck that spoke with the voice of John Virgo. As it slithered downwards again like some cosmic boa constrictor, I heard its mocking, tormenting voice sound once again inside my head.

'You've been snookered,' it said. So the thing *had* seen *Big Break*.

And with that, Jacinta, who was still on top of me and angling my shaft towards the hand of the tall alien with the blades, roared in triumph.

'At last!' she yelled. 'At last, Womankind will rule the Earth, and make the males run around like ants.'

The vision she described was so terrifying that, for a moment, time appeared to stand still. I saw in my mind's eye a society totally upended, where lonely men like me, Paul Ball, Biff Fudge, Ian Haggard, Old Man Gristler, Postman Crawley, Jake Guzman and Steve Hayman would serve no other purpose than to run baths, organise days out and plan meals, sometimes days, or even weeks, in

SPECIMEN

advance. We'd find ourselves taking our other halves to the supermarket while we either waited in the car or walked the dog again, never having time to read our newspapers in their entirety, never again commandeering the entire television night after night for the films only we wanted to watch; always having to share portions of our takeaways, always making morning cups of tea when morning cups of tea were never once proffered in return. The sheer horror of this new society hit me like an electric bolt: a glimpse of hell that would last aeons, with Jacinta and her new species looming over our cowering forms as we ran, blindly, to our next thankless task.

It was the ultimate vision of cosmic horror.

And with it now threatening instant madness, a primal scream erupted from my throat. A scream so potent it was almost orgasmic in its intensity.

Almost? Scratch that. It was *literally* so, as the raised shaft in Jacinta's hand flinched violently and instinctively from the approaching dimension blades, the sudden thrusts of movement tipping my man-hammer into immediate overdrive.

And, despite all efforts to contain it, my seed erupted.

CHAPTER THIRTEEN

There was an almighty shriek from all as my seed-geyser roared upwards. Jacinta screamed and flung herself from the bed, and the little grey men with masks on ran about the room, shrieking in terror.

Which wasn't the reaction I'd been expecting.

Similarly, the tall alien beside me flung the rotating tesseract-fork dimension-blade contraption into the far distance and dived into the whiteness of the surrounding wall as John Virgo yelled loudly from the middle of my brain.

'Now you've bloody torn it!'

'Torn what?' I cried back, still dazed from the eruption and failing to see why everyone was so upset by the successful extraction of my seed.

Then I saw what Virgo was on about.

For I had indeed torn something. Or rather, my seed had. For as I lay there, fighting the urge to nod off, my seed began to boil and sizzle like acid as it landed on the floor of the alien spaceship. Within seconds it had burned through to the floor below, immediately causing the bright enveloping white surrounding us to vanish, and all at once I saw that I was lying prostrate inside the central cockpit of an alien craft, banks of flashing computer screens surrounding me as the grey-skinned aliens fought to control their now rapidly disintegrating vehicle.

Whatever my seed had formerly consisted of, it was now, in a universe controlled by Jacinta alone, evidently a deeply caustic and

SPECIMEN

toxic strain, not just to these beings themselves, but also to the atomic structure of their very own flying craft.

The aliens around me were still shrieking as John Virgo continued to yell inside my head. 'It's burning right through the spacecraft. I told you that seed was a wrong 'un.'

Panicked, two of the little grey men closest to me peered over the edge of the burned-out hole in the floor of the saucer and stared, horrified, as my seed continued to fizz and sizzle its way through the floor directly below. On and on it went, until, with the sound of whatever alien technology powered this craft now grinding to a terrifying halt, a cold burst of night air rushed upwards as the outer atmosphere poured into the exposed gap created by the burning fluid.

Immediately the control panels in front of me began to go haywire, with items of equipment and flailing alien forms flying about the cockpit of their own accord. As the outer winds howled through the craft, I felt the saucer lose balance and begin to upend itself. Then we were careening sideways in a terrifying death spiral towards the ground below.

'Let me fly this baby!' I yelled, but none of them would allow me to, even though I'd done one introductory flying lesson for my fortieth birthday and was, according to the instructor, the best novice pilot he'd ever had the privilege of flying beside. And even though I'd subsequently wrenched the controls too hard and sent us nose-diving into Stalkford Airport's central runway, I had since qualified as a chopper pilot and run numerous combat missions as a part-time Navy Seal.

As the ship continued to descend earthward at speed, I caught a glimpse through the front window of the dome of Stalkford Observatory, over which we'd evidently been hovering for the entire duration of my abduction.

I braced myself as the dome grew nearer and nearer, knowing that at any moment now, unless these aliens had some alternative laws of physics up their sleeves that they were able to manifest in record time, we were going to collide with it head-on.

As we hurtled ever closer, I could spy Fibbford staring up at us, frantically trying to disconnect his hair from the main Fibbertronics circuit board, which had become entangled in the wires previously attached to my finger-ends. I couldn't help but smile as I saw a look of horror cross his face as our saucer descended at speed towards him, on a direct collision path with the observatory's main interior.

Then we crashed into the building.

I grasped on to the side of my bed for dear life as we burst through several floors, tearing down through the main reception area with that weird secretary with an attitude problem. The edge of the saucer clipped her huge spectacle frames, causing us to roll sideways along the dimension-changing hallway, which luckily shrunk as we went, slowing us down, until at long last we shot through the double doors of the building and bounced down the main hill like a runaway tyre into Stalkford city centre itself, at which point the saucer struck a ramp and arced upwards again at immense, supersonic speed before descending once more, this time into a distant patch of woodland bordering Chokewood Forest.

As the trees came up to meet us, I blacked out.

★

I awoke amid the broken, burning wreckage of the crashed spacecraft, hardly believing that I was still alive.

As I struggled to free myself from the crushed cockpit, I looked around frantically among the encroaching flames for Jacinta, all too aware that any hope of mutual interstellar species-making between us was now long gone, yet somehow still feeling touched by our brief moment of comminglement in that whirling wall of multicoloured light.

SPECIMEN

Maybe there was still a chance we could make it together, I pondered in my dazed, post-crash delirium. Perhaps we could put aside our differences for the sake of our respective wallets, if nothing else – and perhaps for Meredith, too, if she could learn to be less prickly in exchange.

But whatever Jacinta had ended up becoming as a result of my imagination escaping and making each of our published accounts of supposed alien abduction come alive around us, there was little sign of her now.

In fact, there was no sign at all.

Suspecting that she had either been flung far from the craft during its fiery descent, or had beamed somewhere else in the nick of time like they do in *Star Trek*, I elected to focus instead on saving myself.

And as the flames licked ever closer to my naked frame, my immediate problem was pain. Pain in my scrotum. I reached down with one hand to assess the damage and drew out a small, solid object that had become lodged between the floor of the cockpit and the folds of my pouch.

A typewriter key ...

I turned it over and saw it was the 'return' key that had previously been attached to my rectal walls. Evidently the sheer force of the impact had dislodged it from within.

Spurred on by the thought that if I could somehow escape this burning spacecraft, I'd no longer be troubled with a crippling pile problem, I staggered to my feet, aware that the flames were getting closer all the time.

Quickly, I put on my clothes, which the aliens had seen fit to hang in a closet adjacent to the main operating theatre. Aware that I had mere seconds left to escape, I quickly ran a comb through my bedraggled mane and rubbed finger-smears from the lenses of my glasses. I could hear the approach of distant sirens, as whatever authority now ran Stalkford rushed to secure the scene of an apparent crashed alien craft.

Whether it was the army itself approaching – who, no doubt, would wish to store the crashed alien dead in concealed military bunkers somewhere in that vast desert situated thirty miles south of the village of Clayston – or Jacinta's own sinister force of alien female taker-overers, neither would get here before the entire craft was consumed entirely from within by the destructive inferno now licking at the very edges of my black leather blouson.

I looked around desperately. There was no way I could escape now, I realised. For the flames were all around me and my life was almost over, destined to end in a crashed alien mothership of my own creation (with additional material from my ex-wife).

My pile problem might have vanished, but all I'd really gained was about thirty-five seconds of blissful, itch-free nirvana.

And then I saw it. A small, almost indiscernible gap in the control panel in front of me. A dark blob amid the vast bank of strangely shaped, multicoloured light buttons. The tell-tale space of a *missing key*.

I flung one of the dead alien pilots aside and leaned in closer to the main control console. The area above the missing button was labelled 'Time Machine Unit'.

I gasped. Could it be true? Did this alien craft somehow possess the ability to travel backwards and forwards in time, as well as spinning around in the sky like a giant firework?

Tentatively, I drew forth the typewriter key again, which I now realised was not a typewriter key from my ancient Chinese typewriter at all, but some sort of *cosmic* key. I held it up against the small gap in the console board.

It was a perfect fit.

Maybe this was my chance. Maybe by putting this button marked 'return' back in its place inside the console section marked 'Time Machine Unit', I could return to a time before all these horrors had come to pass. A time before I'd been abducted by aliens. A time before Jacinta and I had agreed to divorce. A time before I'd even

SPECIMEN

considered the possibility of dreaming up such a ridiculous abduction story in the hope of hoodwinking Joe and Jill Public into giving me all their money in exchange for a cheap and tawdry thrill.

A time before I'd slept with that bloody cursed typewriter and wrought eternal ruin upon the entire face of Stalkford town centre.

I caught the sudden scent of roasting beef, and saw that the surrounding flames were now licking at the sleeve tassels of my treasured blouson.

Without further thought, I slotted the key back into its place and pressed 'return'.

*

I was back in my road. The sun was just rising, and I could spy Postman Crawley already at work, leaving Ian Haggard's driveway and turning immediately up Old Man Gristler's.

'Morning, Nick,' he called out to me.

I held up one hand and tried to grin, though tears were already threatening to fall. 'Morning, Postman Crawley,' I said, turning away so that he couldn't see the raw emotion running through me.

It had worked, then. I was back. Back with the *men*.

I watched as Biff Fudge from three doors down gave his Ford Mondeo another blast of water, before stopping to sip the cup of coffee his wife, Meryl, had just brought him. I smiled as he spat it out and ordered her to bring him another with less milk in it.

There was no mistaking it. Things, thank the Lord, were back to normal.

I opened the gate of my own driveway and tried not to stagger as I made my way up the garden path. I was exhausted, desperate for sleep, but the first thing I needed was a shower. Then some food, maybe, followed by a quick physical frolic with Jacinta if she was home, or myself if not. Then sleep. Blissful, uninterrupted sleep.

It was over, thank God. The nightmare was over.

'Morning, Nick,' said the voice of Steve Hayman, calling to me from the window of his home studio.

I turned and caught the wonderful sight of my neighbour's gentle, prog-rock-career-lined visage. 'Hey there, Steve,' I replied. 'What gives?'

'Same old, Nick. Same old. Where have you been?' he said.

'You wouldn't believe me if I told you, bud,' I said, letting myself in. 'Catch you later.'

And with that, I closed my front door and stepped back into my home.

'Jacinta?' I called out.

There was no response.

'Meredith?'

They were nowhere to be found. And though I searched every inch of the house, Meredith wasn't even inside the airing cupboard where she normally hid when Jacinta and I were arguing.

'Meredith! It's me, kiddo. Daddy's home!'

There was no response. I shivered, a vague, creeping fear growing once again in the area of my vitals. Maybe it was a Sunday, I figured. Maybe they were both out shopping, preparing a huge meat feast for my return. Or perhaps they were taking my stubborn undies down to the launderette again.

But maybe not . . .

'Hi, Dad,' said a voice just behind me.

I prepared to turn around, aware already that the voice belonged to my daughter. Yet something about the tone of it stopped me for a moment. For it seemed different now. Calmer, almost. Centred.

Controlled.

'Is your mother about?' I said, finally turning to face her.

'Of course I am,' said Jacinta, stepping into the room from the front hall and moving to stand beside Meredith. Then another figure stepped into view from behind the doorframe. It was Astrid Hayman.

SPECIMEN

'We're all here,' Astrid said, calmly walking into the lounge before coming to a stop on my daughter's other side. 'We all have a group appointment at the nail clinic later, don't we, Meredith?'

'We do indeed, Astrid,' said Meredith. 'All paid for by Mum.'

'With *your* money,' said Jacinta, looking straight at me – and looking as beautiful as I'd ever seen her, dammit, having re-frizzed her perm since we'd last parted.

'And then we're going to buy yet more new shoes,' added Astrid, as Madge Fudge, Linda Guzman and all my male neighbours' other halves trooped suddenly into the room from the front hall.

Followed by *Roz*.

She was wearing a grey suit, goddammit. And stone me, if it didn't look *good* on her.

'And *you*,' my former editor barked in a hostile tone, pointing a finger in my direction – an action which was soon replicated by Jacinta, Meredith, Astrid and all those crowding other halves – 'will be driving us there.'

'Me?' I said, my voice now a hoarse whisper. For even if I *could* retrieve my catalytic converter from my smashed-up Ford Taurus, it would still take a couple of days to arrange a replacement hire car with my insurance company – and even then I'd most likely only be able to fit four of them in.

'You,' they all said as one. 'You, Nick Steen. You. *You*. YOU.'

So the 'return' key hadn't worked at all, then. Rather than 'returning' me to a particular point in time, it had simply returned me to the *figurative* mothership, meaning the Alien Queen herself. By pressing 'return', I'd simply, and unwittingly, returned myself to Jacinta's side.

To do her bidding.

'No way,' I yelled, and ran towards the window immediately behind me, which was fortunately on the ground floor, meaning I could hurl myself out of it without hurting myself too badly.

But there in the alleyway running along the rear of the house, they stood. Lined up in their hundreds, blocking my escape. Staring in at me, coldly. Waiting for me to make my next move.

I ran my eyes over them. There in the foreground stood Postman Crawley, Jake Guzman, Old Man Gristler, Paul Ball, Biff Fudge, Ian Haggard and Steve Hayman.

But not the Postman Crawley, Jake Guzman, Old Man Gristler, Paul Ball, Biff Fudge, Ian Haggard and Steve Hayman that *I* knew.

For this Postman Crawley, Jake Guzman, Old Man Gristler, Paul Ball, Biff Fudge, Ian Haggard and Steve Hayman, was (or were) *hairless*.

'Join us, Nick,' said the hairless former guitarist of Quorum. Former guitarist, because there was no way Steve Hayman would ever be picking up an electric guitar and shredding his load on it again, I realised. 'It's cake time.'

'No thanks, Steve,' I replied, turning back to face their other halves, who were now gathered in their hundreds around me.

'Look, can we talk about this?' I said, hoping we might somehow come to some arrangement. But instead, Jacinta, Meredith and all the hairless men's other halves began to laugh. Just like those cold, cruel aliens had laughed at me once before, outside the broken ruins of Paul Ball's diner.

A deafening burst of triumphant, merciless mockery. For the joke, I realised at long last, was on *me*.

I watched, helpless, as my own replacement stepped towards me from the gathered throng, slowly drawing what looked to me like the gleaming blade of a familiar-looking kitchen knife ...

... from the folds of its brand-new *apron*.

The End

THE WARNER

I am the Warner
Bewarner O' Mankind
I am Bewarner
Heed my dark, bewarning mind

For I doth warned ya
Oh, how I warned you every time
Hey now, didn't I warn ya?
Seems you've run all out of time

Look around ye and about ye
For the Five Horsemen do doth ride
Yes, that's five horsemen (not horsewomen)
For one more hath joined their side

Now Armageddolypse ist upon us
Two End Times side by side
Armageddon plus the Apocalypse
And did I not say 'Woe Betide?'

Five names did I emblazon
Across this Bursted Land
Rot, Mould, Youth and Lootage
Plus the Skeletal Taxman

For I am the Warner
Bewarner O' Mankind
I am Bewarner
And I've warned ye multiple times

Yes, I dothed warned ya
Yet heed me did ye nay
Now lo, the Dark One scorns ya
And it's too late for thou'st to pray

To the Warner
Bewarner o' Mankind
For he doth hath bewarned ya
Now Five Horsemen do doth ride…

Garth Marenghi

GARTH MARENGHI'S ACKNOWLEDGEMENTS

I daresay I must thank mineself. For the visions. For the dreamscapes. For riding the Night Mare throughout (but not in an *Equus* way). Yea, and I must accept those thanks, too, even if I scarcely possess time enow for the acknowledging, so vexing is my sworn and solemn duty to guide Humanity through these wasted ruins.

But I will do it.

I won't even demand a cheque on this occasion.

Thank you, Garth.

Thank you.

And thank me, too.

Thank you too, Garth.

Thank you.

You're welcome, Garth. And remember, go balls-forward into that hard night.

Already have.

Likewise. i.e. Ditto.

Garth Marenghi

MATTHEW HOLNESS'
ACKNOWLEDGEMENTS

I'd like to thank my agents Matthew Turner, Sophie Chapman and Rhonda Lidgold once more for steering a frequently irascible Garth through his later years. Also Tom, Hannah, Phoebe, Kit and everyone at Hodder for their continual support, advice and encouragement. Also Liam Wheatley for his superb audio editing, Joe Avery for another blinder of a cover and Alisdair Wood for four more fantastic illustrations. I'd also like to thank Nigel Heath for invaluable audio guidance, Bennett Maples at Sonic Fruit, and also Myfanwy Moore once again for kicking the entire thing off. Special thanks, meanwhile, to Joshua Boland-Burrell and all the team at Live Nation for organising and managing Garth's live shows and ensuring his exhaustive rider stays box-fresh at all times. James Harris and Mark Lane at Teashop Productions for their constant support and enthusiasm over a great number of years, and also Phil Canning from Universal Music for his own excellent advice.

Finally, I'd like to thank my family. My parents especially, but also my sister Kate and brother Steve (and their families). My wonderful and hilarious partner Sarah for reading it all first and fixing all the rubbish bits, not to mention adding one or two corkers of her own. And at long last my beloved daughter, Clara, who dug me out of a creative slump by turning a tired werewolf into a vibrant skeleton.

I could never have written these books without you.

Thank you.

DO YOU DARE CRACK OPEN THE *TERRORTOME*?
(MIND THE SPINE)

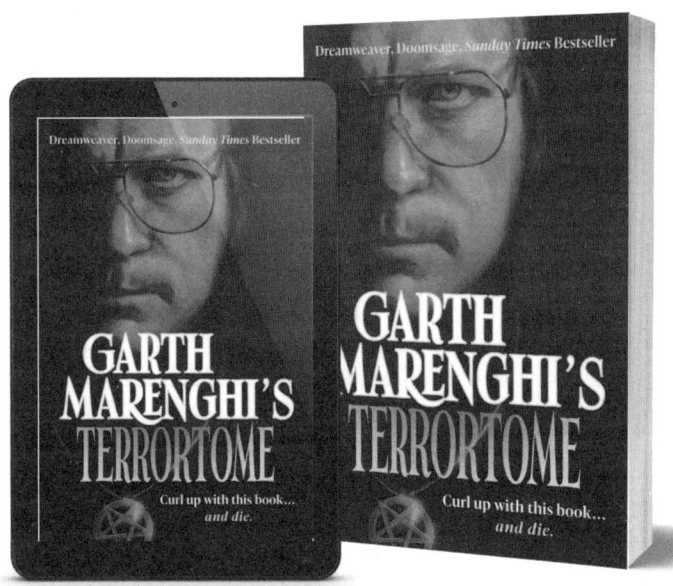

READ ON FOR A SPINE-TINGLING EXCERPT FROM THE HORROR MASTER'S LONG-LOST MULTI-VOLUME EPIC

AN ADMONISHMENT

That's it. You can stop reading. The book is over. The tale is told. My personal contractual obligations have been met. I am, as weaker men would say, spent.

However, Ken Hodder appears to have his own obligations to fulfil (aside from issuing the remainder of my advance) which roughly translates as a number of extant blank pages to fill. He has therefore suggested – *timidly*, I might add – that his imprint fill these with the opening chapter of *Garth Marenghi's TerrorTome*, for the benefit of those who may have finished reading *This Bursted Earth* without having previously read *the preceding two volumes* . . .

Needless to say, with the possible exception of Dermot O'Leary, who also read all three volumes in *completely the wrong order*, I have very little respect for those readers other than a genuine scientific interest in the abnormal functioning of their brains. But on the understanding that reprinting the opening section of the first volume in this trilogy will somehow encourage the demented to visit what they should technically only be *re*visiting, I present, with sincere reservations, the entire opening chapter of *TerrorTome* (for *gratis*, too, I might add).

And to those readers who are encountering the following tale for the first time, I simply say this.

Shame on you.

Garth Marenghi

TYPE-FACE

(Dark Lord of the Prolix)

CHAPTER ONE

So it *did* exist.

I stood alone in the pouring rain, peering in through the window of 'Uniquities Inc., plus Eels', at a machine supposedly invented by Christopher Latham Sholes in 1867, but constructed, according to the price tag slung from its golden carriage-return lever, by a Chinese magician in the latter half of the Tang Dynasty.

I smiled, shaking my head. A bold claim ...

Yet true. For my own research had revealed that Eastern antiquity had achieved, in its long-lost past, a level of technological advancement surpassing even Currys. Yes, the Chinese had invented paper and, thank the lord, gunpowder. But, finally, here was proof beyond all doubt that those ancient sorcerers had also created the humble typewriter.

I turned my face from the glass display and looked around me. This lonely side street off Stalkford's town centre, which I'd never noticed before today, seemed to be perpetually empty. Maybe a small second-hand shop specialising in offbeat mysterious oddities didn't attract major footfall. That or the eels were an issue.

Nick Steen's the name. Perhaps you've heard of me? Yeah, that's right. The horror guy. The insanely rich, multiple best-selling, dark and dangerous-to-know paperback visionary of the dark arts. *That* Nick Steen. If not, you soon will (in fact, you do now). But maybe not in quite the way you imagine. An apposite word, that – *imagine* – and not just because words (like *apposite*) are my trade, or *profession*. For *imagination*, which is the root noun of that previous word

GARTH MARENGHI

– *imagine* – has everything to do with the real-life horrors that were about to unfold.

Imagination . . .
My imagination . . .
Let me explicate.

In my own time.

I turned down the collar of my charcoal tweed blazer over my black polo-neck sweater, smoothed back my full and flowing mane of smoky-topaz hair, then removed the buff-tinted shades of my chopper-pilot days to get a better look.

To the casual observer, the typewriter sitting in the shop window before me resembled a conventional model. Aside from its gold-plated exterior, the only difference appeared to be a set of extra keys surrounding the conventional QWERTYs, depicting obscure archaic letterings and bizarre runic symbols. These stood out, I noticed, at insane psycho-geometric angles only Carl Sagan and myself could have perceived.

But if the rumours I'd heard were true, and this *was* the very typewriter I was seeking, then this bizarre, ancient contraption also possessed certain unique powers entirely its own. For, by some unknown spiritual process long since lost to Man, this machine's original creator had supposedly instilled in it the ability to commune psychically with its owner, allowing him or her (but mainly him) access to hitherto unreachable depths of the subconscious mind, freeing, from the murky swamps of their internal id, the darkest parts of their suppressed imagination.

As a best-selling horror writer, I had to have it. (Also, there was currently thirty per cent off.)

Although I was still the hot news in horror, crafting non-stop the darkest, most terrifying novels of supernatural terror known to

TYPE-FACE

civilisation, sizzling on the publishing plate for nigh-on twenty years and counting, it wasn't enough.

I had too many ideas. Too many tales untold. Too much darkness left untapped.

If I was lucky, I had around forty years of life left. Fifty if I gave up red meat, which wasn't an option. And yet I hadn't even begun to explore the *true* horrors of human existence. Hadn't got anywhere near probing the deeper darkness that exists *beneath* Mankind's basest nature. Hadn't yet drawn upon the horror *beyond* horror, shall we say? That snarling, predatory *hellbeast* lying dormant in our supposedly civilised minds. If I could unleash *that*, thereby teaching Mankind (or Ladykind, if that's important to you) to live *alongside* their own particular corresponding hellbeast, then just maybe I could save all of us from ultimate self-destruction.

Endarken our world for the greater Bad.

(And make more money.)

Which is why I was here now, staring at this damned typewriter.

BUY ME.

I jumped at the sudden sound and looked around me, wondering if the owner had leaned briefly out of his shop doorway. But there was no one there. The street, too, was still completely deserted.

Then who'd spoken?

BUY ME.

There it was again. Coming from somewhere close by, it seemed, yet also immeasurable distances away. A deep voice, devoid of expression, yet possessing an undeniable tone of command.

I SAID, BUY ME.

Again. Was it originating from somewhere in my own head, perhaps? Was I, after twenty solid years at the top of my game, crafting inimitable works of challenging, visionary horror, in fact going *mad*?

GARTH MARENGHI

I looked down at the typewriter again. If I hadn't known better, I'd assume it had shifted forwards slightly on its mock-velvet display, moving closer to the glass pane separating us.

BUY ME.

In an effort to get away from the strange voice in my head, I made my way over to the door and stepped inside. The interior of the shop was dark and gloomy. An old man in a grubby rubber apron stood behind a dusty counter on the far side of the room. He looked familiar.

'Eel?' he asked me, offering up a lidless plastic container clutched in his hand. I walked towards him and glanced inside it. It was an old ice-cream box half-filled with dirty water, with a writhing cluster of black, slimy snake-fish wriggling within.

I looked back up and stared deeply into his cataract-covered eyes. 'I know you from somewhere, old-timer.'

'I'm Moses Unique,' he rasped, chewing on an eel's head. 'I sell ... *uniquities.*' He let the eel slide inside him, swallowing the creature whole. 'Plus eels.'

'I'm interested in that typewriter you have on display in your front window.'

'This one?' he replied, lifting up a large tea cosy on the counter to reveal an identical-looking machine immediately below it.

'So they're a pair, are they?' I asked.

'A *pair?*' he echoed, confused. 'This is the only machine of its kind in existence.'

I glanced back behind me at the window display. A Victorian sex chair now stood in the space where the typewriter had been.

'An exquisite machine,' the old man continued, his oily hands hovering over the contraption's keys. 'Tang Dynasty, no less. Look at that gleaming return lever. This resplendent feed roller. Do your fingers not yearn to hammer hard upon those golden keys? Do you not hunger for the touch of its jewel-emblazoned ribbon reverse

TYPE-FACE

knob? The soft kiss of its diamond-adorned ribbon spool? Do you not dream of feeding your soft paper sheetage through its hard, studded platen?'

'I'm more interested in its *mind*,' I said, curious to see whether or not he understood me. The old man examined me for a moment, a spark of recognition crossing his half-blind eyes.

'Steen . . .' he said, nodding to himself. 'Nick Steen . . . The horror writer?'

'Correct,' I replied. 'But you're not Moses Unique.'

He grinned nervously then, his milky-white orbs darting furtively from left to right. Hell, I *knew* him, alright. But where from?

BUY ME.

That voice again. Whatever it was, wherever it was coming from, it seemed to be reading my innermost thoughts. It too, wanted me to buy the typewriter. And the strange thing was, I now felt like I was being forced. Ordered. *Compelled*. (Not tautologous, as there is a subtle difference between all three.)

I quickly did the math. Despite my fame, I knew I'd be unable to claim ancient antiquities against tax (I've tried several times, but no joy), meaning I'd need to make my savings elsewhere. If I ceased all alimony payments and sent my ex-wife to live in rented accommodation at her own expense, selling all my daughter's non-transportable toys, I might just be able to afford it without dipping into any of my own money.

Given that Jacinta had yet to forgive me for press-ganging our daughter into an early proofreading career, it would hardly come as a surprise to her if I suddenly recommenced hostilities out of the blue. And I wouldn't need to worry about any legal challenge, either. Early on in my career, I'd refused to co-write anything with another human being, including my marriage certificate, for which I'd employed several pseudonyms. So any potential ex-wife would need to descend all nine Circles of Hell in order to extract a single penny from my mounting fortunes. And, if this typewriter really was the one I'd been seeking, those fortunes would soon be mounting even higher.

Soon I'd be writing darker, more terrifying novels than any I'd dared write before. Famed the whole world over as the greatest horror writer who'd ever lived. Then finally, Roz Bloom, my editor at Clackett Publishing, would realise, once and for all, that I *don't need an editor.*

If this typewriter was the one.

The old man swallowed another eel and tapped his finger against the discount sticker.

Was the thing *truly* magical, like I'd been told?

I AM INDEED.

Dammit, that voice *again*. Either I *was* going mad, or some presence, some *force*, seemed to be communicating with me from deep within my own mind. Plumbing the murkiest depths of my subconscious.

And then it hit me.

Maybe the typewriter *itself* was already trying to communicate with me.

YES.

If that was true, there could no longer be any doubt in my mind. The machine perched in front of me truly *had* to be the one I'd been seeking. The key to unlocking my deepest, darkest nightmares.

THAT'S RIGHT. I AM.

I froze. That voice ... That voice in my head ... It was the *typewriter's* voice! As unbelievable as it might seem, the *typewriter itself* was *speaking to me.*

EUREKA.

Then this really was it, beyond all doubt. After an endless, painstaking search of several hours, the hunt was finally over. The machine I had sought was finally in my grasp.

TYPE-FACE

'And will you be purchasing?' asked the old man, with the hint of a sly grin.

'I will,' I replied, pulling out my credit card. 'But I'll need a VAT receipt.'

'Oh,' he said, hands fumbling uselessly in both pockets. 'We only take cash.'

'Then put it on my slate, having first set me up with said slate,' I said, reaching for the typewriter. But somehow it was already there, in my arms.

'Ouch,' I snapped suddenly, feeling my right index finger snag sharply against part of its mechanism.

The old man chuckled, tucking into another eel. 'You have just felt, sir, the delicious, castigating pinch of its dormant ribbon vibrator.'

'Go easy on those eels,' I said. He winked at me.

'Does your rod not harden at the coy wink of its sparkling typebar?'

I ignored him and walked back over to the door, and my Honda Civic parked beyond. Then turned again in a final attempt to place the man's features.

But his face was now masked by the plastic container, which he'd tipped upwards at one corner to gulp down what remained. I stepped outside, yanked open my car door and placed the typewriter down on the passenger seat. Then found myself attaching the seatbelt across its front.

THANKS.

'You're welcome,' I said, getting in beside it and keying the ignition. Before pulling out, I turned to address it directly, realising I would look stir-crazy to anyone passing by. Fortunately, the street was still entirely empty.

'Let me make one thing perfectly clear,' I said, leaning over towards it. 'Yes, you may be ancient. Yes, you may possess untold powers beyond the ken of Man, but from this moment on, you work for me, *capiche*? I'm the master, and you do *my* bidding.'

SURE. WHATEVER YOU SAY.

I grinned, pleased we'd reached an early understanding, and keyed the engine.

COWBOY.

I glanced back for a second, confused, then pulled out on to the main road.

Sucking the blood from my injured finger.